# HARD NEWS

Hearing voices, the men turned toward the house as the portly Dr. Hawkinson came to the doorway. Behind him was Claire Kerry, her face as white as the flowers in the window box. A few steps behind was his father, Clancey Kerry, looking every inch an old man in spite of his hulking frame.

Luther yelled, "Hey, the doc's a'comin' out!"

He hurried to the porch. Cole stayed beside the sorrel. He realized this was no time for him to intrude, even if he was Ethan's brother. He would stay no more than two days, then he would head out and start over. It was a good thought. Time to let go of the past. Cole looked at the people gathered on the porch and felt more lonely than he could ever recall. It was like returning to someone else's life. Like gazing at an oil painting of people; some looked familiar but they didn't seem to be a part of his life, in any way.

At the porch, Luther asked, "Doc? How's the boss? He be up n' roarin' cum the mornin'?"

Dr. Hawkinson cleared his throat. His thick belly rose and fell with a prolonged breath and then he proclaimed, "Ethan Kerry is going to be just fine . . ."

Luther hollered, "Hot damn! I know'd it!"

". . . but he's blind."

# Behold a Red Horse

## Cotton Smith

LEISURE BOOKS     **L**     NEW YORK CITY

A LEISURE BOOK®

July 2001

Published by

Dorchester Publishing Co., Inc.
276 Fifth Avenue
New York, NY 10001

ISBN 0-8439-4894-9

The name "Leisure Books" and the stylized "L" with design are
trademarks of Dorchester Publishing Co., Inc.

Printed in the United States of America.

Visit us on the web at www.dorchesterpub.com.

*To my sons and daughters*
*Scott and Cindy, Laura and Owen, Stephanie and Rob*
*With love*

# Behold a Red Horse

# Chapter One

Strands of buffalo grass waved a welcome as Ethan Kerry reined in the willful bay gelding. Stopping at the crest of a tired mesa, the lean rancher pushed back the brim of his hat to coax any stray breeze that hadn't been run off by the white hot sun. He couldn't remember feeling so tired. His deep-set eyes betrayed the worry that had dogged him since town. Ethan Kerry should have expected this treachery from Sam Winlow. The powerful cattleman had coveted Ethan's ranch for a long time.

His annual stop at the town bank to get a letter of credit for the drive had turned into an ugly nightmare. This would be his third herd taken north over the long and dangerous Western Trail, always as his own trail boss. But this would be the first time his whole ranch was at stake. Unable to look Ethan in the eyes, the bank president had notified him that he could not issue him the letter and that his existing loan would be called in

September, instead of renewed. Full payment would be expected at that time. It wasn't hard to figure out why: Sam Winlow had bought the bank three days ago.

As a younger man, he would have galloped over to Sam Winlow's place and killed him right then and there. But that was a different Ethan Kerry. And before he met Claire. Killing Winlow wasn't the answer now. Maybe it never was. Few of his riders had ever seen the violent side of Ethan Kerry. Those that had, whispered tales of a man savage enough to kill a Comanche war party by himself when they attacked the ranch in the early days. He had pistol-whipped the last three warriors when he ran out of bullets.

A cigarette was rolled with practiced ease, followed by the glow of a match snapped to life on his gun belt. Trying to settle his mind, he squinted into the afternoon's commanding glare, letting the trail of smoke wander through his thick mustache, past his Roman nose, once broken, and up his color-drained face. He knew the hard ways of the Texas prairie well. He had built the proud Bar K out of mesquite, hot winds, and savage Indian attacks. All of that seemed easy next to what he now faced: the likelihood of losing it to Sam Winlow.

The gold coins and certificates he and Claire had hidden away would have to do for costs during the drive. Some of that money was from a Yankee bank he and his brothers had robbed after the War of Northern Aggression. Before, he always asked the bank to provide a statement of ownership of his trail herd, in case he needed it. This time he hadn't even asked, but went to Judge Henry, an old friend from the war, to give him written proof. Henry was glad to help and upset to hear about Winlow's move against him but said that, so far, there wasn't anything illegal about it.

Ethan hadn't asked for his advice; the judge had just volunteered it.

In the green valley below, the land blossomed with his cattle and riders. Usually this majestic sight gave Ethan Kerry great satisfaction. Today, though, seeing his gathered Bar K trail herd only tightened the ache in his stomach as he rested after the ride from Uvalde. More than 2,500 steers and older cows were gathered by his trail crew in this elevated pasture, linked to the hills west of the main ranch house. Men were cutting out cattle or working around a large branding fire, giving each animal a special trail mark on their left horn to identify them for the drive. Animals not yet branded on the left hip were given the Bar K brand. Male calves were castrated as the branding process moved along in an organized fury. Severed testicles were tossed into a bucket for frying as a suppertime treat.

A colorful dance of alkaline dust, hot breezes, horses, sweaty men, and roped steers swirled around the glowing embers. Like most cattlemen, Ethan always had a special trail brand placed on the animals, in addition to the Bar K on their flanks. Within the week, they would begin the trek to Dodge City, Kansas. Of course, none of the men below realized yet how critical this drive had become. Ethan wasn't certain he would tell them. It was his problem, not theirs.

Ethan eased the horse down the soft side of the mesa, his batwing chaps sliding against an outstretched bush as he cut diagonally downward. The bay was four years old and had been selected to join the remuda this year. Ethan liked the horse and had chosen it to ride to Uvalde. It was one of the green mounts being broken at the ranch and would be brought out to add to the trail remuda to replace some of the older horses. The bay was learning fast that the man on his back was boss.

Examining the herd as he zigzagged downward, he silently pronounced it fit for the drive. The familiar song of bellowing cattle, fretting and snorting horses, mixed with the dry scuffle of saddle leather and the raw curses and shouts of cowboys drifted up to Ethan Kerry, filling him with new resolve. Sam Winlow wasn't going to get his ranch. Not as long as he could ride—or fight. Even the odor of burned cow flesh from the branding arrived like an old friend seeking to encourage him.

"Howdy, boss. We about got this here beef ready to go. When do we get the new broncs?"

With long blond hair spinning out from under his hat, a short cowboy with bright eyes wheeled his buckskin horse alongside Ethan. Jared Dancer would be one of his two point riders on the drive and was in charge of the roundup. Ethan had no foreman. Not yet. He held that job, in effect, himself. Not even his older brother was given that much responsibility. Ethan had always liked Luther's description of Dancer: "Ever'body dun know he's short, 'ceptin' him. He reckons he's the biggest he-bull in the valley."

Ethan Kerry grinned, flicked the butt of his cigarette toward the ground. "If I can keep Luther at it, we'll have eighteen ready, maybe twenty, when the herd is. All with at least ten saddles under them."

"Sounds good. Someday I'd like all the hosses in my string to be alike. Wouldn't that be something? A string of all buckskin hosses!"

The tall rancher smiled and nodded approval. Dancer was eccentric but a solid cowman, a superb horseman and loyal to the brand, almost to a fault. If he knew about Sam Winlow's latest move, the fiery rider would be hard to keep from starting a private war. The energetic Dancer wore studded cuffs, stovepipe straight chaps, and a black vest. Around his neck hung a tiny leather pouch on a thin buckskin thong. The Kiowa medicine bag was a gift from an old shaman he had once befriended. Even his horses showed his feelings about Kiowa religion; the buckskin had a small painted symbol on its chest and a wide circle around its right eye, both signs of Kiowa medicine.

"All the signs look good, boss. The spirits are with us. Gave them some tobacco last night—just to make sure." Without glancing down, Dancer pushed the pouch lying on his shirt inside it, as if to reinforce his feelings.

Knowing Dancer well, Ethan Kerry changed the subject. "There's a good-lookin' buckskin in the new bunch you're gonna like. Thought of you the minute I saw him."

"You rode him yet, boss?"

"Yeah, he's a handful. They all are. Green-broke is all we got time for, but they'll all neck-rein and stand quiet for you. Most of the time. A few are slicker and rope broke, not cow savvy, though. They'll just have to get it on the trail. But you'll like this one. May be better than Curly Joe here."

Dancer's eyes told of his interest, and he asked, "How are we picking our strings?"

"Oh, you an' DuMonte can get all of yours first. The rest can rotate. We'll do that . . . Thursday."

"Well, you tell that old billy goat Luther I got first call on that buckskin. That'll give me four, anyway."

"He's already said it's yours. I'm sure DuMonte won't care," Ethan said, paused and continued, "Remind the boys to turn out any stray brands. We aren't heading north with somebody else's beef."

13

Dancer grinned widely; Ethan had repeated that order every day.

"Hello, Preacher! How's it going?" Ethan yelled to the quiet black cowboy ridng toward him.

"Afternoon, Mr. Kerry. We're doing fine."

Ethan knew DuMonte read the Good Book in the morning and at night, prayed on his knees like a child before sleeping, and never cursed or raised his voice. He also knew DuMonte was a sturdy hand with a savvy for cattle and men. DuMonte and Dancer would be his point riders on the drive, just like last year.

DuMonte reined up alongside the two and shook Ethan's hand. Like Ethan, most of the men had taken to calling him "Preacher" because of his devout ways. The nickname was received with patient understanding; he had been called much worse over the years.

"You got plenty of food for two more days, don't you? How's Stovepipe doing with the cooking?"

"Eating like kings, the boys are," DuMonte said with a grin. The floppy brim of his high-crowned hat covered most of his unlined face.

Ethan chuckled. "Good. Kill a steer, one of ours, so they can have plenty of beef. It'll be the last until we reach Dodge. I'll see you in two days with the new remuda and the chuck wagon. We'll pull out Friday morning."

After a few more minutes of answering Ethan's questions, the lean rancher was satisfied, said his good-byes, and loped back up the mesa. His two point riders watched him climb the hillside and disappear over its sun-drenched ridge before returning to their chores.

As he rode, Ethan decided he would go over last year's trail diary one more time when he got home. The leather-bound volume held the details of each day of the drive in his own scrawled shorthand. From it, he had made a master list of work to be done. Most of his men thought the list got longer each day, instead of shorter, as Kerry thought of more things to be readied. Details were the key to success, he reasoned. "Forget something little and something big gets hurt" was one of his favorite expressions. Now everything was nearly ready and he should be excited, like he always was. But he couldn't shake the day's turn of events. In a matter of minutes, he had gone from being one of the region's strongest ranchers to the most fragile.

"I can't let that son of a bitch Winlow sit in my damn mind too," he told himself. The bay's ears flicked backwards to understand.

He patted the horse on the neck and rolled a cigarette. He rode a diagonal trail that took him through a portion of his eastern range. It was the longer way to the ranch house, but he wanted to check out the rest of his herd. No real reason. Just the pride of seeing what he had accomplished. Most of the main herd was there; one- and two-year-old steers, young cows with calves and selected bulls. They had been gathered for the trail cutting and now were drifting back to favorite pastures. A playful calf followed him for a quarter mile before deciding he wasn't fun anymore. The calf's mother had trailed along as well, keeping an eye on her offspring and Ethan.

Pulling a silver watch from his vest pocket, he checked the time and paused to study the picture of Claire on their wedding day before replacing it. Screening the sun with his hand to his forehead, he checked the position of the sun against the watch. If he wanted to be home before dark, and supper, he'd better let this horse have its head for a while.

The drive hadn't even started and he realized he was already missing Claire and their two children. But he always did on the Kansas drives. She was a big part of his success, and a bigger part of his life. No, she was his life. Without her beside him, taming his fierceness into something profitable, making life good and happy, who knows where his gun might have taken him. Instinctively, he patted the Colt at his hip. It had been a year since he had shot at anything, and that was a rattlesnake. Out of habit, though, he cleaned the revolver nearly every night. Ethan Kerry shrugged his shoulders and kicked the bay into a lope. The horse was ready to run.

Dusk was at his heels when he caught sight of the ranch yard. The terrain was accented with an occasional jagged arroyo and scattered mesquite thickets. He took pride, as he always did, in how well constructed the buildings were and how well cared for. This was no rawhide outfit, that was for certain. This was built by a man with an eye for detail and the toughness to get them done right.

Barely visible in the heavy dusk, a Bar K–branded longhorn skull was centered on a crosspiece above the entrance gate. He didn't like the slight tilt of the skull, but didn't want to take the time now to climb the pole and adjust it. Tomorrow he would, and made a mental note of the project. Off to his left was the bunkhouse, a long, low building. No one had noticed his arrival yet; everyone was too busy and the bay's walk was quiet, its wildness left back on the prairie. The breaking corral was a whirl of color and dust. A wrangler was rope-breaking a bay. The horse was becoming accustomed to the wrangler's stretched-out lasso tied to a large piece of sagebrush dragging behind them. Ethan shook his head and grinned; he would join in that battle tomorrow morning.

Two other corrals held horses at various stages of

development. Most of the new animals had been under the saddle at least three times now. A few had "ten saddles" of experience. Some remained saddled; some had their front legs half-hitched together to keep them quiet. Gazing past the horse-breaking area, he saw Claire; she was working on the chuck wagon with the trail cook. Ethan loved to watch her when she didn't know it. A buxom woman with well-earned crow's-feet around her bright eyes, she was carrying something to the chuck wagon. Helping her was the Kerrys' five-year-old daughter, Maggie, or at least she thought she was.

The sturdily built, wide-beamed wagon, with its bentwood bows holding protective canvas, would eventually hold everything for the long drive. The wagon bed was already loaded with the bulk foodstuff—sacks of green coffee beans, flour, sugar, salt, dried apples, pinto beans and cornmeal, as well as boxes of soda, canned goods, and wraps of salt pork and bacon.

Ethan reminded himself that tomorrow he needed to check out the heavy toolbox hanging on the side of the wagon, opposite the water barrel. It should have everything he had put on his list: shovel, ax, branding irons, horseshoeing equipment, hobbles, rods for the pot rack, and extra skillets. But he would check it again, just to be certain. For that matter, he would go over the wagon's contents itself.

Whether it was Claire or her daughter who saw Ethan first would be anyone's guess, because both shouted his arrival at the same time.

"Ethan, you're back!" was louder than "Daddy, you're back!" but no quicker. The tall rancher smiled, yelled, "How are my girls?" and swung out of the saddle.

"Hey, did you tell that Injun-lovin' Dancer that we

got him a ri't smart buckskin?" His older brother, Luther Kerry, yelled from the middle of the corral, where he was twisting the sorrel's ear as a last resort to get its attention. Drawing the rope, with a stray piece of sagebrush attached, slowly toward him, he waved a hand without looking up. Luther was older by two years and slower of mind, except around horses.

"Yeah, he's a mighty happy man," replied Ethan lustily.

Maggie came running toward him, her arms out wide. He would tell Claire about the bank problems tomorrow. No need to make her worry all night. As he grabbed his daughter and pulled her to him, his eyes met Claire's. She knew something was wrong. She always did. He would have to tell her as soon as they were alone.

Night came like a lady to the Bar K ranch, encouraging all the stars but inviting only the softest breezes. As darkness caressed the ranch buildings, sheds, and corrals, the main room of the log-and-adobe ranchhouse glowed with yellow light. Freshly cleaned oil lamps encouraged playful shadows to enjoy themselves in the corners.

One shadow rested near the large fireplace, understanding its sadness in not having a crackling fire. Another elongated shadow kept a possessive arm along the rolltop desk and the ornately carved cabinet that came from the Texas panhandle. Both were pieces of furniture that had been owned by Claire's mother and father. Above the desk were framed tintypes of their parents, taken on their separate wedding days, watching the room with youthful sternness.

Ethan and Claire, with their two children, sat down to supper at the heavy planked table. They were joined by Luther and the two brothers' father, Clancey Kerry.

They were the only men on the ranch now. A hearty stew of calf's liver, brains, heart, lean beef, onions, and sweetbreads, washed with a hot sauce, was Claire's evening treat. Luther called it "son-of-a-bitch stew," but not around Claire or the children. The table was neatly set with Claire's prized white stoneware plates and heavy iron utensils, all the way from Kansas City. In the center was a blue glass vase with a tiny crack trinkling down its side, proudly presenting a fistful of wild bluebonnet flowers.

Luther had difficulty with his chair; he was so bow-legged that it just didn't follow the bend of his legs well. Everyone waited while he pushed the chair one way and then another. He mumbled to himself, then realized where he was and bit his lower lip. Finally, he just plopped down on the seat and strung his legs out like they were in a rowboat.

Once Luther had settled in, Claire looked around the table, rested her eyes on Ethan, and said quietly, "Ethan, would you please say grace for us." It wasn't a question.

"Dear Lord," Ethan began immediately, anticipating her request, "we thank you for the blessings you have given us, this good food, the good weather. Watch over this family while we are on the trail. Watch over us, grant us water and grass—and bring us home safe. Amen."

"Amen," Claire added.

"You betcha," Luther followed, and glanced at Ethan out of the corner of his eye. The rancher blinked away a grin when he saw Claire's frown.

Ethan took a deep breath, smiled awkwardly, and said, "The boys will be through with the branding Thursday. Maybe before. Animals look good and fit."

"Wal, all right," Luther responded with enthusiasm,

19

Cotton Smith

"I'll bet ol' Dancer near peed his britches when ya tolt him about that new buckskin." Luther realized what he had said, lowered his eyes, and asked for Claire to forgive him. She did with an understanding nod.

"By the saints, that be a strange man, Jared Dancer," Clancey pronounced. Whiskey was evident on his breath.

20

# Chapter Two

"Yes, he is that," Ethan agreed, "but Dancer would stand against hell if it was right for the brand. And he can move a herd so smoothly that the cattle think it's their own idea."

Ethan could tell his father wasn't listening and wanted to share his own gathered information. After all, Clancey had never been on a trail drive. He had never been successful at business either, failing twice at owning a general store. The love of whiskey had always been his one great weakness. His wife, and Ethan's mother, had died of smallpox years ago and the big Irishman now lived with his son's family.

"Well, one of the men told me that the strange lad hisself always put his bedroll the same distance from the chuck wagon—and sleeps with a cedar sprig right on top of his blankets, of all things. A cedar sprig, lads—and lasses! Cross me heart, that's what I heard.

More, in fact, but it skips me mind. If you be interested, I can ask again."

"Dad, I could add to the list myself," Ethan broke in impatiently. "Dancer is a superstitious man. It's mostly Kiowa stuff. He lived with 'em awhile. Believes in what they believe. Doesn't matter, I'm damn glad he's on my side. You quit worrying about him."

"Shoot fire, Dancer's a fire-eatin' rascal," Luther added.

"Aye, there be a bit of Ethan Kerry hisself in the lad's fighting spirit, no?"

Ethan's silent nod showed little enthusiasm for the comparison. Finally realizing his report wasn't of interest, Clancey asked, "How about a wee nip to celebrate your trail drive being ready?"

"No, thanks, Dad."

Without being asked, Luther chimed in, "Don't reckon I need no who-shot-john neither, Paw."

Clancey Kerry was a cheerful Irishman who was the opposite of his son, Ethan, in most ways. Some would say Ethan looked gaunt, especially compared to his father's bearlike appearance. But his narrow frame was deceiving, for the rancher was sinewy and strong. He could lift more than most men of any size, and hit harder than most, too, if it came to that. Luther looked more like their mother. Soon all three men were busy with their food, eating in silence as was the habit of most western men.

It was Maggie who first broke into the mealtime reverie. "Daddy, are you taking any little calves along to Kansas?"

"Well, sort of. We expect to have some join us along the way. So we're taking a wagon just to carry them, during the day, so they won't fall behind."

"Won't they miss their mommies?"

"We'll make sure their mommies are close by," Ethan said, with a wink at Luther.

It had been Claire's idea to bring the extra wagon for the calves. Many drovers killed any young born on the drive, not wishing to be held back by their inability to keep up. Ethan would sell them to Kansas farmers.

"Yessir, little Maggie, that thar wagon is a mighty fine place to be if'n yur a little calf. You kin ree-lax and be ri't thar with yur mommy at the same time. Why, that's whar I'd like to ride, but yur pappy won't let me," Luther said, leaning across the table. His eyes were bright and warm. His mouth was looped into a teethy grin underneath a long, droopy mustache. The right side of his face was more wrinkled than his left, like he had squinted with only his right eye, riding in the sun. His clothes always looked like he had slept in them, even when they were new.

"Is Mr. Speakman going to drive it?" Claire asked, her eyes caressing her husband's face.

"Yeah, ol' Ben's got the nursemaid job again," Ethan said, not aware of his wife's growing amorous interest.

Claire stood and walked around the table, refilling coffee cups. This would be one of the last suppers she and Ethan would share before the men left for three months. She would have preferred to be alone with him, but she wouldn't have dreamed of asking Luther and Clancey to eat earlier or by themselves. Returning to her chair, she studied the two brothers, bronzed by the lamplight: the slow and cantankerous Luther contrasted to her tough-minded and controlling husband. They were concentrating on the food and obviously enjoying it. She smiled to herself. It was clearly a compliment to her cooking. Clancey was picking at his

23

food, mostly drinking his coffee, which was laced with whiskey.

Before there was a Bar K, Luther and Cole, the youngest Kerry brother, had followed Ethan Kerry during the war as part of General John Bell Hood's Texas Brigade. After the surrender, they had followed him as guerrilla fighters, briefly carrying on their own private war. That soon led to the outlaw trail. Neither Ethan nor Luther ever talked about those bitter days, at least not that she had heard. Those were times when young men of battle found little to come home to—their guns more comforting than their plows. They had been part outlaws, part rebel warriors not believing it was over—and all hard men who lived by their wits and their guns. Ethan had never kept any of it from her, not even when they were courting.

Folded away in her remembrance box was a yellowed, creased wanted poster, offering a reward for help with the arrest of a gang of confederate bank robbers. She had kept it as a reminder of how they met. The four men robbed a bank in a small Texas border town; she was there with her father. Ethan saw her, and she, him. The bank robbers left quickly, but not before the outlaw leader came over to ask her name and whisper he would return to see her. He found her parents' ranch two days later—an agonizing forty-eight hours when she alternately hoped he would come and then was scared he would.

A month later they were married after he promised to leave the outlaw trail. It was the only time she had met Cole Kerry, six years younger than her husband. Distraught over his big brother's decision to settle down, the young firebrand had left and never returned. She remembered his icy blue eyes looking deep into her soul and shivered. Several years ago, he had written a letter; it was posted in Wichita, Kansas. She knew Ethan kept it, but he never spoke about him anymore. Ethan had decided his brother had been killed somewhere. Claire told Luther she felt Cole was alive; it was a feeling inside her. But she didn't say so to her husband; he would have given her one of those looks that said she was being foolish.

"Daddy, do you like the flowers?" Maggie asked again. "I picked them today—just for you." As an afterthought, she added, "An' for Luther and Grandpaw too."

Ethan felt bad he hadn't said anything before. He wiped his mouth with the cloth napkin and said, "They are beautiful, Maggie. I saw them right away and meant to say something. Thank you."

"Little Maggie, you are ri't nice to put me an' Grandpaw in your pickin'. I reckon you dun brung the spring right inside. They are as pretty as you," Luther added. He leaned across the table to smell the flowers and made a loud sucking noise, pretending one had been pulled up his nose.

"Oh, Uncle Luther, you're so silly," Maggie exclaimed, and laughed. Clancey smiled but said nothing as his oldest son continued performing. Luther would be the trail drive wrangler, as he had been on all the drives. What Luther said concerning horses, Ethan would have to listen to, even though his older brother was more child than man.

Until now, Eli had been silent. The eight-year-old boy, with a full set of freckles across his nose, two missing teeth, and light hair that paid no mind to any brush, was usually brimming with questions. At his feet was curled a gray hound with a white muzzle, named Blue. The ugly dog paid attention to only three people: Eli, Maggie—and sometimes Claire. Not even Ethan could get the hound to mind no matter how much he yelled, threatened, or swatted. More than one cowhand had been nipped trying to get acquainted. Neither Clancey nor Luther ever tried to touch him.

"Dad, how long will you be gone?" Eli asked, not looking up from his plate.

Ethan shot a glance at Claire, blinked his eyes, and replied, "It'll be a long time, son. Probably three months. You know we've got to go all the way to Kansas, then come back."

There was a silence, one that made everyone uncomfortable. Even Luther was without words. It was Claire who finally spoke.

"Eli, it will be a long time for your father to be away from us. But this is what he must do so we can have this fine home." Claire's stern expression didn't match the softness of her voice.

"Dad, can I go with you?" Eli asked, as if he hadn't heard his mother.

"Someday you will, that's for sure. But for now, I need you to be the man while I'm gone."

"Oh, Grandpa will do that."

"Yes, but he'll need your help—an' so will your mother. An' I'll be bringing back some surprises for all of you." Ethan glanced at Claire, whose eyes were as sad as her son's. He looked over at his father, but Clancey appeared in his own world, sipping his coffee.

Luther's pinched face mirrored the boy's, and he sputtered, "It be hard, Eli. We be a-missin' you sumthin' fierce."

Eli's face couldn't hold back the sorrow any longer, and he sprang from his chair and bolted toward the bedroom he shared with his sister. Tears streaked his cheeks. Ethan rose from his chair and followed him.

"Luther, Dad, how about some pie? I baked two buttermilk pies today. A new recipe I've been saving from last year's church social. I want to see what you think. Please?" Claire said without watching her husband and son. She knew how her son felt. It was hard, too hard. Both men declined, but she insisted and they reluctantly agreed that it sounded good.

"Come and help me, Maggie."

Moments later, large slices of pie were set before each chair, including one for Eli and Ethan.

"Ma'am, this h'yar is so tasty, a man would fight a war all by hisself, jest to git sum," Luther praised with his mouth full.

Clancey smiled self-consciously and said, "Aye, t'is fit for the king hisself."

"Well, thank you, gentlemen," Claire said, her face beaming with pride.

Ethan rejoined them, and shortly afterward, a pale, tear-streaked Eli did too. After completing his pie and complimenting Claire on its worthiness, Ethan rolled a smoke and lit it. Luther did the same, although he preferred chewing tobacco, and Clancey lit a cigar. Claire and the children removed the dishes from the table. Eli and Maggie were given the assignment of washing and drying them.

Claire returned to the table with a fresh pot of coffee and filled the cups with a smooth efficiency. She laid a hand on Ethan's shoulder as she poured the steaming liquid into his cup. He put his own hand on top of hers and looked up into her flushed face. Their eyes exchanged love.

"Hey, brother, you never gave us no line on how'd you liked that bay," Luther asked without noticing the interlude between them. He seemed uncomfortable without a chaw of tobacco in his mouth but would never chew in Claire's house, even if she told him that he could.

"That's going to be a good worker, that one," Ethan said, turning his reddened face back to the table and releasing Claire's hand. "He's headstrong—and a little jumpy, for my taste—but he'll take a man a long, long way before stopping."

"Good hoss," Luther reinforced.

"Ah, a hoss-man! Nothing like a hoss-man," Clancey said, waving his hand. To be called a "hossman" was to receive his highest compliment.

"How are the rest coming?" Ethan asked.

"Some, eight saddles. Gittin' them rascals wound down to rattlesnake level, anyway. The boys'll have to take 'em from thar."

Ethan was always fascinated about how Luther seemed to come alive when the subject changed to horses.

"How about the big red?"

"That danged sorrel dun throwed me ever' time. Shoot, that'd be three sittin's for this bowlegged ol' boy. Never seed the like. That red thing'll ram ya sky-high an' never say as much as howdy."

"Is that the one you call Kiowa, Uncle Luther?" Eli asked, appearing interested in the conversation for the first time.

"That be him. Kiowa. Fits 'im, too, I reckon. Wildest thing I seed in a long spell. But, man, he'll be a goer. Yessir, Eli. Strong legs. Big chest. Got hisse'f a heart like a lion, boy. He'll go all day and ask fer passengers!"

Eli smiled, beaming with the attention of the man he admired. Claire touched her napkin to Maggie's cheek, appearing to remove some misplaced pie, but really to avoid watching Luther with her son. Luther's oldest daughter would have been just a little older than Eli.

Luther had joined the Bar K two years ago, after losing his wife and three children to the fevers, then forfeiting his nearly forgotten ranch to the bankers. She never looked at the rawhide face of this grizzled cowboy without remembering the day he rode in and wept in Ethan's arms. She remembered, too, Ethan taking the guns, including Luther's own, from the house when the unconsolable man finally slept. He was worried about his brother shooting himself.

"Think Kiowa will be ready for the drive?" Ethan asked, blowing on his coffee before taking a sip.

"Hard to say. He could jes' stay outlaw—an' we ain't got much time to fiddle with any bad un's."

"Yeah, you're right," Ethan agreed. His mind was filled with the image of that sorrel, a powerful animal he'd traded three steers for with a passing buffalo hunter a month ago. He liked the horse; it reminded him of the sleek, fast mounts they had used in their old outlaw days.

"Now, Luther, you don't really think he's a bad one," Ethan said, returning to the subject. "The only thing wrong with Kiowa is that he was cut. Think of all the fine red colts we could've had."

Jumping in her chair, Maggie exclaimed, "Oh Daddy! Can I have a red colt? Can I, please!"

"How about a nice brown one?"

"All of 'em woulda bin outlaws an' sky-toppers an' sech."

Ethan laughed. "You don't fool me, you ol' goat. You like that big red horse as much as I do."

Claire was eager to share her own achievements in preparing the chuck wagon for the drive. Withdrawing her list from the pocket of her apron, she announced that the wagon was ready and proceeded to read it aloud. Everything that should go in the wagon bed was in place: rope, guns, tobacco, ammunition, a lantern and kerosene, axle grease, even two extra wheels—and all the food supplies. The men listened attentively, fascinated by her businesslike thoroughness. Both Luther and Clancey had helped carry the heavy items from the house and storage shed. The boot and the chuck box, at the back end of the wagon, was also fully stocked. It contained a hinged worktable and a honeycomb of drawers and cubbyholes.

"Let's see, I have packed it with salt, lard, baking soda, coffee beans, vinegar, matches, calomel, castor oil, bandages, needles . . . and molasses," she began reporting.

Her recital included the news that the sourdough keg and coffeepot were in place, as were skillets, pot hooks, plates, cups, utensils, cooking knives, and roasted coffee beans. The coffee grinder was loaded, hanging from a new hook, since the old one had disappeared. The coiled stake ropes for making a corral to hold the remuda at night were in place and the two smoke-blackened Dutch ovens were already sitting by the rear wheel, ready to go in last. Her face was set in an expression that reminded Luther of her husband. He coughed to hide his smile.

"Buckets of grain for the wagon teams aren't in there yet. Luther has promised to take care of that. And there are a few more things I've got to get. Oh, and the water barrel isn't filled," she continued, and looked at Ethan. Luther chuckled. Ethan always insisted on filling the big barrel that hung outside the wagon on the day they left, for good luck.

Of course, Luther knew Ethan Kerry would recheck everything in the wagon before they left anyway. So did Claire. But her goal was to think of everything in advance so that—just once—he wouldn't bring up something overlooked. She had gotten close last year, but he wanted more cans of tomatoes, more cans of peaches, more rope, and a second extra wheel. Claire took Ethan's auditing with a wry smile that seemed to say she understood her man needed to control most things.

"Think you have enough sugar, Claire?" Ethan asked impulsively. "You know the men like their sugar."

"Good thought. I'll add another sack tomorrow."

Luther chuckled and spat, "Better put two in thar. Dancer, he's got a sweet tooth wider'n the Red River."

Claire cocked her head slightly to the side and said coyly, "Gentlemen, does my work pass the test?"

Ethan was the first to answer. "It always does, little lady."

It was Clancey who brought the conversation to Ethan's experience in town without realizing its severity. Ethan thought for a minute, then decided to share the news. He had already told Claire.

"Bad news—the bank won't give me any more time on the loan. They'll be on our porch for payment—all of it—the day we get back. They're not giving me a letter of credit for the drive, either."

"Damn the blackards. By your sweet mither's grave, I swear bankers are hisself, the devil!"

"Well, in this case, I reckon it's Sam Winlow. He owns the bank now."

The big Irishman looked like a prizefighter just hit with an unseen punch. His eyes bulged and his mouth gaped. His face surged into a bright crimson.

"That's it. I'll take that no-good sonvabitch apart meself! The man be having more land and cattle in

31

these parts than any five men. Should that not be enough for the bastard!" Clancey roared.

Luther also appeared stunned, but asked quietly, "Whatcha gonna do, brother?"

"We'll be fine if the drive is successful. I'll have enough to pay them. Just won't have any to set aside for the year coming. We can find another bank, in another town. Claire and I have some money we can use for the trail. Anyway—I don't want a word of this to the men. If they hear this, some will quit and it will make the drive even harder."

"Yah, I reckon you're ri't. We'll keep 'er ri't here."

"Me lips is sealed," Clancey said, and motioned the sealing with his fingers.

"The only way we beat Sam Winlow is get those steers to market. That pays off my loan—and that's the end of it. Winlow can do anything he wants to with that bank, after that."

Looking for something positive to talk about, Clancey asked, "Did ye pay the newspaper again for the wee writin'?"

"Yeah, it'll be the same advertisement as before. Says we've got the range for ten miles around our watering hole."

"Ah yes, and a fine piece of writin' it is. And a grand range, too. That's about as far as any of the noble Bar K beasts would walk to water. I am proud of you, Ethan."

"Well, there's nothing legal about the claim, you know. We still only own those first hundred and fifty acres. But everybody seems to pay a mind if it's in the newspaper. I read Winlow's advertisement, and it says he's got almost all the rest of the range—except ours. An' I'll bet he doesn't own much more than we do!"

Luther stared at Ethan and said, "A few years back,

we'd a'handled hisse'l a mite different, brother."

Ethan caught his older brother's eyes and smiled thinly.

"Yeah, we would have."

# Chapter Three

"Stay with 'im, Luther! I'll throw you a coat if he jumps any higher! It'll be cold up there!" Ethan Kerry roared cheerfully as his older brother exploded skyward on a raw bronc. Leaning his long arms against the top of the working corral, the tall rancher had just finished working out another horse.

The bay, called Rip, was one of the untamed three- and four-year-olds being broken for the trail drive remuda to take the places of older horses. This was the fifth time it had been ridden this week. Midmorning sun had already wrung sweat out of the young day. Hours ago, the rose streaks of dawn had been driven into the dry Texas earth by a golden new hue. The two Bar K men had been working new horses since those streaks were mere slices of crimson in a bleary sky. Ethan hoped to finish today or Thursday at the latest.

Ethan Kerry squinted into the spiraling dust as intense as always. No one paid more attention to details than he did. His cowhands knew full well that every new horse placed in the remuda would have been ridden by him before it got there. It wasn't that he didn't trust Luther, just that it made him more comfortable knowing for himself.

"Nice work, Luther! Make Rip mind ya now. None of that!" Kerry yelled again.

Luther's heavy quirt slapped the terrified bay's withers each time it bucked, trying to connect pain with misbehavior. The animal definitely had the beginnings of a solid trail horse disposition, in spite of its high-spirited antics. There simply wasn't time to break these horses as gently or as completely as he liked. Green-broke would have to do with no more than eight saddles apiece.

"Bring him down to a walk, Luther. Can ya now? Stay with it," Ethan advised. "Walk. Walk. That's it. Good job." Even though Luther was better with horses than he was, Ethan couldn't help making comments.

Like the other four horses worked so far this morning, the bay would soon realize what its duties were. Ethan expected to select twenty of these newly trained broncs for the trail and leave the rest behind for more seasoning or selling off. The best of the green-broke horses would be divided among his men for the trail, with the older animals carrying most of the early responsibility. He was pleased with the progress of all the new mounts, except for a wild-eyed sorral called Kiowa they had discussed last night. Neither he nor Luther had been able to stay on it for more than a jump or two.

"Rip's a feisty one, Luther. Make him mind. Pop him when he does that. No, you've got to do it right then," Ethan said. He liked the look of this young bay, watching it move with experienced appreciation.

He demanded horses with stamina, animals that would perform wisely and consistently. His men always rode good horses. Going to Dodge, excellent mounts would mean the difference between success and failure. He'd seen it firsthand. And this year would be even more important. So far, though, he had managed to put the threat of Sam Winlow from his mind. Claire had been the primary reason for that relief. Her eyes had glittered with fear when he told her about the bank's decision to call their loan. But her words that followed were those of confidence, and her eyes soon matched. The night had been made well again by the sweetness of their bedded lovemaking.

The rancher's own dark eyes returned to the other corrals where the rest of the new horses waited. Dashing shades of bay, sorrel, and dun caught the sun and made a distinctive rainbow of brown. Ten horses remained to be worked today; they were all in the farthest fenced containment. Another eighteen had been worked as much as they would be. Half were in the second corral; the rest were hobbled and allowed to graze at the edge of the south pasture. Luther felt horses lost weight being in any corral, so they were moved out as soon as possible. All of them needed more work, but the trail would have to be the final teacher.

Ethan spotted the unridden sorral and knew he would have to be the one that broke it. That was the way it should be, he decided to himself. "Kiowa, you an' me, boy. You an' me."

His sunburned face was streaked with worry lines and accented with heavy eyebrows and a nose like an arrowhead. Horses like this big red animal were either impossible to break or would become the finest mount in the string. Nothing in between. He shivered slightly at the thought of riding Kiowa and muttered again, "Kinda cool this morning." He snorted at the lie; that was a horse to scare any man, so why deny it?

"Luther, turn 'im around now, will you. No! Don't let 'im get away with that! Take 'im in a circle again. Yeah, keep it tight. Yeah, that's the way," Ethan continued his coaching, and Luther accepted it without comment. He knew his brother meant nothing by it.

"That's the way, Luther. You've got his number. Atta boy," Ethan praised.

In the ring, the cowboy was making Rip turn on command, most of the time. But the horse wanted to run when it was supposed to be walking. Ethan Kerry's eight-year-old son, Eli, was glued to the fence, enamored with Luther's performance as he worked to get the animal to behave as he wished.

The yellow-haired lad got his courage up and shouted out his feelings. "Way to go, Luther! You're the best rider ever!"

Luther's shirt was already drenched with sweat and his shirttail was out, flapping over his battle-scarred batwing chaps. One of his suspenders had popped a button and was also bouncing around. His wide-brimmed hat lay in the middle of the corral.

"Luther, are we going to have to teach you again about putting your things away?!" Ethan yelled.

Luther nodded his head in appreciation, praised the horse as it began to follow his commands without hesitation, "Hot-damn and horny toads for breakfast! Would you look at the fanciness this h'yar dandy hoss is a-doin'. Looks like a Toledo drummer goin' to church on a fine Sunday mornin'."

Luther waved his arms as if accepting the applause of an invisible audience and hollered with a smile,

"Reckon he dun be ready to cum out, Ethan. Yessir, open up them gates o' paradise!"

"Make Rip come walking."

Luther rode out of the corral, keeping the bay to a hesitant walk. But the mustang turned its back away from the gate and sidestepped toward the opening. With a whap of his quirt, he convinced the horse to straighten around. Once out into the ranch yard, he forced it into a walking circle every time the animal attempted to break into a canter, slapping hard with his quirt to reinforce the point.

He stopped the horse and swung down. Holding the reins tightly, he untied a rolled-up slicker on the back of the saddle for the next phase of breaking. He lifted the slicker and let it unravel. With one sweep, Luther covered the horse's head with the oil cloth to get it used to unexpected sounds and scary activity. A few minutes later, he swung back into the saddle and continued the slicker training. His legs tightened in anticipation of the bucking that would surely come as he spread the long raincoat over the horse's head, but the horse remained calm.

"Wal, a ri't smart hoss you be, Rip," Luther praised. They rode past two horses, worked earlier, tied to the long hitching rail next to the bunkhouse. All of the green horses remained saddled until the tack was needed. The extra time wearing saddles and bridles gave the mounts another lesson in their new responsiblities.

Ethan looked away from his brother's exit and instinctively sought Claire. His eyes first caught the red and white flowers peeking out from adobe windowsill boxes under the two front windows of the main house. To the far right was a small rock cooling house and a stone well. Down the hill and closer to the corrals was the bunkhouse and the connected cookhouse. Little Maggie was playing with a rag doll on the front porch. Blue lay beside her, watching quietly. Movement at the front door porch drew the dog's eyes there.

Claire came out of the door, headed for the loaded chuck wagon. She was carrying a box; he figured it was tobacco. Last night, when they were alone, he suggested adding more sacks of Bull Durham and more wedges; tobacco would be scarce where they were going, and might also be a good trade offering with the Indians, if that proved necessary. As if sensing Ethan's observation, the handsome woman glanced toward the corral. Her smile was a rainbow to his eyes. He smiled back. *God, I'm going to miss her!* he thought.

After trotting Rip around the open ranch yard, Luther took him to the rail with the other worked horses. He patted the bay on the neck and walked over to a water barrel next to the bunkhouse made of cottonwood logs. His leathery hands were cupped together to bring the liquid coolness to his sunburned face. He glanced at the watery-eyed dun standing alone, tied to a scrawny cottonwood twenty yards away.

Fighting distemper, the thin-flanked animal coughed as a running sore glared from under its lower jaw. Luther was thankful the disease hadn't spread to others but felt sorry for the horse. He couldn't resist walking over and patting the weak animal.

"Now, don' ya be a-frettin'. Ya gonna be fit as fiddle in no time, boy," he said softly.

After talking to the sick horse, he walked past the bunkhouse and the roofed breezeway that connected it to a small stone cookhouse, and headed back to the corrals. He was actually excited inside, except for the part of him that would never be the same, that would never be anything but pain. Riding horses was one of his favorite things in the world. That and fried chicken. Keeping busy also kept his mind from betraying him with images of his dead wife and children, seeping out from that black place where he kept them locked away. Luther didn't think he would ever be strong enough to accept that ache full-on again.

Eli came running to be near his idol. "Hi, Luther! Did you like that hoss? Was he tough to ride, huh?"

The cowboy put his hand on the boy's shoulder as they walked along. His own daughter, Rebecca, would have been about this age. Luther blinked away the memory and said, "That Rip's gonna work out real fittin', Eli. Hope I git 'im for my string." Eli's eyes shone with being told such important information as they ambled toward the corrals.

"I really like the twelve we've picked so far," Ethan yelled as Luther and the boy advanced.

"Reckon they'll do."

"What about that dark brown?"

"No. That boy, he dun be gelded."

"Too bad. No reason to add to our problems, though. How about that bay you worked first thing this morning?"

"No, that thar animal's a stargazer."

"That's a damn shame. Fine-looking horse. You think you can break him of that?"

"Leave that rascal hyar."

Ethan knew his older brother was right. An animal that held its head up high, instead of a natural position, was a dangerous mount. It was either excitable by nature or had been worked too hard, too early, with a bit in its mouth, and tried to stay away from that pain by keeping its head high. Either way it would take patience to break the habit, and they didn't have that luxury now.

"You think there's eight more in there worth taking?"

"Oh, yeah, big brother, I reckon so. Ain't gonna be easy, though."

"Have you given Claire the extra lariats, leather, and the rest of your horse gear?"

"Sure nuff," Luther answered with a smile. Ethan had asked him that three days in a row.

Ethan said, "I'm gonna get Kiowa ready."

A frown split Luther's forehead. He looked at the tall cattleman and his silence told much.

"One more time. If I can't stay, we'll give up on him for now. I promise," Ethan answered the unspoken question.

Luther remained silent for a moment and spat, "Thar's other'n we should be a-workin' instead, if'n ya want nuther eight."

"You're getting old, Luther," Ethan teased, and lightly slapped the man's shoulder. Luther smiled wanly.

"Wal, let me be a-straddlin' that thar red a'fur ya. Then ya kin jump on 'im," the grizzled cowboy said, and spat a long brown stream of tobacco juice at the jutting corral post.

"No, Luther. You've already ridden twice this morning. It's my turn. Besides, he threw you yesterday. Remember?"

No more words were spoken. Luther and Ethan headed for the holding corral. Luther stalked the big sorrel skittering among the other horses. With laid-back ears and wide eyes, they broke away from the south rim of the corral and flowed around Luther standing in the center. As the sorrel glided past, Luther darted his lasso toward its flashing front legs. Seconds later Kiowa was on the dusty ground.

"Atta way to busy him!" Ethan yelled, and pounced on the downed animal to hog-tie its front legs together with a soft hemp rope. Luther came behind him with another rope to tie one hind leg and connect the lariat to the hog-tied front feet for further control.

It was Luther who had insisted on the value of fore-footing instead of neck-roping a young horse. He kept showing Ethan how a horse roped by the neck would fight, convinced its life was at stake. The fearful animal would run until choked down, and that could mean an injury as well as pulling the cowboy around. That certainly didn't help calm the animal for the next time, either. Roping the forelegs made it easy to pull the animal on the ground without harm. In minutes, a horse was under control and saddled. Just like now.

Around the sorrel's eyes, Luther knotted a blue kerchief and then began the saddling. The horse took the bit without shaking its head, but worked the metal bar in its jaws, not liking what the piece meant. Led by Luther, Kiowa walked into the main corral quietly and made no attempt to struggle or kick. Luther held the powerful sorrel's head with both hands tight on the bridle as Ethan untied the bindings at its legs and removed the rope. Ears flat against its head were the only indication the big red gelding was disturbed by this handling. Luther took the lariat and quickly rolled it in his hand.

"Reckon I'll be a-takin' a ride on 'im first, brother," Luther said as he advanced, trying to act casual about it.

"Thanks, Luther. Later you can."

"Lemme ride 'im first, Ethan. I knows 'im."

"No, this time he's mine."

Luther mumbled to himself, but Ethan couldn't make it out.

"Cum on now, knothead. Ya be a-mindin' your manners, ya hear me . . . or we dun gonna make stew outta your sorry hide," Luther blurted as he grabbed the animal's ears and twisted them to keep its attention on the pain while Ethan removed the blindfold. He mumbled something else that Ethan couldn't understand either.

Ethan rechecked the cinch and bridle one last time and swung into the saddle. Luther released the animal's ears and grabbed the reins close to the bit. A wave of the rancher's hand signaled Luther to let go and stand back. Luther's worried face was quite readable as he walked toward Eli, who was watching from the rail. He avoided looking at the young boy and leaned against the corral fencing, fiddling with the coiled rope in his hands.

The red horse stood absolutely still, as if checking to see if it was really free. There was no mistaking the explosiveness in this animal. Like one of those Fourth of July fireballs Luther enjoyed so much, the sorrel's first move was straight up—an arching back-bending jump, leaving Ethan's breath back with the onlookers. Horse and rider hung in the sky, caught on an invisible hook. When they returned to the ground with an earth-rattling jolt, Ethan's shoulders snapped backward. Kiowa bucked again, even higher than the first time, came down, and spun viciously in a circle twice, then three times. Suddenly, the sorrel reared, standing up straight.

Luther yelled, "Jump!"

The tall cattleman was off balance when the horse returned its front feet to the earth, only to buck again. Ethan rocked back and forth, then sideways; his legs swung uncontrolled, like they were being yanked. His outstretched right arm grabbed the air, fighting to stay in the saddle. His left hand held the reins with every ounce of his strength, now reinforced with fear. With blurring speed, the sorrel's head came backward as Ethan's face came forward. The impact was a poleax blow to his head. The cattleman's eyes flew back in his head and he left the saddle in a frozen pose. He hit the ground with his shoulder, and the sorrel slammed its back hooves at the unconscious man's head. The sound was a sickening whack.

Luther's lariat caught the red animal by the neck and pulled the wild animal away from the unmoving rancher. After tying it to the corral railing, he quickly turned and wobbled toward Ethan as fast as his bowed legs would allow. Eli was already kneeling next to his father, his hands frozen midway toward Ethan's head. The imprint of the hoof was an outline of red on the side of Ethan's temple; a thin streak of blood ran from his mouth; his body was limp. His chest heaving, Luther caught up and leaned over Eli's shoulder to look.

"Son, ya he'p me lift yur pappy. I'll carry 'im to the house. Cum on!"

"I-is he dead?"

"No, no, he ain't. But he dun took a hard 'un to his haid. We'uns gotta hurry, son."

Eli pushed with all his might. Grunting under the weight, Luther lifted the unconscious rancher into his arms and carried him toward the front porch. Walking backward, Eli couldn't take his eyes off his father's bloody head. The boy was white-faced with fear, but no tears had broken through. As if by premonition, Claire Kerry met them on the front porch. Her eyes glittered with fright, but her voice was forced into a calm order. Luther saw the tiny trembles grabbing at the corners of her mouth.

"Please carry him inside. To the bed. Luther, you ride for Dr. Hawkinson. Hurry . . . please!" As if disconnected from everyone, Eli nodded slowly, like a tree branch in a high wind; he looked again at his father's face, then at his mother's as it disappeared into tears. The boy's trance twisted into uncontrolled anguish, and he began to weep.

# *Chapter Four*

In a crowded corner of the hot Uvalde, Texas, saloon, an old man played a worn guitar, lost in the memories of the song. Around him swirled the cacophony of men laughing and talking, while a dark-haired white woman, a tall blonde with heavy rouge, and two Mexican women served them. Four well-dressed men were playing a serious game of poker in the corner. Chips, gold coins, and certificates were scattered among the players. At another table, five plainsmen played for drinks. All of the tables were filled; the saloon was busy even at this early hour.

From the midmorning shadows of the main room, the outlaw Cole Kerry sat alone at a table with a long scratch across its surface. In his lap was one of his ivory-handled, silver-plated Colts. It was easier to get to when he was eating, a habit he had learned in battle. The gun had come from a sidewinder holster on his bullet belt at the front of his waist, butt toward the ground, barrel parallel to the belt. The second Colt sat in a regular holster on his right hip. Both weapons were set to be drawn with his right hand.

His light blue eyes hunted the room for trouble as he gulped down his second plateful of beans, chilis, and torillas and nursed a bottle of tequila. This was his third day in this small Texas town. Weeks back, he had outrun a posse that had tracked him into the Nations before quickly losing their courage and going back home to their wives and sweethearts. He didn't blame them; riding through the Nations wasn't a thing to take lightly.

Only a few federal marshals ever dared it, and did so rarely. It was like entering another world, one without law of any kind—a vast, uncharted world where outlaw gangs roamed without fear after attacking border towns in Kansas and Missouri. Scattered throughout the rolling hills and thick forests, war parties of Kiowa and Comanche waited to pounce on unsuspecting riders, in stark contrast to the civilized tribes of Cherokees, Creeks, Seminoles, Choctaws, and Chickasaws who occupied the Territory legally.

In Abilene, Kansas, he had killed a man over a woman and wounded another. Kathleen Shannon was her name, and she was as Irish as it sounded. It was the first woman he loved, or thought he did. She wasn't beautiful, at least not not by most men's standards. But there was about her a bewitching presence that made him want to be with her all of the time. Dark crimson hair framed a plain, freckled face that became radiant when she smiled. Cole had never seen a woman smile and talk at the same time like she did. Large brown eyes explored his soul, seeking something only her own soul knew. Even now, the warm sweet smell of her filled his mind. It shouldn't be that way, but it was.

She had made it clear she didn't want to see him again and that she was going to marry Webster Stevenson.

That was the man he killed. Webster Stevenson's father was a prominent businessman, and the son was raised to feel he was royalty, even though Abilene was still essentially a cow town. Webster and two friends had come to the saloon after Cole had been told by Kathleen that she was going to marry the young townsman. Her face didn't smile that day. They intended to send him running, but he wouldn't.

Cole downed Webster and one friend with his fists, then the second friend pulled a pistol, as did Webster. Both men fired at him, striking Cole in the right leg and creasing his right shoulder. Cole's returned shots—while on his knees—killed Webster and hit the friend in the chest. Witnesses said it was self-defense, but that didn't matter. Webster's father arranged for a posse, and they were eager to put a rope around his neck. The long ride and the reason for it lay on his tongue like old milk. Only the tequila seemed to help erase it and the ache in his leg. He took another swallow of the fiery liquid and winced as it exploded in his throat.

Several days of unshaven beard couldn't cover a deep cleft in his chin or the boyish charm in his hard face. His nose held the faint memory of being broken once by his brother, Ethan, in a scuffling match. He had returned the favor. Cole hadn't seen Ethan or Luther, his oldest brother, since he rode out angrily. That was ten years ago. He figured his older brothers probably thought he was dead.

After leaving Texas as a young angry man, Cole drifted northward alone with little purpose, except to hurt the North somehow. His fuming was mostly embarrassment at the South having to admit defeat—but partly his natural tendency to fight. He robbed a Yankee bank in Ohio but found no satisfaction in the deed, only Union troops chasing him for a week.

For the next decade, he rode both sides of the owl-hoot trail, sometimes selling his ability with a gun, sometimes riding with other outlaws. He drifted from one raw Kansas town to another. Once he even accepted a sheriff's badge briefly—after a friend, who had worn it proudly, was murdered. Cole had killed the two men responsible. Since then, he had crisscrossed the plains, mostly as a hired gun for cattlemen.

The Nations was the perfect territory for the lawless to hide until they were ready to strike again. He had spent a lot of time there. Few lawmen ever went into the Nations and lived to tell it—much less tracked outlaws openly. It was a lonely life, but one that suited him. Stopping at several Texas trail herd campfires he met along the way for supper awakened the yearning to return, before he recognized the idea for what it was. He had never had the urge to see his older brothers again—until now.

Uvalde! Who would have thought he would have ever returned to this place! The town had changed much since he left. Of course, he recognized a few of the buildings, but he hadn't seen anyone he knew. Once he crossed the Red River, Uvalde had been a magnet to his mind. Tomorrow, he would ride out to see if he could find the Bar K and his older brothers, Ethan and Luther. Wouldn't that be something!

"I reckon you're through with this h'yar table."

The words broke into Cole's daydreaming. He looked up to see four men standing near him. The tallest, and closest, was the one who had addressed him, and the apparent leader of the group. Cole heard the stocky cowboy say, "Git him movin', Everett. I'm plumb thirsty."

Everett's elongated face was braced by muttonchop sideburns and accented by a blubbery lower lip. Everett's suit and pants were newly store-bought but too small for his long frame. He wore a new hat, too. A day in town had been busy, it appeared. Whiskey inflamed his eyes and increased the snarl of his mouth. He was expecting fear to show on the seated stranger's face, followed by a quick desire to leave.

Behind Everett were three cowhands: a sloe-eyed, younger man; a stocky brawler with an uneven beard; and a blue-shirted man with a discolored right eye. A white scar crossed the brow of the disabled eye. The side of this man's mouth was jammed with tobacco. Everett referred to him as Cherokee, telling him that the stranger was getting ready to leave. All were carrying pistols. Cole could also see a knife holstered at Everett's waist.

In the shadows, back against the saloon's southern wall, stood a large, wide-shouldered man with his arms crossed, waiting. Cruel, bulging eyes loomed in the grayness and wanted to pop from the large man's face. Cole was certain the foursome worked for him. The young outlaw's attention was drawn momentarily to the wide-shouldered man. He wore a dark pin-striped suit, a silk cravat, and a white, round-crowned Stetson.

Here was someone used to having his way, Cole thought. Haughtiness distorted the man's round face, made smaller by the extended eyes, stickpin nose, full dark beard, and arching eyebrows. The tall blond waitress stopped to greet him, and he ran a hand familiarly over her arms and breasts as he talked to her. She smiled self-consciously and nodded her head. His savage smile reminded Cole of the senior Stevenson.

Cole's casual manner aggravated the Cherokee because he didn't respond in any way to Everett's demand. Instead, he picked up his coffee cup with his left hand, letting his right go to his lap. Cole's eyes were aimed at the bar across the room.

"Didn't ya hear my friend?" Cherokee asked brusquely. "He said git."

Everett chuckled. "Now, Cherokee, this h'yar gentleman was just leavin'. He jes' didn't understand, that's all. See that big fella back thar? That's Sam Winlow. This is his table."

From under the table, Everett heard the distinctive sound of the hammer of a gun pulled back. He froze. His friends hadn't heard it. Cherokee stepped toward the table, set to dramatize his point by spitting on Cole's remaining food.

"Swallow it—or your guts will be plastered on that wall," came the warning from Cole. Cherokee stopped, his once-glaring eyes widened. He hadn't expected resistance; no one ever did when a Walking W rider wanted something in Uvalde, especially with their boss, Sam Winlow, with them.

"He's got iron under thar, Cherokee," Everett said, examining more closely the seated man in front of them. He made a quick decision.

"I reckon we dun made a mistake, mister. Thought you was through an' all. Sorry."

"Tell your friend to swallow that mouthful of brown. I've been riding trail for too damn long to put up with the likes of your sorry asses. Do it." Cole's eyes were slits, but the brightness of anger shone through.

Sweating, Everett glanced back at the man in the shadows, then turned to his blue-shirted friend. "Swallow the tobacky, Cherokee."

Looking at his taller friend in disbelief, then over to the hard stranger at the table, Cherokee took a deep breath and swallowed. He blinked his eyes to hold back the tears unleashed by its bitterness.

"Tell your boss—what's his name—that I don't move for bug-eyed assholes. Say it, I want to hear you say it."

"Ah, boss . . . ah, he says he don't . . . ah, move for bug-eyed assholes." Everett's voice cracked with the pressure of fear from both sides of this situation. His face cried for relief.

Sam Winlow's face crackled with hate. His bulging eyes became hooded daggers toward Cole, and he waved his men to go. The four turned away and left Cole alone again. He watched them move to the far corner of the saloon and repeat their interruption of an occupied table. It worked this time. Three cardplayers quickly removed themselves from the sought-after location. The large man in the shadows walked forward like a crown prince at a coronation. The cowboy called Cherokee pushed back a chair for him to sit in. The blond waitress was invited to sit with them, and she reluctantly did. Cole went back to his food and his thinking.

After he spent a day or two with his brothers, he was giving strong thought to heading back to western Kansas and joining a buffalo-hunting outfit. A few herds were left, and the hides still brought good money. The other idea he'd been chewing on was to head for Dodge City and open a saloon. From what he'd seen the last time he'd ridden through, the town was a gold mine, what with all the trail herds headed there, instead of Abilene, Ellsworth, or Wichita now. One thing was certain: He was tired of running.

"What else can Maria do for you, senor?" asked the raven-haired Mexican waitress, leaning over the table to fill his coffee cup.

She looked up to assure herself that he saw her ample bosom revealed as the scooped neckline of her blouse fell away. Cole's dark eyebrows arched in appreciation, and he grinned mischievously. Maria returned his response with a light touch of her fingers on his hand.

"Sweetheart, give me a minute and I'll be right with you," he said, his smile warm and beguiling.

It was time to relax, he told himself. And a great way to forget Kathleen Shannon and all the trouble she had brought him. Cole Kerry pushed his wide-brimmed, black hat off his head. The leather tie-down held it at his neck as he rose from his chair. He returned the Colt to its holster, tossed a coin on the table in one fluid motion, and grinned again.

"Lead on, sugar."

"*Sí,* Senor."

His spurs brushed the wooden steps as he followed her up a creaky staircase to a half-floor consisting of three small bedrooms. He tried to brush trail dust from his vest and the faded pants that disappeared into his boot tops just below his knees. The task was hopeless, and he quit after a few swipes. It was too hot for the black coat he wore, but he liked it. A black silk kerchief hung loosely around his neck, showing a collarless shirt that had once been blue and now was torn where Webster's bullet had severed the cloth. No one would mistake him for a cowman or a clerk. He looked dangerous in spite of his easy smile. A bullet hole in his upper boot explained his limp. The ache in his leg was a dull, constant pain.

An upstairs bedroom greeted Cole and Maria with one candle atop a dilapidated cabinet. An iron-framed bed was the only other furniture in the gray room. One wall featured a window that overlooked the alley. A lopsided painting of a horse decorated the opposite wall. Cole felt compelled to straighten the picture as he entered.

"Sugar, while you get yourself all ready, I'm going to lay right down here and wait," Cole Kerry explained, tossing his hat on the floor and unbuckling his gunbelt. He laid the weapons on the cabinet next to the bed and stretched out on the faded red bedspread. It felt good to his wounded leg. Kathleen came to his tired mind and caressed the weary thoughts bundled there.

Surprised at his casual approach, and lack of interest in holding her or taking off her clothes, Maria removed her blouse with a shrug. She turned around proudly to watch the lust fill his face. Instead, she saw a man sound asleep.

"*Senor*, are you ready for sweet dessert?" she purred. The response was a light snoring.

She repeated the provocative offer, this time leaning over him to let her breasts trace lines across his face. Soon, she realized the affair was over. The handsome man before her had released himself in another way. Maria reached into his right front pocket and found nothing. Moving to the other side of the bed, she tried his left pants pocket and was rewarded with two gold coins. She kept one and put the other back.

"*Adios,*" she whispered as she rebuttoned her shawl blouse, closed the door, and returned to the cacophony of the saloon.

An hour later, commotion downstairs shook Cole awake. He came out of a deep sleep, struggling to pull himself from the murky world of dreams and back into the reality of the tiny room. For three heartbeats, he had no idea of where he was. He muttered, "Kathleen, where are you?" Consciousness finally shoved away the stupor of fatigue. He wanted to go back to sleep, but the noise below was growing. It had to be a fight. There were better places to rest anyway, he thought, and remembered why he was upstairs. He checked his front pockets and discovered there was only one coin. He chuckled and shook his head. His hotel room would be quiet—and safer. A good night's rest would prepare him for his short trip to the ranch. When he admitted it to himself, he was fearful of going. It had been so long, and he left spitting such venom. They probably wouldn't like seeing him again.

Swinging his feet to the floor, Cole shook his head, picked up his pistol belt, and looked for his hat. His movements were like a puppet's; he pushed away the deep tiredness wearing on his soul. Suddenly remembering, he felt his back pocket for reassurance the folded letter to Kathleen was still with him. The lone sheet was comfortably settled there. It was the third he had written; the other two were burned in campfires. They were filled with hate. This letter told his real feelings: He loved her and wanted only happiness for her. Yet he had not posted the letter at the last trading post he had passed. He couldn't bring himself to do it.

As he cleared the first half of the staircase, the trouble in the saloon below was evident. It was the same four cowboys who had riled him earlier.

Two of them held a bloody cowboy while the tall Everett pummeled him with his fists. An older gentleman was being held by the one-eyed Cherokee. Most of the saloon crowd watched from their chairs, offering anonymous encouragement to the cowboys. Those at the bar had drawn closer to fully enjoy the spectacle. None attempted to intervene. Cole saw the well-dressed, large-eyed man from earlier, sitting at the same table and sipping whiskey, apparently with little interest in what his associates were doing. The blond waitress sat beside him; his hand rested on her thigh exposed below a shoved-back green skirt.

"What the hell you think you're doin', old man? You think you kin jes' come in here. . . . and ask for our town doc?!" growled Everett. He was doing the slugging and obviously enjoying it.

Stepping back, Everett took a deep breath, momentarily fatigued by the beating given the trapped cowboy. Everett shook both of his hands to rid them of the soreness acquired by the blows. On the floor, not far from the cowboy's battered hat, lay Everett's new one. A bald-headed man handed him a bottle, and Everett took a long swig before returning it. He liked being the center of attention.

In midstep, Cole Kerry realized who the battered cowboy was. Luther! It was Luther! His oldest brother! The one who had cried when he showed up as a too-young recruit to ride with his brothers against the North. Reenergized by the bitter liquor, Everett returned to his task with a lopsided snear. His fist slammed into Luther's midsection. After wincing, Luther slowly looked up and spat in Everett's face.

"Why, you goddamn sonvabitch, I'll teach you!" Everett yelled, wiping his face with the back of his reddened hand. He reached for the knife in the sheath on his left hip, dangling from an old belt that also held a holstered revolver.

"If you pull that blade, you'll never see another day."

Cole Kerry's words ripped into the tense air like a sharp saw into dry wood. Everyone stopped watching Everett and looked for the source. It was as if the words had drifted in from some strange place disconnected from the beating. Who would dare make such a statement?!

The tall cowboy's head swung like on a swivel, his

angry eyes searching for courage in any of the onlookers. Finally he saw Cole standing casually at the foot of the staircase and knew where the challenge had come. Cole's right arm rested on the rickety bannister.

"Thought you left. Don't think I heard you right, stranger," Everett accused.

"Sure you did. But I'll say it again, just so you get it straight. I said you an' your asshole friends are yellow cowards. Afraid to face this man by yourself. I think that's what I said."

Everett sputtered in disbelief, "Why, you . . ."

"No, that's not what I said. That's just what I thought," Cole continued, his eyes penetrating Everett's face. "What I said was—leave my friend alone . . . and do it now. That's what I said, wasn't it? Or did I say you would die if you pulled that knife? Yeah, that was it. I get it mixed up sometimes. Too much riding alone, I guess."

Chuckling danced through the attentive audience, fascinated anew by the interruption and the man who caused it. Luther stared at the young stranger across the room through half-closed eyes. Recognition of who it was slowly clicked inside him. He muttered, "Well, I'll be damned. Cole. Li'l brother, it dun be you, ain't it?"

"You're about to get in over your head, mister. Move on," Everett threatened.

Cole pursed his lips, shook his head slowly, and replied, "Tell your friend, the one that likes to swallow tobacco, if he moves any closer to his gun, I'll put a bullet in your brain. And his. And tell your bug-eyed boss over there to keep his hands on that lady's leg where I can see them."

"Quit it, Cherokee. You fool! I'll take care of this," Everett snapped without looking around.

"Good," Cole replied. "I thought you looked like a man who hadn't been kicked in the head . . . too many times."

Loud laughter skipped across the room behind the tall cowboy, engulfing the more constrained chuckles. Everett's eyes searched the crowd again and abruptly silenced it. He looked back again and was surprised to find Cole only two steps away.

"How tough are you when the man can hit back?" Cole said in a low, even voice.

# Chapter Five

A calm passed over the tired outlaw and, instantly, everyone seemed to be within thick molasses, with every movement slowed to a fraction of its normal speed. Without turning his head, Cole saw the grizzled drunk on the far left scratch his ear. Behind Everett, he saw the sloe-eyed cowboy and the stocky one tighten their holds on Luther's arms. His vision caught Cherokee biting his lower lip nervously, while to the far right, he saw the fat clerk whisper to the wide-eyed, whiskey-cheeked man next to him.

He saw the rancher who led these men was now turned toward them; gone was his pretense of not being interested. His bulging eyes analyzed Cole. Both of the big man's hands were on top of the table, his hands wrapped around the half-empty glass of whiskey in an overstated demonstration of nonengagement. The waitress was gone. Everything was within Cole's vision, yet all of his concentration was on Everett. During a fight he was aware of all detail, big and little, and yet afterward could barely describe what happened. It was one flowing decision. He couldn't remember when fighting wasn't this way. The entire room was in his sight while focusing on Everett, directly in front of him. It was an inner quiet, like some unseen force that took over his body and directed it. Ethan said it was the instinct of a fighter; their Irish father said it was the power of the wee spirits around his youngest son. Regardless of the reason, there was something about this kind of moment that made him feel alive.

"You're gonna . . ." Everett screamed, and swung a heavy-armed haymaker at Cole Kerry's face.

Cole's left forearm stopped the blow, pushing it harmlessly past his ear. He ducked at the same moment and followed the parry with a vicious right hand that drove deep into Everett's stomach. The tall cowboy gasped as his breath disappeared and a fire of pain ignited. A heartbeat behind came Cole's left fist, removing any remaining wisps of air in the man. The tall cowboy bent over, grabbing at his midsection, his mouth open, spittle dripping from his mouth. Cole threw a blurring right jab that connected at the bottom of Everett's jaw. Those standing near the fight heard the jawbone pop.

The rest of Cole's frustration was released with a savage combination of two well-placed punches: a short hammer again to the cowboy's tortured stomach and a final smash to his nose. Blood sprang wildly across the room. Everett crumpled and sank without knowing to the floor. The two disbelieving cowboys holding Luther flinched at their leader's collapse.

Taking advantage of their unsteadiness, the bloody-faced Luther yanked his right arm free of the stocky man's softened grip and swung his freed fist into the belly of the surprised, sloe-eyed cowboy holding his left arm. Just as the cowboy's grip released, Luther kneed him in the groin. Regaining his balance, the stocky man reached for Luther, but something made him look first at Cole. The young outlaw mouthed, "No." The man froze. Luther grinned at Cole Kerry and returned to the bent-over, sloe-eyed cowboy.

"Ya git to goin' straight ta hell, ya yeller bastard," Luther growled, and finished his counterattack with a full swing of his right fist into the groaning man's unprotected chin. The cowboy's body arched in response to the blow and flipped backward, finally sliding up against the bar.

During this commotion, Cherokee regained his courage, released the older man he held, and went for his pistol. His hand had pulled the gun halfway from the holster when his mind registered that Cole Kerry was already holding a thumbed-back Colt. No one remembered seeing him draw the silver-plated gun.

"My maw told me never to start anything I didn't intend to finish," Cole said, his smile inviting a response. "What'd your maw tell you?"

Cherokee's hands shivered toward the ceiling, letting the gun slide harmlessly back into its holster. Somewhere in the back of the room came a long sigh of relief.

"Luther, it's mighty good to see you," Cole said with a sly grin, returning his pistol to the sidewinder holster. "What brings you to town?"

"Came fer the doc, Cole. Ethan's got hisself all banged up by a kickin' hoss. Big red mean outlaw. Hit 'im in the head. It's bad," Luther answered, paused, shook his head, and proclaimed, "Gawdalmighty, boy, it be good to see ya. By golly, if'n ya don't 'pear a day older than when ya hightailed it outta hyar."

"Neither do you, Luther."

"Now, that thar sounds a wee like Paw's kinda windyin'."

"What's with these bastards? How come they—"

"They's Walkin' W men, Cole. Reckon they do the biddin' o' that big sonvabitch Sam Winlow. Over thar. He dun got hisse'f all fixed on gittin' Ethan's place."

"I want to thank you for . . . for stopping this. Ethan Kerry is a friend," Dr. Hawkinson, the older man restrained by the two Walking W riders, interrupted. His thin voice struggled to sound professional and without fear.

"Good. Sounds like we'd better ride, Doc. You got a horse handy?" Cole asked. Before the doctor could answer, the young outlaw turned around to look for the bug-eyed man. Sam Winlow wasn't in the saloon.

Streaks of pink in the late-afternoon sky signaled the opening act of dusk when Cole, Luther, and the doctor rode into the Bar K ranchyard. Clancey was pacing back and forth on the front porch, stopping occasionally to sip from a small flask.

"Aye, an' it's been a long wait for ye, Doc Hawkinson. Good that you are here, t'is," Clancey Kerry greeted heartily as the the three men entered the open ranch yard. Luther headed directly to the main corral where the rest of the horses were milling, while Cole and the doctor advanced toward the house.

"Hurt bad is me fine son, but your good hand, guided by the God of me blessed mither, will make him well. This I know, Doc," Clancey pronounced without acknowledging the new rider.

Claire and the children were inside with Ethan. Cole thought he would have recognized his father's voice anywhere. The big man looked smaller than Cole remembered. He tried to think kindly of him; their troubles as father and son should be long ridden over. He wasn't sure, though, if his heart agreed with his logic. A shiver ran through him, and he wanted to turn around and ride out.

"We came as fast as we could," Dr. Hawkinson said as they trotted toward the main house. He expected the big Irishman to recognize his third son.

When that didn't happen, he looked at Cole for permission to announce him. Cole pulled the brim of his hat down farther to shield his upper face and shook his head slightly. It wouldn't have mattered; the big Irishman had already turned and gone into the house. His voice could be heard outside, trumpeting the doctor's arrival. Cole held the reins of the doctor's horse while he dismounted at the porch. Dr. Hawkinson retrieved the reins and wrapped them carefully around the hitching rack adjacent to the porch.

"They will be glad to see you, Cole. They could use you now, I suspect," Dr. Hawkinson said.

He pulled his bulky saddlebags, filled with medical supplies, from their latigo straps. Laying them across his right arm, he brushed off the trail dust from his suit with his left.

"I appreciate the thought, but not right now, Doc. This isn't the time. You take care of Ethan first. I'll let them know when you're finished," Cole replied, acknowledging to himself that he just couldn't barge into his brother's home after the way he left and the time that had passed. It didn't feel right; he wasn't certain now that he should have even come and fought the inner desire to leave.

"Whatever you wish, son."

"Good luck, Doc."

Dr. Hawkinson half-trotted up the porch and disappeared into the house. Leaning against the saddle horn,

Cole stared at the ranchhouse; his gaze gradually took in all of the other buildings, noting to himself how well constructed they were and how well cared for.

"Looks like Ethan built it, all right," he said to himself. "Everything in its place and nailed down tight."

He wheeled his black horse around and headed toward the corral, where Luther waited.

"Ya should be hyar. With your brothers," Luther said quietly, his eyes remaining lowered.

Cole thought his slow-witted brother was going to cry. He remembered Luther as always protecting him from Ethan's roughhousing when they were boys. He had continued to protect him, or tried to, when they were part of the Texas brigade. How long ago that seemed. More like some other life, or some other people. Cole knew the grizzled man in front of him was so worried about his brother that he couldn't think. Yet the young outlaw could think of no words to comfort him. From Luther's description on the ride from town, it sounded bad for Ethan. What could he say to Luther that wouldn't ring hollow—or sound foolish?

"I got a likin' fer this hyar black," Luther said, relieving Cole of the difficulty of making his older brother feel better.

The wrangler leaned down and ran his hand down the horse's lower front legs, then checked each hoof. He repeated the examination with the back legs, stood, and pronounced, "This one'll run all day an' ask fer passengers." Cole recalled that it was one of his favorite expressions about a strong horse.

"You know your horses, Luther. This ol' boy took me from Abilene, down through the Nations, to here. Never asked for quarter. Never got it."

"I'll take 'im to the barn. Grain and water hisse'f."

"That's mighty nice of you, Luther. He'll probably

not know what the grain is for. Been living on buffalo grass for a long time!"

Luther spat a long stream of tobacco juice, glanced at the silent ranch house, and asked, "Did ya see many cow drives as ya was a-droppin' down?"

"Sure did. Camped with three different outfits coming across the Nations. Made me think of you boys."

"Any Injun trouble?"

It was obvious Luther wanted to talk about anything that would keep his mind off of Ethan.

"Once, but I was lucky." Cole shook his head. "I was beat tired and stopped for water. Wasn't paying attention to anything but drinking—and a band of Comanche warriors came up on me like I was some greenhorn. They flat caught me napping. They were wearing paint and showing fresh scalps. Their head man was one tough-looking hombre. Painted red on half of his body, top and bottom. Red feathers, red breechcloth. Red paint all over his horse. A white horse it was."

Luther asked, "Wonder if his ol' bare ass be a-painted red, or ha'f red?"

Cole chuckled. "I didn't stop to check. I swung on top of ol' Black and burned grass outta there."

"They chase ya down?"

"No, I guess they got what they wanted, the watering hole. An' I guess they had enough scalps for the day."

"Never kin figger Injuns," Luther acknowledged, scratching his unshaved chin.

"You got that right. At least, I can't."

With an uncertain frown on his face, Luther suddenly asked, "Why did ya up n' leave us back then, Cole?"

"Seemed like the thing to do at the time, Luther."

"Ya shouldn'ta have left us, li'l brother. We needed ya."

Cole cocked his head to the side and smiled. He knew it was a statement of caring. They continued to talk as Luther took Cole's horse and headed toward the barn. Cole followed, marveling at the older man's ability to shake off the saloon punishment. His right eye was half swollen shut and his lower lip was puffy, sawed at the corner and scabbed over. His movements were stiff at times; Cole knew most men would be bedridden after such a beating.

But the rawboned cowhand hadn't said a word about it. Cole decided no one would know how much in pain he felt either. Same old Luther, the youngest Kerry smiled to himself. On the hurried return, Luther had thanked Cole for his help, told him what had happened to Ethan and the problem with Sam Winlow and talked nonstop about the Bar K.

"What do you keep in here?" Cole asked after they left the stable and paused beside a large, split-log building with its double doors opened. He noticed dirt had been well packed around the foundation timbers, with trenches dug to lead the water away. The barn was protected the same way. That would be Ethan, he thought.

Luther patted the wall and spat a long stream of tobacco juice for emphasis. "We'uns hammered this hyar shed together last fall. Dun keep most o' our tack in thar. Chuck wagon, too. It's up by the big house ri't now. Mrs. Kerry, you remember Claire, don't ya—she's bin a-stewin' over it, gittin' her ready for the drive."

"Looks sturdy."

"Well, ya know'd yur brother." Luther blinked hard to keep away the wetness that was attracted by his words.

Cole nodded and asked, "Care for a cigar?" He

pulled a black cheroot from his inside coat pocket.

"No, thank ye. Got mese'f a ri't fine chaw a-workin'."

Cole bit off the end of the cigar, spat it toward the ground, and lit the smoke. They continued walking; Luther described the ranch with considerable pride, mentioning places where family incidents had occurred. Cole enjoyed listening and knew his brother needed the release.

"How long have you and Ethan been together?"

Luther gulped, spat another string of tobacco juice, and continued, "I joined 'em, ah, two year past, I reckon it were."

The hitch in Luther's voice signaled that this was a subject Cole shouldn't pursue further. Luther looked away at the horizon, blinked away the growing dusk, and rolled his neck to relieve the pressure that the last question had brought to his mind.

Ten feet from the shed was a tall tree stump, at least four feet tall and that much wide. Its upper edges were jagged from the rest of the tree being ripped away by wind years ago. They were walking past when Cole noticed that the stump had names carefully carved in it: "Ethan Kerry," "Claire Kerry," and "Luther Kerry" were in one cluster. "Clancey Kerry," "Eli Kerry," and "Maggie Kerry" were scratched into place slightly to the right of the first group. Another cluster of names featured Cole's late mother, "Alice Kerry," and two names that must be those of Claire's parents, "William Johnson" and "May Allison Johnson." And off to the left was a wobbly version of "Cole Kerry."

"Ethan, he dun started it all. That'd be his carvin' thar," Luther described, pausing to admire the misshapen stump as if he were seeing it for the first time. Spitting a thin stream of tobacco juice in the opposite direction, he continued, "Oh Claire, she dun came ri't down on the need to add the names o' her kin. They's dead, ya know. An' then as the rest o' us came along, Ethan added that bunch thar."

He paused, pointed at Cole's name, and said thoughtfully, " 'Bout a year ago it was, I reckon. T'were the day after Claire dun tolt me she were sur ya was still a-'kickin'. I figgered she dun it. Never said, though. Jes' one day Ethan an' me walked past h'yar an' thar it were. Like them spirits had dun it. Made Ethan happy to see it. Shore nuff, it did. I ain't spittin' in the wind. Nossir."

Luther looked toward the ranch house, and the sigh that followed was more like the bitter howl of a winter wind.

"How long has Paw been here?" Cole asked, trying to get him talking again. Luther's eyes shifted to examine the younger man's expression without appearing to do so. Cole's face was cut stone.

"Oh, I reckon ol' Clancey's bin a-strollin' around h'yar nigh onta the beginnin'. Leastwise, since Ethan had hisse'f this hyar place on its feet an' a-goin' strong."

"Has he changed much?"

"Nope, reckon he ain't, Cole. Lots a' holes in that thar ol' boy. Guess Pappy dun mean well, though."

"Yeah, guess so."

"Pappy'll be right smart proud to see ya, Cole."

"That's all right, Luther. I didn't come to see him. I came to . . ."

"I know'd that, Cole, but I reckon he'll be puffed up like a rooster in the mornin'."

They strolled on with Luther pointing out things of interest and without speaking more of the elder Kerry. They came to a stone-lined well across from the bunkhouse and stopped beside it. Cole was impressed with its construction. Luther leaned over to pick up two buckets without comment.

"Better be a-throwin' sum water upta them hosses. Them boys is a-lookin' a mite restless."

"I'll give you a hand."

"Cole, I shoulda bin atop that red hoss." Luther's face was torn with anguish. "Shoulda bin me. I know'd he were a outlaw. I knowed it."

Cole put a hand on his oldest brother's shoulder and said, "Luther, this wasn't your fault—an' no one thinks it was. If a man's around horses long enough, he's likely to get hurt. That's the truth of it. Ethan knew that—and there's no way he would have let you ride that sorrel. I haven't been here, but I know my brother. It's going to be all right. Ethan's a tough man, you'll see."

Luther wiped his eyes with his shirtsleeve and busied himself with gathering water. He seemed satisfied with Cole's answer and spoke no more. After lowering the buckets, one at a time, with the rigged well rope, they each carried two full buckets toward the corral. Luther's bowlegged stride jostled the water and splashed some on his chaps and boots.

"Gol durn it! Can't never git the hang o' this walkin'. Work oughta be dun on the back o' a hoss," he muttered, and grinned at Cole, who smiled back.

Two trips filled the corral trough as the horses crowded to it and pushed their muzzles deep into the cool wetness. Some weren't thirsty; instead, they swirled around the far side of the corral, searching for freedom.

Luther stopped next to where Cole stood at the side of the bronc-busting corral fence and watched him examine a sturdy brown horse. He spat a thick string of tobacco juice and growled, "Pardon my guldarned nosiness, Cole, but what brung ya, through the Nations an' all—to Uvalde. After all them years o' nobody knowin' whar ya was. Hellfire, Ethan dun figgered ya was dead. Said so hisse'f."

Cole turned toward him, expecting to see Luther's eyes peering at him in hard judgment. Instead, Luther's crinkled face carried an impish grin and he looked more like himself again.

"Well, Luther, I guess the first reason, I was running from a posse that wanted to put a rope around my neck."

"Oh. That be whar ya got the ketch in your leg?"

Luther's face couldn't hide the disappointment in having his gut hunch being true. Cole saw it and tried not to smile, realizing the man had deliberately opened a line of conversation most men wouldn't attempt. He told him about his experience in a few sentences, leaving out none of the important details—except that he couldn't stop thinking about Kathleen, in spite of what had happened.

"Cole, ya shoulda dun cum back sooner."

Pulling a square of tobacco from his shirt, Luther cut off a piece with a small pocketknife and pushed the tobacco into the right side of his mouth. His jaw looked like a big squirrel with a bunch of acorns. He offered the remaining square to Cole, but he declined. Cole told him about the reason he was being chased. Luther nodded.

"After I saw what ya dun in town, I figgered you was a bad man. No offense, Cole," Luther spoke with the new chaw gaining moisture as he headed the conversation toward a new goal. He spat a lightly colored stream of tobacco juice and frowned at its quality.

Cole said, "None taken. Glad I was there. Mighty sorry about the reason for it, though."

"Yah, wal, sounds like ya dun picked the wrong gal." Luther growled. "Real sorry. Never did like that thar Abilene town nohow."

For the first time, Cole smiled about it. "Well, his pappy was rich. I guess that's what it was all about. I don't know, Luther, guess I didn't know her like I thought."

"Ya reckon the doc should take a look-see at that leg o' yurn?" Luther asked. "An' yur shoulder?"

"No, that's all right. I was lucky, only hit the fat part of my calf. It'll take time, but I'll be fine. Kept moss on both places while I was coming through the Nations," Cole said, staring down at his right leg and feeling the pain more than he wanted to admit. "Got some new pants at the trading post but just couldn't part with these boots. I'll have to let that hole be a reminder of Abilene."

"Reckon as how ya'd just as soon fergit 'bout her."

"Yeah. Not so easy sometimes."

"Yah, I know'd what ya mean. Sum days ya wished ya could fergit all o' it—and sum days, ya jes' wanna chew on the good stuff over an' over," Luther said, looked away, and changed the subject. "That bug-eyed bastard Winlow, he dun wants this spread bad, Cole, like a mean boar needin' food. Shoot fire, his cows dun already look like they's havin' two an' three calves ever' day. Them riders o' his'n dun brand ever'thin' they kin put a rope on. If'n he be a-hearin' Ethan is hurt, he'll be over hyar like a buzzard circlin' somethin' dead."

71

# Chapter Six

"Cole, will Ethan dun be a'ri't?" Luther's voice was suddenly dry. His eyes were a dog's looking for his master.

"Wish I knew, Luther. Wish I knew," Cole replied, and placed a hand on his brother's shoulder.

"Claire'll dun want ya to stay, Cole. She dun windied of ya now an' then. 'Bout the ol' days."

"That's nice to say," Cole replied, watching a long line of smoke curl upward from his cigar. "I'll stay, for a day or two. If you put me to work, anyway. Reckon there are a few things left to get done for your drive."

"If Ethan be down, thar ain't gonna be no drive."

The grizzled cowboy continued his bluster to himself, spitting out barely heard sentences while looking at the ground. Luther's face paled, and his lip trembled for an instant.

Cole took a deep breath and said, "Why don't you lead the drive, if Ethan can't."

Luther turned toward Cole and smiled. It was a friendly smile, yet bemused, like a poker player who's just been called, with only a small pair in his hand.

"Cole, ain't no way them drovers is gonna foller me. Don't blame 'em none either."

"Well, isn't there somebody that knows the way?"

"No man know'd that trail like Ethan. He's an ol' prairie wolf. Even has his notions down in book scratchin's."

"Writing?"

"Yep."

"You mean he keeps a diary on the drive?"

"That's it. In that thar book, he dun keep the whole trail. I seed the scratchin' a time or two." Luther spat again. He watched with approval this time as the brown spittle soaked into the ground.

"Well, why don't you boys just follow it yourself?"

"Cole, I cain't figger no scratchin's. Neither kin Dancer. DuMonte kin, fer sur, but it takes Ethan to do the reckonin'. I know'd pieces o' the trail, so do they. But the men wouldn't take to it nohow."

"What about going in with another drive?" Cole asked.

"All gone. Most are a month out, I reckon. More maybe, fer sum. Onliest one, 'sides us, left here—be Winlow. Ethan dun like this hyar time the best. Yessur, he be partial to the grass full green. He waits fer it."

Luther's attention turned to Cole, who had again glimpsed the sorrel called Kiowa at the bunkhouse tie rack.

"I were gonna shoot that red hoss after he dun kicked Ethan. Claire wouldn't let me nohow. She said Ethan cared a lot for 'im, no matter what." Luther answered the unasked question.

Without further conversation, Cole walked over to

the saddled sorrel. Luther went with him, studying his younger brother's limp. Cole ran his hands along Kiowa's neck and chest, feeling the horse tremble under his touch. The sorrel's ears laid against its neck. Cole talked quietly to the animal, but the horse remained tense, like it would explode if he touched it in the right spot. Kathleen's hair was almost the color of the big horse's flowing mane and tail. A shiver ran up his spine at the coincidence.

He could see her smiling at him, laughing and pointing out one of the red birds she loved so much. He felt sorry for himself and then thought of Ethan. He touched his hat brim. A tiny red feather was still there, stuck in the hatband. He'd forgotten. It was the only thing he had to remind him of her. She had given it to him on their first picnic together. He started to pull the feather from the band, then stopped as he heard Luther spout his promise to kill the horse tomorrow.

"Tomorry, I'm gonna shoot 'im anyway."

"Too bad. Good-lookin' animal. Will you let me have a go at 'im first?" Cole said, speaking quietly.

"He be a killin' hoss, Cole. Break a man's heart—an' back."

"Not saying I can ride better than you. Figure not many could, Luther."

A trace of satisfaction slid across the wrangler's mouth.

"But what if we took him down to that long creek bed, close to town. With all that heavy sand. Make him run down in that wet stuff until he's worn slick. Claire might like that better than killing."

Cole sounded like a man who had been thinking about the horse for longer than it appeared. "I have a hunch if we can push him past that first explosion, there might be a good animal waiting. I think he's just plain scared, Luther. An' got enough in him to make a man pay for it."

"Cole, he could dun break hisse'f a leg in that thar sand," Luther observed.

"Might."

"Then we be havin' to kill 'im."

"So, what have you got to lose?"

Hearing voices, they turned toward the house as the portly Dr. Hawkinson came to the doorway. Behind him was Claire Kerry, her face as white as the flowers in the window box. Cole remembered her only as being upset with him; her face was strangely unfamiliar. He thought she was quite attractive and didn't remember that either. A few steps behind was his father, Clancey Kerry, looking every inch an old man in spite of his hulking frame.

Luther yelled, "Hey, the doc's a-comin' out!"

He hurried to the porch. Cole stayed beside the sorrel. He realized this was no time for him to intrude, even if he was Ethan's brother. He would stay no more than two days, then he would head out and start over. It was a good thought. Time to let go of the past. Cole looked at the people gathered on the porch and felt more lonely than he could ever recall. It was like returning to someone else's life. Like gazing at an oil painting of people; some looked familiar, but they didn't seem to be a part of his life in any way.

At the porch, Luther asked, "Doc? How's the boss? He be up an' roarin' cum the mornin'?"

Dr. Hawkinson cleared his throat. His thick belly rose and fell with a prolonged breath, and then he proclaimed, "Ethan Kerry is going to be just fine—"

Luther hollered, "Hot damn! I know'd it!"

"—but he's blind."

Luther's reaction sucked the air from the porch. His

hard eyes squinted for the truth. "My God, Doc, that thar's . . . sumthin', ya know'd, temporal. He's gonna see . . . onc't his headache goes away, right? Heard tell o' men gittin' wham-kicked in the haid and losing their eyes fer a day or—"

"God didn't give me that wisdom, I'm sorry to report. Ethan's eyesight might return tomorrow . . . or a month from now . . . or maybe, not ever," Dr. Hawkinson said, staring straight at Cole in the distance, not daring to glance at Claire Kerry. "I've recommended to the family that he go to someone with more . . . than me. There's a good doctor in Kansas City I know."

Tears lashing his cheeks, Luther trembled, "T-t-thar be n-n-no drive, i-i-is thar?"

Ethan's father answered, with his thick Irish accent and his eyes toward the ground, "Aye, it be hard to say right now, me son. By me sainted mither's grave, all wrong it is. All wrong."

Her eyes soft and sad, Claire turned toward Luther and whispered, "Luther, I don't want you to do anything to Kiowa. Please, Luther. Ethan loved that horse. He talked about it all the time. I—I think it reminded him of the . . . old days. Promise me, Luther."

"Y-yes, ma'am. I, uh, ya got my word on it."

"Thank you, Luther."

Grim-faced, Luther looked away, caught Cole's questioning stare, and answered it by dropping his eyes to the ground. As if a door had slammed in his face, Luther staggered backward, then spun around and lumbered toward his younger brother. Cole patted the wild sorrel on the shoulder and watched him approach. A red sun wrapped long shadows around Luther, his face sagging with sadness, his hooded eyes casting an unreachable pain.

"E-E-Ethan dun be . . . he be . . . blind," Luther reported, swallowing back the emotion that jammed his throat.

"He's . . . he's blind?!"

"Yeah."

"Oh, my God! I'm sorry, Luther," Cole replied, wishing he could think of more healing words.

In Ellsworth, he had dealt with a blinded man once. Cole didn't like recalling the man had shot himself after months sitting outside a saloon, living on handouts. The thought sped through his mind as he placed a comforting hand on Luther's shoulder.

Clancey returned to the solitude of the house without realizing his youngest son had come home. Dr. Hawkinson waved feebly as he rode out. Cole raised his arm in response. Luther just watched him leave, then stared at the Bar K brand on the longhorn skull.

"Cole . . . Cole Kerry?! Is that you?!" The high, nervous voice was Claire's.

"My God, Cole . . . it is you! Oh, how wonderful! Ethan will be thril—" She covered her open mouth with her hand.

"Ya be goin' to see her now," Luther said, his voice quivering, his eyes reddened with sorrow.

Cole Kerry nodded and managed a thin smile. An old memory darted into his mind of his older brother being upset when the sixteen-year-old Cole joined them in Hood's army. Uneasily, the young outlaw patted the sorrel and walked toward the house without further words or eye contact. Luther sighed and tried to say something, but it came out an anguished grunt. Night was taking charge as Claire Kerry stood on the porch, watching him advance. Cole looked away toward the corral, more out of discomfort than a desire to see something. When he looked back, she was holding hands with two children: Maggie on the left and Eli on the right. The boy appeared dazed, disbelieving; the younger girl was only sleepy and desiring to be held by her mother. Next to the boy was a large, gray hound with a white muzzle.

The creak of wood as Cole stepped onto the porch was a boisterous intrusion upon the silence. Removing his hat and bowing his head slightly, he greeted the grieving woman he only vaguely recalled, "I'm very sorry . . . about Ethan. If I can be of any help to you, ma'am, just ask."

Her eyes wide but clear, Claire nodded. Only that tiny tremble at the corner of her mouth gave away the emotion within. Her face was so still, Cole wondered if she was holding her breath. But the rhythm of her substantial bosom told him otherwise. He blinked his eyes to force a concentration on her face; he could feel the redness at his neck for his inadvertent attraction to her breasts. She didn't appear to notice his wavering attention.

He could handle men, could read their intentions easily and was usually effective at determining if they would fight and how well. Women were a different matter. Certainly he hadn't seen the truth with Kathleen Shannon. He thought she wanted to marry him, and he was drawn to the idea like nothing he could remember. But that didn't matter now. Nothing in his past seemed to prepare him for judging how a woman would react, or how best to talk to one in this situation. He had found it hard to talk to Kathleen at first. She was the one who sought him out. Later he told her everything about himself, about leaving Ethan and Luther, about missing them, about wanting to see them again someday. How foolish that all sounded now.

It was Claire who spoke first. Her voice reminded Cole of a solemn priest he'd once heard, comforting yet distant. "Please call me Claire. May I call you Cole? Thank you for helping us, Cole. Dr. Hawkinson told me what you did in town. I am sorry we didn't greet you earlier—but we didn't know. You know you are welcome here . . . for as long as you can stay. This is your home too."

"Thank you, ma . . . Claire. That's very generous. But I'm just passing through. Thought it was time to . . ."

"I understand. But we want you to stay as long as you can. Ethan will be pleased to se . . . want to talk with you as soon as he wakes up."

"I would like to see my brother now, if that's all right."

"Yes, yes. Of course you would. Please come. He's asleep, but you can see him. Supper will be ready soon too."

Across the grounds, Luther was releasing the red horse into the main corral. Cole glanced in that direction again and felt strangely alone. Yet the woman before him couldn't have been friendlier, considering what she had just been through. He returned his attention to her, holding his hat with both hands at his waist. Seeing Claire deal with the awful blow dealt her family made his own troubles seems hollow. He studied her, and it was healing. He shifted his weight to his left leg to relieve the ache in his right.

"Cole, this our son, Eli . . . and our daughter, Maggie. Children, this is your uncle Cole. Your father's brother. He's been . . . away for a long time."

"Pleased to meet you, Eli . . . and you, Maggie." Cole extended his handshake to the boy and touched the brim of his hat in a greeting to the little girl, who giggled at the adult attention. Eli stared at him, said nothing at first, then asked, "Are you really my uncle, like Uncle Luther? I like him the best."

"Eli!" Claire admonished.

"I am really your uncle, Eli. But the way I see it, Luther is the best too."

"That's not what Maw says, she—"

"That's enough, Eli," Claire interrupted, and said, "Please come inside. Ethan's father—your father—will be excited to see you. It's been so long, Cole. We were . . . worried about you. I . . . I need to be in the kitchen. I'm afraid I—I—I wasn't . . ."

With a wave of her hand to reinforce her invitation, she turned quickly toward the door and went inside, guiding her children ahead of her. The ugly dog slipped inside beside them. Cole was certain she was crying and didn't want anyone to see. He admired her strength. What must be whirling through her mind? As a courtesy to her, Cole unbuckled his pistol belt and laid the weapons down a few feet from the doorway. Behind him, Luther had stopped at the well, jammed his shirttail back inside his pants, and was washing for supper.

Inside the house, Cole was taken by the warm sense of family. He couldn't remember the last time he'd been in a real home. His eyes feasted on the main room, built with a man's tenacity and decorated by a woman's love. A bittersweet sensation. He'd long forgotten what a home was like. How he envied Ethan Kerry! The thought caught in his throat, and he coughed. More than once he had fantasized about having a home like this, leaving behind his unwanted reputation as a man of the gun and going someplace that didn't care who he was, only who he wanted to be. Would Kathleen want a life like this? With him? He tried to imagine them married—like Claire and

Ethan. His hand touched the unsent letter folded in his back pocket.

A chill drove through him, bringing the realization that this family may have been changed forever. The thought made him ashamed to be in the house. Delicious smells of boiling coffee, frying beefsteek, and potatoes crept into the room, pulling him away from his own emptiness. Claire stood in the middle of the room, wiping away the sadness from her cheeks. The two children had disappeared into the kitchen. Pointing toward a darkened room off the main area, she said, "Ethan is in there. He's asleep."

Cole nodded as Claire left for the kitchen without further words. He walked slowly to the bedroom entrance. A solitary candle softened the room's melancholy. Its yellow glow caressed Ethan's bandaged face. His eyes were covered with a folded white cloth that encircled his forehead. He was unconscious or sleeping. Cole thought he was sleeping.

Cole stepped silently into the room and sought a closer look. Ethan appeared much older than he remembered, but that was enhanced by his injury and the wavering candlelight. His older brother was his idol in many ways, not just the ranch and family. It was always Ethan that people sought for answers; it was always Ethan that men looked to for leadership. The awfulness of his brother being blinded was a stone in his mind. Ethan Kerry had everything going for him: a fine family, a growing ranch. Was it all gone into darkness?

Cole couldn't shake the question: What would he do if he were Ethan? He wondered if a bullet would be his answer, like the man he knew in Ellsworth. Cold sweat had followed his silent affirmative answer. The hand on his shoulder surprised him. It was Luther.

The big, slow-witted man said, "It dun be finished, ain't it?"

Cole didn't answer the oddly stated question, but he understood the meaning. He glanced at Luther without speaking, trying to think of something comforting to say, but found no such thoughts.

"A man without no eyes ain't a man," Luther stated flatly as a follow-up to his own question.

"Only knew one blind man before. Sad thing," Cole finally said, abandoning his search for words of comfort. The darkness of the room had torn away his own confidence. "Sat outside a saloon every day. Took handouts from folks passing. I gave him food from time to time. Damn!"

"Ethan ain't no man who be sittin' by no saloon," Luther said, his words edged with anger and frustration.

"I didn't say he was, Luther."

What was he supposed to say? Ethan Kerry was a dead man and didn't know it. If there were more words coming, the noise of Luther and Clancey in the other room broke the thought. Silently, both men glanced once more at their stricken brother and left the bedroom.

"By the saints of me homeland, the young lion has returned," the old man bellowed, standing in the main room with an exaggerated wide-spread stance of command. Eli and Maggie were at his side, along with the dog.

The elder Kerry extended his huge hand, then pulled Cole to him for a bear hug. Cole was surprised and pleased at the warm reception. The last time he had seen his father, the big Irishman had cursed him for following his older brothers into war. His father's refusal to talk to him about his mother's death had silently separated them years before.

Clancey had referred to her death as if she were out on some extended errand and due back anytime. That madness had gone on for months until the boy finally challenged his father on the reality of such talk. It hadn't gone well then, and Cole realized the big man wasn't accepting Ethan's blindness either.

"Did you meet these two youn'uns. This fine scrappin' lad is Eli . . . and this little darlin' is Maggie."

Cole responded matter-of-factly, "I've met Eli and Maggie. They're somethin to be proud of."

The big man ignored the compliment and proclaimed with more of a grin than his wrinkled face wanted to handle, "I hear you tore the teeth outta of the wolves in town, you did!"

Cole wasn't sure of what to say. Luther spoke for him, "Cole be one hard hombre, Paw."

"Aye, Luther, by God, me bet he t'is. Come this way, Cole, me boy, have a wee taste of good Irish whiskey with me. I need meself a swallow or two, Lord be if I don't. You, too, Luther."

Cole knew the big Irishman wanted everything to be like it was, with his son, Ethan, in charge. What father wouldn't, he mused to himself, and felt sorry for Clancey Kerry. As the old Irishman ambled out of the room to get the whiskey, the big dog trotted away from Eli's side and toward Cole. The young outlaw realized his father had come as close as he would, or could, come to apologizing for the way he had acted when Cole left him.

In a voice seeking authority, the boy said, "That's Blue. He don't take kindly to strangers none."

# *Chapter Seven*

Smiling warmly, Cole squatted to greet the beast's low, growling advance. The little girl stared at Cole's face.

"That thar hound'll bite ya, Cole," came Luther's terse warning.

Cole spoke quietly to the approaching animal, "Hello, Blue. Tell you what, if you don't bite me, I won't bite you."

With that, he held out the back side of his right hand for the dog to examine. After a few studied sniffs, Blue stepped closer to Cole, the dog's muzzle even with his face.

"Cole . . ." came Luther's unfinished alarm.

"We're fine. Blue's just trying to figure out if I can do what I said. We're going to be friends, aren't we, Blue?"

Cole's hand went easily to the animal's neck and scratched the short gray hair on the powerful frame.

"Wal . . . I'll be!! Ol Blue dun tore a damn hideful

off'n many a feller, Cole. Spit in my eye, if'n you can't talk dog," Luther exclaimed, his hands on his hips, and looking around for a place to spit for good measure, then remembering he was inside the main house.

"Come here, Blue." The boy seemed disappointed in the dog's lack of aggressiveness toward this man.

"Your master's calling, Blue. Better go," Cole said, petting the animal on the head as he stood. The big dog trotted back to Eli, wagging his tail happily. The frowning boy mumbled to the animal, then walked back into the kitchen with the dog at his side.

Under his breath, Luther praised, "Maybe ya dun gonna ride that red hoss."

Outside, a horse whinnied from the corral, followed by angry squeals. Two green mounts were arguing about dominance. Luther stepped to the doorway, but nightfall gave away only moving shapes. Without waiting for any further comment, he left for the corral. Clancey Kerry returned with a hand-carved, inlaid tray holding a bottle of whiskey and glasses. He laid it down ceremoniously on the opened rolltop desk in the corner of the main room and immediately began pouring the brown liquid into the glasses.

He passed the brimming glass to Cole, then raised his toward the ceiling. "To me young son's return."

"Here's to Ethan's full recovery—and fast," Cole added, silently pleased at the tribute.

"Ah, yes, may me other son find the light again. By me sainted mither's grave, so shall it be!" the old man demanded, and swallowed his drink in two ravenous gulps. Cole sipped the fine whiskey, savoring the excellent taste.

"Glory be! I need me a wee more o' that fine elixir," Clancey said, and laughed. He poured his glass to the brim, insisted on adding to Cole's glass, and fixed another for the absent Luther and left it on the tray.

Claire Kerry reentered, her face glowing from closeness to the cooking. Her tired smile sought Cole's face. Their eyes met for an instant: The young outlaw felt like his soul was being inspected and figured Luther had shared the news about his being a wanted man. Cole glanced at Clancey Kerry, who was now downing Luther's glass, which he carefully refilled along with his own.

"Luther tells me you had some trouble—in Kansas," Claire said. Her eyes were soft, her face worn from hiding the agony.

"Yes, ma'am . . . I did." *That was fast,* he thought to himself.

She continued, "He said a man tried to kill you and you had to defend yourself, and his friends chased you out of town."

Cole looked at her quiet face, trying to determine if she had deliberately left out the reason why it had happened, or if Luther had.

"Luther left out the reason, Claire," he responded without thinking further.

Her expression told him Luther had, indeed, shared the whole story, and he was pleased that he had volunteered to tell it. This was clearly Claire's way of measuring him. He explained what had happened.

"I can't imagine a woman worth anything would do that to you," she said, and a smile passed across her mouth so quickly he wasn't certain it had ever been there. He felt a blush encircling his neck and face.

Claire turned to her father-in-law. "Grandpaw, I would appreciate a little of your whiskey."

Surprise filled the big man's face, but he quickly poured her a drink and politely offered it. His eyes would not meet Claire's. The bitter liquid contorted her face as she tasted it. Cole expected her to tell him more about Ethan's condition, now that she had the liquor's courage.

But no such conversation came. Instead, she smiled and asked him about Kathleen. He talked easily about her, even showing her the red bird feather on his hat. She asked if his gunshot wounds needed tending. He felt foolish talking about them, compared to Ethan's injury, but her concern was genuine. Cole was surprised that she wasn't put off by his gunfighter reputation. He wondered if it was because Ethan had once been quite good with a gun too.

Swallowing the last of her whiskey, she excused herself, left the room, and completed the meal's last details. Returning with a plate of steaming cornbread, she directed the men toward the supper table. Cole assisted Claire with her chair as Clancey and the two children took their seats. She thanked him, slightly embarrassed by the attention, and watched him go to his chair next to the just returning Luther.

With her hands folded in her lap, she bowed her head to say grace. Cole lowered his hands to his lap and watched her in silence.

"Gracious Lord, we thank you for this food. Fill us with your love and grace. Be with our men as they undertake the long drive to Kansas. Grant them your strength and wisdom. Thank you for bringing Cole back to us. Thy will be done. Amen," she prayed without any signs of emotion.

Luther opened his eyes and looked sideways at Cole, who looked back. He thought it was a strange prayer with no mention of her husband lying in the other room, blind and unable to lead anything.

Clancey Kerry blubbered, "God save us. Let's eat, me lads, before cold she gets."

Luther ate in silence. The elder Kerry continued to drink, ignoring the food in front of him. Claire Kerry didn't seem to have much of an appetite either, preferring to talk with Cole and ask him questions. Occasionally, she took a small bite; most of the time, however, her fork just moved the rest around on her plate. For him, however, the meal was excellent and he tried to balance his enjoyment and answering her without out a filled mouth.

"Cole, have you ever been on a cattle drive?" she finally asked.

"No, ma . . . Claire, I haven't. My work with beef has always been on the eating end."

She smiled, and it was geniune. "Ethan has led two successful drives into Kansas. This will be his third."

"I imagine my brother is very good at it."

She continued, driven by an inner need to return everything to normal, "The herd will go through the Indian Nations. That's the scariest part, besides the rivers and the weather. You came through there, didn't you?"

"Yes, Claire, I sure did."

Luther looked up from his plate and observed, "Cole near dun lost his hair to a Comanche war par—"

Claire frowned, and Luther swallowed the rest of his thought. He went back to eating and said no more. She told Cole how her husband was known for his attention to details. A forced laugh was the preamble to sharing how he always checked her loading of the chuck wagon and always found something he wanted to change. Cole realized she was locked into place emotionally. She wanted everything to be the same as it was before—and if she talked like it was once, it would be again. The more she talked, the more Cole was convinced the doctor had told them Ethan Kerry would remain blind, regardless of what anyone did—something he hadn't shared with Luther.

The old man interrupted her presentation abruptly to ask, "Pray tell, how many times be ye battling the red savage, me boy?"

"Times? That's an interesting question. Haven't really kept count. I guess, well, ten or so times. Somethin' like that, I suppose. I spend a lot more time staying out of their way than fighting them."

"Win any medals, me lad?" Clancey asked, leaning over his plate toward his youngest son.

"No medals. Unless you count a bullet in my leg and one across my shoulder."

His father's face brightened, but Cole couldn't read what was on his mind. Just when he thought Clancey Kerry was going to ask another question, Claire Kerry asked Luther when the new horses would be ready. The wrangler's face hid his feelings, and he told her they should be ready tomorrow. She expressed her pleasure at the news and offered the expectation that Ethan would be up and around tomorrow or the day after and would want to move out as soon as possible. Not knowing what else to do, Luther nodded and forked an imaginary piece of food.

Continuing her performance, Claire asked Luther about the horse that had blinded her husband. "Luther, I don't expect anyone to try to break the red horse. At least not for now. You can leave it behind with us when you an' Ethan are on the drive. He can work him all this winter. That's too good a horse to waste."

Hesitating, Luther said, "Cole, he be figgerin' the red kin be broke."

She was silent a moment, studying first Cole, then Luther. Finally she said, "Cole, that's not necessary. Ethan can do it this winter."

"A hoss-man ye would be, Cole?" Clancey's question caught the back end of her unfinished question.

"Not as good as Luther—or Ethan, but I generally stay on what I put a saddle on."

Luther grinned at the compliment and stared at his youngest brother like they had just met. Claire's contrived conversation had only served to make Luther more depressed. He didn't want supper to end, because it meant going to a dark bunkhouse and facing the fear that the Bar K was finished.

"Is Dad gonna see again?" Eli suddenly asked.

He could no longer hold back the question. Lucy was playing with a cloth doll, absorbed in another world. Her brother's bluntness apparently didn't register.

"Of course he is, Eli. We pray it so, and God listens to prayers. Your father has a cattle drive to lead." Claire's face couldn't mask the hurt of the question as she responded.

Her answer was one she was desperately trying to believe herself, Cole thought, but it wasn't the one she should have given. A boy should be told the truth. He remembered, as a boy about Eli's age, being told by Clancey that his mother had gone away on a long trip and would be returning soon, when she had actually died of the fevers. He wondered if young Eli would see through the lie as he had and hate the teller for it. That was the first crack in the relationship between the elder Kerry and his youngest son. Cole wondered if Claire realized the emotion she might be triggering in the boy. But then, he thought, Claire wasn't Clancey—and Eli wasn't him—and what did he know about raising children anyway.

Eli's face sagged; the frown that followed indicated he was sorting through his feelings about a God that would do something like this in the first place. Con-

fusing thoughts were shoved into his young mind: the
sadness of knowing his father was seriously hurt; the
odd assurance by his mother that he wasn't. Cole read
the boy's face and remembered; Claire had made a mistake in not telling him.

"It's bedtime, children. You run on, and I'll be in to
listen to your prayers."

Maggie asked sweetly, "Can we go see Daddy first?"

Swallowing back the emotion, Claire gently said,
"Not tonight, sweetheart. Daddy needs to sleep. Tomorrow you can . . . see him."

"Can Uncle Luther come to hear our prayers?" Eli
asked.

*Uncle.* What a strange and wonderful sound, Cole
thought.

"You betcha," Luther said.

"Al-l-l right!"

Exploding from his chair, Eli headed for his room,
with Blue only a step behind. Maggie yawned and me-
andered there, pretending to walk her doll alongside
her. Luther jumped from his chair and waddled bowlegged toward their room. Cole decided to take advantage of the moment alone with Claire and Clancey
Kerry. But the old man hummed an Irish tune to himself, one that Cole vaguely recalled—and, like his
granddaughter, was somewhere else.

Looking into his coffee cup, Cole said politely,
"Claire, thank you very much for this fine supper. It's
been a long time since I had home cooking—or even
been in a home."

"Thank you, Cole. It wasn't much, I'm afraid."

"How long be you with us, Cole, me lad?" Clancey
asked, mentally returning to the table; his eyes were
glazed with whiskey. "Will ye be ridin' with us to Kan-

sas? Me, myself, will be leading the drive. Likely it is."

Cole was thankful for the change of conversation, but he caught Claire's exasperated expression.

"I'll be ridin' on. You have enough troub—"

"Troubles? We have no troubles. We'll be fine, Cole. We've had a little setback, but we'll be fine." Claire's tone was harsh.

"Begging your pardon, Claire, but things aren't fine—and the sooner you come down on that fact, the better you're going to be thinking. Ethan is blind. You have to find a new trail boss—or not make the drive. Can you afford to do that?"

His tone was hard, his eyes flashing. He paused, knowing his words hurt, but he kept on.

"Wishing won't change things, Claire. Neither will talking like nothing has happened. The doc said Ethan was blind—and was going to stay that way, didn't he?"

"W-w-well, he did say . . ."

"Say it. Ethan is blind."

Tears flooded her face. She mouthed the words "Ethan is blind." But no sound came.

The drunken Clancey roared out of his chair and challenged the young outlaw, "Returning son or no, ye'll not talk that way. Stand and prepare to taste me fists."

"Sit down, Clancey, and shut up. I'm talking to Claire, not you. Go and drink something." The elder Kerry shrank from Cole's angry words.

"I am sorry to make you cry, Claire. I'm not being cruel. I wouldn't be talking this way if I didn't think you were strong. You've got to face the truth. Until you do, you won't make good decisions. I know, I've made some pretty stupid ones that way."

She nodded, biting her lower lip and breathing

deeply. Tears were turning her cheeks into wettened red circles.

"After all these years, I wouldn't claim to know Ethan. But I always looked up to him. Reckon I still do. He's quite a man, but now he's a blind man. You've got to sit down with him and make some hard decisions."

Cole leaned forward on the table and looked into Claire's watery eyes.

"Maggie can wait, but you've got to tell Eli. He knows, and he'll resent your not telling him. I know. Clancey pulled that stunt on me when our mother died. I've never forgotten it. He has, though."

He stood and handed her a napkin, and she let it claim her face. As she buried her eyes in the cloth, she nodded her head in agreement.

Cole sat down and asked, "Has he been able to talk yet? Does he know?"

"Y-yes, h-he knows. D-Dr. Hawkinson told him."

"Now, don't you fret, me lady, old Clancey hisse'f will lead the lads to Kansas. Aye, what a grand time it shall be!" Clancey boasted, regaining his bravado and walking to her side and patting her with his huge hands.

Her pained eyes were sufficient answer, although the old man never saw the response. Cole felt sorry for her and pitied his foolish father. He owed them nothing, and more than that, he could do nothing for them. Except what he had tried to do: get her to face reality. But he wasn't a cattleman, he wasn't a trail boss, and he sure wasn't a doctor. He would ride on, after helping Luther with the sorrel.

"T-thank you, C-Cole," Claire whispered.

# Chapter Eight

"Get up, Kiowa! Run, you big red, run!"

Cole yelled at the sorrel from the bank of the creek bed. Luther hurled his best threat at the racing mustang, "Run yurse'f all the way to hell an' back, ya crazy hoss!"

Both men had a rope around Kiowa's neck; each rode a horse on an opposite side of the wet creek bed with the sorral in the middle, down in the sand-laden creek bed. Taut lariats wrapped around saddle pommels kept the animal from running up the bank in either direction. This was the chosen breaking ground Cole had described earlier. A mostly straight strip of wet sand cradled by steep banks. Water filled the channel only when the heavy rains came, but enough dampness remained to create a thick gravelly soup. An old, wooden bridge crossed it fifty yards to the east, a tribute to the days when its banks held water most of the time.

Neither shout was needed; the savage horse was out-running both of their horses, even though the sorrel was plunging through the deep, clinging sand of the long creek bed. Cole wondered if their lariats or their cinches would hold under the strain. Back and forth they ran, first in one direction, then returning, forcing the sorrel to fight through the heavy sand. The sticky mire covered its hooves and ankles, and clung halfway up its legs like a second skin.

At first, the fiery horse had stood on its hind legs, crashed downward, struggling against the ropes, then bolted westward toward the white sky and freedom. Kiowa's head and tail were up, signaling defiance. Long red mane lashed the air as it raced—a singular flag of strength. But their ropes controlled the sorrel's destiny. Luther cracked the whip in his right hand to keep the horse running. They had been working it this way for two hours, and Kiowa continued to roar down the creek bed, slashing against the energy-sucking sand, always faster than their own horses.

"Luther, I've got to switch," Cole yelled across the creek bed. "Can you hold him, or should we tie him to that tree?"

"Reckon I kin hold 'im."

Taking turns, they moved to new horses, already saddled, giving the sorrel a brief chance for relief, tying their worn mounts to the same snarled cottonwood. The sorrel stood with its legs apart in the sand like a prize-fighter between rounds. *My God, what a horse,* thought Cole as they pulled Kiowa into running again, half dragging it back through the sand. It was like holding on to a red lightning bolt. Their new mounts were soon running with open mouths. But the sorrel's mouth was still closed, ears laid back, flesh still cold, nostrils blowing an invisible fire.

Cole had worked many horses before, but this sorrel was a rare beast. If they could bring its fearful energy under control, Kiowa would be a horse to lead men on. Over and over, challenging the sand, struggling against the ropes, the sorrel's eyes glared, but gradually his head began to lower. Froth lay across its glistening body like icing on a cake. Finally, the riders stopped. Kiowa was heaving, tongue hanging out, trembling; his head was low, his body rippling with convulsions. The red horse lay down in the sand.

"We dun kilt 'im," came Luther's evaluation, a sadness in his voice.

"No, we have made the first step, Luther. I'll give him water," Cole said, and dismounted, tying his second horse next to the first two.

After waiting until he felt the animal could handle drinking, he walked downstream where a small pool of water was trapped among the rocks and dipped his hat into the cool liquid. His right leg ached from the hard riding. Trembling, the sorrel accepted the water and Cole stroked its long neck as the horse drank. He repeated the watering trip and petted the horse again. This time Kiowa stood, shaking his body so hard Cole could feel the vibration.

"Let's try to saddle him, Luther. If he's too much after all this, there's not much we're gonna do. That would've killed most horses."

"Reckon I should be a-hobblin' him?"

"No, I think we're gonna be fine."

Carefully, Cole laid a saddle blanket over Kiowa's back and then a straight fork saddle. The animal hunched and shivered at the new weight but didn't attempt to throw it off. Built for bronc riding, this saddle had extensions built on each side of the fork below the horn. A rider could hook his knees under them for better balance on a bucking horse.

"Be mighty careful," Luther warned, holding his lariat tight with the loop around the sorrel's neck.

Cole slid his hand under the horse's belly and slowly tightened the double cinches, talking softly to Kiowa as he worked. With his eye on the sorrel's hind legs, Cole completed the saddling while Luther moved closer, sliding his hands down the taut lariat.

"Now for the tough part," Cole said, and laughed.

"He won't be a-takin' that thar steel."

"Grab his ears and let's see what happens."

Luther twisted the sorrel's ears while Cole tried to engage the bit. Although the sorrel's head was lowered and unmoving, its teeth were locked defiantly together. Cole wrapped his hand around the animal's lower jaw and pushed his fingers through its mouth to the spaces behind the teeth on each side. He pressed the back edges of its mouth against the lower teeth. In response to the pain, Kiowa's mouth opened and he shoved the curb bit into place. A few seconds later, the leather bridle was over its ears and belted in place. Luther held the horse's bridle with both hands.

Taking a deep breath, Cole stepped into the stirrup and said, "Luther, let's see what we've got."

For an instant, both men thought the horse had been completely whipped. The great Kiowa stood with his head down, absolutely unmoving. A terrible shiver ran from his chest to his tail. Cole wasn't fooled, though. He waited, and suddenly the sorral threw back its hind legs and slammed them against the midday air.

The big red horse took off running and kicking, in spite of the weighted sand and its tired state. Cole did his best to keep the sorrel in the creek bed, and after twenty steps, the animal slowed to a trot; in another ten, it was walking. He patted the sweating side of the horse and smiled back at his brother.

"I'm gonna let him out of the creek bed."

"Ya be careful, Cole. He be a devil hoss. He'll fool ya."

"Yeah, could be. Let's see."

With a touch of his spurs, he turned the sorrel toward the northern side of the creek bed and felt its powerful glide from the sand to the rocky embankment and up onto the flat prairie. Cole's body moved in easy syncopation. He nudged the animal into a canter. To his surprise, the sorrel gathered itself into a smooth lope.

"How about that!" he yelled back at Luther.

"Shoot fire!"

After twenty minutes of keeping the horse at a steady lope, running him mostly in wide circles, Cole returned to Luther and invited him to take the horse. It served two purposes: Cole needed to catch his wind and the horse needed to know someone else.

The rest of the afternoon was spent with both taking turns riding the sorrel, never letting the animal have a chance to fully recover its awesome strength. When the cinnamon sun slid into a late-afternoon position, both men were soaked in their own sweat, a match for the tired red horse.

After several long swigs from a canteen, Cole wiped his forehead with a shirtsleeve and announced, "Think it's time for me to head into town."

"What ya be a-needin' thar?" Luther asked, surprised and fearful.

"A girl there owes me something. You can head back to the ranch."

"Will ya be a-cumin' back—an' lightin' for a piece?"

"That would be mighty tempting, Luther, but I should be riding on."

"What do ya reckon's gonna happen to us?"

Cole thought for a moment before replying. He didn't have an answer. At least not one that sounded very good. The only thing the Bar K could do now was to find someone else to drive the herd, or sell it off. If they sold it off in Texas, it was tantamount to losing the ranch. But what choice did they have? Ethan Kerry probably needed to be moved to town, where it would be easier to get doctoring. His brothers were welcome to the small amount of money in his saddlebags if they wanted it.

Maybe a blind man could help with some kind of storekeeping. No, that didn't make any sense, a man needed to see to help folks, to make sure they paid, Cole challenged his own thought. He had no answers. Rolling a smoke and lighting it, Cole repeated what he had just been thinking. Luther deserved that, he reasoned, even if he wasn't smart. It was the same advice he had given Claire earlier.

Luther listened and stated, "Ya could flat lead us, Cole. The men'd foller ya. I know'd they would."

"Coming from you, Luther, that's a real compliment. I take it as such and thank you. But I don't know cattle."

"We got lots o' boys that be a-knowin' their beeves. I know'd hosses. Ethan be knowin' the trail better'n a batch o' Injuns."

"Well, I know that, Luther, but—"

"Bin a-chewin' on this, Cole. Hear out a stupid ol' man, will ya? Please. I ain't blowin' no smoke in yur face nohow. Look, Ethan kin dun ride in the chuck wagon, big as ya please—and he kin tell ya what he's a-seein'—inside his haid, ya know. In there, he kin still see, Cole. He know'd the way like nobody I ever seed. He be a-tellin' ya what he's a-seein' and ya kin lead us. We kin do this, li'l brother. I know'd we kin. If'n ya'll do it."

Cole took a deep breath in silent wonderment at his brother's wild idea. What would anyone think? Whoever heard of a blind man guiding a trail drive? What would Ethan say?

"Oh, Luther, that'd be quite a stretch. I think you-all need to sit down and figure out a way to sell the herd."

His face more unreadable than usual, Luther untied the waiting horses and said, "You gonna ride Kiowa?"

"Yes, it'll be good for him."

"Kiowa's gonna be a good hoss, I reckon, maybe."

"He's got the makin's, Luther. But he's a lot of horse." Cole stroked the sweating animal's neck and flanks, talking softly to it.

Luther headed out for the ranch, leading the extra horses on rope halters. Cole watched him go, telling himself that a romp with Maria was just what he needed. He deserved it. Luther's idea was a foolish one; no one in his right mind would attempt a drive that way. About as foolish as the idea he had been thinking about—of robbing the Uvalde bank and getting Ethan's money that way.

Yet something about Luther's half-cocked idea had hooked his mind in a way he hadn't felt since the War. Would this be possible? The idea of leading men in a difficult adventure struck his soul. But what a silly notion. Who was to say Ethan would be interested in the first place? Why would his brother turn his herd—his ranch—over to a wanted man?

Luther was almost out of sight now, just three specks on the edge of the world. Cole rechecked the cinch and swung into the saddle. The sorrel tensed but relaxed its great body as Cole spoke words of encouragement and patted its neck. Town was less than thirty minutes away. He could have a little tequila, buy some cigars and see Maria. But he didn't move. Kiowa stood quietly waiting for direction from the thing on his back.

"Well, Cole Kerry, what are you going to do now? Keep running?" he asked himself out loud. "You sure don't have a woman waiting for you anywhere!"

The sorrel's ears snapped toward him to catch meaning from the noise. He shook his head, laughed, and swung the sorrel toward the ranch and touched its flanks with his spurs. Kiowa was running in two strides and gaining ground on the returning Luther. A smile raced across Cole's face almost as fast as the horse ran beneath him. A few minutes later, Luther heard the advance, turned in the saddle, and was amazed to see his brother coming toward him.

"Wal, howdy, Cole. That thar were either the fastust spin with a lady a cowboy ever did have—or ya jes' missed my comp'ny sumthin' fierce."

Luther had the sweet look of a little boy who has been told Christmas is coming early.

Cole started to play coy and ask what his brother was talking about, but he knew well what he meant, and this was no time to kid with Luther. Instinctively, Cole studied the double gunbelt at his waist and answered, "Winlow isn't going to take away what Ethan and you have built. Not if I can help it."

Luther glowed and said with sly smile, "Ya kinda like ol' Luther's idea, do ya?"

"The more I think about it, the better it gets, big brother. Risky, for sure. But if Ethan's interested, I'll do it. We'll jam that herd right up Winlow's ass."

Luther roared and then had to say it again so he

could laugh again. They rode for minutes without talking. Cole swallowed; his words were hard.

"I . . . ah, I'm a wanted man, Luther. For the first time, it hurts way down inside to admit it. For the first time, I—I care about what . . . you an' Ethan will think. Ethan may not want to turn his herd over to a wanted man—and I couldn't blame him."

Luther's demeanor never changed; his eyes locked onto the trail ahead. His question was little more than a whisper: "I reckon Ethan'd be a-puttin' ya at his back in a fight ov'r jes' about anybody. Yessur, I know'd he would. So would I."

Cole told him the details about the gunfight in Abilene. His face curled with anguish when he admitted his hate for Webster Stevenson because Kathleen had picked him for her husband. "Luther, why did he come after me? I would've left town. If I couldn't have her, there wasn't any reason to stay."

"Reckon a feller a-bringin' two others along to fight another fella ain't carryin' a lot o' courage. He figgered you'd be a-comin' fer him," Luther said, his eyes concentrating on the trail ahead and his mind obviously more focused on his brother's declaration to lead the drive.

"I know that. I just wish . . ."

"That thar lady's no lady, Cole, an' ya know'd it. Fergit that wish. Ethan dun wishes fer his eyes, little brother. Ya kin be that thar wish," Luther said, and looked over at his younger brother.

"Luther, you make it hard for a man to feel sorry for himself," Cole said, turning his head toward the big man and grinning. For the first time, Kathleen's face was only a blur in his mind. He saw her but he didn't.

"I reckon Luther know'd his little brother purty

damn well, even if'n ya ain't bin 'round. Ya would do to ride the river with, yessir."

When they eased into the ranchyard, long strokes of red, purple, and gold were signaling sundown. They were laying the wet saddle blankets over a corral post to dry when Claire stepped out on the porch and called.

"Cole, would you come in, please? Ethan would like to se . . . talk with you."

He yelled back, "Sure thing, Claire, I'll be right there as soon as I wash up."

With a shallow pan, Cole jerked water into it from the well pump and washed his face and hands, letting the cool water soften the sun's work on his tanned skin. He looked at his shirt streaked with sand and sweat; it wouldn't do. He went into the bunkhouse and pulled one of two remaining shirts from his saddlebags and put it on. His gunbelt was laid on the bunk where he had slept last night.

Newly lit lamps throughout the dark house gave it a spotted appearance as he approached. He hoped supper was soon ready. How quickly a man gets to expecting things, he thought. There wasn't any reason for him to assume that a meal was being prepared, but he knew it was.

"Hello, Cole," came the salutation as he stepped on the porch. It was Claire, just inside the front door.

"Ethan is waiting for you."

"Well, I would like that. How's he feeling?"

"He says he feels better."

With that simple declaration, Claire led him again to the gray bedroom, where new candles turned it half orange. In the corner, sitting in a chair, was Ethan Kerry. His eyes were hidden with a white bandage, folded and wrapped around his head. A purple welt on the right side of his forehead was swollen and angry.

Inside of it, a half-moon cut threatened to burst open again. He looked more like a statue than a man.

"Ethan, Cole is here."

"Hello, Cole, it's been a long time. I hear you've turned into quite a man." Ethan's voice carried a tinge of self-pity.

"Just trying to be like my big brother. Nothing's changed," Cole replied, holding back the easy-to-say phrase about how good it was to see him. His mind caught the agony of the key word "see" and wouldn't let it out.

Ethan stood up slowly and held out his hand into the space between them. He waited for Cole to place his own correctly for a handshake. Cole wasn't sure of what to do, what to say. As soon as their hands connected, Ethan pulled him into a hug. From the corner of his eyes, Cole saw Claire leave the room.

"I'm sorry about your accident," Cole mumbled as they parted.

"Yeah, it wasn't what I had in mind. Thanks for helping us."

"I've been thanked plenty."

"Claire tells me you broke Kiowa today. She saw you riding in," Ethan said. "That's quite a horse, isn't it. Reminds me of the ones we used to ride. Back then."

Cole told him how they had worn the horse down in the sandbed and Ethan wanted to know more. Claire returned to the room and announced that supper was ready. She asked if Ethan wanted to eat with the others. He nodded affirmatively. She walked to his side and took his hand and forearm in hers and began guiding him uneasily toward the door.

"Cole, what am I going to do?" he said without turning his head.

Cole's response was a surprise even to himself: "You and I are going to lead your herd to Kansas."

# *Chapter Nine*

The small bedroom shrunk into a box without air. Ethan Kerry spun away from his wife's hand, back toward where Cole stood. The rancher's face was red with unreasoned fury; his white bandage made the contrast even more severe.

Claire's expression was that of a woman who'd just seen a horrible accident but had to look again to see if it was really true. She stared at the young brother with her mouth open, stunned.

Staggering toward where he thought Cole was standing, Ethan screamed, "Godammit, man! You think that's funny! You think this is like breaking some goddamn horse! Can't you understand? I can't see anything! Try getting up in the morning and walking around with your eyes shut. Try it! That's me, goddammit. Me! Only, I can't open them. Not ever! I'll never see my wife, or my kids, again. I can't see how my little brother has grown. Hell, I'm nothin' but a piece of furniture." A tear betrayed him, slipping under the bandage and down his cheeks.

Cole responded calmly, "Ethan, I reckon you misunderstood me. I figure a lot of men would be stopped by this accident. Most, maybe. I just had a hunch you wouldn't. I haven't seen you in a long time, but you're still the big brother I looked up to. That's all. I meant no disrespect. I was giving it."

Claire recovered enough to place her hands once again on her husband to guide him to the other room. Ethan put his hand on his wife's arm to indicate he didn't want to leave. His breathing was heavy, gasping like he had run a long race.

Cole continued, "Ethan, I will lead your drive . . . if you're interested—and if you'll go with me. You know every inch of that trail in your head. All you have to do is see it in your mind—and tell me what's there. If you need help, your diary's right there."

Like an attorney presenting his case to the judge, Cole outlined his own qualifications: "I'm the best man for the job, assuming there isn't a good trail boss around. And there isn't. I know horses and men. I can fight—and find water at the same time, if need be. I've been all through the Nations—and Kansas. An' I'm your brother."

Ethan stood unmoving with his back turned; Claire urged him to walk toward the supper table. Cole saw the man's back straighten and his jaw rise, his shoulders shifted. Gently but firmly, Ethan removed his wife's hand from his arm. He stutter-stepped in a circle in an attempt to face his younger brother. He ended up headed toward the bed.

"Cole, do you know what you're saying?" he asked, unable to hide the lilt in this voice.

"I sure as hell do. Pardon me, Claire," Cole answered.

"Where would I ride?" Ethan asked, adjusting his body toward his brother's voice.

Cole smiled. It was obvious his brother liked the idea.

"Seems to me, the chuck wagon makes the most sense. . . ."

"You mean next to that pain-in-the-butt Hayden?"

Cole laughed. "Yeah, sometimes you'll ride a horse. Next to me. I'll tell you what I see, and you can tell me what's coming and what we ought to do."

"Who's in charge?"

"Me. I'm the trail boss. But it's your herd."

"I'm the only trail boss the Bar K has ever had. Why do I need you?"

"If you can get the men to follow you without me, you don't."

"You think they won't?"

"Do you?"

Claire interrupted, finding her voice and trying to resume control. "Ethan, dear, this isn't the kind of conversation you should be having right now. You need rest. After a few weeks, everything will be fine again."

"Claire, that's not true and you know it. Doc said I was blind, pure and simple. Nothin's gonna change it. Either we get the herd to Kansas—or we lose everything."

"But—but—Ethan, y-you c-can't. You j-just can't."

"Because I'm blind? Say it. I can't do it because I'm blind."

"Y-yes, you're blind. You can't do this . . . to me, to your family."

"What am I supposed to do? Sit around and let you all starve? Or—or go into town and beg? How about that, is that what you want, for me to beg? I can't even go rob a bank with my brother. Or should we just sit here and wait for the vultures like Sam Winlow!"

Cole winced at the verbal jab at him but said nothing. Tears flooded down Claire's white face. She had no way to argue, no way to explain, without hurting the man she loved. Cole wished he had a woman who loved him like that. Until this moment, he realized that he didn't really know what love was.

"Cole?" Ethan asked slyly.

"Yes?"

"I'm hungry, how about you?"

"Sounds mighty good."

"All right, let's go eat and we'll talk more later . . . about this crazy blindman's bluff idea of yours. Lead on, my dear," Ethan said with a bold grin.

With that, Claire blinked her eyes and wiped the wetness from her cheeks with her apron. She struggled to bring her emotions under control for the sake of the others. Cole was proud of her, but she avoided his eyes. Retaking Ethan's arm, she led him into the main room, pointing out the position of chairs and tables so he wouldn't walk into them.

"Here's the small table, Ethan, the one where we spilled all the coffee, just a little more to your right. That's it."

Ethan's step was brisk, in spite of not seeing. He walked as normally as possible, but caught the edge of his knee on the last chair between him and the dining area. He winced but was determined not to show that it hurt.

Claire ignored the encounter. At the supper table, he stood in place while his wife pulled back his chair and pushed it forward again slowly. He felt for the familiar chair arms, tracing his hands around the edges until satisfied he knew which way it was facing.

He sat and sighed—an involuntary emotion, but one that spoke loudly. She pushed him closer to the table. The two children had eaten earlier and were in their room. Luther was already at the table. Clancey Kerry never showed for supper; he had been sleeping off the day's whiskey since early afternoon. After the rancher said grace, without referring to his injury, the men tore into the meal of beef stew and fresh loaves of bread with enthusiasm. Cole looked at Luther and winked; the wrangler wasn't sure why but chuckled anyway. Continuing to chuckle beyond the joke's value, he poured four heaping spoonfuls of sugar into his coffee cup.

Methodically, Claire told her husband what was on his plate. "Ethan, the potatoes are on your right side, like three o'clock. Here's a piece of bread."

She cut the potatoes and meat into smaller sizes for him to eat easily. Cole saw the man's face turn crimson in embarrassment over being treated like a child and not being able to help it.

"I want some coffee," Ethan suddenly proclaimed.

"It's right here," she said gently, picking up the cup and holding it close to his right hand until he took it.

"Just put it straight down when you're through," she whispered.

"Goddammit, woman! I can put down a coffee cup."

Everyone tried to avoid watching Ethan Kerry while they ate, except for hidden glances. They were drawn by curiosity: Could he find his mouth without seeing? Occasionally Claire would dash her napkin to his mouth to clear away traces of stew. Each time his resentment grew, but he said nothing. After supper Luther started to leave, but Ethan asked him to stay. The oldest Kerry brother looked uncomfortable, fearing the announcement of no drive; or worse, the sale of the ranch; or almost as bad, a long discussion about Ethan's blindness.

Ethan spoke, a serious timbre carrying his words. "Luther, our long-lost brother here has an idea. I want to know what you think about it. You have always been loyal and true, so I expect the truth. Hard and straight."

Ethan paused and ran his tongue over his lips, apprehensive about what Luther might have to say. Luther rubbed a leathery hand across his whiskered chin and growled, "Speakin' straight has dun got this sorry hoss-breaker in quicksand more'n onc't. But that thar's the way I figger on floatin' my stick, anyhow. Trot it out, Ethan."

"Cole here thinks we can make the drive—with him as the trail boss . . . an' me as the guide. I can tell him where we need to be, what we should be looking for. You know what a stickler for details I am." Ethan forced a laugh.

Luther didn't know what to say. He looked again at Ethan, at Claire, back to Cole, and finally broke into a wide, toothy smile.

"He dun stole my idea! That no-good rascal! I tolt him that thar was what we should be a-doin'," Luther announced, slamming his chest with his fist and grinning from ear to ear.

"Well, I'll be! Your idea!" Ethan struck his thigh with his right hand. His own smile was as broad as Luther's. Claire's mouth became a jagged cut of disbelief.

"Cole'll keep us ri't safe through all that thar Injun country," Luther enthused.

"Well, now, wait a minute, my brother," Cole interjected. "Let's don't make this too good. You know the kind of country we'd be riding through. Indians are likely to be any place in the Nations—out of it, too, for that matter."

"So, Luther, you don't think the idea is totally crazy."

Ethan encouraged more response while he searched the table with his right hand to find his coffee cup. Claire took his fingers and directed them to the handle. He drank and returned the cup to the table. She was the only one to see the slight trembling as he set it down again.

Luther scratched his nose again, looked at his finger, and declared, "If'n yur up to goin', Ethan, we'd best be at it. I figger two more weeks an' we be runnin' outta grass an' water sumwhar in Injun country."

Ethan didn't respond, and the room became quiet as each man took the plan inside himself to let it simmer. Eli's sneeze from the children's bedroom was like a thunderbolt, and Claire flinched in her chair. But the blind rancher sat with his arms folded, unruffled, a determined jut to his jaw. He said nothing. Claire stood and excused herself. She got only a few feet away before the tears came again. Ethan cocked his head toward the muffled weeping as she hurried into the bedroom. Gradually he turned back again to the table; Luther was making a point to Cole.

"Now, Cole, you know'd us drovers ain' takin' to no heavy-reinin' when it cums to orders an' sech. All ya gotta do is whisper an' we'll be a-runnin' circles around ya to git 'er dun."

"If the rest of the men are like you, Luther, I don't think I'll be needed. But don't tell the boss, will you?"

Luther wasn't certain what it meant but nodded approval.

"Cole, why do you want to do this? What's in it for you?" Ethan asked.

"A better way to go north than riding there alone. I'm not in a hurry. Figure to join a buffalo-hunting outfit up that way. Dodge City is a good place to do it. That and, say, two hundred dollars when you sell the herd."

"What about that posse—from Abilene, wasn't it?" Ethan asked.

Cole glanced at Luther. His expression gave him away; he was the one who had told their blind brother. It didn't matter. Cole planned on telling Ethan anyway.

"I killed a man there. He and two friends of his wanted me out of town. They tried fists and that didn't work so well," Cole said. "So they tried guns. I can shoot better than they could. Problem was, he had a rich pappy. Hell, he was there, pushing his kid on. But I figure those boys have long since gone back to their bedrooms."

"T'weren't his fault, Ethan. I know'd, that thar other feller, he dun—"

Ethan interrupted. "It doesn't matter. I'm sorry you had to face that alone. Luther says you took lead in the leg and shoulder."

"Ya dun as bad, Ethan," Luther blurted. "We all dun things we didn't want to do, I reckon. We're jes' damn glad you're hyar, Cole. That's all that counts, by God."

Ethan was annoyed. "I know that, Luther. I'm talking with Cole. How bad were you hit? I hear you're limping."

"The bullet went through my calf without busting anything. I'll be fine."

"You had no choice?" Ethan's voice had an edge to it.

"Than to kill him?" Cole's response had a smiliar

112

raw tremor. "If two men came at you with guns, Ethan . . ."

"I would've killed both of them."

Cole cocked his head to the side. "But I reckon there's a poster there somewhere with me on it. I've ridden owlhoot—and hired out my gun. Didn't seem to matter much, until I met . . . I would understand if you didn't want an outlaw leading your herd. You sure don't owe me anything."

"Like as not, we'll run into some buffalo hunters in the Nations, though most are west of there. If we do, are you leaving us?" Ethan asked, already changing the subject.

"Not unless you want me to. I said I wasn't in a hurry."

"What if I don't agree—to the money?"

Cole laughed. "Well, I decided it was something I wanted to do . . . before I put a price tag on it. You tell me what's fair."

"The price is fair. I'd like to chew on this a day or two. That all right with you? Besides, I'm mighty weak . . . from that damn kicking I got."

"Of course. It's a big decision. I'll understand if you don't want to do it. But I'll try to change your mind, big brother."

Ethan chuckled and asked, "Anyone got the makin's? I'd like a smoke right about now."

Luther was the closest and handed him a pouch and papers, laying them in his opened palm. Conversation was forced as the men were drawn to Ethan's attempt to roll a smoke. He managed to separate one paper from the others and crease it. With his teeth holding the drawstring, he opened the bag and began sprinkling tobacco along the edge.

Tobacco fragments skittered on the table and his lap.

One end was stacked higher than the other, but the job was nearly as good as a sighted man could do. Ethan laid the bag on the table after drawing the string tight in his teeth. His closing of the cigarette was a disaster. Tobacco fled everywhere, leaving him with a nearly empty paper at his tongue. Luther glanced hopefully at Cole, but he was watching Ethan. Each man worried about the blind man's reaction to this failure.

"Which one of you peckerheads is gonna keep me in smokes while we're out there?"

Laughter exploded in the tense room. With tears huddled at the corners of his eyes, Luther retrieved the smoking materials, rolled a new smoke, and said, "H'yar be a bran'-spankin' new one, brother o' mine."

A match followed the placement and Ethan inhaled, letting a white string of smoke wander toward the ceiling. Cole silently watched the display of caring from the grizzled cowboy, who would have denied to the point of fighting that he had done anything more than happen to have a cigarette ready. Luther turned away and blew his nose into a bandanna from his back pocket. Blue wandered into the room, looking for something to eat, and eventually went to Cole.

"Well, Blue, how you been?" Cole greeted the ugly dog, and scratched its ears.

Luther shook his head, amazed at the animal's friendliness toward his younger brother. The wrangler had long ago given up on attempting to even go near the mean-tempered cur.

"Cole, that dog doesn't like anybody," Ethan said, equally surprised, "except Eli and Maggie."

"That thar boy be as good with dawgs as he be with hosses, Ethan. Ya shoulda seed how he brought that thar red hoss 'round, pretty as ya please!" Luther jumped in his chair as the realization of his offensive statement hit his brain. His face paled and his eyes widened like those of a man who's about to be killed. Ethan didn't respond to either the comment about "seeing" or the taming of the sorrel. He drew slowly on his cigarette and let the smoke busy itself around his bandaged eyes before vanishing toward the ceiling.

"Boys, I'm mighty tired," Ethan finally said. "Would one of you be kind enough to help this blind fool to his bed? We'll talk more tomorrow. That work for you, Cole?"

"Of course."

Luther helped Ethan to his bedroom, pointing out the obstacles in front of them as they walked. Cole went on to the bunkhouse. Claire was sitting in a rocking chair, reading her Bible. Ethan thanked his older brother for the assistance and said he could make it from the doorway. Luther hesitated, but watched as Ethan pulled away from him and walked stiffly forward in short steps, measuring the distance as he moved. His knee hit the bed in midstride, and he dropped his cigarette.

"I'll get it," he responded quickly, and kneeled to trace the ground. He found the cigarette and held it up toward Luther. "I'm through with this. Will you put it out for me, Luther?"

"Of course." Luther took the cigarette and excused himself. "I'll be a-sayin' my good-nights now. Claire, I do thank ye fer the good chow. That was mighty carin' with all that be a-goin' on."

"You are welcome," Claire answered politely but coolly. "Now I hope you will be as caring about us."

"Claire! What's the matter with you!" Ethan shouted.

"All of this talk about you going on the drive is nonsense—and you know it, Ethan Kerry. I can't believe you, of all people, would be so, so foolish. And you, Luther, how could you? How could you repay us like this?"

"That's enough, Claire." Ethan took a half-step toward her chair.

Luther's face was stone as he answered, "I reckon this be the ri't thing to do, Claire. Maybe the onliest thing. I ain't backin' off that. Sorry ya don't side with it."

"Then, then, why don't *you* buy the herd? Or you an' Cole. I don't care . . . just, just . . ." She couldn't finish the thought, and tears took the place of her anger.

Luther was unsure of what to say or do next. Watching the woman's anguish cut him hard. He held the smoking cigarette with the fingers of both hands at his waist like it was a precious living thing.

Ethan's tone was comforting for both of them. "Luther, leave us now. My wife has been through much these last two days. Harder on her than it is on me, or you, I reckon."

Luther nodded and turned away. His concentration was so intense as he left the ranch house that he didn't see Eli standing in the far corner of the darkened main room. The boy was crying. Next to him was Blue, sitting on his hunches, trying to understand. Eli went to the window and looked outside at the gray stillness and the shadowy silhouette of Luther walking slowly to the bunkhouse. He saw a tiny light spin to the ground as Luther tossed his father's cigarette. For the first time, the night scared the boy. With a catch in his throat, Eli spun around and ran to his bedroom. His eyes blurred with tears; his mouth blubbered with saliva. Blue raced beside him.

Back in his parents' bedroom, Claire fought hard to hold back her own tears. This was no time to release the anguish that bubbled within her, she knew that. She must be steadfast. Headstong and courageous, Ethan was vulnerable in a way neither of them could have imagined yesterday.

"Claire," Ethan said, sitting on the edge of the bed, slump-shouldered, his head down, holding his hands together as if praying, "I can't see my hands, Claire. I can't see our house. I can't see Maggie's flowers. I can't see her—or Eli. Lord God, I can't see you."

"Ethan . . ."

"I'm worthless. As worthless as a chunk of crappy sagebrush blowing around. How can I build a cow-calf outfit when I can't even see one? Not even that scrawny thing Eli's been keeping in the barn."

Ethan's shoulders heaved with the reality of his condition. He fought back tears for only the second time in his life. He hadn't even cried at his mother's death, but when Cole angrily rode away, the tears had come.

"My little brother comes riding in and thinks it's no big deal to take a herd to Kansas. Hell, he's no cowman; he's a gunfighter. An outlaw. You'd think he would've learned something in all these years. Hell, whoever heard of a goddamn blind man telling somebody what to do on a cattle drive?" Ethan continued, squeezing and unsqueezing his hands to hold the emotion in place.

"My darling, we will get through this. We will."

"How? How, Claire? If a damn Comanche came to the door, I couldn't protect my own family. Goddammit, why didn't that red horse just kill me! How can this be happening? Lord God Almighty . . ."

"Ethan. Ethan. Please. Blasphemy won't help us," she said, gripping the Bible tighter with both hands as if it could keep her from falling off the world.

Ethan raised his head. The strained veins in his neck

and forehead were raised and pounding with anger. "Maybe God'll strike me dead—and everybody will be better off!"

Claire could hold back the sadness no more; a waterfall burst down her pale face. Her sobbing was intense, unstoppable; her body heaved with the release like a small sapling being whipped by a storm.

"Oh, Claire, oh, Claire, I'm sorry, I'm sorry," Ethan cried, stood, and stepped toward her.

His knee hit the end table, and he staggered backwards. Regaining his balance, the rancher directed himself toward the sobbing. His fingers found her arm, then her shoulder, then her soaked face. He pulled her to him and held her tightly, and began to weep. At the crack in the barely opened doorway, the small eyes of a boy peeked in.

# *Chapter Ten*

Cole Kerry awoke from a fitful sleep laced with nightmares about Sam Winlow burning a whole herd of cattle while an outlaw with flaming red hair watched with glee. The sun was snaking through the window. It was the first morning he could remember when his first thought wasn't about Kathleen.

Loud talking near the ranch house slipped through, along with the yellow rays. He lifted his head and saw that Luther and Ethan had already left the bunkhouse. After dressing quickly, he stepped to the doorway and saw six riders talking to Ethan, Luther, and Clancey at the ranch house. Stray words wandered downhill, but not enough to make out the conversation. Claire wasn't in sight.

Cole first recognized Sam Winlow, then the scar-eyed cowboy named Cherokee who had held the doctor at the saloon. He didn't see Everett or any of the others from that fight. He stepped back into the bunkhouse and buckled on his gunbelt. But a thought roped his actions: this may be what his brother wants, and he should stay out of it. If Winlow offers a fair price for the trail herd, it might be for the best. Ethan wouldn't sell him the ranch or his young stock; his pride wouldn't allow that drastic a step. At least not now. He should stay out of it.

"Kerry, I'm giving you a fair deal—an' you know it," Winlow said, exasperated at the rancher's earlier negative reaction. The haughty cattleman was dressed in trail gear, including heavy chaps bearing the Walking W brand.

"There isn't any way in hell you're gonna get that beef to market. No trail boss worth his salt is around to lead them without you. Except for Benson—and he works for me. Fact is, our drive started yesterday. We're leaving here to catch up. We've just got time to take your herd along. How about it, Kerry?"

The morning sun's commanding glare was bothering everyone except the blinded Ethan. He stood on the porch with one hand resting against the split-log railing. Luther was uneasy, his eyes darting from one armed rider to the next, expecting trouble. Ethan's father was stern-faced, struggling with a hangover.

"What's the matter?" snarled Cherokee. "Ya got a twitch or somethin'? Maybe we oughta finish what we started. Stand still while my boss is talkin'."

"That's enough, Cherokee," Winlow ordered. "We didn't come here to cause trouble. We came to help."

"Like a coyote a-he'pin' chickens," growled Luther. The stream of tobacco juice that followed was full and glorious, catching the right front hoof of Cherokee's horse. Startled, the animal lifted its splattered leg, flagged its ears upright and backed up, wanting to bolt.

Cherokee cursed and struggled to bring the frightened animal under control.

"Excuse me?" Winlow said, his bulging eyes glaring at the cowhand with contempt.

"I dun said, you was nuthin' but a burr on a coyote's butt," Luther snapped, and spat tobacco juice again in the direction of Cherokee's horse. This time the brown spittle plopped in the dirt; the horse studied it for a moment to be assured there was no threat.

"Now, see here, Kerry, I didn't come here to be insulted. I came for business. Let's go inside where we can talk in private."

"Aye, t'is the polite thing to do, Mr. Winlow. Perhaps a wee taste of Irish whiskey would be a good way to . . ."

"No, that's not necessary," Ethan cut off his father. Neither Clancey nor Luther could have guessed what would have come next.

"Luther, would you ask Cole to join us, please?"

"I'd be ri't proud to do jes' that. Was a-hopin' you'd say that."

"Well, good. Winlow, there are a hellva lot of things you don't know about—and one of them is the whereabouts of good trail bosses. I'd like you to meet mine. Then I want you off my land—you've already ruined my breakfast."

Winlow turned to watch Luther head toward the bunkhouse, then spun back to Ethan on the porch. Winlow spoke sarcastically. "What's this all about? You trying to make me believe you've got some savvy trail boss hidden away—just for the occasion. Come on, Kerry, what do you take me for?"

"You wouldn't want to hear it."

Cherokee snarled, "Come on, boss. We can run over this blind piece of crap. You don't have to take this."

"See here, Kerry, you're testing my patience. I came to buy your herd. I didn't have to. I could just wait and get your ranch the easy way. I was trying to help."

"Sure you were, Winlow. That price wouldn't buy five hundred head, and you know it. I may be blind, but I'm not stupid. As for your friend here, tell him I still know how to use a gun. It may take three bullets instead of one, but I'll take you if he starts anything."

Winlow and his men watched as Luther and Cole headed toward the house. Cherkokee whispered in Winlow's ear.

"You asked if I had a savvy trail boss hidden away. Yeah, I do, Winlow. My brother. I'm turning my herd over to my brother. An' I'm going too."

Clancey Kerry shook his head to clear the cobwebs that made him think his son had just said he was going on the drive.

"Kerry, don't be a fool! You can't see! Brother or not, he'll run off with your beeves and leave you sittin' in the middle of Indian country," Winlow snarled.

"The problem with you, Winlow, is that you think all men would do what you would do. Like coming in here an' throwing a few dollars in my face, hoping we're so desparate we'll jump for it. You're one sorry sonuvabitch."

"Why, if you weren't blind, I'd . . ."

"Don't let that stop you, Winlow, come on. I hear your men need that kind of edge too."

"Mornin', boss," came Cole's greeting as he walked between two Walking W riders, acting oblivious to the heated exchange. Luther followed him like a pet dog. Luther noticed his youngest brother was walking slower than usual to hide his stiffened leg.

"Mornin'," Ethan responded warmly, turning his head in the direction of Cole's voice. "I was just telling these men from the Walking W you were going to lead my herd to Kansas. They asked to meet you before leaving."

Cole tried to hide his surprise; his glance at Luther didn't help. The grizzled cowboy had swallowed his chaw in response to Ethan's statement and his face was like a startled deer's, only red. The disturbing entry into his throat immediately occupied his attention. Clancey stepped back inside, unable to cope or unaware of the significance of the moment. Cole recovered mentally, reminding himself that this might be nothing more than a negotiating ploy by Ethan to get Winlow to raise his price.

"Boss, I've met this one . . . and this one." He pointed to Winlow and Cherokee. "Haven't had the pleasure of the others. But I've seen their like before . . . under rocks."

Cole leaned over to pick up a burnt match on the ground as he finished his sentence. When he straightened, sunlight bounced off the cocked Colt in his fist, aimed at Winlow's stomach.

"Hey! What the hell's this?" demanded Winlow, yanking on his reins in an involuntary reaction to the sudden appearance of the gun.

"Winlow, tell your men how close you came to dying—and why."

The big man glared at Cole, his ugly face distorted into hate, and growled, "You heard the man, let him see your hands. Cherokee, get away from your goddamn gun!"

Cheroke flinched and drew his hand away from his holstered pistol like it had touched a flame. Cole's eyes ripped at Winlow's confidence while the black nose of his Colt stared unmoving at Winlow's heart. Gradually he was convinced Winlow's men had raised their hands sufficiently and eased the hammer down on his Colt. He returned it to the sidewinder holster near his belt buckle. Winlow's relief filled his face.

After inspecting his men for their compliance, Winlow turned back to Ethan. "You're really enjoying this, aren't you? There'll be a time, Kerry. There'll be a time. Your brother—if he is your brother—is nothin' but a gunfighter. You're turning your herd over to a no-good drifter."

"He is my brother, Winlow, but I don't reckon you'd know anything about family," Ethan replied, his voice hard and clipped, like the heavy click-click of a Winchester being cocked.

There was an instant of complete silence, a flicker of time when Winlow knew he had said the wrong thing but it was too late to grab the words out of the air. Out of the corner of his eye, he caught the curious grin of Luther, standing on the porch with his arms crossed, imitating the stance of his brother, Ethan. Cole's response was a razor to Winlow's courage.

"Today is your lucky day, Winlow. I'm going to let that go, since you're on my brother's ranch. But you'd better pray I never see you again. Nobody messes with the Kerry brothers—an' nobody calls me a no-good drifter."

The evil rancher blinked, inhaling to push away the shiver before anyone saw it. He had expected a downtrodden bunch and a beaten Ethan Kerry ready to make any kind of deal possible. This wasn't working well; he had no doubt the gunfighter meant what he said. Through the doorway came Claire Kerry, her face betraying a lack of sleep. Her jaw was set and her eyes were darts. Winlow realized this was his last chance.

"Good morning, Mrs. Kerry. We came by to offer our sympathy for your husband's accident. It's a sad thing to see a good man cut down before his time. I've offered to buy the trail herd, and I hope you'll convince him to listen. It'd be the best for you and your children. Our herd's already moving, so we have to know now."

Cole looked at the woman, and she caught his eyes before focusing her attention on Winlow.

"How gracious of you, Mr. Winlow." Her response was syrupy. She cleared her throat, holding her hand to her mouth, and looked at Luther. Her smile brought a puzzled frown to his leathery face.

Returning her attention to Winlow and his pasted-on courtesy, she said, "I can't imagine why you would think we have any need for your help. Good day to you."

Before anyone else could react, she added, "Luther, Cole, would you mind seeing these men find their way out. I know there's much to be done for the drive. I believe my husband wants to leave today."

Cole couldn't help grinning. "You heard the lady, Winlow. We've got work to do. Ride on."

"You'll rue this day, Kerry, you're nothing but a blind fool!" Winlow spat and yanked his horse around, spurring it viciously into a gallop. His riders followed. Cherokee looked back and yelled something, but no one could understand.

"Well, boys, we've got work to do. What do you say, trail boss, can we do it?" Ethan held out his hand.

Cole walked over and grabbed it. "We can, Ethan. We will."

He looked away to see Claire. Her eyes were bright with wetness and her lip quivered, so she bit it into submission. He knew it had been a long night for both of them. A stray thought of Kathleen wandered through his conscious mind, and he wished she were standing beside him, like Claire was with Ethan.

Winlow's leaving triggered an energized sense of urgency, as if moments were being counted against them. Luther actually trotted to the corral to ready the new mounts and gather any last-minute tack. Eli ran after him, asking nonstop questions. Claire bustled to the chuck wagon with Maggie at her side. Hayden, the trail cook, was already there, reviewing his domain with pride. Ethan grabbed Cole's arm and said, "Let's go inside. I want to read the first pages of my diary again. If we forget something now, it's hard to make up for it."

Cole took his brother's arm and led him into the house. Clancey was nowhere in sight. Sounds from the kitchen indicated he was there, drinking. As they walked, Cole felt a tenseness within Ethan, but dismissed it as no more than the excitement he felt himself. Sitting side by side at the table, Cole read aloud from the leather-bound book. Ethan was so focused and so much in command that Cole expected him at any minute to rip off the bandage and announce he could see again. As Cole read, he became more and more impressed with the thoroughness of the notes. They ranged from extensive trail descriptions, to comments on the riders' daily attitudes and each day's meals, to assessments about the herd's condition, to concerns about the horses, to the weather.

Only once did Ethan waver from the business at hand. That came when Cole read a remark about the brilliance of the second day's sunset. "I'll never see one of those again, Cole," he muttered. "Won't even know if it's a sunny day. How'd you like to trade eyes?" Cole was silent.

Like a returning dream, Cole realized how thorough his brother was in his thinking. Not a detail was left untouched in their preparation, or unsaid. The man's blindness heightened his intensity to cover all the possible considerations of the trail, if it was possible to do so, and he recited every important step they would take on the first days out. Cole tried to absorb what he needed to know, letting pass those things Ethan should be leaving to him to decide and knew it, but couldn't resist saying anyway. Cole recognized they would have plenty of time to adjust to each other's style.

It was Luther who broke into the review, coming to the front door and yelling, "Wal, brothers o' mine, are ya gonna talk 'bout it, or is ya gonna do it? We best git to goin', if'n we've a mind to. Ever'thin's ready."

Ethan took a deep breath and said, "Better get out there, Cole. I'll be along. Want to say my goodbyes to Claire and the kids. Let them know I'm in here, will you?"

"Sure."

After telling Claire, Cole retreated to the bunkhouse, gathered his gear and placed it in the chuck wagon, then headed for the corral to saddle the big sorrel. Ten minutes later, he saw Claire open the front door and cross the open ranch yard toward him. She had been inside with Ethan; the two children remained there. There were no tears, no sniffles, just those bright eyes that had searched his soul earlier.

As Cole placed the bridle on Kiowa, she stopped in front of him and said, "Cole, I believe God sent you here for this. I believe you will get the herd through and keep my husband safe. Don't let him fight himself. It will be hard. Hardest on you, I think. But you can stand up to my Ethan—and still love him. Thank you for doing this."

She kissed Cole on the cheek and turned away. He stood watching her go, savoring the words. Even with blindness, his brother had far more than he did: He had a woman who stood beside him through life, and together they had two happy children. Could there be anything better than that? He reached into his back pocket and felt the waiting letter. Should he give it to Claire to post in town later? *No, not now. Not this way,* he told himself. *Maybe I'll post it at one of the general stores on the early part of the trail. Yeah, that's what I'll do.*

Commotion at the porch broke into his thinking. The chuck wagon pulled up in front of the house. Slamming open the front door of the house, Ethan strode forward in his chaps and spurs. He was alone. Wobbly, but alone. A weather-beaten hat was low on his forehead. His hands were at his hips, above the comfortable pistol belt, in a defiant, open stance. Only the bandage around his eyes gave away reality. God, if ever a man looked like a cowman, it was Ethan Kerry—and it was now, Cole muttered. But knowing the situation also made Ethan appear almost like a clown.

"Let's go, Cole!" Ethan yelled authoritatively. His voice carried a hint of fear only a knowing man could hear. "Where's Hayden?"

"Right here, Mr. Kerry. Just a minute and I'll help you up."

Claire appeared beside Ethan, along with Eli and Maggie. She tried to assist him down the porch steps without appearing to do so. He was walking faster than he should and stumbled. She held him up, but he yanked his arm away from her. "I can find the damn wagon by myself, Claire."

As if she had never heard the comment, Claire guided his hands to the waiting chuck wagon and his boot to the iron step. He grunted and swung into place, losing his balance and careening off Hayden, who was unwrapping the reins from where he had just placed them around the whip pole.

"Goodbye, Ethan, I love you," Claire said, tears taking over her face in spite of her unspoken resolve. "Eli, Maggie, tell your father goodbye." She waited for their responses and then added, "Good luck, Hayden. Do you have everything you need?" She didn't wait for the answer and yelled, "Good luck, Luther! Good luck, Cole!"

Cole swung into the saddle and led the procession out of the ranch yard toward the waiting herd. Earlier, Ethan had repeated the directions at least six times. Behind him rumbled the chuck wagon with a stoic Hayden and a fidgety Ethan. Farther back, Luther drove the twenty new horses to add to the trail remuda. Cole inhaled deeply, looked back at Claire and Maggie. Eli was running beside Luther, crying and asking to go along. Cole waved, and Claire waved back. She looked down, and Maggie waved too, and Cole returned it. Soon even the ranch house was a small blur, and then it disappeared. A feisty midday sun soon turned horses, riders, and the wagon into bronze.

Ahead was a long roll of crumbling hills and desolate mesas that could hide anything in this part of Texas, even Comanche war parties. Old habits die hard, so his caution was instinctive. He eased the red horse across a sandy divide and over its lip onto a wide expanse of prairie grass, with the others close behind. Suddenly before them was an unending brown sea of cattle.

The Bar K trail herd was a majestic sight, one he had expected but couldn't really comprehend until now. Nearly three thousand steers and older cows were milling across this elevated pasture. Horsemen moved in an easy rhythm with the herd. Some waved. As soon as Cole rode into the camp, he knew trouble was brewing. He'd been around groups of men too long not to pick up the signals. Luther helped Ethan down from the chuck wagon while most of the men watched the activity. Several turned away from the sight of a blind Ethan Kerry.

Munching on a biscuit, Jared Dancer, the blond cowboy in stovepipe straight chaps, left his squatted position by the fire and quickly made his way to Luther. The grizzled wrangler and three other riders were moving the new horses into the rope corral. After talking a few minutes, Luther went grim-faced to Cole and Ethan. A brief huddle ended with Luther leading the blind rancher to the front left wheel of the wagon, where he could hold it with his right hand for balance. Cole walked a few steps behind them.

"It's a good day to ride," Ethan said with as much bravado as he could generate while his men gathered around him. He was nervous but tried not to show it.

Under the wide bandage tied around his head, his eyes opened and shut in agitated rhythm to his continuing declaration. "Boys, I've got some things to tell you. I reckon you already know the first, though. . . . I'm blind. Can't see a thing. Everybody's going to want to play cards with me!"

A murmur through the gathering was less than Cole thought there should have been. He studied the hard faces of the riders in front of him.

"But the rest is good. Our drive is on. We're leaving now. I want to move the herd fast. Get 'em away from home ground before they realize it. Cole Kerry, my brother, will be trail boss. He's knows well the territory we're going through. But I'll be going along to . . . help too." Ethan's voice trailed off slightly as he came to the end of his speech, a recognition of the awkwardness he felt.

Cole took the introduction and stepped forward. "Men, this is not how you thought it was going to be. Everyone knows that. But things'll go easy if we work together. I'll take my orders from my brother. You'll take yours from me. I don't expect to be giving many. You know what needs to be done. Our job is to get this herd, nice and fat, to Kansas."

No one spoke.

Finally, Ike Jenkins, a balding, plump cowboy with a nervous twitch to the left side of his face when he talked, broke the silence. "Stranger, we don't know who you are, or why you're here. Mr. Kerry says you're his brother. I hear you're a gunfighter. Some of us aren't so wound up about heading for Kansas—following a stranger and a blind man. No offense, but why don't you sell to another rancher, Mr. Kerry?"

Muffled agreement followed. Most of the riders stared at their boots as if each had just discovered a foot problem.

Ethan answered, "Ike, I'm sorry to hear you won't be going with us. You can get your pay at the house tomorrow. Anyone else not want to go?"

Cole smiled to himself. It was a gutsy move, but one he should have expected from his brother. Cole followed up on what Luther had just told them. "Ike, how much did Sam Winlow pay you to say that?"

"What! What the hell you talkin' about?" Ike responded, his eyes involuntarily going to Cole's gunbelt. "I ain't talked with nobody. Jes' worried, that's all."

"Really. Winlow and some of his men rode through here no more than two hours ago. Sam Winlow talked with you private-like—or do you want to call me a liar?" Cole's eyes cut into Ike's face. The men around Ike Jenkins stepped away from him.

"W-w-wait a minute, I ain't takin' no lead for Sam Winlow," Ike Jenkins exclaimed, shaking, and lifting his hands. "He gave me a gold piece jes' to say I was worried, that's all. I woulda done it—"

# *Chapter Eleven*

"Ride on, Ike." Ethan's words were bullets. "Luther, see that he takes only his own horse. Not one of ours. I want him out of here. Now."

"You sonvabitch! All of you . . . you're crazy. This is crazy! Ain't no way you're gonna get thar. Hellfire, boys, you're gonna be followin' a blind man!" Ike spat as he stamped toward the remuda with Luther following him. Dancer handed the fired cowboy an already saddled horse and slapped its rump as he was swinging up. Horse and rider went bounding off toward the south.

Ethan resumed the discussion. "If you decide you don't want to make the drive, you'll have a job when we get back. If you decide to go, you're going all the way. I may be blind, but I'm not a quitter.

"This man here, my younger brother—Cole Kerry— knows men and how to get them through the rough country we'll be crossing. He knows Indians and how

133

to kill them without being killed, if it comes to that. He knows horses. In case you weren't watching, that's Kiowa he's riding. The red horse none of us could ride. He broke it yesterday. I know the trail to Kansas, maybe better than anybody. We've got Dancer and DuMonte at the point. An' Luther's got better horses than anybody has ever seen. Together we're going to get this herd to Dodge City. Who rides with us?"

From the back side of the gathered cowboys, Luther yelled, "By cracky, boys, it's gettin' late in the day. Jawin's through. We got us a herd to move—an' she's goin' today to that grassy hole near the twin buttes."

"T-hat's n-n-n-near t-twelve miles, L-Luther," Jip Jersey responded, his stuttering more pronounced because he was excited. The cowboy prided himself on his manner of dress, a form of personal compensation for his vocal problem. A navy blue, pin-striped vest, completely buttoned, set off a full silk cravat; this was his standard dress on the trail or off of it. That and star-emblazoned batwing chaps and a curled white hat.

"That's why you got to git into yur guldurn saddle, Jip. An' don't talk no more about it. We ain't got time for you to git out another of your rattlin' speeches."

Laughter followed, then excited banter as men began moving toward their saddles and gear. Luther was immediately busy roping out designated mounts. The men would be allowed to select the rest of their personal strings of ten horses over the next couple of days. Cole didn't want to wait any longer to get going. Ethan had told him the country north dried out quickly this time of the year. Luther would oversee the horse choosing; Cole and the two point riders would select their strings first. The rest would rotate selections, choosing one animal at a time.

Enthused by the drovers' reactions, Cole sought Jared Dancer as the first man to meet. Described by his older brother as both hot-tempered and fearless, Ethan had told him the point rider was superstitious and had some strange habits, but that Dancer's abilities far outweighed his idiosyncrasies.

Smiling, Ethan had added, "Dancer'll always be looking for signs—good or bad. He'll always put his bedroll the same distance from the chuck wagon with a cedar sprig over his blankets. Has to ride his string of horses in a certain order that even Luther can't figure out. There's more, but it's all harmless stuff. Mostly Kiowa. Lived with them awhile. He holds big store in their thinking. But he's a damn good man to have on your side. You'll like him, Cole."

The short rider was checking his saddlebags as Cole approached and held out his hand.

"Dancer, you an' DuMonte take the lead and I'll catch up with you. I'll stay back until we get everything moving."

A braided leather quirt dangled from his left wrist as Dancer replied enthusiastically, "Cole Kerry, proud to be ridin'with you. Your medicine looks strong."

Cole smiled, remembering Ethan's description. He noticed the cowboy's black-handled Colt resting on his right thigh for a left-handed pull. Deciding not to comment on the unusual positioning, he outlined the initial drover assignments as a courtesy to Dancer. After a brief exchange about timing, Dancer excused himself, spun around, and headed for the remuda with a bounce to his walk.

"Hey, Luther, I want that dun with the black feet! I rode him first on last year's drive!" he yelled toward the swirl of dust and horses. "Don't nobody touch my saddle—I'll get it."

Without glancing down, Dancer pushed his small

medicine pouch, hanging from his neck, back inside his undershirt as he ran. The superstitious point rider never took off his favorite good-luck charm, not even to bathe. Cole continued his rounds, introducing himself and shaking hands with each cowboy he came to. Following Ethan's suggestions, Cole assigned men to the flank and swing positions along the already moving herd.

Looking more like a black professor than a cowboy, Harold DuMonte was stuffing his Bible into his bag to put in the chuck wagon. Cole knew the man was quite religious from Ethan's briefing. His older brother had said, "You know, Cole, both of my point riders are spiritual as all get-out. Different directions, though. One's Christian and the other's Kiowa. Not sure which is the best, come to think of it."

Cole's greeting was cordial but brief.

"Howdy. I'm Cole Kerry."

"I'm very glad to meet you, Mr. Kerry. Harold DuMonte is my name. But everyone calls me Du-Monte—or Preacher."

"Heard that. We're going to need the good Lord on our side, DuMonte. Counting on you to help us with that."

"Yessir, Mr. Kerry. I will be praying."

"You'll be riding point too. You an' Dancer head on out whenever you're ready. I'll catch up."

"Yes sir." DuMonte almost smiled.

Gray-haired Ben Speakman was an older man, a former rebel captain under Longstreet's command, and prone to long and thoughtful answers to questions, according to Luther's warning. Speakman's left arm had been amputated after the great battle of Gettysburg. With his left shirt cuff pinned to his shoulder, he saluted when Cole approached to meet him. A well-used pipe completed the man. Speakman's legs could no longer take riding a horse on a drive like this, but he could handle the calf wagon just fine.

Cole figured not too many men would dare to call him "nursemaid," or "mother cow," or any of the other nicknames drovers liked to call the calf wagon driver. At least not to his face. Anyone who did could count on a long-winded response that started with the importance of young cattle, slid to the significance of mothers in general and his, in particular, and ended with a few comments about humor. As far as Luther knew, no one had stayed around for the complete thought.

"Reporting for duty, Cole Kerry," Ben Speakman snapped with a twinkle in his eyes. His tanned face was a war map of wrinkles and squints, and his back was slightly bowed, but his manner was alert. Faded buttermilk pants carried the faint hint of a yellow strip down the sides. Cole observed that Speakman carried an early-model Colt dragoon, a heavy pistol that used paper loads instead of shells and often misfired. Evaluating another man's weapons, and how he carried them, was as natural to Cole as introducing himself.

"At ease . . . Captain," Cole said with a warm smile, returning the salute, reminding himself not to ask this engaging man about the war; he didn't have time to listen.

"If you're anything like your brother, ridin' with you will be sunshine, water, and hot chow," Speakman said cheerfully, vigorously puffing his pipe. He lifted a bawling calf into the wagon, awkwardly holding the animal in place with the stub of his left arm as he swooped and lifted with the other. Four other calves were already on board. With that success, he went after another, hiding behind its mother.

He chattered as he closed in on the skittish calf. "I

remember the first time we pushed 'em north. You couldn't believe what we ran into. Comanches, my God, they were thicker'n flies on an old molasses jug an—"

"I'm mighty glad you're along, Ben," Cole replied, and walked on.

Cole introduced himself to Gus Oleen, a dour Swede who was unhappy about a missing sock but even grumpier over the news that he was riding drag. However, he made certain Cole was out of earshot before griping about the assignment. The next drover Cole met was the complete opposite of the grumbling Swede: gap-toothed and happy Mike Henderson, whom everyone called "Stovepipe." The new trail boss smiled when he shook Stovepipe's hand, remembering that Luther had indicated the nickname hadn't come from his lean, bullwhip frame but from a whore describing the size of his manhood.

Stovepipe Henderson had a new pair of leather gloves and was eager to show them to the new trail boss. After listening to Stovepipe discuss the importance of good gloves, Cole excused himself and continued his introductions to the trail drovers. He chuckled to himself as he headed toward the next rider. It was difficult to imagine anyone as thin as Stovepipe being so well-endowed—or so fascinated with a new pair of gloves.

Standing by himself, surveying the activity, was a compact snarl of a man named John Davis Sotar. Cole observed him as he drew closer. The man's pistol belt wasn't something an ordinary drover wore. Sotar's cutaway holster rested on his left hip with the pistol handle forward. Silver studs lined both the holster and the belt. The walnut grips of the short-barreled Colt were inlaid with a silver star on each side. While a star was a familiar adornment for a Texas cowboy, Cole thought the man was more likely from Missouri. Sotar's voice carried the distinctive twang of the Ozark hill country. A cattle drive was a good place to disappear if a man needed to—and Cole had a feeling Sotar did. As they shook hands, Sotar's manner was more challenge than welcome.

Cole noticed that the bottom of Sotar's left earlobe was gone, most likely the result of a too-close bullet. As they talked, the fingers of the man's right hand were in nervous motion, with his thumb and forefinger rubbing a constant circle. But if Luther vouched for the rider, and he did, Sotar must be a steady hand. Cole shook off the concern and looked for another drover to meet. Sotar studied the bullet hole in Cole's boot as he walked away.

The last rider Cole met before riding out was a half-breed Sioux. Everyone called him Abe because his Sioux name, Ablakela Sunkawakan, Calm Horse, started with that sound. Already, he had a reputation for ignoring an order he didn't like, no matter who gave it. His skill with cattle left some room for that independence. The half-breed, with long black hair under a shapeless hat, clearly liked Cole Kerry, seeing him as a worthy leader.

"Cole Ker-rie. Damn," Abe greeted his new trail boss.

Cole had been warned that the half-breed knew little English and that which he did know was laced with curse words, a product of the saloonkeeper who raised him.

"Abe, I hear you're good with cattle. Glad to have you with us."

Abe's eyes widened in pleasant surprise. "Yes, cattel. Cole Ker-rie. Damn."

Cole said, "I want you to ride the left flank. Understand?" The flank rider position was two-thirds of the way back from the herd's lead steers; the swing rider position was a third back.

"Abe know, Cole Ker-rie. Damn. Yatahey."

Cole smiled, shook his head, and left to find Kiowa and Ethan Kerry. He would have a long time to meet the rest of the crew. Maybe too long. Already seated in the chuck wagon, Ethan greeted his younger brother lustily: "Take 'em to Kansas, Cole!" Under a white-hot sky, the dry prairie blossomed with mounted riders. Like an orchestrated symphony, men and animals moved in a harmony of brown and black. Hot breezes, seemingly from a giant smithy's firebox, created dances of dust beside the endless stream of moving cattle.

Overhead, a red-tailed hawk hung against the sky. Cole Kerry caught a tiny flicker of light in the hills to the north. Reflection off field glasses, he thought. Who would be watching a herd of cattle move out? No, that wasn't the right question. Who would be watching *this* herd move out? There was only one possibility. Sam Winlow.

Soon, the afternoon sun was racing to beat them to the two slump-shouldered buttes ahead. The excitement of the drive's start had long passed, and the heat of the day ate into alertness. The herd wasn't happy about being pushed along this fast. Rotating horses frequently kept the men at an advantage, but the steers were still on familiar ground—and definitely not used to moving together. That's why Ethan Kerry wanted them driven hard tomorrow and the next day. Strange surroundings and tired animals were a good combination. Once the cattle were beyond land they had grazed on, the herd would be allowed to enjoy the greening grasses and fatten as they moved north.

Sounds of scuffling cattle, creaking saddle leather, bawling steers, and the insistent calls of cowboys working the herd were a symphony across the sunbaked plains. At the front, Cole Kerry was riding his third horse of the day, a stout bay Luther recommended. His mind wandered off the trail and onto the dead man he had left behind in Abilene and the woman who was the reason for it. For a moment, he wanted to race away and leave all this new responsibility behind. He blinked, and reality returned with the prairie's heat. As he turned in his saddle, his eyes sought the chuck wagon off to the side of the herd. Ethan was sitting silently alongside T. L. Hayden. It was too far away to see Ethan's expression, but he was sitting stiffly. Cole chuckled to himself and wondered if the cook had said anything to his brother. Ethan was an intimiding man, even if he was blind.

Behind him, an uproar broke his daydreaming. He swung the bay around to see what the pandemonium was about, but the horse resisted the idea. His spurs added the necessary encouragement, and it turned and held in place as Cole stared unbelieving at the raging tumult. The middle of the herd was a storm of dust and noise; steers lunged toward the freedom of the open prairie, running in every direction; men and horses were swallowed in the roar. Even the cattle in the front of the herd were disturbed and beginning to trot, glancing nervously backward to see if they should run too.

Whatever caused the stampede didn't matter for now. Cole reined the bay in the direction of a hundred streaking beasts, and the horse was at full speed in three strides. DuMonte and Dancer were ahead and attempting to turn one bunch of wide-eyed steers thundering together. Out of the corner of his eye, Cole could see Sotar and Abe racing to catch up with another group. Scattered yells were swallowed by the excitement.

Cole raced past both point riders to a large speckled steer, leading twenty others. The bay tore up the remaining space in seconds. As if looking for a reason, the beast slowed, then came to a shuffling stop as Cole cut in front. The trailing animals mimicked his action as if they never had any intention of doing anything else. Waving his lariat to get their attention, Cole turned the steers and headed back.

The bay stutter-stepped, threw its head and wanted to run again, but Cole held the reins tight, forced it to walk, and the sturdy animal obeyed. He liked the horse and its friskiness. As usual, Luther's judgment about horses was accurate.

They met another ten steers walking in the wrong direction; the cattle were easily persuaded to turn around and join the speckled steer and his group.

The stampede was over. Just like that. Cattle would rather walk and eat than run. Now came the slow, time-eating work to bring the scattered animals together again. Steers and cows were spread over the prairie, uncaring of their disruption and forgetful of the reason for it. Everywhere he looked, riders were prodding bunches of cattle back into one long body. In the distance, the remuda had stopped, and Luther was ready to receive more horse changes than usual.

Jip Jersey rode alongside Cole, pushing eighteen steers in front of him. His face was white with tension and streaked with sweat. "A-A-A b-b-buffalo came out of t-t-that ravine r-r-right in front of m-m-me. D-d-didn't s-s-see it, n-n-no how."

"Yeah, that can happen in a hurry, Jip," Cole said,

waving his hand to keep the steers heading in the same direction. Cole wondered to himself if Jip would have worried about the buffalo even if he had seen it.

Jip shook his head, looked down at his horse's wet chest and legs, and apologized. "D-d-d-didn't mean t-t-to wear h-h-him out, r-r-really. I—I was h-h-headin' for the r-r-remuda when it h-h-happened, M-M-Mr. K-K-Kerry."

"You go on, Jip. I'll keep these heading the right way. Your horse needs rest."

"T-t-thanks, M-M-Mr. K-K-Kerry," the stuttering cowboy said softly, and peeled his tired horse away and toward the distant horse herd.

Cole wore out the bay riding back and forth along the half-mile herdline, checking to make certain no one was hurt and that the steers were being located. Finally, he switched to a rangy brown mustang and continued his assessment. For the next two hours, the Bar K men gradually regained control. After the herd was resettled and moving quietly again, Cole and Dancer set up a counting point at the front. Standing on each side of the collected herd, the two men counted the passing animals. The only difference was the way each man kept track: Dancer placed a pebble in his vest pocket for every hundred animals counted; Cole looped a quick knot in the end of his lariat to designate the same amount.

As the drag riders pushed the slowest steers and cows past, Dancer yelled across, "Got ourselves some extries! Sixty-one by my count. Must've caught some range stuff."

"I've got sixty-four," Cole answered. "Tell the boys to keep an eye out. Ethan doesn't want someone else's beef along."

"When we put 'em back on the trail tomorrow, we should get most of them. I'll pass the word," Dancer said, removing his hat and wiping away the afternoon's sweat from his brow.

The herd moved easily northward, with the lead steer, Whistle, out front. This was the second trip to Kansas for the rangy steer with the V-shaped right horn. Last year, it had proved to be a steady lead animal and was brought home to do it again. Cole switched to the fiery Kiowa and expected the worst. The sorrel was responsive to the slightest command, intentionally or otherwise, and Cole was pleased with the animal's attitude.

A late-afternoon sun beat them to the buttes and was resting on the top ridges when they reached the night's bedground. Working the herd in a huge circle, the Bar K men began the process of adjusting them to their first stopover. Watering had already been accomplished at the swollen creek meandering through the region. Patiently, the riders gradually tightened the circle, slowly easing the cattle into their evening stand so they thought it was their own idea.

Cole looked over his shoulder and again saw the chuck wagon and the calf wagon lumbering into view. In the far distance, he could see the remuda drinking at the creek. He swung his horse and galloped toward the wagons. Ethan would want to know that the herd was accounted for. "Did we lose any?" Ethan asked as Cole rode up beside the chuck wagon.

# Chapter Twelve

Cole assured him they hadn't lost any cattle but had actually gathered sixty head of range stock to boot. Ethan grinned and repeated what Cole had expected, that he didn't want to have anyone else's cattle in his herd, even if they were pure mavericks. Cole said the men were going to cull the strays in the morning as the herd got back on the trail. Ethan stated his approval of that plan, adding a few comments on how he wanted it done.

T. L. Hayden looked straight ahead at the horses he was handling; a bored expression defined his square face as the two Kerrys talked. Ethan was nervous, filled with details he wanted to share and, as yet, still savoring the excitement of the drive like a kid eating a stick of hard candy. He seemed out of place sitting in the chuck wagon, his chaps and spurs of no use there, but he wore them anyway. The dust-streaked bandage cov-

145

ering his eyes was a constant reminder of the new world he must stay in.

After reporting the herd's numbers, Cole listened as he rode alongside the wagon, except for providing a brief description of the bedground for the blind rancher. Earlier, Ethan had asked the cook to tell him about the area, but Hayden's attempts were more frustrating than enlightening. It was a three-sided mesa, nudging two buttes to the northwest. Thickets of mesquite belted the front of the grassy elevation. Only one tree enjoyed the ground: a wind-battered cottonwood with its right half gone, stripped away by lightning, from the looks of the charred scar.

Surrounding one side of the mesa was a creek that spun westward at a direct angle and ran away into the dusty horizon, searching for a river. Spring rains had built up its courage. Grasses of varying length covered the area, except for a giant hand of odd-shaped rocks. It was exactly as Ethan had outlined it in his diary. Almost eerily so. It was an excellent bedground for a herd: elevated land, good grass, and good water.

Cole rolled a cigarette and handed it to his older brother. Before Cole could strike a match, Ethan had one of his own flashing. Cole rolled and lit a second, for himself. As they drew closer to the herd, he watched the men move the herd like musicians with a familiar song. He was leader enough, and confident enough, not to interfere or posture with needless orders. He eased his stiffened leg out of the stirrup to let it straighten. The lower calf had cramped on him earlier.

"Cole?" Ethan asked as the white lines of smoke strolled across his suntanned face.

"Yes?"

"I like to use the wagon tongue to point the way for

the next day's direction. Makes it easier when you're leaving before light."

"Makes good sense to me."

"Cole, make sure the herd isn't crowded. Especially the muleys. I hate those hornless things—they're always crowding together and causing trouble. They'll be jumpy for a few days. Not used to traveling as herd, I reckon. I've seen one crowded steer start a whole herd stampeding," Ethan continued, paused, exhaled, and finished. "That was when I could see."

Hayden glanced at Cole; the cook's haughty eyes were like those of someone who has just heard a dirty joke. When there was no response from Cole, Hayden quickly returned his attention to the horses. He eased them to the east, having decided on the location for his domain.

Cole cocked his head to the side and said, "Hayden, the men will be mighty hungry tonight. They used up a lot of nerves getting started. I want them to have plenty to eat."

"Hayden and I already talked about keeping it kinda light. You know, it's going to be a long drive—and we sure don't want to overuse our supplies early on. No need to make them think it's going to be a picnic all the way."

Hayden smiled victoriously, like a panther watching another cat leave his territory. His eyes met Cole's, and the smile evaporated into a thin retreat. This was definitely a man the cook didn't want to cross. He'd heard the stories, and Cole's two-gun rig was a constant reminder of his reputation. Cole himself held his tongue; supper wasn't worth an argument. Talking over the details of the meal while riding together was a natural thing for Ethan and Hayden to do—although every time he glanced at them, neither was talking. He figured it was more of a decision expressed about the meal—from Ethan—rather than a two-way conversation.

But he didn't like having his command intruded upon, even slightly. It was a weakness, he realized, perhaps born from being a man of the gun, not a cattleman, or from being alone too much. Patting Kiowa's neck, Cole started to say something when, across the field, a steer broke loose from the flow and raced for home. Two more followed.

Long curved horns sliced past a green-broke horse ridden by the youngest drover on the drive, and the mustang reared. Completely surprised, the inexperienced cowboy grabbed for the graying sky first, then for the saddle horn, but it was too late. He tumbled backward, stirrups rising in the air, and his horse bolted toward the buttes.

"Got some steer troubles. I'll be back," Cole said as he yanked the red horse toward the sudden activity.

"Keep an eye out for the bad ones," Ethan yelled back. "We'll probably have to get rid of them."

Several riders were chasing the steers, so Cole spurred the big sorrel into a full gallop after the runaway horse. Waving off pursuit by the others, he swung wide to cut off the animal without its sensing pursuit. Chasing a horse was a good way to make the thing run harder, he thought. Kiowa was responsive and quick, showing no signs of being tired. In less than a minute, he was parallel to the loose horse. From twenty yards away, Cole studied the animal enjoying its freedom; the horse was adding an occasional hop to its running and paying no attention to Cole's advance.

Swinging to his left, Cole closed in. Nostrils flared as the freed horse suddenly realized recapture was imminent. As the smooth-running sorrel slid alongside the loose horse, Cole reached down and grabbed the bouncing reins. Seconds later, the two were trotting together. He pulled the escaped horse closer to him, patted its sweaty neck, and talked softly, trying to calm the animal. Kiowa seemed to understand its role and walked quietly.

In minutes, they were back at camp, with the runaway horse striding with its head down. Ethan had assigned the first two night riders and dismissed the rest. Ferguson and Jip took the first watch, normally the easiest, but for the next few days the cattle could be easily stampeded anytime. The young cowboy everyone called Loop was waiting with a coiled lariat in his right fist at his side, red-faced but unhurt.

"Thanks, boss. It won't happen again. I—I—I was just . . ."

"Don't worry about it. Glad you weren't hurt. Better have Luther check him over good to make sure he didn't hurt himself either," Cole said, handing the reins to the young man

"Yessir, Mr. Kerry, I will."

Watching the teenager take his tired horse toward the remuda, Cole couldn't remember being called "Mister" before. Loop was the youngest Bar K hand but had already proven himself skilled with a lariat— hence the nickname. He never seemed to be without a rope in his hands. Even he was beginning to favor the nickname over his real one, Josiah Hedricks, of the Fort Worth Hedricks. Sporting brown hair to his shoulders, the young cowhand was short, compact, and agile as a cat. Old Ben Speakman had recommended the youngster to Ethan, and the rancher had liked the boy immediately.

Following the young rider, Cole rode over to Luther's rope corral where the horses were already in

place and grazing. Seven horses were hobbled; the rest
wandered freely. He joined the others unsaddling their
mounts. Cole ran his hands over the sorrel's legs,
picked its hooves with a pocketknife, and turned the
animal over to the busy wrangler. Loop watched the
new trail boss, trying not to be obvious about it, and
duplicated Cole's actions with his own horse.

"Good hoss," Luther observed.

"Yeah. Better hobble him, though."

"That's what I is a-figgerin' on doin'."

"Good."

Luther smiled. Cole noticed that the wrangler's
hands carried fresh rope burns, the badge of honor for
wranglers. Cole sensed a formality that hadn't been
there before and assumed it was brought on by Cole's
becoming the trail boss, a major authority figure in his
older brother's eyes. Loop brought forward his horse
and asked Luther to check it carefully. Cole patted
Loop on the back and left for the main camp. Luther
himself watched his younger brother leave with curiosity in unreadable eyes.

As he passed cowboys spreading their bedrolls and
relaxing, Cole looked for Ethan, didn't see him at first,
then realized he was sitting crosslegged on the ground
as DuMonte and Dancer gathered wood for a campfire.
Cole was struck at the naturalness of Ethan Kerry sitting there, drawing on a fresh cigarette, except for the
bandage around his eyes. Behind them and close to the
herd, old Ben Speakman was letting the calves out of
his wagon so they could join their mothers for the
night.

"Look out!" the old-timer yelled as the handful of
frisky calves changed direction, for some reason known
only to them, and ran as a group through the camp.
Like mesquite balls blown by the wind, they bumped

against one another and anything in their path. One brown calf with a white spot around its right eye stopped to examine Ethan while the others pranced on. The rancher realized what the hot breath meant, laughed, ran his hand along its back, and patted its head. The others zigzagged their way back to their mothers, urged on with waving arms and hollering.

"Now, here's a good one for you. He's going to be another Whistle. Not afraid of anything," Ethan said with a wide grin.

Dancer came over and gave the small animal a swat on the rump to move it along. In instant response, the calf kicked out with both hind legs, popping against the point rider's thigh.

"Hey! Get along now!" Dancer exclaimed, and waved his arms at the reluctant calf. Instead of running, the calf shuffled its legs a few feet and remained close to Ethan.

As he strolled toward them, Cole yelled, "Now, there's a youngster that knows who's boss!"

Speakman laughed, grabbed the calf by the ear, and led it away from Ethan and toward the herd. Dancer stomped off, brushing his chaps to wipe away the sting of the tiny hooves.

Ethan turned toward the voice and responded, "Glad you're back, Cole. Heard we had some ornery steers and an unseated cowboy. Loop all right?"

"Yeah. Busted his pride a little."

"They'll be lookin' for things to spook on tonight, probably tomorrow too," Ethan advised, and took another drag on his cigarette.

"Yeah, we'll push 'em hard again. By noon, we should be off any land they know. That should help," Cole replied.

"You learn fast, little brother," Ethan said, and

151

grinned. "I figure the trick to trail driving is three things: watch your cow's feet, watch your horses' backs, and watch your men's stomachs." He laughed at his trinity of "watches."

"Sounds good to me."

"Trouble is, you've got to see to do them."

Cole didn't respond. After hitching his gunbelt to make the weight more comfortable, he eased himself into a sitting position beside the blind rancher. Cole's leg ached, but it often did after long riding. Out of the corner of his eye, he noticed that John Davis Sotar was studying him, pretending to work on a saddle cinch near his bedroll. Had he met the man before this drive, Cole wondered, or was it simply one man good with a gun being interested in another? Ethan's ongoing advice yanked Cole's attention away from the mysterious rider.

"They'll be skittery at first light. By the way, this short grass will be wet with morning dew when we move out. Hooves'll soften if they go through it much. Isn't there taller grass to the east? Should be drier, I reckon."

Cole smiled and rolled a cigarette. Of course there was taller grass in that direction. "We'll ease 'em that way when we move off the bedground."

"Goldarn it, Cole, I'm sorry. Sometimes I get stuff running through my head and I just have to get it out. Damn!"

"Hey, I don't want to find out about something I should have known, after it's happened. You just keep on telling."

Pursing his lips like he had sucked on a lemon, Ethan was silent. His right hand touched the bandage as if it helped his thinking, and he said, "Would you mind bringing over my dun? It's just, well, I'd like to have him staked out next to my bedroll. That's how I've always done it before. I know it doesn't make much sense, but . . ."

"I'll take care of it. Plan to do the same myself. Learned the idea from the Indians. Did you know a Comanche warrior will sleep with his best war horse ready, just outside the wickiup?" Cole said, shifting his stiffened leg again.

"Reckon we all had the same idea. The more I think on it, I'll do my own saddling. It's a sorry man that can't saddle his own horse," Ethan said, and patted his younger brother's hand.

"When you want to go over your diary for tomorrow?" Cole changed the subject.

"After supper all right with you?"

"Fine."

"That sounds good. I'd like to do a diary this time, too, Cole. Will you take down the words?"

"Of course. It's a good idea."

They talked for a few minutes longer. When Cole finished his cigarette, he excused himself and left to find Luther, DuMonte, and Dancer. Luther would be on a horse, he figured, no matter what he was trying to get done. The cowboy had told him the only honorable work on foot was roping in a corral or branding; the rest wasn't worth doing if it couldn't be done on horseback. Cole figured the man would catch and saddle a horse rather than walk twenty-five yards. He smiled to himself. Luther was at the edge of the camp, on horseback, talking with Dancer. Good, he needed to talk with both men.

# Chapter Thirteen

The night sky was sullen, intent on keeping the moon and stars from taking their rightful places. A new set of nighthawks had taken over, and the herd was quiet. Cole Kerry lay awake. So far, sleep had come only in short pieces. The amazing outcome of the day wouldn't leave his mind. What had started as a confrontation with Sam Winlow had ended with the Bar K herd's first day on the trail to Dodge City, Kansas.

Was this drive really doable? He recited the positive side to himself. Why did those advantages keep coming up short in his mind? He wasn't a worrier; that was something Ethan did. Ethan was thoroughness and rock; he was instinct and fire. Maybe the reason for the feeling of a shortfall was his assessment of himself. He wasn't a trail boss, a guide for a bunch of mindless cattle and their nursemaids; he was a man of the winds. Free to go where he wanted to go. Why had he let his emotions get away from him and into this? He didn't owe his brothers anything, nor did they owe him. He and Ethan were not the same men they were a decade ago; they barely knew each other, or at least the men they had each become.

And what about Luther? Why did Luther's approval mean so much to him? Luther had always been his protector. Back in their childhood days when the Kerry boys scuffled constantly with each other, it was always Luther who stepped in when Ethan got too rough on their young brother. As Cole grew, he began to realize that Luther was different, slower in mind and action. Had he simply responded to some deep, unstated urge to pay Luther back for all those times he watched over him? Was that it? Or was it to prove to Ethan he was now the better man?

Cole was beginning to think his oldest brother held certain ideas, certain thoughts more deeply than either Ethan or himself. The big unreadable man had a sense of family that Cole didn't have, coupled with a sense of respect for their father that Cole didn't share and likely wouldn't. It was more than that, something Cole couldn't wrap words around. After all, this whole thing was Luther's idea. It wouldn't have occured to Cole, at least he didn't think so. And he didn't think Ethan would have suggested it either. Yet here they were, riding on the whim of a man whom people considered stupid.

Gradually, his thinking drifted to Ethan's blindness and stayed there longer than it should have. Even if they got the herd through, what was his brother going to do? How could a ranch be run without seeing? His whole herd could be run off and Ethan wouldn't know until it was too late. He thought again of Claire, Ethan's strong wife. She might be the edge his brother would need.

Yes, Claire was strong enough for both of them, if it came to that. She had been strong enough to let him go on this crazy endeavor—but what choice did she really have? From what Ethan had told him, the bank would take the ranch if his loan wasn't repaid. Sam Winlow was a shrewd man for making that purchase. With the bank's ownership, he immediately controlled the destiny of most businesses and ranches in the region. Who could fault a bank for deciding a loan was to be paid?

What about this Sam Winlow? There was no question this man wanted the Bar K, but how far would he go to get it? Cole had dismissed him at first as someone with a ravenous appetite—lots of bark, little bite. A man who got where he was by pushing and shoving others out of way—and gambling on none of them fighting back. Maybe Cole was wrong. Maybe Sam Winlow was every bit as tenacious as he was shrewd. A man didn't live long in this country misjudging other men or their intentions, he said softly to himself.

Kathleen. Kathleen. He wondered what she might be doing now. Did thoughts of him ever enter her mind? Was she looking for a new husband already? Of course. "Or three," he said aloud. Jealous heat filled his face. How stupid, he thought, and the warmth gradually went away. He tried to think about what tomorrow would bring, just to get away from the quicksand she brought to his mind. It was over, he told himself. Yet sleep seemed farther away than before.

The night was easing toward cold; the day's heat had been swept away hours ago. Even his saddled night horse was sleeping—standing with its head down, twenty feet from his bedroll. Luther had told him the horse would remain wherever the reins were dropped, but Cole preferred another level of security, just in case, and had added a rope halter and lead rope wrapped around a large box-shaped rock.

Ethan was also apparently asleep; his bedroll and night horse were thirty feet away. Strange, Cole thought, that he would be lying awake instead of Ethan; it was his older brother who always did the worrying. He had been more of a father growing up than Clancey Kerry ever was. A soft memory lifted itself into his tired mind: the day Ethan and Luther rode off to the War and left Cole with their mother and father. The night before, Ethan had given his younger brother a three-page letter of things he was expected to take care of while they were gone. Cole had burned it after they left—and cried.

Cole's reverie was disturbed by somebody starting to snore loudly in a high octave. He thought it was DuMonte, lying under a colorful quilt some forty feet from him. The black man was easy to like, Cole thought. His religious energy was real, and the trail boss respected that; DuMonte wasn't one of the "look at me, I'm a churchgoer" types he had seen all too often in too many towns. Tomorrow, he would tease DuMonte about his snoring and the black man would smile gently and say something like, "Bless you, Mr. Kerry, I'll try not to do that again." No, Cole decided, he wouldn't mention it; the good man might think he was serious.

Across the open field were the shapes of other sleeping men and the last orange sparkle of a dying campfire. Someone was talking in his sleep; likely it was Stovepipe Henderson. The cowboy was like one of those music boxes that kept playing the same song over and over when it was wound up. Stovepipe never stopped talking during the long drudgery of the day, either—at least he hadn't so far. Cole wondered if the man was ever unhappy. Studying the otherwise silent camp, he noted that Dancer had placed his bedroll exactly as Ethan had described. Even in the darkness, Cole could see a cedar spray on top of the superstitious cowboy's blankets.

On the other side of the campground, a horse snorted a challenge from the rope corral. The demanding sound reminded him of a bugle call. Cole knew instantly that it was Kiowa. The sorrel was probably angry at one of the other horses. No, wait! Something moved next to the far corral stake! His mind caught it before his eyes realized what they were seeing. Cole was immediately alert.

It wasn't his imagination. A man was there, and it was far too early for anyone to be saddling for the next nighthawk turn. Cole stared into the darkness, letting his eyes adjust to its uncertain mysteries. Forcing his vision to push through the night's curtain, he could see a man kneeling near the farthest stake of the rope corral. Kiowa had muscled its way through the herd and stood, next to the rope, pawing the ground and fighting the restraints of the hobble rope.

The man glanced around to see if anyone was watching. The shadows would not allow any definition to his face or features. Annoyed by Kiowa's posturing, he waved his hat at the sorrel in an attempt to back it away. The motion only served to anger Kiowa more; its neck mane bristled and the horse gave another shrill whinny. Realizing the futility of trying to frighten it, the man jammed his hat on his head and returned to his task.

Cole grabbed a pistol from the gunbelt lying beside him and snapped into a low crouch. He stalked toward the remuda with his feet bare and only his pants on, advancing silently toward the suspicious figure. He was a few steps away from the silhouette when the man turned around and jumped at the sight of the advancing trail boss.

It was Gus Oleen! The Swede's derby was half-flattened on his head. His knee-length chink chaps brushed the ground as he squatted, but Cole immediately noticed the man wasn't wearing spurs. For an instant, Oleen looked like a startled deer but quickly recovered his composure—and explained his reaction.

"Yah, Mr. Kerry, you scare me, you did. Yah, 'round the hosses, I hear a noise. Maybe a cat, I vas a-thinkin'."

Stopping and letting the gun in his hand rest at his side, Cole said skeptically, "What were you going to do if there was one, let the horses loose?"

As he spoke, Cole thought he heard muffled footsteps ever so lightly in the darkness on the far side of the remuda. Or was he just misreading night sounds? A half-bent-over scrub oak in the distance became fatter for an instant as if someone ran past, or was it his imagination?

Oleen's eyes widened and furtively glanced at the stake, then the remuda, before he spoke. "No, Oleen vas not untying the rope, I vas making sure she vas tight. Yah, that is so."

Cole started to question him further, but a soft step caused him to spin around, his body in a low crouch with his pistol cocked and ready. It was Luther lumbering toward the corral.

"Hey thar, boss! Ain't no call to be aimin' that six-shooter at me. It's too damn early fer that," Luther said. His smile was more reflex than comfort. His hat was on his head in a cockeyed fashion, and he wore boots over his long johns. Luther's face was etched with sleep; lines of concern layered his forehead; his mouth was open, like that of a man surprised and then frozen in place; his eyes were big and round, searching for answers.

"Sorry, Luther, I'm a little jumpy, I guess."

"You all be a-callin' a meetin' to talk hoss? Ya dun stirred me from my beauty sleep. Figgered it must be sumthin' that can't wait fer sunup, so I dun come a-moseyin'."

"Oleen thought he saw a panther prowling around the horses," Cole replied, his stare never leaving the nervous Swede.

Barefoot and in his long underwear, Dancer came running with a pistol in his hand. He stopped beside Cole, winded, his eyes wide with excitement. Old Ben Speakman was up and headed their way. DuMonte was coming too. Cole was impressed at the alertness of these men and was becoming self-conscious that he had created enough noise to wake them for nothing.

Dancer surveyed the corral without speaking. Speakman wobbled beside him, the old Civil War dragoon in his hand. The veteran cowhand looked into Cole's face and growled, "What's up, boss?" It was the first time Cole could remember seeing him without a pipe in his mouth.

"Oleen here, thought he saw a panther, but it's gone now," Cole reaffirmed.

"Yah, it vas that, a big cat, Lut-ter. But it is gone."

Dancer observed, "Didn't know there were any around here. Strong medicine, the panther. Wish I'd seen it."

"Well, you kin sur nuff look fer tracks come sunup, Dancer," Luther said. "That oughta tell us straight out if the Swede's seein' things ag'in—or if'n they be a catamount 'round an' about."

With that observation, the other men looked at

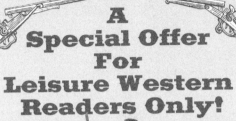

# A Special Offer For Leisure Western Readers Only!

## Get FOUR FREE* Western Novels

Travel to the Old West in all its glory and drama—without leaving your home!

**Plus, you'll save between $3.00 and $6.00 every time you buy!**

# Get Four Books Totally
# F R E E* –
# A Value between
# $16 and $20

Tear here and mail your FREE* book card today!

PLEASE RUSH
MY FOUR FREE*
BOOKS TO ME
RIGHT AWAY!

LeisureWestern Book Club
P.O. Box 6613
Edison, NJ 08818-6613

AFFIX
STAMP
HERE

Oleen. He was tolerated by most of the men in camp, but not well liked—mostly because the thick-framed cowboy had a tendency to gripe about everything from the temperature of the coffee to the hardness of his bunk. Of course, he never did so within earshot of Ethan, or now Cole. No one did. Griping was one thing Ethan wouldn't tolerate. The job was a tough one, and he didn't want men around who couldn't handle it. Everyone assumed his young brother would be no different.

Perhaps a worse trait than his constant griping, Oleen was stingy. In town, he always managed to let others buy the drinks. His wardrobe consisted entirely of clothes the other hands had tired of and given to him. No matter what the situation, he always had a precise reason for not using his own money, or not being able to lend a piece of rope or leather or whatever, when asked by one of the drovers.

"Oleen, this h'yar cat didn't git at yur money poke, did it?" Luther said with a grin. "That'd be sumthin' to gander at, watchin' you chase a catamount across Texas to git yur money back."

Speakman laughed the loudest as the gathering of riders chuckled. Luther glanced at Cole, but the youngest Kerry brother hadn't heard the joke; he was already walking toward his own sleeping area. Luther watched him for a moment, then returned to Speakman, telling about the dangers of a mountain lion being close by, which drifted into the tale of the time he had run into a she-cat and her offspring. Luther interrupted to remind Oleen that he had imagined seeing a grizzly last year. DuMonte soon headed back to bed, and Dancer followed, after both examined the ground near the corral. Speakman resumed talking, and kept at it to Oleen all the way back to their bedrolls.

As Cole pulled the blankets into place, his mind was swollen with new worry: What was Oleen doing at the corral? Was he really looking for a panther? What else made any sense? The man was a longtime Bar K hand; Ethan trusted him, although Oleen wasn't a top rider. What if he was untying the rope corral as it appeared? What if there was someone else at the corral? Who? Why? Cole knew the answer; that part was easy. If the horses were freed, the drive would be delayed until they were rounded up. That would take all day, maybe longer. It would also deflate the thin optimism of the drovers, bringing back the worry that hid only a blind man's eyes away.

His mind wouldn't let go of the situation, but the pictures in his mind remained shadows. Maybe the shadows had betrayed his eyes and Oleen was merely checking the rope as he said. Maybe his ears had made more of the night than was warranted. Maybe he was being too much the outlaw and not enough the trail boss.

If Oleen had heard a panther, he was being conscientious to chase it away. If they found tracks in the morning, it would be obvious the Swede was right. If they didn't find any, it only meant the rider had been mistaken. Nothing more. What man in the wilderness hadn't seen things that weren't there? Cole replayed the scene again and again, searching for a sign of either approach. It was important to determine: One way Oleen was protecting the horses; the other way, he was trying to hurt the drive.

Why would the Swede want to do that? The only answer was Sam Winlow. There was nothing in the middle. Would Winlow pay Oleen to disrupt the drive's progress? Was it possible Winlow could have convinced the cowboy that working for him was the

Swede's best path for the future? When would Winlow have approached him, if he did? No one had told him about Oleen talking with Winlow, like they had about the turncoat Ike Jenkins; so Cole had to assume the rider was always with the group or in their sight.

As far as he knew, Oleen had been with the herd gathering since the start; that left no time to see Winlow, other than when the rancher rode into camp. Yet Cole had a hunch the man wasn't as loyal as Ethan had said he was. A whiny man with a strong sense for saving money might easily be drawn to getting more—especially if the man was convinced the drive wasn't going to make it anyway. In the morning, he would ask Luther whether a hand could disappear long enough during a roundup to meet with someone without the rest of the riders knowing about it. He would also look for cat tracks, marks he doubted would be there. He wished he was wrong.

As his younger brother finally gave up to sleep, Ethan Kerry lay on his waterproofed bedroll tarp with its heavy quilt. His fingers tugged absentmindedly on one of the closure rings. The ache in his head was unrelenting, like it often was, waking him every hour. If he lay very still for a few minutes, the pain would go away. It always did. Listening was his main connection to the world. He had heard the commotion at the corral, and Luther had told him the reason: The Swede was seeing things again. Why hadn't Cole given him the courtesy of coming by and telling him?

He chuckled to himself, remembering last year when Oleen thought he saw a grizzly near the herd one evening when he was riding nighthawk. Ethan wondered if he wrote about the incident in his trail book. He would tell Cole tomorrow. His brother was seeing things too. He needed to concentrate on getting the herd through and quit worrying about shadows.

Grazing a few yards away was a saddled trail horse—his favorite, a line-backed dun with black stockings. On past drives, he had always slept with a saddled horse near where he slept, in case of an emergency. His young brother did so now, as the trail boss; the blind rancher slept with his horse close by for the feeling it gave him of the way the drive should be.

When he stopped to think about it, this whole thing was like a dream. Here he was, virtually helpless, and had turned his fortune, and the well-being of his family, over to what amounted to a stranger, even if he was his brother. The headache passed. He rolled over on his stomach and caught himself trying to look around the campground to make sure things were as they should be. It was black. Not night. Black. His blindness rammed into him.

He groaned and bit his lip. What good was a blind man on a cattle drive? What good was he to anyone? Could he stand never seeing his wife again? Not watching his children grow up? Never seeing the prairie after a rain? Or a sunset? New grass in the spring? A leggy calf attempting to walk for the first time? Or a wet colt searching for its mother? Never being able to judge a new horse just by the way it moves in a corral? Or check his cattle by riding through them?

Depression rushed through his mind and pushed him against the ground. He drew himself into a ball, wrapped his arms around his knees, and squeezed as tightly as he could, trying to make the awfulness go away. Suddenly, he couldn't breath. He jumped up, then went to his knees, then to all fours, his chest heaving to regain the air it needed to survive. Finally, he rolled over on the bedding and lay there, drenched in a cold sweat.

His fingers touched the butt of the pistol lying close to his bedroll. The metal was icy, smooth, and strangely inviting. Images of Claire and his two children sitting around their dinner table stopped his hand from going further. He buried his face into the bedroll and prayed for sleep.

# Chapter Fourteen

Five hundred miles became a blur of dust, sweat, cattle, and unending days in the saddle. The Bar K range was over a month behind them, and the incident with Gus Oleen was a forgotten incident in the daily challenges of moving the cattle northward. Although the herd had stampeded twice more, they had lost only a handful, and the cattle were gradually settling into the rhythm of the drive and, importantly, taking on weight.

The only other bad incident was a day when they ran into a wall of flies turning everything into a maddening swarm that almost drove the herd into a stampede. Cole shivered when he recalled the drovers frantically waving blankets, coats, and ropes to swat away the thick cloud of insects. Finally, they had pushed through the insanity and back into daylight. Ethan said there must've been a buffalo herd that passed through a few days before. He criticized his younger brother for not riding far enough ahead to spot it, and Cole knew he was right.

Morning was a heavy gray; dawn hadn't begun to think about adding brightness to the sky. Ethan Kerry sat fully dressed on his bedroll. A headache was thundering inside his temples. So far, sitting without moving hadn't helped any. He had refused to take the laudanum Dr. Hawkinson had given him. The unopened bottle was in his saddlebags, but he was tempted this morning. Sorely tempted.

He sat quietly, his bandaged eyes closed anyway, taking in the familiar song of a waking trail camp. Rattling canteens and jingling bit-chains mixed with the dry scuffle of saddle leather, the fretting and snorting of horses, the tremor of men yawning and cursing things lost in the night. Even without seeing, he knew it was Stovepipe Henderson singing to himself. Wouldn't it be great to wake up happy-like every day? the blind rancher thought. Ethan's saddled trail horse added a gentle rhythm of grazing. If he concentrated, he could hear the distant cry of a coyote saluting the coming dawn. All of it curled around the constant murmur of the herd itself.

Listening was more than his main connection to the world. He had found the skill was beginning to give him an unusual edge in judging men. In the past weeks on the trail, he had become adept at hearing the things between a man's words, things unspoken but meant; he could sense if he was nervous, confident—or lying.

Most of the drive was like a disjointed dream that he should be able to wake up from and see. See the dawn as the streaks of rose took their position of leadership over the gray. See the camp come alive. See his Claire. He missed his wife and children terribly; he always did on the trail, but it seemed more so this time. Claire was a remarkable woman; he knew few wives who would have understood his need to go, a desire far apart from money, a desire as strong as breathing itself. If he hadn't gone, he was beaten. He was worse than nothing. He was a standing dead man. She knew that.

He was learning to savor the smells of the drive. The smell of dew-laden buffalo grass in the early morning, of horses and leather, of the sweat of hardworking riders, of fresh coffee and sizzling bacon, even the distant smell of cattle waste. With those odors came the pictures in his mind that his eyes could no longer deliver.

"Get up, you lazy bastards! Come an' git it, before I throw it in the creek!" T. L. Hayden hurled his usual morning call to the sleeping crew. The sound of the acid-tongued cook was comforting. At this time of the day, he was the supreme authority and reveled in it. To Hayden's left, the Dutch ovens were offering their sweet aroma of freshly baked biscuits to join the smells of coffee boiling and bacon frying.

A bobolink told Ethan someone was coming, then he heard the gentle jingle of spurs and the whisper of chaps against tall grass announcing the arrival. Ethan thought it was Cole, although his stride sounded about the same as Luther's. His young brother had a slight limp, but Luther was so bowlegged, their walking sounded identical. He thought that surprising. Last night, Ethan and Cole had reviewed his diary, just as they had done every night since leaving, with Cole reading and Ethan interpreting his own notes and adding layers of direction.

After the first week, though, Cole delegated the responsibility for keeping a diary on this year's drive to DuMonte. The black man's patience was a better match for Ethan's penchant for detail. Ethan wasn't pleased with the idea of the switch, but after the first night DuMonte was a fixture with the blind man. If DuMonte was bothered with the task, he didn't say.

Cole had gotten over the incident at the corral with Gus Oleen, or at least Ethan figured he had. Ethan's colorful description of the cowhand declaring he had seen a grizzly around the herd on last year's drive helped his brother when no cat tracks were found. But that didn't make it right for the Swede to be whining about the drive not making it, as Speakman had quietly relayed last night. Ethan planned to tell Cole, in case he didn't already know. There was no room for gripers. Especially not now.

Today they would cross the Red; his notes about last year's crossing said "We were lucky. Gentle. Six inches. Quicksand, far bank." He knew this mysterious river could go from wading depth to over twenty feet in a matter of hours. It was a time of significant crossing. On this side, they were a part of Texas and Texas law. On the other side, they would be riding into the wild lands of the Indian Nations, where Kiowa and Comanche war parties could deliver punishment quickly and savagely. Not to mention the gangs of outlaws who found sanctuary in this strange creation of the federal government.

Of course, mounted police forces from any of the Five Civilized Tribes—Cherokee, Choctaw, Chickasaw, and Seminole—might stop a herd and demand payment to cross. In his heart, Ethan knew the crossing was why he awoke earlier than usual. It was the painful thought of being forced to ride in the chuck wagon— on a ferry, no less—when they crossed. This would be the first time he hadn't led the herd through these significant waters.

Not leading hadn't really bothered him until this moment. He had tried hard not to feel sorry for himself, but he was this morning. Ethan Kerry was no different from the bedrolls and the Dutch ovens, just part of the stuff that had to cross differently than the men and horses and cattle. For a moment, he resented his young brother. His brother was nothing but a gunfighter: no family; no responsibilities, not really. Why, he had even killed a man over a woman who had spurned him. Why shouldn't he be the one who was blinded, instead of me? Shivering, Ethan stopped the negative thoughts and sighed.

Last year was the first time a ferry had been in place, and it had been easier than building a raft to get the wagons across and well worth the extra expense. But he had never thought the ferry would ever be carrying him too. Instead, he envisioned himself on a horse swimming in the deep, swift water, a great herd coming behind him with his men fighting the challenge of the current with him. Sometimes Ethan forgot about his blindness, especially in the mornings when he awakened and wisps of dreams were heavy about his mind. In his dreams, he was never blind. Unrelenting gray always brought him back to reality. It was no dream, only a never-ending nightmare.

But he couldn't bring himself to let anyone, except his brothers, see him without the bandage around his face. It didn't feel right. His hand touched the cloth around his face, and he sighed. He didn't want the men to see his lifeless eyes.

"Mornin', boss, how about some coffee?"

It was Cole. He held a steaming cup toward Ethan; the rancher reached for the brisk smell with both hands.

"Got it," Ethan said. He held the cup close to his mouth, judged its hotness, blew on it, and sipped carefully. The rancher was grateful for his brother's off-handed way of handling his blindness, as if it wasn't anything more than a turned ankle—or wasn't there at all. Most of the drovers were reluctant to use the word "see" or any phrase about "seeing" when explaining something to him. It made for some unnecessarily awkward moments. Not Cole. He didn't even treat Ethan like a brother; he treated Ethan like a man. Simple as that. Ethan regretted even more his earlier feelings about him; he should be ever grateful, not spiteful.

Ethan asked, "You ever cross the Red at this spot before?"

"No, I haven't. Figure it isn't much different than east of here, around the Station."

"No, no, it isn't."

"I sent Abe out to give us a look-see on the crossing. Figure we should hit it about noon, maybe a little before. Let's hope she's sweet today, like last year," Cole said, sipping his own coffee between sentences.

He didn't tell Ethan that the half-breed had left last night during the darkness. Cole had spotted someone watching them from the far hill yesterday. The sun was setting at the time, but enough daylight remained to sparkle off of something out there. It wasn't a natural something, either. Maybe he was worrying about nothing; maybe running from a posse had made him too jumpy. Or maybe it had taken Sam Winlow this long to realize they weren't going to be stopped naturally, and he was going to try to force the situation again. Cole never figured the cruel rancher had given up on his greedy mission: to get Ethan Kerry's herd—and his ranch.

The more Cole thought about it, the more he realized hitting the Bar K herd shortly after they had crossed the Red River would be an excellent strategy. All of their guns would be in the chuck wagon, placed there along with clothes and boots to keep dry while they swam across. What a perfect time for an ambush: no weapons, and everyone relaxed after the treacherous crossing. The wagons would be en route from the ferry landing and easily intercepted after the main ambush and the herd was taken. He had decided not to share his discovery. Not yet, anyway. It was nothing more than a hunch—and maybe one that was too much imagination and too little sleep.

Abe was to use the ferry and work his way downstream to where they intended to cross. Cole had found him to be a reliable scout. If there was going to be an ambush, he felt certain the half-breed would find out, where others wouldn't, and get away without their enemies knowing he was close.

"You kinda like using him that way, don't you?" Ethan asked.

Cole responded with a cornered smile. "Never thought about it much before. I like . . . , well, I like what he sees. More than what I see, even. Abe picks up things most men don't—and it keeps me in a position to lead and make decisions. Do you have a problem with that?"

"Oh, no, Cole. Didn't mean to sound like I did. I like your style. It's different than mine—but I like it. I probably would have gone myself. Your way makes sense, though."

Cole wasn't sure how to take this conversation. His brother liked to control things, that was his nature. Was Ethan making conversation, or was he trying to tell him something he wanted changed?

"If you'd rather I do it myself, Ethan, I—"

"Hell no, Cole. You know me. I'm always taking things apart and looking at them, just to see if we're doing it right. Besides, you're the trail boss, not me."

Cole surveyed the camp, watching it come to life. The men were up and moving, except for Oleen. The Swede wasn't one of his favorites, and it wasn't just the corral encounter. Cole wasn't certain the man could be trusted, dispite Ethan's protestations to the contrary. As Cole watched, Oleen finally threw back his blankets and sat up. He was fully dressed except for his boots and hat. Loop, dressing nearby, winced at whatever Oleen said.

Brusquely, Ethan handed his younger brother a two-page letter to Claire, dictated to DuMonte last night. This morning, the last page sported a scrawled "I love you. Ethan" wandering across the sheet.

"Lost the envelope. It's around here somewhere, dammit," Ethan said, embarrassed at both his romantic addition to the letter and the misplaced envelope.

"Here it is," Cole said, retrieving it from the corner of Ethan's bedding.

"Give that . . . letter . . . to Hayden to post at the settlement, will you?" Ethan asked.

"Sure."

"Better give him a list of supplies we need, too," Ethan advised.

"He knows what we need better than I do, Ethan. Besides, you two went over that last night. At least, that's what he said."

"Oh, yeah, come to think of it, we did."

Returning to the most important event of the day, Cole started to share the concern that was growing within him, but Ethan began giving advice.

"Watch for the glare off the water, Cole. If the beeves see it, they won't go in. The men'll have to watch for quicksand if the water's low. Especially along that far bank. Sounds like the cattle are good an' thirsty. Are they? Were the boys able to keep 'em out of the water last night?"

"Yeah, they haven't drank—and they're letting us know it," Cole responded, sipping his coffee and marveling at his brother's consistent attention to the smallest detail.

"Good. That should make things easier for us at the Red."

Cole took Ethan's arm and helped him to his feet. With Ethan holding on to his forearm, they walked across the open campground toward the chuck wagon. Six riders had already gathered there. After tossing their bedrolls and gear into the wagon, they were eating a breakfast of beans, bacon, and biscuits, and washing it down with hot coffee. Conversation was only beginning to live, born in an occasional comment about the river ahead.

Four riders were with the herd; they had the worst shift of the night, the "rooster-tail watch," Luther called it. They would eat after new riders took over; most likely that would be Cole and the two point riders, with the rest filling in as soon as they got saddled.

Only Loop and Speakman were talking continuously, and they were arguing about the best length for a lariat. Loop proclaimed in a high-pitched voice, "I'm tellin' you that twenty-two feet, yessir, twenty-two feet is what a man wants in his ketch rope. Git close and git 'er done, I say."

The old Confederate shoved the last of his biscuit into his mouth and spoke with it poking out the side of his cheek. "Sonny boy, if you was to use a longer reata, say thirty or thirty-five feet, you wouldn't have to get so dang close—and your horse wouldn't have to work so dang hard. That's why your horses are getting worn out. There's a real art to working with a rope, son. I've seen men make 'em do tricks you couldn't imagine. Once—"

Zeke Ferguson, with his fat belly and marbled face, nodded as he held his plate close to his mouth for faster intake. Speakman glanced at him, inhaled, and stepped away without stopping his story; the man smelled of acrid sweat and cow manure. The old cowhand bumped into Luther, who realized the reason for the Speakman's sudden movement.

"Guldarn you, Ferguson! If'n you don't git washed inside and out when we cross the Red, you're gonna ride drag by yourself all the way to Kansas! Phuu-eee!" Luther bellowed to the enjoyment of the others. Ferguson glanced at him with a hurt expression but said nothing.

Out of the corner of his eye, Luther saw Cole coming with Ethan and nodded his head in greeting. Cole returned it with the same motion. His floppy hat pulled low across his face, Harold DuMonte stood off to the side of the gathering hands; the black man was drinking his coffee and intently reading his Bible. Ferguson stepped over near him.

DuMonte looked up, smiled graciously, and said, "Good morning, Ferguson. The Lord has given us a beautiful day, hasn't he?" Without waiting for a response, he resumed his study.

A few steps from the eating area, Ethan's boot caught a rock halfway submerged in the ground and stumbled. Cole hadn't noticed it as he passed. Ethan grabbed Cole with both hands, and the trail boss swung his left arm around to keep him from falling. The men stopped eating and watched in silence. Although the talk of Ethan's blindness had been one of the crew's early campfire subjects, interest in the topic had faded as familiarity took hold and things had gone evenly.

Besides, a blind man riding in a wagon didn't seem helpless, especially when the trail boss regularly sought his opinion. But now they were reminded again of the man's vulnerability.

"Sorry, boys. This good-for-nothin' trail boss ran me into a rock," Ethan said with a laugh, straightening himself. Light chuckles followed that didn't match the tightened faces.

Spitting for emphasis, Luther said, "Guldarn it, Cole. Thar be onliest one rock to all o' Texas, an' ya steered the boss ri't into it! That'd be a li'l brother fer ya."

Both brothers laughed. The blind rancher pushed his opened hand against Cole playfully, and the youngest brother said, "Well, Luther, I was just following the advice of my big brother. When I was a kid, you told me there weren't any rocks in Texas!"

"Wal, now, thar ain't quite what I tolt ya. I said rock's 'bout as useless as a wart on some purty gal's backside!" Luther finished the exchange.

That brought true laughter, and the men relaxed and returned to their eating. More shadow than shape, Hayden stood in front of the opened tabletop, now filled with the day's fixings. With exaggerated movements, he dealt heavy portions to the cowhands passing in front of him. Each held a tin plate in one hand and a tin coffee cup in the other; most nodded their acceptance without speaking.

"What are you lookin' at, Jersey! Those are the best damn biscuits you'll ever have in your whole sorry-ass life!" Hayden spat as the stuttering cowhand watched his plate being filled. Jersey replied mildly, "T-t-they l-l-look very g-g-good."

"That's goddamn better," Hayden advised, and turned to the next cowboy, Gus Oleen, who was working up his courage to ask for a second biscuit.

"Y-y-yah, an' I vould be liking a second biscuit. A long time it is 'til eating again," he said with his eyes averted.

"What?! Two biscuits?! Who do you think you are?! An' you can call me *Mister* Hayden." The cook snorted his disgust at the request and placed a single biscuit on the Swede's bulging plate.

Jared Dancer was the next man in line. Arrogantly, Hayden threw back his shoulders and snarled, "An' you'd better clean your plate, Dancer. I don't want to see any of my food wasted like last night."

Dancer's eyes instantly became flames; his mouth, a thin line of trouble, matched the furrow of his forehead. Hayden realized he had pushed too far with the wrong man and quickly said, "I was just kidding. How about some coffee, good an' hot." The point rider held out his cup without taking his eyes from the nervous cook; Dancer remained coiled for anything he didn't like coming out of Hayden's mouth.

"If you pour any of that on my hand, I'll jam this plate down your fat mouth," demanded Dancer, his hot temper pushing itself into his face. "It's too early for any of your silly crap."

Luther saw the exchange and said, "Hayden, ya sure are one hard sonvabitch to deal with—but ya sure as hell kin make biscuits. Near makes yur sourpuss worth it all—when I dun sink my teeth into this hyar sweet thing. But ya be real careful, now. Dancer hyar's mean nuff to git into a bitin' contest with a rattler—an' give it first bite."

He slapped the feisty point rider on the back and grinned. Dancer chuckled and moved away. Hayden accepted the compliment and the bridge away from Dancer's ire. Hayden knew he was a coward; his sarcasm covered it sometimes, but not always. His eyes

177

followed Dancer, who walked over to DuMonte and began eating. In minutes, both men left to get their morning horses.

With Hayden preoccupied, Oleen lifted a second biscuit from the pan warming on the closest Dutch oven. He walked away, shoving it into his mouth. A step later, he stopped and yowled, spitting out the steaming hot pieces of biscuit all over an unfortunate passing sagebrush. Hayden shot him a look of surprise but was pulled back by Cole's request.

"You got any more for a couple of hungry hands?" Cole held out two plates and two cups for the cook to fill.

"You bet, Mr. Kerry," Hayden said with what passed for a smile. Cole took the first filled plate and cup to Ethan, who sat sprawled on the damp earth. Cole returned moments later with his own food and coffee. Luther moved beside them but was nearly finished with his breakfast. The wrangler's hardest work of the day would begin in minutes: roping horses for each man.

"Mornin', Luther," Cole said as he sat down. "Everything all right with the horses?"

"Got three lame."

"How bad?"

"Two weeks, maybe three."

"Anyone with a string short more than one horse?"

"Loop. He be two short."

Ethan suggested that Cole talk with the young rider to keep him from working his mounts too long before changing them. Cole agreed, as Luther stood like a schoolboy holding his empty plate and cup with both hands.

"What hoss ya takin' this mornin'?" Luther's dark eyes sought Cole's face but showed no emotion.

"I'll ride Bramble. Switch to my black at the Red."

"Good river hoss."

After laying his plate and cup on the chuck wagon table, Luther lumbered methodically toward the makeshift corral of ropes and stakes holding the horses. Most were quiet this morning, but not the hobbled Kiowa. The powerful horse was taking charge; the other geldings swirled around him as he bit and kicked to get control in spite of his rope shackles. Dancer and DuMonte strolled over to Ethan and Cole. Both men led their horses and sought their orders for the day.

"You want to let 'em drift awhile, Mr. Kerry? Mile or so, following the tongue?" DuMonte asked.

"Sounds good," Ethan said. Cole nodded and glanced at the tongue of the chuck wagon, pointed due north.

"We'll count 'em when we push the herd onto the trail," Cole added, and placed the last piece of bacon in his mouth.

Dancer nodded agreement, pulled on his hat, and added, "No watering, I reckon."

Ethan said, "Yes," and Cole nodded his assent. Ethan rubbed his forehead in response to the throbbing that hadn't gone away yet.

"That'll mean the crick a half mile west will be about as welcome as a wet dog at church," Dancer said, and looked at DuMonte. The black cowboy smiled.

Ethan mumbled that thirsty cattle would be easier to go into the river. He was distracted by the violent pain in his forehead that refused to go away. Cole rolled his tongue across the inside of his mouth; he was still hungry. Maybe he would grab another slice of bacon and a biscuit to eat on the way. He looked up to see if any food was left. Oleen was getting a second plateful, and so was Ferguson. But it looked like both bacon and biscuits remained; he wasn't interested in more beans.

That was the way Ethan liked it: plenty of good food and good horses for his men. Cole had readily agreed with the approach. However, the cook had become accustomed to having Ethan ask for a daily accounting of the food used.

A commotion at the corral interrupted their discussion. Jip Jersey's bay had decided it didn't want to work this morning and was trying to throw the cowboy with a series of high, jolting jumps.

# Chapter Fifteen

Onlooking drovers were yelling encouragement: "Ride 'em, Jip!" "Stay with it, boy!" "That'll cure the stutters!" "Just like a church social!" Finally the horse decided it was nothing to get excited about and stopped the bucking as suddenly as it had started.

Laughter and cheers followed the stuttering cowboy's attempt to yell his victory: "T-t-t-the h-h-hell w-w-w-with you, hoss."

"Sounds like a little 'good mornin' to ya' between hoss an' cowhand," Dancer said. Everyone laughed, and DuMonte added, "That's why a morning prayer is a good idea."

Pointing at a small red symbol on the chest of Dancer's dun horse, Cole said, "I've seen that before. Sign of the 'Sun Boy.' One of the Kiowa gods, sort of, isn't it?"

"Yeah, that's the 'Sun Boy.' Had a dream about him

last night," Dancer explained. "Figured we might need some help—crossing the Red."

Cole nodded without speaking; his mind was also on the river, and he knew Ethan's was too. Many herds were lost crossing rivers, and the Red had taken more than its share. DuMonte smiled without commenting, and both point riders left for the herd.

"Don't worry about me, Cole. Just help me get over to the chuck, where I can get some more coffee and wait for Hayden," Ethan said casually, but there was more he wanted to say.

Cole was silent, guessing his brother wasn't finished.

"Cole, I'd give a whole hellva lot to ride across the Red. With you. At the head of the herd. I know it sounds stupid an' it's not fair to ask . . . but I just can't handle going across in a ferry."

Cole Kerry tossed aside the last swallow of his coffee with a flick of the cup, trying not to overreact to Ethan's request. The last thing he needed was another thing to worry about with the crossing. Yet how would he feel if the tables were reversed? The image of the blind man begging beside the saloon door burst into his mind.

"Seems to me you should be the one leading us out of Texas." The words came out of his mouth hard enough to force the ugly memory into mental retreat. At the same instant, the thought of letting his blind brother ride into a possible ambush made him shiver.

The lilt in his brother's voice was umistakable and reinforced the rightness of Cole's response: "Thanks, Cole! I sure appreciate that. Now, if she's bein' a real hellcat today, I won't expect you to keep your word."

"We'll be fine. Let's see if Luther can find us a couple of horses and you can ride with me now."

Ethan walked beside his younger brother, sliding his

boots against the ground and placing his right hand on Cole's shoulder for guidance. Cole knew his older brother hated the dependence more than he hated not seeing. Who wouldn't? Ethan Kerry was a fighter, not a cripple. That's why he had to tell him that he was worried about being ambushed by Sam Winlow's men after they crossed the Red.

"Tell me what you see, Cole."

The request surprised Cole, then made him feel guilty. He stopped, looked around, coughed, and said, "Sky's yellow. Gonna turn nice an' blue, though. It'll be a hot one. The steers are on their feet, easy-like. Whistle is throwing his head. I think he's trying to tell us he's ready . . ."

"That Whistle, he's a rascal, isn't he?"

"Yeah, more like a big dog than a cow, it seems to me."

"Go on . . . will you, Cole?"

"Well, looks like we've got four men with the herd. The rest are either waiting for a horse from Luther—or saddling one," Cole continued, his eyes searching the campground and his mind struggling for the words to match what was there. "Luther, he's sweating like he was shoveling coal. Sotar is sitting by his bedroll—looks like he's cleaning that fancy star pistol, putting in new loads. Speakman's got a new rope out of the chuck and is showing Loop something about it."

"Something is bothering you, Cole. Did I go butting in again? You know me, I don't have—"

"Oh no, Ethan, not that. I—I . . . well, I've got a feeling Winlow is going to try something after we cross the Red. I can't shake the idea that it's a perfect spot for an ambush—and Indians would be blamed."

Cole explained his concern about seeing the field glass reflection yesterday, about the advantages of an ambush after they crossed, and about sending Abe out last night. Ethan was silent, and Cole wondered if his brother was angry that he hadn't shared this earlier.

"Thanks for telling me. An' for not wanting me to worry too. God knows I am a stewer," Ethan finally said. "What are we going to do if Abe tells you they're waiting?"

"Got a plan I've been chewing on. Let's talk while we ride."

"I'd like that."

The herd moved easily northward, with Whistle out front. The men had an easy way of collecting the herd, keeping the rear no wider than the swing, yet without letting them bunch together and get overheated and slanting them away from the creek. They were moving into a new kind of country, leaving the treeless arid plains and finding themselves in rich bottomland, thick with timber and bushes, and flush with wild game.

Riding beside Cole at the front of the herd was the blind rancher on a black horse called Hoolie. Ethan couldn't help the wide smile on his face, in spite of the river's possible treachery and Winlow's too. While his appearance was happy, his mind was tightened around the threat of ambush. With great energy, he explored options aloud with his younger brother.

Cole was pleased there was no wasted discussion about how unfair it all was, or suggestions about readying the cattle, or how dangerous the river itself might be, or even if it was likely Winlow's men would really be waiting for them. Instead Ethan sounded like a briefing officer providing Cole with every detail he could recall about the terrain north of the Red River, where Winlow might wait.

"What if they open up on us while we're crossing?" Ethan blurted.

"They won't. Winlow wants your herd too—and they would lose a lot of beef that way. Shooting at us in the river would spook them. Besides, they could only get those of us in front. Our boys in the back would have time to get away. Maybe take part of the herd with them. No, they'll wait until we're all across, relaxed and laughing."

As they rode, Ethan took a Bull Durham bag from his shirt pocket and smoothly rolled a cigarette. He fumbled for a match in his vest pocket, found it, and lit the smoke before Cole could get a match of his own.

"Say, that's pretty good," Cole said appreciatively.

"Not bad for a blind man. Been practicing while riding in the chuck. Not much else to do, you know."

"We got any tobacco left?" Cole teased.

Ethan laughed and slapped his thigh. The black horse pricked up its ears to determine the meaning. Cole reached over and patted its neck. Ethan seemed unaware of his horse's alarm.

Ethan Kerry restated his brother's strategy: "So you're going to put some men with the wagons when they go across on the ferry—and let them sneak up on the bastards."

"Yeah, if Winlow's men are not too far from the river, we can get them in a crossfire before they know what's happened."

"I never would've thought of an ambush. I just . . ."

"There might not be one, I'm guessing."

Ethan turned in his saddle, back toward the herd, then resumed his regular position. Cole assumed it was an old habit. The blind rancher rode silently, smoke pausing occasionally near his bandaged face. Cole wondered what he was thinking.

Finally, Ethan spoke again. "Why don't we just sit

on this side—and wait for them to come at us? Seems safer."

"If we do, they win. If we stop long enough, we won't have food to make it. When we finally do get around to crossing, they'd still be waiting. I'd prefer to sting 'em hard. Make the price too high."

"You think Winlow will leave us alone after that?" Ethan asked, unable to hide the anxiety in his voice.

"He might, if we hit 'em hard enough."

"Cole . . . my boys ain't much for gunslinging, but don't count them short. They all ride for the brand. Dancer hasn't got a scared bone in his body. Sotar, I reckon he's got the look and will be the best. Old Ben, he'll be good, even with one arm."

"Yeah, he could talk 'em to death, given half a chance."

"Hell, maybe you ought to send Stovepipe and let him whip out that long wacker of his—and make 'em feel downright unmanly," Ethan cracked.

Cole forced a chuckle. It wasn't like his brother to make jokes, especially off-color ones. Was his brother hiding something from him?

Ethan's face twisted into a box of wrinkles and worry lines as he said, "Used to be . . . you could stack me alongside most—with a gun. Not in your class, Cole, but I—"

A wild turkey jabbered its annoyance and stopped Ethan's sad assessment as Abe came loping back from the river. Cole thought to himself that a knowing man could tell an Indian rider from quite a distance: He rode differently from a white man, the way he swung his quirt and dug in his heels at every jump.

"Cole Ker-rie. Damn. River is lady. Damn. We cross this high," the half-breed reported before his horse had completely stopped beside them. Abe moved his hand to show the water was chest-high while mounted.

Pulling on the brim of his hat to keep the advancing sun away, Cole asked, "Any signs of an ambush?"

"Yes, Cole Ker-rie. Damn. Eight men with long guns. Came morning. They wait. By the long thicket."

"Well, you called that one," Ethan said, shaking his head and throwing the butt of his cigarette to the ground.

Cole exhaled, his tanned forehead squeezing into a row of worry, and said, "How far from the bank?"

"Past flank rider."

That was the half-breed's way of measurement. It meant the distance between the front of the herd and a flank rider's normal position a third of the way back.

"Sound like they're in that hedgerow I told you about," Ethan said.

"Thanks, Abe. Good work," Cole complimented the half-breed scout. "I want you to go back with Dancer and two men. Take your rifles. You'll hide in the wagons when they cross on the ferry. Speakman will give you another gun. I want you to catch those boys waiting for us from behind."

"Take hoss, Cole Ker-rie?"

"Yeah, tie them to the wagons. Better switch yours out, though—he's done his work for the day."

"Where Cole Ker-rie and his guns?"

"We'll be coming from the river and hit 'em both ways at once. Can you get close without being seen?"

"Yes, Cole Ker-rie. Abe can. Others maybe not so. Too white. Damn."

"You'll have to help them."

"You don't waste any time," Ethan observed to his brother.

"Old habit. I'd rather charge than be charged at."

"Seems like I remember that."

"You ought to. You're the one that taught me."

Cole turned back to the half-breed and said, "Abe, don't tell anybody yet about our plans. Dancer will come to you when we're ready."

"Abe no speak, Cole Ker-rie. Damn."

"Good work, Abe. Thanks."

Ethan mumbled a similar response as Abe kicked his horse and galloped away. Cole waved at Dancer to join them from his position beside Whistle and the front of the herd. Under his breath, he said, "I'm going to tell Dancer first, Ethan. Then DuMonte."

"Whatever you think best."

"Come on."

Dancer rode up and heard the problem. The fiery point rider's face darkened and his words came out of the side of his mouth where a slight grin had appeared. The point rider touched the medicine bag beneath his shirt with his fingers.

"Pick your men. Tell Hayden and Speakman, too. I want you moving out as quick as you can."

"I'll take care of it, boss."

His eyes dancing with challenge, Dancer yanked his horse away from the herd and loped toward the wagons. The lithe rider was a strange mixture, Cole thought, half devil-may-care and half spiritual. But he liked Dancer and knew it was partly because he reminded him of himself at a younger age, only without the superstitious bent. Cole quickly told DuMonte what was facing them, that he was sending Dancer and Abe, along with riflemen in the wagons, to flank the ambushers. The religious cowhand's face was unreadable as he listened. When he spoke, his eyes flashed with a hardness Cole hadn't seen before.

"Well, you had Winlow pegged right, Mr. Kerry. It would be like him. He wants your brother's spread somethin' awful. If he figures we're going to make it, well, he's got to stop us."

"Spread the word. I want everyone armed when we cross."

Cole wasn't ready for DuMonte's next response. He expected something about praying.

"It's going to be hard keeping guns dry in the river," DuMonte advised.

"Got a better idea? I'm open."

"I'll rig us up a raft. Put the rifles and a box or two of bullets on it and bring alongside me when we cross. I can lead it with a rope-tie from my horse. How's that?"

Ethan quickly responded, "Make sure it's good and tight, though. Lash everything to the raft. If it turns over, you'll still have 'em."

"Go to it, DuMonte," Cole said.

As DuMonte spun away, Ethan said, "Told you he was more than a Bible-thumper."

Throughout the rest of the morning, riders took turns going over to the chuck wagon and depositing clothes and equipment they didn't want with them at the river. Chaps, shirts, pants, and boots were left in the wagon bed, next to bedrolls and other gear. Pistol belts were unbuckled and dropped off too. Long johns and hats became the uniform of the day. Riders made a second stop to leave their Winchesters where DuMonte was busy rigging a small raft of downed poles and rawhide.

As soon as the gear was loaded, the chuck wagon took off with two saddle horses tied behind. Inside were Dancer and Sotar. In the wagon loaded with small calves, Oleen rode beside Ben Speakman. Two more fresh horses were tied behind the vehicle too. Cole watched them slide behind a treeline and disappear over the crest of the hill. He needed to give them an hour before they hit the Red, at least an hour. Oleen and Sotar probably wouldn't have been his choice of men to go, but he trusted Dancer's judgment; good marksmen were needed, not nice folks. He instructed Dancer to wait to shoot until he heard the herd coming. That would mean help was close. The firing would likely stampede the herd, but after their work in the river it shouldn't be too hard to round them up again.

At the chuck wagon, Cole and Ethan shed their clothes like the others, leaving only their hats.

"Are you tossing in that fancy gunbelt I've heard so much about?" Ethan asked sarcastically. The tone of the remark surprised Cole, but he let it pass. There was enough tension in the day already.

"No, I'm going to give my belt to DuMonte so he can bring them over. Along with my rifle. Only, I'm keeping a six-gun for the river. Just in case."

"How you going to keep that iron dry, little brother?"

As he rolled a bandanna into a tight string, Cole explained to Ethan what he was doing. With the cloth looped through the trigger guard, he tied the bandanna around his neck. The gun rested awkwardly on his upper chest, but it should remain dry. Earlier, he had tied a knife to his left forearm with a leather thong to cut the bandanna and grab the gun quickly. A handful of extra cartridges were stuck in his hatband.

"Maybe I should carry a pistol, too. What do you think, little brother?"

Cole looked at his brother and saw a twisted face trying hard to deal with the agony of not seeing, of not being able to fight, of not leading. Here was a man who built a ranch out of prairie reduced to a puppet, at least in his mind.

"Sure. I'll rig one for you."

"Don't pet me on the head like I'm some kid, Cole. I can still whip your ass, even if I can't see."

Hayden walked around the corner of the wagon, heard the last sentence, and retreated to the front again.

"I'm interested in whipping Winlow's ass, not yours, big brother. Do you want this pistol around your neck or not? We've got a lot to do before the Red."

Ethan froze as the comments bounced into his face; his mouth curled into a thin string, and he swung his right fist at the direction of Cole's face. The blow caught him off guard and landed squarely against his cheek. Cole staggered backward, reeling from the blow.

"What the . . . ? What the hell's the matter with you!"

"Come on, Cole. Come on. Let's see how tough you are against a helpless blind man. Come on." Ethan spoke with a fury; his face was crimson, his teeth tightened in a wide grimace; the tendons in his neck pulsed like a raging river.

For an instant, the flash through Cole's mind was that of a younger brother fighting for respect from his older brother—so long ago it seemed to be someone else's life. He took a deep breath and opened his fists. He didn't remember clinching them.

"I'm going to switch our horses for the river," Cole said in a hoarse whisper. "When I get back, you can let me know if you want a pistol tied around your neck or not."

He turned, grabbed the reins of both horses, and walked away, leaving Ethan sputtering and half-swinging his fists in the air. When the young trail boss reached the remuda, Luther had their river horses pulled from the remuda. Cole's own black horse and Hook for Ethan were standing quietly beside him. Cole told Luther of the plan. His oldest brother seemed disgruntled.

"I know'd. Dancer dun tolt me. Sotar too. My brother dun come a mite late with his windyin'."

"Sorry, Luther, I—"

"Don' matter none. I seed ya fightin' with Ethan. Why?"

"We weren't fighting, Luther. Ethan took a swing at me, that's all."

"Our brother don' feel like he be a man, not seein' an' all. Ya gotta he'p bring back the panther inside his heart, Cole."

Cole didn't know what to say. It was one of the most unusual statements he'd heard his oldest brother make. Why was Luther blaming him for something Ethan did? It wasn't his fault Ethan was blind, for God's sakes. He stared at his oldest brother and fumed, biting on words that shouldn't be said but seared his mind wanting out.

"Look yonder," Luther said, and pointed in the direction of the chuck wagon.

Across the open stretch of land came Ethan Kerry, a pistol tied around his neck with his bandanna. His choppy strides were closer to that of a drunk than his own as he reacted to the changing level of ground. His hands were thrust forward to warn him of obstacles. He stepped into a shallow hole, stumbled, and fell. Cole started to run to him, and Luther grabbed his arm.

"No, brother. That's what I bin a-sayin'. That thar panther dun needs to fight the land. He'll hate you if'n ya don't let 'im."

Shaking his bandaged head, Ethan pushed himself to his feet again, brushed off the dirt from his chest, and resumed his task. Luther and Cole stood and watched their brother zig and zag toward them, narrowly missing a scrub oak tree and its gnarly branches.

Luther spoke first as Ethan neared them. "My brother dun needs his river hoss, I reckon. It's ready fer leather." That was it. No words of concern, no expression of wonderment at the blind man walking by himself. Nothing.

"Where's Cole?"

Cole stiffened. Not more of this.

"I'm right here, Ethan."

"Good. I want you to punch me right in the face—for being such a stupid ass. God Almighty, why would I take it out on you? Hell, I wouldn't even have a drive if—"

Cole interrupted. "Let's get these catfish saddled, big brother. There's work to be done."

He winked at Luther, and the big man smiled. The saddles were readied quickly, with Luther insisting Ethan do his own tacking. The sinewy rancher attacked the task with relish, finishing only a minute longer than his sighted brother. Soon they were riding again. Cole glanced back at Luther, and his oldest brother waved. Cole waved back. Side by side, the two Kerry brothers rode. Ethan's horse had its head down and was walking quietly. The gentle manner relaxed Cole, who worried that the animal might suddenly bolt as any horse could. Anticipating the concern, Ethan reminded Cole that he was blind, not stupid, that he still remembered how to rein in a horse.

# Chapter Sixteen

Ahead was the majestic Red River. Clay sediment from upstream had gradually turned its high banks into dull crimson, matching the brackish shade of the flowing water. Even the timber guarding the shoreline carried stripes of red, a reminder of the river's ability to become a savage beast overnight. There was an aura about this river that was almost magical, especially to trail-driving Texans.

Today, the Red looked like it had no desire to be fierce. The river had divided into several smaller channels, separated by shallow bars of crusted red land leading into the main flow of the river. It was swimming depth and wide, wider than Cole had remembered when he crossed farther downstream. Abe had reported accurately, and Cole said so to Ethan riding beside him.

"We're here, Ethan. It looks as good as it gets."

The blind rancher held up his chin as if to see the river and asked, "Any reflection?"

"None."

"Good, let's bring 'em on."

"You give the call, Ethan," Cole Kerry said, and watched his brother accept the suggestion and give the command himself.

"Squeeze 'em down!" Without hesitation, Ethan yelled to the advancing drovers. It came with a hint of nervousness.

Smoothly, the men began to narrow the width of the herd for the crossing. It was a proud moment for Ethan Kerry, and he bit his lip to keep emotions from bursting through. For the moment, the possible ambush was forgotten. Earlier, Ethan had advised letting the horse herd take the water ahead of the cattle. As if on cue, the string of extra horses began to lope forward, parallel to the herd, pushed by Luther and Ferguson. Whistle would be encouraged to follow right after them, and, hopefully, the herd wouldn't hesitate.

Dismounting, Cole held his horse, loosened the cinch, and looked over at Ethan, who had swung down by himself and was doing the same thing.

"Better loosen your cinch. Horses get all swoll up when swimming," Ethan coached. Cole knew this well from other river crossings but said nothing. He was having second thoughts about letting Ethan ride the river, but it was too late to worry about it.

Ethan looked over as if to check on his younger brother, but only grayness reached his brain. "I know you're worrying about me, Cole. Don't. This old hoss'll get me across just fine."

"I'm not worried, I know you'll do fine. Luther's headed our way. We'll be in the Red in minutes. I'll bet we have some red cattle before the day's over."

"Isn't that something? If the water's moving slow,

we always get red stripes . . . across everything. Damnedest thing a cowman'll ever see."

Both men caught the significance of the word "see." Ethan sucked on his teeth to let out the feeling; Cole exhaled and patted the rump of his horse.

"I'll be right beside you."

"If ol' Hook starts heading the wrong way, just tell me. I'll splash a little water in his face. Opposite side. Reins aren't much good in water, you know. You should be grabbing mane."

Cole smiled grimly. There were times when Ethan's counsel was too much like being a child again. He knew the man meant no harm; it was just his way. Details made the difference between almost winning and victory—that was Ethan Kerry's creed—and none were left unattended if he had anything to say about them.

A whisper through Cole's mind brought back the time when they were boys and his older brother taught him how to clean and load a pistol. Not how to shoot the gun, but how to clean and load it right. Over and over, Ethan had demanded his little brother repeat the process until Cole had become angry and thrown the gun across the yard. It had gone off, and they had both flung themselves to the ground. That teaching episode had ended in a wrestling match; Luther had stopped it.

Cole smiled to himself when he recalled bringing home a half-dozen grouse and his big brother demanding to see how many loads had been used. When Ethan discovered it was six for six, there were no more lessons about handling a gun. Cole realized, for the first time, that his older brother had been more father than brother.

Cole Kerry eased his horse down the soft, red-rocked ford with Ethan at his right side. They entered the quiet channel, and the two animals drank briefly. In another minute, they were swimming and both men were stretched prone on the water, over the horses' backs. A fistful of mane was the only connection to the mounts. Cole watched his brother fearful he might lose his balance, but Ethan appeared as comfortable as a man in a rocking chair.

"Man, can you smell the river, Cole? It's fresh, ah, sorta sweet almost. I can't find any words to put around it," Ethan said joyfully.

Surprised at his brother's sensitive observation, Cole grunted agreement and looked back to see the remuda advancing. Swinging their coiled lariats overhead, Luther and Ferguson trailed the thundering remuda. Without a pause, the horses splashed into the shallow channel and headed for the far bank. Several stopped to drink, but the drovers kept them moving.

A few yards farther, they were swimming smoothly, their glistening backs and heads gliding above the dark water. In the lead was Kiowa, with Luther's rope around its neck. The fiery horse nipped at a bay who tried to swim past. As the last horse entered, DuMonte gave the lead steer a holler and pushed his horse behind the animal to prod him along. Whistler stopped at the water's edge, eyed the surroundings, drank deeply, and stepped confidently into the magical river.

Behind the rangy steer came a brown stream of cattle to intersect with the brackish current. Men whooped, whistled, and swung their lariats to keep the cattle from thinking about the crossing. In minutes, Whistler was leading a double-filed line, swimming straight for the far shoreline. Riders pushed their horses to the downstream side of the herd to keep it from drifting. Cole glanced from Ethan to the horses behind him to the trailing herd and back again.

"They're coming, Ethan. They're coming."

"Are the boys getting downstream so they won't drift on us? That's an easy way to lose cattle."

Cole inhaled deeply, annoyed by the question, but answered it anyway. "Yes, they're all in place."

"All kinds of problems crossing rivers," Ethan yelled. "An undercurrent can take a man so fast. Better watch the bank for quicksand."

"Right."

"I've seen a man get cramps right in the middle of the damn river and drown before anyone can get to him," Ethan jabbered on. "Cole, did you love that gal in Abilene?"

It wasn't a question he expected from Ethan. Cole didn't think his brother even knew of the situation, since they had never talked about it. A splash of water caught his frozen-open mouth. Choking and spitting, he tried to answer but couldn't. Ethan chuckled.

"I, ah, thought I did."

"Did you talk to her—after the shooting?"

"No. I was pretty busy, getting ahead of that posse."

"Maybe she wanted someone who could give her a good home. Women want that, you know," Ethan said. "Selling your gun isn't real stable work."

"Maybe so," Cole replied. "Women like Claire are hard to find. You're a lucky man, Ethan."

The phrase came out before he could stop it.

"Oh, yeah, real lucky. I'll never see her face again. Or watch my son ride across the Red like this. I'll never see—"

"Didn't mean it that way. At least you've got a wife and kids."

"Forget it, we've got a herd to get across. Or you do." As he finished, a lap of water hit Ethan in the face. He choked and spat. Cole glanced over at him.

Cole's forehead furrowed, then he broke into laughter.

"Well, damn, little brother, I near swallowed half the Red and you're splitting a gut laughing," Ethan growled in jest. "Am I still going straight?"

"Splash a little on the right side."

"How's that?"

"Again. Yeah, that's it. We're halfway."

"Thanks, Cole," Ethan said, his face looking straight ahead. "I know this was piling on the worry for you."

"You're mighty welcome, Ethan. I wouldn't have had it any other way. Just don't fall off. I can't swim."

Ethan laughed, swallowed more water, and said, "That would pay me back for the stunt I pulled this morning. How's your jaw?"

"About like getting kicked by a mule. Brought back memories of you kicking my butt and Luther trying to stop it."

Ethan didn't respond right away, then said, "You know, Luther lost his wife and his three kids—to the fevers. He couldn't stomach working on his ranch after that, and the bank took it. After he came to us, I took all my guns, and his, out of the house, put 'em that little shed, and locked it. I was worried . . . but he's never talked about it since."

"I didn't know, Ethan," Cole said, and wondered why he was telling him this right now.

"Our big brother may not be the fastest, but I'd never bet against him when it comes to grit."

"I wouldn't bet against either of you."

"Oh, Luther's a lot tougher than me."

Cole wondered if Ethan was trying to tell him something beyond Luther's past. His thoughts were reconnected to the river as both horses stepped onto the soggy bottom as the waters began to shallow. Cole swung back into the saddle, grabbing the reins that lay knotted across his horse's neck. He started to tell Ethan to do the same, but his brother had already slipped into his saddle. Cole wondered what it must be like to be blind. He shut his eyes for a few seconds in an involuntary test, then opened them.

Remembering his pistol, he took the knife from his arm, leaving the tied leather in place, and cut the bandanna. The silver-plated Colt never felt better in his hand. He stuck the wadded bandanna inside his long johns, looked back over his shoulder, and waved to Luther, who returned the greeting with no expression on his face.

Shaking their bodies to rid themselves of the river, the extra horses trampled up the bank and over the top. Kiowa remained in the lead and kicked at a buckskin, who dared to make the mistake of trying to be first up the embankment. Luther and Ferguson brought the remuda into a tight bunch and talked them into stopping near the two waiting brothers. For the first time, Cole realized that Kiowa was wearing a rope around its neck, held by his brother.

Luther yelled, "This hyar Kiowa is the he-cat o' the hosses, Cole."

"Looks like it. Luther, hold 'em here. Ethan, stay with Luther, will you? I'm going to check on the herd and get my guns."

"Winlow! I forgot all about him!" Ethan exclaimed, and yanked on his wet bandanna to retrieve the handgun.

Cole saw the struggle and handed him his sheath knife, brushing it against Ethan's shoulder. "Here, use my knife."

"I can get it."

"Suit yourself. I couldn't get mine undone and had to cut it."

Ethan took the offered blade. After sawing on the kerchief until it let go of his gun, Ethan straightened his back and said, "Hey, a smoke would be mighty fine right about now." He spun the revolver in his hand with the ease of a man used to handling a gun.

Cole watched the display of dexterity, chuckled, and said, "I'm fresh out."

"Ya kin have a piece o' my chew." Luther grinned. " 'Course, it dun bin in my mouth for a while."

"I'll be back later," Cole announced, turned his horse, nudged it with his knees, and loped back to the river.

"Luther, that brother of ours has grown up strong," Ethan said. Luther was quiet for a moment and answered, "Yeah, I reckon he's a fire-eatin' warrior, like Maw . . . and you."

"Like Maw, anyway."

At the river, several hundred steers had cleared the bank and the full herd was a fat line connecting Texas to the Nations over the waterway. Cole rode alongside DuMonte, who was concentrating on the progress. His dripping horse stood quietly on the shore. Beside the black cowboy was the raft laden with guns. The blanket lining the top of the raft was soaked, but the guns and the ammunition boxes appeared dry. Drenched steers struggled past him, headed for grazing.

"Hey, Loop! Over here. Quicksand!" DuMonte yelled and pointed for the benefit of the young rider swimming his horse alongside the herd. The cowboy glanced at him, waved a hand, and splashed his horse's face to head in the direction of two animals struggling belly-deep in a yellowish-gray circle near the western edge of the slick bank. Stovepipe was already there and climbing down from his drenched saddle.

"Stovepipe fell off, but he got his horse back,"

DuMonte reported as a greeting as Cole reined up beside him. "Only time I haven't seen him laughing and happy. He was spewing water like Jonah's whale!"

"Maybe he should've wrapped his doodad around the saddle horn."

DuMonte's polite chuckle carried embarrassment at the risqué remark, and Cole felt sorry he had said it.

"Half the time I never know if that sprout hears me or not," DuMonte said, changing the subject and referring to Loop. "Sometimes, I think he does it on purpose to rile this ol' man. He's gonna get thrown if he doesn't start getting his horse's head lined up with his rope. One of those steers is gonna yank him and his hoss right smack into real trouble. You watch and see. Lord help us."

Cole nodded, but DuMonte's comments barely registered. His attention was on the raft. Dismounting, he retrieved his gunbelt and strapped it on over his wet underwear. The ground was hard and uneven on his bare feet, and he walked gingerly. He shoved fresh loads into both Colts before returning them to the holsters. Empty bullet loops were quickly filled from one of the ammunition boxes. Long ago, he had begun carrying bullets that would work in both his handguns and his rifle. Grabbing his Winchester, he reloaded it and swung back into the saddle.

"DuMonte, you're in charge of the herd. Ethan and Luther are just over that ridge, waiting. When you get there, move 'em along the trail just like my brother says."

"Where are you going, Mr. Kerry?"

"I'm going on ahead to check on the Winlow boys."

"Thought we were going to do that together."

Cole put his hand on the black cowboy's shoulder and said, "DuMonte, it's better this way. This is going to be a gunfight—and I'm better at it than most. I reckon Dancer picked the best shooters already. I'd rather not give them a bunch of targets if I don't have to."

"Boss, it isn't my place to say—but you aren't riding lonesome anymore."

"It'll be fine, DuMonte. Winlow's boys will think I'm riding point and let me get close. Close enough to hurt the bastards when Dancer opens the ball."

"You know, Mr. Kerry, just because I read the Bible doesn't mean I can't handle a gun."

"I never thought otherwise, but we're going to do it my way. I need you here. Besides, I might save us a stampede if I get far enough ahead."

Cole told him to have the men take their guns as they passed but to stay with the herd. With that, he kicked his horse into a gallop and swung east and wide so that he wouldn't have to face Ethan or Luther again. DuMonte watched him go, ignoring the cowboys struggling with the two trapped steers behind him. Mournful bawling reinforced the seriousness of the situation.

Under his breath, the controlled point rider muttered, "Please, Lord, keep him safe. He's heady, but he's good. Please, hear me, Lord. Amen."

DuMonte swallowed hard and turned toward the quicksand problem. "Don't pull on his head, Loop! We'll have to get a rope around each leg, Stovepipe."

Reining up beside two windblown cottonwoods, Cole Kerry brushed the nearest branch with his outstretched hand. His other arm cradled a Winchester. The touch was a silent tribute to Ethan Kerry's description that they must pass these trees before reaching the long hedgerow where Winlow's men waited. His eyes searched the forested rim of the open meadow for signs of something that shouldn't be there. According to

Ethan, the hedgerow was another quarter mile away.

He smiled when he remembered Ethan's words: *Cole, you'll see those two trees perched on that ridge, like two lonely folks who wandered into the prairie and got lost. Stay to the right. You're only four miles, due north, from where we'll camp.* The young trail boss muttered aloud, "The man sees better when he can't!"

In the distance, two rifle shots clattered through the valley, then another, then a dozen. Distance gave them a ghostly dimension. Cole nudged his horse and bolted toward the shots. He was halfway across the clearing when a rider cleared the rock-stubbled ridge a hundred yards away. It was Abe, slapping his horse with a quirt and headed his way. The half-breed saw Cole, waved his arm over his head, and reined the charging mount in the young trail boss's direction.

Cole slowed his horse and gradually brought it to a halt as Abe approached. Obviously, somebody's ambush had begun. He hoped it was his men doing the ambushing and not the other way around. Seeing Abe made him wonder. The half-breed stopped his horse hard; its hind legs dug into the damp earth, spraying mud and grass. Cole's mount stutter-stepped away from the sliding horse, but the trail boss quickly quieted the animal. He waited for Abe to speak, but the trail boss's face was filled with questions, his eyes laced with challenge. The half-breed glanced at Cole's now drying long underwear and a soft grin worked its way onto his face. Cole had forgotten what he was wearing.

"What's going on, Abe?"

"Goddamn, Cole Ker-rie. Shoot too quick. They fear us. Run."

"What?"

"Shoot too quick. No get close. Win-low men get

hoss. Run far. We no kill. God-damn, Cole Ker-rie."

The significance of Abe's report ripped away Cole's energy. What had happened?

"Are you saying one of our boys started firing . . . too soon . . . and gave the Winlow men a chance to get away?" Cole restated what the half-breed had told him. Abe's words were clear enough. It was Cole's mind needing the repetition.

"Son of bitch. Cole Ker-rie. That so. No kill. They run."

"Did you chase them?"

"We chase on foot. Shoot. Our hosses with wagon. Damn."

"Can we—you and me—swing around and cut them off now, somewhere on their back trail?"

"No, Cole Ker-rie. Abe get hoss. Follow quick. They go far. Abe track to Win-low camp. Yes? Damn. You want go Win-low camp?" Abe responded, his dark eyes searching the trail boss's face. "No Abe fault, Cole Ker-rie. Damn."

"I know that, Abe. You did fine. Guess I was hoping for too much. Who was it, who shot too soon?"

"Abe no know. Me crawl. Get close for see. Eight Win-low rifles. Wait in long bush." The half-breed made hand signals to describe his actions.

"Go on."

"Abe turn. Wave others close," Abe continued, waving his arm briskly to mimick his command. "Gun shoot. Abe turn back. Win-low men all jump, yell. Run for hosses."

"Was it Dancer?" Cole asked, but he couldn't believe the fiery point rider would give away their advantage so easily.

"Abe no know. Damn. Swede maybe. Maybe Soo-tar. No One-Arm."

"Well, take me to our men."

Cole Kerry could hear the Bar K cowboys talking before he saw the two wagons and tied horses among a sentinel of cottonwoods. Abe looked at the trail boss and pointed; Cole saw the gathering at the same time.

"Hey, shut up! Someone's a-coming!" came a hoarse command from the trees. It was John Davis Sotar's Missouri twang cutting through the distance.

"It's Abe and . . ."

"Cole Kerry is vith him, by Jiminy."

"Oh hell, we're gonna get it now!"

"It wasn't my fault. It was you, Oleen, you stupid son of a bitch."

"Ya, you shut up. . . ."

Reminding himself that these men weren't used to gunfighting, Cole rode into the small clearing and sought Jared Dancer. The peppery rider rolled his shoulders to relieve the tension and met Cole's stare with his own flashing eyes.

"Boss, it was my fault. This was my command. I let you down, I'm sorry. They got away."

Before Cole could respond, the one-armed Confederate soldier, Ben Speakman, added his observation. "Mr. Kerry, sir. Young Dancer did everything you asked him to do. He was the victim of a soldier getting too anxious. Happens to the best of us. The man fired when he should have been advancing, sir. All of us have done that one time or another, I reckon, sir. I remember at Shiloh, there was . . ."

It was difficult to resist grinning at the old Rebel's military-sounding report. Cole looked around at the men who were staring at him, rifles resting in their crossed arms. Jared Dancer. John Davis Sotar. Gus Oleen. Old Ben Speakman, the former Confederate officer with one arm, held his Colt dragoon in his right hand, resting at his side and still talking about some Civil War battle. Even T. L. Hayden was armed, with a double-barreled shotgun. Something about his serious posture seemed comical to the trail boss. He wondered if the cook had ever fired the thing. Hayden's smirk reminded Cole of his own attire, and he chuckled to himself at what he must look like to men who hadn't crossed the way he had. But this wasn't the time for levity, and he waited for more information.

"It was all that stupid Swede's fault," Hayden burst out. The corners of his mouth gave away the satisfaction he felt in placing blame. "He started firing before we even got ten feet. Stupid fool."

"Yah, you are stupid one," Oleen stammered. "They saw us, one uff them saw us, he vas goin' to shoot. I yust did it first. You vould have bin dead. You veren't watching."

The Swede's face was swallowed in crimson; his eyelids blinked rapidly as his eyes sought someone in the group to support his viewpoint. His gaze came to rest on Sotar.

"Sotar, he shot too, yah. He vas right beside me, he vere, yah. Sotar saw him. Sotar shoot vhen I did, yah. Before, maybe. Yah, it vas so."

John Davis Sotar had been watching Cole, an unmeasured danger in the Missourian's flinty eyes. Of all the men on the drive, Sotar would be the most dangerous in any fight, Cole knew. Except for Ethan, if he could see. With Oleen's accusation, Sotar stepped backward as if to let the words fall in front of him. His eyes sparkled with hate, his right hand moved toward the pistol at his hip, then a calmness took over. The words that followed were disconnected from his vengeful reaction.

"Sorry, Oleen, you must be mistaken. The first I

knew about it was hearing your shot. But if you say there was a man there, I ain't challenging it. Reckon I was looking down at the ground to see where I was going to crawl next."

"Yah, but . . ."

"Be real careful, Oleen, you're headed toward calling me a liar."

# Chapter Seventeen

Hayden chuckled at the description; the one-armed Speakman nodded. Oleen was frightened. Cole could read men well, but he wasn't certain about either Sotar or Oleen. Was Sotar in cohoots with Winlow somehow? Or Oleen? Were the early shots a result of being overeager—or a calculated warning?

"Well, boys, they sure as hell didn't get done what they wanted," Cole advised, placing one hand over the other on his saddle horn. "Maybe you scared them into taking care of their own herd, instead of messing with us."

He didn't feel nearly as positive as the statement, but he needed to end this situation before it became a shouting match that would solve nothing. Or worse. There was no doubt in his mind that Sotar would kill Oleen if it came to that, and he wouldn't look back. That was the edge a gunfighter had: He didn't care about taking another's life. Everything about Sotar indicated he was such a man.

Cole saw all of their faces change, like sunlight touching a morning flower, as he relieved them of failure, and continued, "Let's get on back to the herd. When I left, everything was doing all right, but they'll be needing help as soon as we can get there. As you can tell, it's mighty damp back there—and we're a little short on clothes."

The men smiled at his attempt to be lighthearted and went for their horses. Looking over at the half-breed sitting quietly on his horse, Cole added, "Abe, I'd like to mosey down Winlow's back trail a ways. Just to make sure they don't double back. Will you show me where they headed?"

"Yes, Cole Ker-rie. Goddamn."

"I'd like to go with you, boss," Dancer said. His voice was submissive.

Cole's first impulse was to agree, but it wasn't where the man was needed, and he said simply, "Thanks. I'd like that, Jared, but I think DuMonte will be needing you more. All of you."

The sentence had barely finished when Hayden snapped the lines of the chuck wagon and headed south. Behind it came the calf wagon, noisy with small animals, with Speakman at the reins. The three riders mounted their horses and followed. None spoke as they loped toward the unseen river.

The sun's last red streaks were lying on the horizon when the half-breed Abe and Cole Kerry returned to the relaxed camp. The Bar K drive had settled about four miles from the river in a bedground that was just as Ethan had described. Surrounded on three sides by a winding dry ravine, the clearing was level with sufficient grass at least for the night. A thicket of blackjack curled halfway around the clearing's edge.

The blind rancher had declared that a celebration was in order after the successful crossing of the Red River and the breakup of the ambush. He ordered Hayden to get out three bottles of whiskey. Ethan kept one for himself. Around the camp, tired drovers were laughing about the river and passing the other bottles from man to man. The threat of ambush was forgotten, at least for the moment.

Speakman was sitting on a log next to Ethan, reading him a letter from Claire that he had picked up at the settlement. Ethan's face was pulled by the emotions roaring through him as Speakman droned on, embarrassed by the task of reading personal thoughts between a married couple. The settlement was the post for trail letters coming and going. Ethan's fist held a bottle of whiskey, taking a swallow with almost every sentence.

Sotar and Ferguson were quietly talking; Ferguson was the only one looking as dirty as before the Red. DuMonte was lying on his bedroll reading his Bible. Stovepipe, Loop, Oleen, and Jersey were with the herd. Venison steak was sizzling over Hayden's stove, courtesy of Sotar, who had shot a three-point buck on the way back. Fresh onions, potatoes, and carrots were cooking, too, purchases from the settlement.

Luther met the two riders as they pulled into the happy setting. He was sitting alone, on the edge of the bedground, staring outward. His Winchester lay in his lap. A brown, stocky mustang was saddled and standing quietly, the reins resting easy in his tanned hand. Cole figured his brother would rather saddle a horse to ride ten yards than walk across the bedground, if he had the choice. It was like Luther, he thought, to be the one standing guard when everyone else was relaxing. Luther stood as they approached, taking the Winchester into his cradled arms.

"Any sight of 'em bastards?" Luther asked, working on a new chaw. His breath carried a light whiskey odor; his fingers tapped against the rifle stock.

"No. They rode hard," Cole answered, swinging down from his horse. "The way I figure it, they won't get back to their herd until early morning."

"Think they'll double back?"

"Might. From now on, you, me—and Dancer and DuMonte—will take turns standing guard at night. In addition to the nighthawks." Cole spoke as he loosened the cinch on his saddle.

"Makes sense to me. My beauty sleep ain't be doin' much good nohow. You gonna tell the boys?" Luther asked, and spat.

"No reason not to."

"They come again, Cole Ker-rie. You must kill all. Damn," came the half-breed's harsh assessment before he shoved his heels into the tired horse and headed for the night rope corral.

"I hear tell Oleen upped and fired too quick-like," Luther said.

Cole yanked the saddle to the ground, dragging the saddle blanket along. He pulled his Winchester from its sheath, looked at Luther, and repeated what he had been told about the encounter.

"Wal, Oleen's a solid hand," Luther said defensively, shifting the chaw from one side of his mouth to the other. "Ain't my favorite com-pan-ion, mind ya, but ya cain't count him low on account o' this h'yar shootin', Cole. Coulda happened to any of us."

Cole looked at his older brother with eyes that questioned the remark.

Luther accepted the unspoken challenge and said,

"Now, I could be remindin' a young feller o' the time he took it upon hisself to attack a whole passel o' Yanks, 'stead o' waitin' for his friends."

"That's not exactly how it was," Cole said with a tired smile, "but that's the second time Oleen has been, well, on the wrong side of a situation."

"Dancer took it hard, Cole," Luther interrupted, as if he didn't want to hear Cole's accusation. "He wants bad to show you he can handle hisse'f."

"He's got nothing to prove to me."

"Maybe you oughta tell him that. He's a-wearin' his skin real thin ri't 'bout now."

"Where is he?" Cole looked in the general direction of the camp but didn't see Jared Dancer.

"Saw 'im wander out that away. Prob'ly talkin' with them spirits he dun takes a shine to."

"I'll find him. Then I need to talk with Ethan."

"None o' my never mind, but I'd stay away from that ol' boy fur a piece."

"Why?"

"Well, that brother o' yurn, he were mad as a bull who didn't git the cow when the news dun came 'bout ya a-goin' on ahead without any o' us. Lordy, he was a-spewin'!"

Cole couldn't think of anything to say. Both men knew Cole's decision was the right one. Ethan's personal agony over his condition was beginning to wear on the trail boss. Cole's eyes revealed the unexpressed feeling, and Luther read them easily. Luther's mouth twisted underneath his droopy mustache, and the wrinkles on the right side of his face seemed even more pronounced than usual. Luther stared at the yellowing sky as he continued talking without looking at Cole.

"The way I track 'er down, Cole . . . Ethan, wal, he's got hisse'f all stirred up. Bein' blind an' all an' then

213

a-havin' that Winlow bunch circlin' us like a pack of wolves. Wal, that thar's a mighty big load to carry 'round, I reckon. Dun tear a man apart . . . inside. Like a swoll-up crick a-bangin' again' sum beaver dam."

Luther paused, glanced at Cole, who was rubbing his horse with a handful of grass, and returned his gaze to the sky as he talked. "Cain't say as I dun blame Ethan. No sirree, cain't say as I do. Reckon I'd be a ri't hard feller to handle in the same path."

"Get to the point, Luther." Cole's voice was low, and his growing frustration wasn't hidden to his brother.

Luther smiled away the obvious tone of the younger man's voice and said, "Like I were a-sayin', crossin' the Red like ya did, lettin' him ride along . . . now that was good, real good. I were ri't smart proud o' ya. I really were."

He stopped and stared at Cole, expecting some kind of response. There was none other than the trail boss lifting his saddle and swinging it over this shoulder.

Luther knew his time for further talking was short. "But it t'were bad too, I reckon. Made Ethan want more, ya know'd. Made him dun miss ever'thing— more, if'n that's possible. Ya an' I don' know what it's like not to see. Nossir, we don't. An' when he dun heard you was a-goin' at 'em by yournse'f, well, I reckon . . . it made him, well, like he wasn't nuthin', ya know'd. Man like him jes' can't handle not bein' ri't there. Leadin'."

"I've done everything I know how to do, Luther," Cole said as he started walking toward the rope corral, leading his tired horse. The ground hurt his bare feet. He stopped and asked, "What am I supposed to do? I know he's hurting—but I—I . . ."

"Thar ain't nuthin' you kin do, li'l brother . . . that

you ain't already dun. One more thing, a'fer I dun fergit. Ethan got hisse'f a letter from Claire. Yessir, Speakman picked it up at the settlement post, he did, as a fact. Ethan asked the ol' man to read it to him. Speakman tolt me he never saw the like, our brother's face a-twistin' an' a-turnin'. Bad, Cole."

"Yeah, a woman can do that to a man, I guess."

Luther smiled and spat. "Wal, now, sonny boy, you ain't the first man to miss a woman. Nohow."

"Didn't say I was."

"Whadda ya miss most?" Luther asked, and looked away. "I—I kin still smell her. My Lizzie. She an' my kids . . ."

"I know about your awful loss. Ethan told me. I'm sorry, Luther. I'm mighty sorry." Cole was surprised at the sudden admission. It was the first time Luther had ever mentioned this awful tragedy in his life. Cole wondered if Ethan had told him about their river conversation.

Luther took a long deep breath and said, "They's waitin' fer me, ya know'd. Up thar somewhar's. Jes' hope I kin measure up an' be with 'em sumday. Them two youn'un's'll be all grow'd up, I reckon." His face trembled, and he squeezed shut his eyes hard to keep the emotion in.

Cole hesitated and finally said, "Big brother, the good Lord will have to take you. Nobody else will be able to handle all of his horses."

Luther rubbed his chin, shook his head, and said, "That'll be nuff o' that. Don't know'd what dun come ov'r me, dang it all. A man's got to ride on from death. No other way. No sir, no other way."

Taking the cue that he wanted to change subjects, Cole said, "I didn't even ask you about the herd."

"By cracky, if'n we didn't lose nary a one. Near did,

though," Luther said, his face showing appreciation for the new direction. He told about DuMonte directing the task of pulling the brown-and-white steer out of the quicksand by its four legs. Cole laughed at the telling. It was amazing how Luther could make him feel good no matter what, and how his old brother could seal off such an awful memory and go on. It made him feel a little silly to be pining over a woman who didn't want him.

"Say, how 'bout a little snort. The boss, ah . . . Ethan . . . dun passed around a couple of bottles of who-shot-John to celebrate gittin' past the Red," Luther said, putting his hands on Cole's shoulder.

"Sounds good, but I think I'll go see Dancer first."

After discovering the point rider was stretched out asleep on his bedroll, Cole Kerry headed back to the small campfire where the laughing and talking had grown louder. He passed the chuck wagon where Hayden had talked Loop into grinding a new sack of coffee beans for the reward of a stick of peppermint that came in each Arbuckles sack.

"Loop, you wouldn't mind if I gave this stick of candy to the boss, do you?" Hayden said sarcastically.

Loop gulped and said, "Oh, oh, of course not. I . . ."

"The candy's yours, Loop," Cole responded. "How soon's chow, Hayden?"

Loop immediately jammed the entire stick in his mouth, grabbed the grinder, and enthusiastically began cranking again. Trying to sound mature and learned, he asked, "Ever wonder why they used up so many letters to spell 'coffee'? Seems to me they coulda saved a 'e' and a 'f.' "

Hayden ignored Loop and said, "Be ready in another fifteen minutes, twenty at the most."

Cole nodded and put on his left-behind clothes.

Fifty feet away, Speakman was reading Ethan's letter in halting phrases, more indicative of his being uncomfortable with the situation than his reading ability. He held the unfolded pages with his one hand and eyed the writing as if it were something that could attack him at any moment.

" . . . Remember, my dear, what we talked about doing. It is a good way if the others agree.

" 'There is a letter here for Cole from Abilene. It is a woman's handwriting. I hope it is good news. The postal clerk brought it to the house two days after you left. He was not certain if there was a Cole Kerry at our ranch, but that was the address. It was very nice of Mr. Robertson to do this. He is a busy man, I am sure. I gave him a glass of lemonade and a piece of a fresh apple pie I had just baked. I was not very happy with the crust, but he said it was good. He told me most of the people in town knew about your trail drive and were astonished to hear you were going in spite of your accident. They do not know my Ethan well.

" 'My prayers go with you. Please greet Luther and Cole and the other men for me. We miss you and love you. I am very proud. Eli counted to a hundred last night. He was so proud. Love, Claire.' "

Speakman paused and said, "Here's that other letter. You want me to give it to Cole?"

"No, no, I'll take it to him," Ethan responded, and held out his opened palm for Speakman to place the folded envelope. The blind rancher shoved it into his back pocket and asked for Claire's letter. He took a long swig of whiskey, folded the letter, and placed in the same pocket.

Behind them, Cole headed their way. "Here comes Cole now," Speakman said, and issued a warm welcome. Ethan's back straightened at the approaching jingle of spurs.

"Well, whadda ya know, here comes my brother, the almighty gunfighter who doesn't need anyone's help. Did you think you could take 'em all on yourself?"

Cole's eyes met Speakman's worried expression before he responded, "They're gone."

"Probably heard about your reputation as a gunfighter." Ethan's words were laced with envy and frothed by whiskey. "Maybe tomorrow you can move the herd all by yourself—to make up for it."

Without another word, Cole Kerry turned and headed back toward the chuck wagon—limping slightly, if anyone watched him closely. His glance caught the cook's stare; the cold in Cole's slitted eyes made Hayden regret his curiosity, and he resumed stirring a bowl of biscuit dough with a vengeance.

Ethan noted the change in direction and yelled, "Hey, boys, that there is Cole Kerry—the boyfriend killer. Yeah, he's so good with a gun that he shot down a man who didn't like him messing with his girlfriend. Tell 'em all about it, little brother. Abilene, it was. Stevenson, that was the city boy's name, wasn't it, Cole? That's why my little brother came to Texas, they ran him out of Kansas. Come on, Cole, everybody'd like to hear about you gunning down that fellow."

The men at the campfire were stunned. John Davis Sotar's eyes widened; he choked, and a strange expression locked onto his gaunt face. The old soldier Speakman stood, stepped toward Ethan, and reached for the whiskey bottle at his feet.

"What do you think you're doing, goddammit! This is my whiskey. My whiskey! All of this is mine. Do you understand?!"

"You've had enough, Ethan," Speakman said, his

voice even, but filled with quiet determination.

Ethan put the bottle to his mouth, swallowed three times, and snapped, "Oh, it's you, Speakman. What are you doing? Sidin' with that gun-totin' kid brother of mine? He put the whole herd to risk today. My herd, goddammit! My herd, do you hear me, Speakman?"

The one-armed Speakman ran his tongue across dried lips, trying to hold back the response within him. It came anyway.

"We wouldn't be here, *Mister* Kerry, if it weren't for your brother."

"Oh, I get it. N-nobody in his right mind would follow a blind man, is that it, S-Speakman? Say it. Lemme hear you say it."

Speakman stared at Ethan. The blind rancher forced another swallow of whiskey, and brown dribbles rolled down his chin. Both hands, shaking slightly, gripped the bottle tighter to subdue the nervous reaction. Unlike his usual wordy self, the old Rebel soldier spun and left the campfire, headed for his bedroll.

"Where you going, S-Speakman, you one-armed son of a bitch?! I'm the one who gave you a job—not my brother. I can hire you—and I can fire you. You hear me, Speakman?" Ethan's face was glowing crimson as his words blistered the still-dusky air.

Speakman stopped in midstride, as if the words had surrounded him, and his shoulders rose and fell. He turned slowly and walked back toward the campfire. His face suddenly aged; his words came softly, each one pronounced with deliberate care.

"You can do that, *Mister* Kerry. Anytime you want. And I can ride away. Anytime I want. You are blind. I have one arm. Every man here carries a hole of some kind in him. Some you can see right away. Some take more looking.

"Life gave us some of those holes from the start. Some we gave to ourselves, one way or the other. But it isn't the weakness that measures a man, it's how he deals with it. You, sir, are a man I respect. And I don't give that easily. Don't make me lose it."

From the opposite side of the camp where he stood guard, Luther shoved the Winchester into its saddle boot and mounted his horse. He spat away the whole chaw in his mouth and kicked it into a lope toward the gathering men. Wiping his lips with his sleeve, he studied the madness in front of him as he advanced. His wrinkled face was a war map of worry. Ethan was standing and yelling. Speakman's words had only lathered his drunkenness into more of a rage.

"Where are you, C-Cole?! Goddammit, c-come here and face me like a man. Can't you stand up to a s-stinking blind man? L-look, I can't see," he roared, and grabbed the bandage from his face, yanking it free.

He held the whiskey bottle in one hand and waved the bandage over his head with the other, like a Comanche warrior celebrating the taking of a scalp. His unseeing eyes stared at the sky. Cole laid down the tin plate he had just selected for supper, spun around, and began walking back toward his brother. Hayden shoved the venison steaks around on the big frying pan, pretending not to watch.

"I am right here, Ethan," Cole said.

"Come on, let's s-see—ha ha ha." Ethan started a challenge and then laughed hysterically at his use of the word "see."

Cole waved the others away, his eyes catching each man's stare and saying more than any words. Speakman stepped back, gingerly crossing behind the log near his feet. So did the fat Ferguson, but he stumbled on the same log and fell flat on the ground, unable to catch himself. Ordinarily this would have been a moment of great laughter, but it was greeted with only a stony silence.

Sotar watched Ferguson fall and looked back at Cole advancing. There was an unnoticed sense of coiling within Sotar. He didn't move, standing next to Ethan. If Cole was aware of the man's symbolic alignment with his brother, it didn't show. The trail boss moved across the flat ground with his hands at his sides, eyes on the drunken Ethan. For the first time, most of the men were aware of the youngest brother's limp. Awakened by the shouting, Dancer came to the campfire and stood behind Sotar. His low whisper was heard only by the lean gunfighter. Sotar's head moved slightly in response.

Attempting to break the tension, DuMonte spoke from the other side of the campfire. "Mr. Kerry, it's been a long day for all us. Why don't—"

"Shut up, DuMonte. I don't need any Bible-thumping from you. Where the hell is my little brother?"

Luther reached the campfire before Cole. He swung down, handed the reins to the sweaty Ferguson, pushed Jip Jersey aside, and, in two bowlegged strides, stood in front of Ethan.

"W-who is this?! G-get out of my way, goddammit!" Ethan said, waving his hands in front of him and brushing against Luther's left arm.

"It'd be me. Luther."

"Luther? What the hell are you doing here? Get out of the way. I've got business with our little brother."

"Naw. Naw, I reckon ya don't."

Ethan opened his mouth to speak, but no words came out. His whiskey-bleary mind tried to understand his brother. But the fire within the blind rancher roared on.

He set his jaw and snarled, "Get out of the way, Luther. This has nothing to do with you."

Pushing out awkwardly with both arms, he caught Luther's chest full force. The oldest Kerry took the blow with a half-step backward, his own arms never raising to deflect Ethan's assault. He caught his balance in time to intercept his youngest brother, placing a firm hand on Cole's shoulder to slow him as he strode toward Ethan.

"Cole. Naw . . . please," Luther grunted; he was close to crying.

Cole didn't look at his oldest brother, grabbing Luther's forearm and shoving it aside without losing a stride. Luther stared at his relieved hand as if it were something separate from his body. His droopy-mustached expression was a pleading one. Cole walked swiftly around him to get to the staggering Ethan. With a hitch of his gunbelt, Cole stopped in front of his blind brother.

"I'm right here, Ethan. What do you want?"

Ethan cocked his head at the sound, trying to locate the person behind the words.

"Thought you'd run away an' hid, boy. Like the time the Indians came to the house when we were kids. Remember? Can you stand up against me, Cole? I'm no lovesick city boy, you know. Just a blind man." Ethan's words split the deathlike stillness of the gathered men.

Cole's response was to step even closer, less than an arm's length from his brother. He reached out and touched Ethan on the right shoulder, and the blind man responded like he had been hit. Behind them, Du-Monte's whispered plea, "Oh Lord, please," rang into the raw air.

"I'm right here, Ethan. Reach out and . . . see for

yourself. You can't miss. You can pull that pistol any-time you want," Cole said calmly.

Ethan's hand straightened slowly and reached Cole's midsection before it was half extended. The blind rancher dropped the whiskey bottle and it exploded at his feet, spraying the remaining liquid on his boots and the ground. The blind rancher's hands shook for an instant before he regained control of his roaring emotions.

Cole watched Ethan's hand withdraw to a position near the gun at his hip and continued. "Nothing to it, Ethan. You draw and I draw. You can't miss. I can't either. That's what you want, isn't it? Both of us will die. Right here. You won't have to be blind anymore. That's what you want, isn't it?"

"You son of a bitch," Ethan snapped, grasping the handle of his Colt.

"Come on, Ethan, bring it to me. Dying's easy. It's living blind that's hard. I don't know what kind of courage that must take. I really don't. But let's get this over with. Winlow can have your ranch—and do with Claire and your kids what he wants. That's their prob-lem. You and me, we won't have to worry about it any longer. Come on, Ethan, pull that iron. I'm ready if you are."

Somewhere a coyote howled, and the lonely sound drove itself deep into the tense camp. Only Luther moved. His eyes blazing with hot tears, he lumbered between his two brothers, surprising both men.

"I gonna die . . . first," he said, his chin up, tears rac-ing down his wrinkled face.

"Get out of the way, Luther," Ethan growled, push-ing unsuccessfully on his oldest brother's chest. "Get out of the wa—"

Ethan's face knotted into white anguish. His hands

came up to hold the bitter torment ripping at his soul.
He leaned over, his body trembling. In the next moment, he was on his knees. Cole looked at Luther, and
the big brother reached out his hand to touch the trail
boss's shoulder. Neither spoke.

A few feet away, Dancer was the first to speak.
"Every man, git. There's chow yonder. Go on, git. This
is over."

Relieved by the suggestion, every man turned away
as the last word echoed across the open bedground.
Except for Sotar. He hesitated, but Dancer encouraged
his leaving too. Sotar muttered something and joined
the others, with Dancer close behind him.

Cole and Luther stood, watching Ethan. Luther put
his hand on Cole's shoulder. Ethan's pained cry tore
into them: "My God, why have you done this to me?
Why?"

Stepping closer to his distraught brother, Cole leaned
down and pulled the pistol from his holster. Ethan
didn't realize it was gone; he was hunched down on
his knees, holding his head with both hands. In a whisper, Cole said, "Keep this—at least for tonight." He
handed Ethan's gun to Luther.

# Chapter Eighteen

An insecure moon struggled with thickening black clouds before surrendering to their swelling appetite. With their dominance came the smell of rain, but it didn't matter. The camp had dropped into welcomed sleep as a refuge from Ethan's drunken madness, except for Cole Kerry and the nighthawks. Sleep would not come to the young gunfighter as the senseless fury of his brother's rage festered within him.

He couldn't let go of Ethan's bitterness and the desire to ride away from it. He owed them nothing, he kept telling himself. Nothing. They could find their way to Dodge City without him, he told himself. Luther knew the way; so did Dancer. They could make it if he left, and maybe Ethan would feel better too. If Winlow attacked, so be it; everyone had to fight sometime. Or run.

Ethan's whiskey-driven words brought Kathleen's bitter farewell to Cole's mind, and it clung there like rancid moss. He could see her face like it belonged to a stranger. She told him again that she was going to marry Webster Stevenson and that she couldn't see him anymore.

"Cole, I have something . . . to tell you." Kathleen bit her lower lip to keep it from trembling. She looked down as if to gain courage, then lifted her head, holding her chin high. "I—I c-cannot see you again. I—I'm going to marry W-Webster Stevenson."

Cole was stunned. His first reaction was an awkward grin, as he waited for her to smile and laugh at the joke. He knew she cared nothing about the boorish young man, whose father's wealth was the son's only claim to achievement. Neither smile nor laugh nor chuckle came. He tried to say something. Anything. But there came no sound from his throat. Silence was a growing wall separating him from the woman he loved. How could this be? He stared at her in disbelief, like she had cut out his heart and held it in her hands. Tears breaking over her face, she reached out for him, but he turned and walked away. He never saw her again.

After packing his few things, he saddled his horse to leave town and stepped into the closest saloon to swallow enough whiskey to obliterate the pain in his soul. He wore his two-gun belt, against the town ordinance, and declined to give them to the bartender, stating he only intended to stay for a drink. He could think of no reason to remain in Abilene. A half hour later, Webster Stevenson, red-faced and angry, entered with two friends, both eager to fight. Sinister smiles signaled their collective intent.

"Cole Kerry, you're not welcome in Abilene anymore."

As Cole turned toward Webster's challenge, the senior Stevenson stepped behind the threesome. His folded arms matched furrowed brows in a practiced intensity. Cole hadn't met either Stevenson, but he knew who they were. Everyone in town did. Vincent Stevenson was a handsome, arrogant, and powerful man who expected his words to be followed without question. The son had the arrogrance, but this was an empty posture with nothing to back it up except his father's accomplishments. Physically, the only similarity was their tall stature: Webster's face was puffy and ruddy; his father's was chiseled and hard. Vincent Stevenson smiled his approval at his son's declaration.

"You got what you wanted, Stevenson, let it alone. I'll ride on when I'm good and ready. Don't be a fool and push it," Cole spat, and returned his attention to the bar and the bottle waiting to help him.

"He's mocking you, Webster," Vincent Stevenson growled under his breath. "I want him begging—an' bleeding."

Webster felt the shove of his father's hands against his back. He glanced at both friends for reassurance, grinned awkwardly, and walked across the open saloon floor toward Cole. The saloon became smaller; patrons stopped drinking, gambling, and talking to watch. The fat-bellied farmer standing next to Cole eyed him nervously, picked up his own bottle and partially filled glass, and shuffled to the far end of the bar.

"You're gonna be sorry you ever met Kathleen Shannon," Webster screamed. His pulpy face was alive with twitching eyebrows and whiskey-enhanced eyes. This wasn't his idea; he looked over his shoulder at his father, who sneered his encouragement.

After emptying his whiskey glass, Cole nodded at the frightened farmer and turned back around to face his closing adversaries. He should have been scared;

instead, he was annoyed. He stared at the elder Stevenson standing at the wall closest to the door. With no sign of emotion, Cole said, "Better take your boy and his playmates home, Stevenson. I'm in no mood to play."

Vincent didn't like the attention and looked away. At that moment, Webster rushed forward and swung at Cole's head. The outlaw parried the wild blow and drove a vicious left jab into Webster's stomach. The young townsman groaned and doubled over. Cole ducked the first friend's immediate roundhouse punch and sent him crashing into a poker table with a jolting right uppercut. Cards and money danced in the air, and players cursed. The second friend hesitated, then pulled a pistol and fired twice. The first shot slammed into the unpainted wall, and the second hit Cole in the lower leg. He crumpled and drew a pistol as his knees hit the floor. He fired as the shock of his wound tried to take control of his body. The second friend spun backward, grasping a bloody chest.

Out of the corner of his eye, Cole saw Webster yank a pistol from under his coat. Webster's first shot ripped along the top of Cole's right shoulder, bringing a crimson line where it passed and severing the cloth. From the same kneeling position Cole fired once more. Webster slumped against the bar and gurgled blood. His eyes fluttered and stared without seeing. He was dead; Cole's shot had ripped through his heart. Cole struggled to stand. His lower leg and boot were red. Vincent Stevenson had vanished.

He jerked upright to remove the terrible memory; she had no right to stay with him this way. It wasn't his fault she didn't get what she wanted: Webster Stevenson—and his money. Had he fired to kill because of who his adversary was? That question had lingered close to his conscious mind since the gunfight. Yet he knew he hadn't. He hadn't started the fight, hadn't gone looking for trouble. He had just ended it. He left town shortly after that, fighting consciousness from the loss of blood and the shock of his wounds. Minutes ahead of the father's paid posse.

Laying back down, his tense mind dragged him again to his crazy death challenge to Ethan, then to long-ago days when he idolized him, on to the terrible emptiness his brother must feel, to the gnawing threat of Winlow somewhere ahead. A stream of disjointed memories pushed him into the black hole of an outlaw trail that had been his recent life—and finally once more to Kathleen. He reached over to find his unfinished letter to her and held it. This time he didn't resist her entry into his being but welcomed it. He shut his eyes and breathed deeply, reclaiming the delicious smell that was her body. A clean sweetness softened the night and let his feverish mind release him to sleep. A fat drop of rain spattered against his cheek. He made no attempt to alter its slide across his face. Another followed.

"Mr. Kerry. Mr. Kerry! The herd's moving!" Stovepipe yelled above the heavy rain.

Cole awoke from a dream, shaking his head to leave behind Kathleen making love to him. It was 2:30 A.M. and the night was soaking black. Groggily, Cole grabbed the slicker that was spread over his bedroll to keep it as dry as possible and put it on. He had never undressed, not even his boots. He rarely did anymore. A light drizzle had begun before he went to bed and had grown nasty. Steers never settle down in this kind of weather. Cole wasn't surprised the herd decided to keep moving, just disappointed that his dream was interrupted and he was returned to the reality of his brother's hatred.

"Get everyone up, Stovepipe. We've got a long night ahead of us."

"Yes, boss, I'll git ri't to it. Most of 'em are."

Cole quickly folded his bedding, carried it to the chuck wagon, and tossed the damp blankets inside. He woke Hayden, sleeping under the wagon, and told him to get ready to move out.

"What the hell we doing? It's the middle of the night!" Hayden sputtered, more asleep than awake. His brain suddenly recognized whom he had just yelled at.

Hayden coughed and said, "M-Mr. Kerry, sir, should I make some coffee for the men, sir?"

Cole squatted beside the wagon and growled, "If you can find a way to do it, get at it. If you can't, get packed. We've got a herd to catch."

Returning to his shortened sleeping spot, Cole mounted his best night horse, a steady bay called Hawk. Already saddled and bridled as usual each evening, the horse was ground-reined to a log not far from his bed. The camp was a murmur of muttering, jingling spurs, sloshing boots, snorting horses, and bellowing cattle as the skies continued to empty themselves. Somewhere close, he could hear Old Ben Speakman rattling on about a rainstorm he had been in that had gone on forever. Then he heard DuMonte call him "Noah" and laugh.

Cole couldn't see the jagged hills that bordered to the west, or the creek fifty feet to the south. He could barely make out the faces of the soaked drovers wearily retaking control of the herd as they shook off their own dreams. He was loping toward the front of the heard when he remembered Ethan. Was his brother awake? Had anyone checked on him? Surely Hayden would, or DuMonte. His conscience wouldn't let him go further, so he spun the bay around and headed back into the breaking camp. He heard Ethan before he saw him.

"Why the hell didn't we have more men mounted before this?" Ethan challenged Hayden, who was tossing cooking gear into the back of the wagon as fast as he could reach the pots, pans, plates, and utensils.

"Where the hell are we headed? Does anybody know?!" Ethan yelled again. "Where's my damn brother? Is he still asleep? Wake him up, Hayden, I want to know where we're going, goddammit."

Exasperated, the cook stood up with an armful of plates and said, "Mr. Kerry, your brother rode out of here twenty minutes ago. I imagine he's at the head of the herd. It looks like they're headed north—where the trail is."

There was silence, then Ethan muttered, "Well, by God, that's where he should be. Don't leave anything behind now. We can't go trailing stuff behind us across the Nations. Did you get the coffee grinder? Don't forget the coffeepot. How about the cups? Luther has a way of leaving 'em everywhere. Can you see where he slept? Any of the food get wet? I hope not. We haven't got food to waste, you know."

Hayden frowned and continued loading without responding. Cole watched for a few seconds longer, then returned to the herd. The night would be long enough without carrying more of Ethan's anger with him.

The first rider he passed was Loop. The young cowboy's face was utter despair. Cole reined his horse until Loop was alongside him.

"What's the matter, Loop? They'll be all right. They don't liking sleeping where it's wet any more than we do."

"Yessiree, Mr. Kerry. It's not that. I don't mind riding all night. Not one bit," Loop said from under a soggy hat with streams of water pouring over the wide brim.

"But what?"

"Well, sir, I—I couldn't find my boot, Mr. Kerry."

Cole looked down and saw that the young rider's right foot was bare; his sock was covered with black mud.

"Where'd you lose it, Loop?"

"I—I—I couldn't find it . . . when I got up. Didn't want to leave the herd—"

"You go back, Loop. Take all the time you need. You're going to need that boot. I'll cover your place until you get back."

"Would you . . . I mean, could . . . Thanks you, Mr. Kerry. I'll sure hurry along. I figure it's right around my sleepin' place."

"I'm sure it is. Now, get." Shaking his head, Cole watched the young rider gallop back toward the empty camp.

Gradually, a new day wrung out the rain clouds about the time Loop returned with both boots. Cole switched to Kiowa, and the big red horse was eager to run. In swift strides, they returned to the front of the herd. In contrast, men and animals slugged forward, paying no attention to the lessening moisture as the first streaks of dawn sought them from the east. At the front of the herd, Cole Kerry rode through memories of Kathleen like it was a fresh-bleeding wound. But the steady clop-clop-clop of his horse's hooves brought him around to the broken hills they were moving through. He felt his back pocket, and his half-written letter to her was gone. Gone! In the night's fury, he had dropped it. *Just as well*, he told himself. His new mistress was the trail drive, and she was a demanding one.

He looked back at the herd stretching out behind him for miles. Bobbing heads told the story of half-sleeping men in the saddle. Cole was proud of the men. Breakfast was a cold can of tomatoes eaten in the saddle. No one had griped. Maybe Oleen had complained to Loop, but not that anyone else heard. They just kept switching wet saddles onto new drenched horses and stayed with the moving mass of steers. The late-morning sun was drying the uneven land fast. Glistening buffalo grass stretched upward to meet the warmth. His stomach asked if he had forgotten about it. Waving his arm, he caught Abe's attention and the half-breed galloped forward.

"Mornin', Abe. Ride ahead and see if there is a good spot to curl the herd. Everybody needs rest," Cole said.

"So be it, Cole Ker-rie. Damn," Abe responded, laid his quirt alongside the horse's withers, and thundered toward the green ridges ahead.

Cole watched him disappear over the hillside and gradually let his mind return to Kathleen. He didn't resist it; he encouraged it. Her skin was luminescent in the soft moonlight of yesterday. Her body was ecstasy against his. Time passed without his being aware of it, lost in her love. Fifty yards ahead was a long row of elderberry bushes with a tight battalion of cedars and oak trees stationed to the rear.

Sunlight danced off something in the underbrush, then was gone so quickly the mind wanted to reject the occurrence at all. It interrupted his wonderful daydream. But Cole's instincts knew instantly what the glitter meant. Someone was waiting to open fire as they rode past, or maybe just waiting to pick him off. How many? The underbrush was too thick to make out anything. Cole had spurred Kiowa into a run before he acknowledged to himself it would be good to know the answer. He always preferred charging, and now was no exception. If too many ambushers were there, at least his men would have a chance to save themselves and the herd.

Closing to within twenty yards from the reflection point, he hoped whoever was there would hold their fire, thinking the trail boss was simply trying to catch up with his scout. He aimed the big sorrel in a parallel line, fifty feet from the bushes, and slid to the far side of Kiowa. Pulling a pistol as he moved, he extended his body forward to let him fire underneath Kiowa's neck. His left hand held the reins and kept him balanced with a fistful of mane. In a passing thought he wondered what the red horse would do when he fired.

Wham! Wham! Wham! Wham! He fired into the blurred underbrush as fast as he could hammer the gun. Kiowa jerked his head upward but didn't break stride. Within the bushes, a grunt and a scream trailed his charge. His two additional shots whistled through the trees. A dozen yards past the area, he pulled the big horse to a hard stop and spun around, reholstered his first gun, and drew the second. Rifle bullets cut the sky around him as he charged back. This time he slid his body to the other side of the horse, his right fist holding the mane and reins and his face and shoulder extending beyond Kiowa's chest. Wild-eyed and sweating, the red horse thundered toward the bushwhackers. Cole fired twice into the same area with his pistol in his left hand. He wasn't as good with his left hand, but it would have to do. A man stood, his face covered in blood, and attempted to aim a rifle that wouldn't stop shaking. He shriveled into the underbrush and disappeared.

A hesitation later, a lone shot sliced the edge of

Cole's exposed right arm. The instant numbness forced his right hand to release control, and he fell from the thundering horse. Another bullet danced next to his body as he thudded to the ground. His gun jumped out of his hand and his head crashed against the prairie. Kiowa raced toward the herd, stirrups swinging in a jerky waltz, as DuMonte and Dancer galloped toward the downed trail boss. Behind them came a hurrying Luther. DuMonte's Winchester was in his hands; Dancer touched the medicine pouch at his neck and pulled his black-handled Colt.

In the front of the herd, steers bawled with interest in the new noises but were too tired to respond aggressively to the gunfire. Two flank riders moved flawlessly to the front of the herd and brought it to a stop. As if nothing was wrong, most of the steers began to graze. The lead steer, Whistler, surveyed the land ahead, determined the sound was not worthy of more inspection, and joined the eating.

Both DuMonte and Dancer wheeled into the underbrush, ready to fire, and saw two unmoving bodies. They heard a galloping horse but couldn't see through the trees. Dancer rode forward to check further, while DuMonte returned to the downed trail boss as Luther reined in his horse beside him. Dazed, Cole looked up to see a worried Luther kneeling beside him. DuMonte remained in the saddle and waved the herd on.

"Wal, I seed the youngest Kerry ain't changed much. You all right, little brother? I don't spot no blood, 'ceptin' on your arm h'yar," Luther reported, his half-wrinkled face stern with more concern than his words indicated. He rolled back Cole's sleeve to inspect the flesh wound.

"Huh? Oh, yeah. Ohhh, that stings, dammit," Cole

responded, and tried to bend his right arm. His brain brought back the reason for the pain.

"Hey, where are those bastards? Did—"

"You cut down two, and the other jaybirds is a-runnin' so fast they's prob'ly outta the Nations by now. I reckon ya saved a lot o' Bar K boys from bein' shot plumb outta the saddle."

Dancer returned, dismounted, and reported that the others had escaped. He recognized one of the dead ambushers.

"I don't know the other fella, but the short one was Pete Dykes, from over San Antonio way. Never thought of him being much of a cow-man. Mostly sold his gun," Dancer advised. "Reckon he won't be selling it no more. He's deader 'n a doornail."

From his saddle, DuMonte grunted, "Winlow. Lord save us from the valley of death."

"Yeah, I reckon," Dancer agreed. "How'd you see those bastards anyway, hunkered down in that brush?"

"I saw . . . a gun barrel . . . reflection. Knew it wasn't rabbits," Cole answered, his mind dragging from the fall.

Luther spat and said, "Course, it never occured to this hyar hard head o' yurn that thar mighta bin an army a-waitin'. Hellfire, we'd better git some kerosene on that—"

Cole interrupted. "I'm all right. Abe should be back soon. I want us to stop as quick as we can. The men are worn out and the cattle are ready."

"Don't suppose you'll get much of an argument out of anyone on that idea, Mr. Kerry." DuMonte grinned. "My stomach is snapping at me something fierce. Praise the Lord for some hot chuck."

"Anybody see Kiowa?" Cole remembered, and asked without responding to DuMonte's comment.

"Yeah. Saw that red devil a-comin' at us like a bad dream. Didn't wait to ketch 'em, though," Luther said, and spat a fresh stream of tobacco juice. "Sumbody'll git 'im if'n he don't run all the way back to Texas. I'll go an' git yur black fer ya. I reckon as how ya kin still ride."

Luther was halfway mounted when Dancer pointed toward the returning half-breed. After being told what happened and being assured his boss was all right, Abe reported what Cole had hoped to find. Their destination would be an open grassland less than a mile away. It was off the regular trail, and that appealed to Cole as well. The grass was high and thick, with a fat pond just to the south of them, according to Abe's sign language. The half-breed said no herd had been there in a long time.

"Pass the word, boys. We're stopping there," Cole said with a tired smile. "We'll count the herd to make sure nothing strayed."

"Damn, Cole Ker-rie, the men will sing," Abe said, paused, studied the dead bodies, and added, "Son of bitch. Cole Ker-rie great warrior."

Dancer galloped along the herd, telling the good news to each rider down the left side as well as what had happened. DuMonte took the other side and told the rest of the men. Luther returned with Kiowa; Jip had grabbed its reins when the sorrel slowed down. Cole remounted and took the lead. Returning to the remuda, Luther passed the chuck wagon and yelled the news about stopping.

Ethan's face became crimson, and he blurted, "What are we stopping for, Luther?! We've still got a hellva long way to go. This isn't some Sunday-go-to-meeting."

" 'Cuz we all bin a-ridin' the whole soak-assed

night, that's why, Mr. Kerry. Judas priest, our tails are draggin' an' so's our beef. You know'd better'n that. See fer yur—" Luther growled back, stopping at his unfortunate suggestion.

Ethan folded his arms and said, "What was all the gunfire about? I'd think somebody'd be smarter than that by now. We could've had beef everywhere."

"Your brother dun kicked up some Winlow boys a-waitin' to cut us down. Nailed two o' 'em. By hisse'f. The other'n lit out for safer country. Reckon he saved us from a bunch o' empty saddles. Or worse. Never seed the like. That boy'd charge hell with a glass o' water, drink it, and keep a-goin'."

"He should've thought about the herd."

"Aw, them beeves never paid no never mind. They's plumb wore out from galivantin' all night long."

Ethan was silent.

Tentatively, J. L. Hayden asked, "Ah, shall I move out, Mr. Kerry?"

"Well, hell yes, Hayden. You got gut-hungry riders, man. Don't you know that? Do I have to make every goddamn decision on this drive? Get the hell in front so you can get at breakfast."

"Yessir," Hayden answered, and shrugged his shoulders to Luther, who shook his head. The cook swung the wagon wide of the herd and popped the reins to get the horses into a trot.

"Luther," Ethan bellowed. "You make damn sure the herd is counted. We could lose a bunch after a night like this."

Luther listened and shook his head. "Yeah. Cole's dun already settin' it up."

"Well, it's about time he got ahead of something on this drive." Ethan's face was hard.

Luther stared at his brother and then rode away silently.

238

# Chapter Nineteen

After a hot breakfast and a nap, Cole Kerry went to Luther to determine the status of their horses. His arm was stiff but otherwise unhurt. His dreaming had been fitful, a swirl of images that made no sense, of his being blind, of Ethan taking Kathleen from him, of a shoot-out with a gunfighter with no face. The afternoon sun was as hot as the night had been wet, but the herd grazed quietly, enjoying their new bedground.

From his position watching the steers, Loop waved and Cole waved back. Luther was shoeing a bay, using his weight to keep the animal off balance as he worked with its right hind hoof. He finished with a last bang of his hammer and let the leg go slowly through his hand. The big man patted the horse on the rump as Cole approached. Luther's eyes were happy to see his brother.

"How ya doin', boss? How's that shootin' arm, stiff as a board?" Luther asked with a twinkle in his eyes.

"Oh, it's fine. How about yourself?"

"Hellfire, I jes' woke up. Yessiree, jes' did. Gittin' too old fer that all night crap. Ever'thing I own is wet as hell too."

"We didn't lose any beef. What about horses?"

"Yeah, we dun lost one."

"What happened?"

"Ferguson's brown. Dun went into a prairie dog hole an' snapped its leg like a stick. Sorry thing to see."

"Is Ferguson all right? I didn't see him at breafast?"

"Oh, he's a mite skinned up. But he never were no handsome fool anyways. I kilt the brown. Back thar," Luther continued, and swung his arm in the direction of where they had come. Cole looked and saw the tiny, dark shapes of buzzards circling against the light blue sky.

"I didn't hear any shot."

"Used my knife. Didn't want to risk spookin' the beeves. 'Sides, you dun all the shootin' we needed fer the day."

As they talked, Cole looked over the remuda and spotted Kiowa. The big sorrel was unsaddled but wet. Without turning to see for himself what his brother was looking at, Luther said, "That red hoss is a good 'un."

"Yeah, sometimes," Cole responded absentmindedly. "I probably should've shot him after he blinded Ethan—and kept riding."

Cole paused and looked at his oldest brother, wondering if a lecture was coming next. Luther's eyes were welling with tears.

"Little brother, ya mustn't hate Ethan. He . . . he . . . he be a-fightin' the devil. Inside hisse'f. It is not you. It's darkness he dun be a-fightin'. Chewed on it all night. Dun counted them raindrops like a greenhorn a'fur gittin' my ass up."

"Yeah, me too. Maybe I should ride on. Maybe that would make things better. You can get there without me now."

" 'Bout like askin' us to all step into quicksand. Thar's no way we're gonna git to Dodge without you a-leadin' us, Cole." Luther's face was a tortured squint.

Cole wasn't interested in hearing more, started to change the subject and ask about tomorrow's river crossing, when a call came out from the north end of camp. It was Speakman yelling.

"Indians! Indians coming."

"Probably a Cherokee Light Horse patrol, come for a toll on our crossing," Cole guessed.

"Yeah, last year them Injun police stopped us an' wanted a whole ten cents fer each damn head. Kin you beat that? Ten cents a beef. But Ethan, he dun paid up. Gave 'em a steer to boot."

Riding slowly toward the Bar K herd over a slanted hill, bristling with trees, were fourteen painted warriors on ponies decorated for war. As they moved into the sunlight, it was readily apparent they weren't Cherokee mounted police.

Luther spat and growled, "Kiowa. Sons of bitches look like they's fancyin' fer a fight. What do ya think, Cole?"

"Don't know. See if you can find Abe—or Dancer, will you? Tell them to join me. Quick."

"I reckon Dancer kin speak sum ri't smart Kiowa. Dun heard him a time or two. Don't know 'bout Abe. Injun's a Injun, I reckon."

"Get the men ready. Spread out. But no shooting—until I do."

"Wal, you keep them fine Colts handy. Them blood-thirsty Kiowa are likely to do most anythin'. Kin ya use yur shootin' arm?"

"It'll be all right," Cole said, immediately flexing his right arm to relieve the stiffness. Luther observed the exercise without commenting. Both men went purposefully in opposite directions: Cole with a confident stride toward the arriving war party, and Luther, as fast as his bowlegs would waddle, to find the two riders.

As Cole passed DuMonte, the black cowboy suggested, "Mr. Kerry, they need to hear the word of the Lord."

The trail boss glanced at him and kept walking. He loosened the thong protecting the hammer of his sidewinder-holstered Colt and answered, "I've got the word of the Lord, right here, if they want it."

The war party rode slowly with their right hands held high as a greeting of friendship. Their faces and chests carried patterns of colored paint. Each warrior had cut his hair on the right side of his head to display bone and silver earrings, the traditional hairstyling of a Kiowa warrior. The rest of their hair was long, braided, and wrapped with fur skins. A small scalp lock hung down the left side of each warrior's head. Pendants of red, yellow, and green flew from leather thongs around their braided hair. Some were further accented with small silver disks attached to the braids.

Eagle feathers were stuck in their scalp locks, except for one warrior who was wearing a broad-brimmed white hat, evidently a trophy from a recent raid somewhere. Another wore a full feathered headress, but he didn't appear to be the leader, just an honored warrior showing off his coups. Three wore long-sleeved buckskin warshirts; another four wore bone breastplates over bare chests; two wore white people's shirts and one was in a woman's blue gingham dress; the rest wore only breechcloths.

At least half were carrying rifles, a mixture of Springfields and Spencers; the rest held bows and arrows and lances shortened for use on horseback. Cole could also see a few revolvers shoved into leather waistbands. Dried scalps dangled from rawhide shields, thong bridles, and lances. *These boys have been busy*, Cole thought as he approached, working his right arm to return its mobility. His limp, from the soreness of his earlier spill, was again pronounced.

The Indians waited on their ponies as Cole Kerry came toward them. Behind him were the sounds of men retrieving rifles from the chuck wagon and selecting firing positions. He stopped in front of the warrior who appeared to be the leader and raised his right hand in welcome. The handsome-featured man sat on a steel-gray horse, painted with the record of successful battles as well as spirit medicine. He wore the head of a wolf as a headdress, with its dark skin draping across his shoulders and back. A magnificent warshirt was beaded in yellows, blues, and whites and accented with scalp locks. His face was slashed with a wide band of black paint from his hairline to his chin and across his right eye.

"Hau!" The confident war chief followed his greeting with a longer one in Kiowan. The trail boss couldn't follow the nasal, choked-off words but understood the supporting sign language. He was being told the Bar K was riding through Kiowa land and must pay to pass. The war chief stated, making grand flourishes with his hands, that Cole and his men were responsible for the killing of the buffalo and for violating the treaties signed by the Great White Father.

For this, he demanded one hundred head of cattle as payment. He claimed to be speaking for Dohasan, the greatest of Kiowa war chiefs, and added that his warriors were the Taupeko, the Crazy Horses, an important warrior society. His meaning was clear. This war party was one of seasoned warriors. By the time the warrior finished his demands, Abe was standing on one side of Cole and Dancer on the other. The half-breed grumbled under his breath, *"Sica sunka!"* Cole recognized the Lakotan phrase for "bad dogs."

A sullen warrior pushed his horse forward alongside his leader and gave a belated introduction of the war chief who had just spoken. The warrior said his leader's name was Black Wolf. *Guikongya.* The spirit of his ancestor, by the same name, gave him invincibility against the *taibos*, white men. Black Wolf was also a respected Keeper of the Ten Grandmothers medicine bundles and could not be killed. After completing his introduction, the warrior reined his horse back to its earlier position behind Black Wolf.

Cole turned to Abe and said, "Tell him that we don't agree with what he says—and that we don't intend to pay him any cattle. But don't insult him."

Abe said he didn't speak the Kiowa language; Dancer asserted that he did, but Black Wolf didn't wait for the interpretation and challenged, "Me know English. We run away white man's cows."

Cole looked him hard in the eyes and said flatly, "If you try it, you die." His words were supported by his own sign language. The other warriors grunted and muttered to each other. One held high a coups stick in reaction.

Raising himself to his full height, the war chief declared, "We die as warriors, not as hungry women and children. You die with us."

Cole answered, "No. You will die as thieves. Not as warriors. At the end of a rope." His sign language supplemented the declaration. "You will hang first."

The war chief winced and said, "Black Wolf has more warriors."

Not waiting for Dancer to help him, Cole answered in English and sign language that his men could handle three times as many and already had done so. Dancer's eyes widened, and Abe exclaimed, "Son of bitch. Damn."

Dancer took two steps, faced Cole with his back to the war party, and whispered, "How about giving him a gift, boss? One warrior to another. No payment. No nothing. But a gift, that's different. That's respect."

"Good idea."

Dancer stepped aside, and Cole proceeded. In English and with sign language, Cole offered Black Wolf a gift of friendship, proven warrior to proven warrior. The gift would be six steers, a sack of sugar, some tobacco, and a jar of molasses. Cole asked Abe and Dancer to find Luther and retrieve the beef and other items. Abe left immediately, glad to be away from the Kiowas.

Before Dancer headed back, he said proudly to the war chief in a stilted Kiowa dialect, "I am blood brother to Wind Hawk. He is shaman. Do you know him?" He held out the small medicine pouch worn around his neck.

Black Wolf listened and spat toward the ground. "Wind Hawk is old woman. I spit on his coward ways."

Dancer stood for a moment, absorbing the sarcastic response. His eyes averted to the tiny pouch at his neck and his hands slowly rose to touch it. After the brief tribute, Dancer's flushed face bounced upward to meet the glare of the haughty war chief. The point rider's eyes were transformed from embarrassment to challenge.

Folding his arms in front of him, Dancer snarled in

Kiowa, "Wind Hawk's medicine is strong. I cannot be killed. Black Wolf knows nothing, it is clear. Here he stands as a child before a real warrior, Cole Kerry, and knows it not. See his arm? He kills two today who would take from us. Two with far stronger medicine than Black Wolf.

"With him rides his brother, a powerful shaman who sees not in this land but only in the spirit world. Beware, Black Wolf, your coming was foretold by him."

Cole observed Dancer's long-winded speech in admiration. He had no idea what was said, but the war chief's face changing from purple to white told him it wasn't about picnicking.

To complete his presentation, Dancer faced the trail boss again, bowed ceremoniously, and whispered, "I told him you hung the moon—and that Ethan was a medicine man, able to see in the spirit world but not here."

"All right, what do I do now?"

"Nothing. Let's see what he does. I'll go help with the stuff."

"What if he wants to see Ethan?"

"Hadn't thought of that."

"Great."

Dancer chuckled and walked away. Black Wolf stared at Cole Kerry with admiration in his hard eyes, and a touch of fear, then smiled.

"Black Wolf has gift for great warrior . . . friend . . . Coal-ee Care-rie."

With that pronouncement, he leaned back and told the closest warrior to dismount. With no expression, the warrior jumped down from his gleaming black horse, walked forward, and handed the braided reins to Cole. The trail boss nodded his thanks.

The war chief asked if he could see the "shaman who

sees only in the spirit world." Cole said the medicine man was currently in the spirit world. Black Wolf was disappointed but dared not to say so. Cole saw questioning in the war leader's eyes, but it quickly passed. From the chuck wagon came Abe, carrying a sack of sugar and a small jar of molasses. In response to Abe's news, Luther and Jip Jersey were pushing six steers toward the war party. Dancer was a few steps behind the half-breed, carrying a small sack of tobacco in his outstretched arms like it was a treasure.

Curious, Oleen peeked out from behind the calf wagon and asked, "Vat are you doing, Dancer? Vhen are ve going to shoot, by Jiminy? Red heathens, they are."

"Shut up, Oleen. Everything is going to be fine if you don't do something stupid like you did at the Red."

The Swede gasped and responded sarcastically, but Dancer was already past and concentrating on his performance. Staggering from behind the chuck wagon, Ethan Kerry wandered into Dancer's path and onto the path of the steers. He had just awakened. His hair was wildly swirled from sleeping, his face drawn with the retreat of whiskey from his body. Dancer went around him without missing a step, and decided to run back to Cole, passing the surprised Abe. The half-breed wasn't certain if he should run too, and began a jerky jog toward the war party.

Ferociously, Ethan shouted, "Where are those bloody redskins?! I'll kill the bastards. They can't have any of my beef!"

Luther and Jip Jersey reined their horses to avoid running into the gyrating blind rancher. Ethan's hand accidentally slapped the neck of Luther's horse, surprising the animal as well as Ethan, who didn't know anyone was close. Startled, the horse sidestepped, and Luther cursed.

He yanked the horse under control and leaned over toward Ethan and said, "Ethan, by God, we dun got this'n handled. You're lookin' like a liquored-up fool."

"What!" Ethan yelled, his voice hoarse with strain. "What did you say?"

"Ethan, you know'd damn well what I jes' said—an' I ain't whistlin' in no wind. Git back."

"You're . . . you're fired. Goddammit, you're fired, Luther!" Ethan screamed as loud as he could, waving his arms like he was batting away a horde of bees.

Calmly, Luther looked at the stuttering cowboy and said, "Come on, Jip, we'uns got some beeves to deliver." He touched his spurs to his horse and moved out. Dancer followed.

Ethan continued his ranting. "Goddamn you, Luther, you come back! Don't you go giving away my beef to any godforsaken redskin!"

He pulled his pistol from the holster that had slid to the front of his belt and raised it in the direction of the two riders. His thumb dragged across the hammer but didn't pull it back. His chin fell to his chest as his gun hand lowered to his side. The gun thudded on the ground.

Squinting to hold back tears, he cried out, "Hayden, get over here! Bring me my bottle."

Cole watched the encounter as he waited for the men to return with the gifts and saw Ethan's gyrations. Almost out of breath, Dancer arrived with the tobacco sack and handed it ceremoniously to Cole. Behind them came Abe with the sugar and molasses, followed by Luther and Jip pushing along the steers.

With concern in his voice, Black Wolf asked, "That no-see shaman?"

Cole took the gift, winked at Dancer, and said loudly, "Yes. He is the . . . ah, medicine man who sees only in the spirit world. He has just come back—from there—and he's angry that he can't see in this world. He blames you. I will tell him you are not to blame."

Cole turned toward the chuck wagon and yelled in a singsong voice, "This is Black Hawk. He is not to blame for your not seeing in this world. Do not send the spirits after him."

Dancer got the hint and repeated the message in Kiowan, reinforcing it with sign. The Kiowa war chief frowned, turned to his warriors, and explained what Cole had said. A murmur of concern passed through them.

Without waiting for a response, Dancer yelled to him in Kiowan, "Get back, your medicine is not right! The shaman brings bad spirits! See them coming!"

"Aiiee!" exclaimed Black Hawk, and swung his horse around and kicked it into a gallop. The rest of the war party wheeled their horses in a hurried retreat. The Bar K men watched as the war party disappeared over the ridge and began whooping in celebration. Nodding his head in agreement, Luther said he would ride out to make certain they did leave and congratulated Cole on not having to give any cattle away.

Cole examined the gift horse, handed the reins to Dancer, and said, "That was Dancer's doing, not mine. Here, this is yours. Too bad it isn't a buckskin. You saved us cattle—and scalps. Thank you, Jared. That was mighty smart thinking."

Blushing, the point rider took the horse, his eyes bright with recognition, and explained, "Had a hunch, that's all. Glad I could help. Reckon I'd better thank the Kiowa spirits real good tonight."

"I think you should," Cole replied, patting him on the back.

# *Chapter Twenty*

A month passed, and more, with each day thickening the wall between Ethan and Cole Kerry. The young trail boss no longer sought Ethan's advice, and the blind rancher didn't offer any. A sullen Ethan Kerry rode in the chuck wagon, rarely speaking to anyone— and only harshly when he did.

Ethan's horrifying performance at the Red River camp had been repeated by every man so often that it was no longer worth talking about. So had Cole's shoot-out with the Winlow men. Every rider had his theory about Cole Kerry's past, and no one wanted to ask the trail boss about it. A few stories, real or imagined, were surfacing about his ability with a gun. Only John David Sotar questioned the likelihood of their being true.

The chill between the two brothers was apparent, even to the vague Ferguson and the immature Loop. Across the wild territory, days and nights had become a long rope of tension, growing tighter with each sunup. Ethan wasn't eating much but drank often from a bottle that no one could take from him. Not even Luther. Ethan's sleep usually came only after the alcohol had stolen his consciousness. Even the gentle DuMonte finally refused to write his drunken ramblings—mostly about Cole's ineptness—in the diary for him.

Ethan told the Bible-reading cowboy that he was fired, but DuMonte had ignored the tirade. Ethan had forced Hayden to take up the task; the rancher didn't realize Hayden couldn't read or write, and the cook was afraid to tell him. Watching the dour Hayden sit next to Ethan in the evenings, making nonsensical marks on the diary's pages as the rancher rambled on and on, provided comic relief from a sad situation.

At least there had been no sign of Winlow's men since the attempted ambush at the Red. Working with Ethan's old diary, Luther's memory, and Cole's overall sense of the region, the Bar K riders had worked their way through the Nations. They had crossed the Washita, Canadian, and the North Canadian. Even so, they geared themselves for a possible attack with each crossing. The threat wore hard on the men. Worrying about Indians, the river crossings, and the weather was enough without the burden of Sam Winlow men lurking somewhere, but Cole Kerry kept them moving.

Abe had spotted a band of Kiowa crossing their trail two miles ahead, but nothing ever came of it. He had also discovered an isolated farm, and that turned out well. Cheerfully, the farmer traded them eggs for a night of cow chips in his pasture from bedding the herd there. The eggs were a tremendous treat. They also left him a young calf in exchange for a sack of dried apples, another of corn, and three apple pies his wife had just baked.

The men ate well, but their full stomachs couldn't take away any their concern about the growing lack of water. Since the storm, the land had become parched and cracked. The closer the drive got to the Cimarron River, the drier the land became. Grass was losing the battle with a relentless sun and no rain. In some places, wide patches were crisp and brown. Day after day, the hot sun pressured the earth to give up its remaining moisture. Day after day, water holes that should have been adequate were little more than brackish mud. Banks of one larger pond had been torn apart to let the precious water seep away into the cracks in the land. Everyone knew it was Winlow's doing. Cole, Du-Monte, Abe, and Dancer were riding almost around the clock to seek out bedgrounds with some kind of water.

After one such fruitless scouting effort, Old Ben Speakman told Cole and Luther a long story about how they could find water by watching swallows carry mud for nest building in their mouths. With great pride, he pointed out that a water hole lay in the direction the birds came from. Luther told him the only problem was that they hadn't seen a swallow in two weeks. The Rebel veteran agreed that would create a flaw in his plan.

Ethan's only contribution during this stretch was to complain that the herd would "soon be as blind as I am," referring to a common, but temporary, condition among thirst-starved cattle. His remarks were directed at Luther, the only rider he talked with anymore, except for occasional demands for details from Hayden. Luther reminded him that they were traveling later than they ever had, and everyone knew that would mean dry spells. Ethan hadn't liked the response.

So far their intensified effort had produced results and the herd was kept more or less satisfied with water, even though it had usually meant going far off the trail to get it. Last night's bedground was typical. Two miles west of the main trail, it hadn't been grazed recently. It was an outlaw camp Cole had used running south. A shallow pond was shielded by high ridges to the south and east. A partially dry arroyo cut off the north, but the cattle weren't likely to move far from the water anyway.

Tonight's destination was an open grassland, backed by a half-moon of low hills. However, no one was certain if the stream there was in good shape. Abe had been sent ahead to determine the situation. If it was bad, they would seek an alternate campsite, one that Luther remembered from two years earlier. It was three miles farther to the northwest. Neither men nor animals would like that decision, but it would be less risky than another restless night without sufficient grass or water.

Behind Cole Kerry, the herd was crossing an uneven prairie, braided with ribbons of brown-tipped buffalo grass and rich with midday sunlight. His mind was racing through yesterdays, remembering his brother Ethan taking on most of the family's responsibilities when barely in his teens, because their father's love of whiskey made him inept. He recalled the time when Ethan whipped three boys of his age—at the same time—after they had beaten Cole before school one day.

It annoyed him that he kept returning to positive times with Ethan, in spite of his brother's rage. But he had accepted his responsibility to get the herd to market, regardless of how Ethan acted. After that, he wouldn't see either of his brothers again. Ethan had made it quite clear that such a separation was preferred. Cole's mind wandered to what he was going to do after they finally got to Dodge and delivered the herd. Right now, joining a buffalo-hunting team had less appeal than it once did. The idea came again that he should buy a saloon. Dodge sounded like a great place to do that. Raising horses crept into the corner of his day-dreaming, and that led back to Luther, then to Ethan.

Yet every time he thought about his future, Kathleen entered without warning. The ache for her had not dulled, only been accepted by his soul. It angered him that she wouldn't leave. She had no right. *Quit it! Quit it!* he muttered to himself. Wisps of dangling memory were washed aside by his determination to focus on the day. *Just remember that somewhere up here Winlow is waiting*, Cole advised himself. *Winlow is waiting. He has to be. Winlow is waiting, and I'm his first target.*

From a bent-over tree, challenged by the winds of many years, came a red bird that flew in front of Cole's horse. Both rider and animal jerked their heads in response. Cole reined hard to keep Kiowa from following its desire to bolt. After the sorrel resettled, he remembered that the bird was one of Kathleen's favorite things. It was like her soul had swept in front of him, to remind him of their time together. He reached up to his hat. The red feather was gone. He nodded and watched the bird fly away and said, "Goodbye, Kathleen. I hope you find what you're looking for."

Across the valley, a rider appeared as a small gray shape. Abe was returning at full gallop. Birds flew into the air as he burst through the heavy grass. He couldn't have reached the proposed camp and returned in this length of time. Something was wrong.

"Cole Ker-rie! Damn! *Ona!* Fire! Son of bitch!" came the agitated call from the half-breed, his long black hair flying as his horse thundered toward the advancing herd.

254

"Over here, Abe!" yelled Cole, waving his hand.

He tried not to guess what the trouble might be. Probably nothing more than that the scout had found some buffalo and wanted permission to hunt them. Cole hoped that was the reason; the men could use a taste of buffalo meat for a change. A few yards before reaching the trail boss, the winded outrider reined his bay hard; its back legs jammed into the packed earth to bring horse and rider to a skidding stop. Abe caught his left-behind breath before reporting, but his normally stoic expression was torn with fear.

"Cole Ker-rie. *Itancan*. Damn. *Ona!* Big Fire! Come to kill all! Plenty die. Damn. Son of bitch."

As he spoke, the scout simultaneously made the sign for "big fire." Cole thought the hand symbol image was especially scary. *A prairie fire! Coming at them? How could this be?*

"Come, Cole Ker-rie. Damn. See. Quick, you come. Damn."

"Show me, Abe," the trail boss said, and motioned to Dancer and DuMonte, his point riders, to hold the herd.

Cole kicked Kiowa into a lope, and Abe spun his winded mount around and chased after him. Several strides before he reached the ridge, Cole entered a giant invisible box of heat. The sensation took his breath away; Kiowa shivered but continued with firm urging. At the ridge's crest, he swallowed hard at what was happening to the open expanse beyond. As far as he could see in either direction, an unending wall of fire was eating the land and voraciously seeking more.

The rising smoke blotted the sky as if the flames were eating it as well. Even the roar of crackling grass and sagebrush captured his mind. A frightened deer bounded past him, frantically searching for safety. He could see eight buffalo running toward him—black hulks against the bright orange inferno, as if they were leading the flames toward the ridge. A skinny coyote scurried beside them.

Kiowa's horse's nostrils flared, and its red body trembled and shied fearfully. The shrill whinny was a cry to escape. Wild-eyed, the animal wanted to run. Cole reined it in place, stroking its neck and talking softly. But its hooves continued to dance on the dry ground. *What could they do?* There was no way to push the herd fast enough to the east or west to get around such a massive prairie fire.

Abe eased beside him. "See, Cole Ker-rie. *Itancan.* Damn."

"Let's get back to the herd, Abe. We've got minutes," Cole exclaimed, and spun Kiowa. The horse needed no urging and was running in two strides.

The young trail boss skidded Kiowa to a hard stop next to the waiting point riders and told them of the oncoming inferno.

Dancer's eyes widened, and he touched the medicine pouch at his neck. The superstitious cowboy admitted, "I should have known. The signs were there this morning—in the bug trails. And last night with the owl."

"Lord, be with us in our time of peril. Amen," DuMonte quickly murmured.

"Let's turn 'em and run for last night's bed. Maybe the fire won't jump that arroyo we crossed early on. Any better ideas?" Cole asked.

"We'll have to stampede 'em. They won't go back easy. Some'll keep walking right into it," DuMonte said, frustrated by his horse nervously spinning in a circle, wanting the opportunity to run. He glanced at the wall of flame engulfing the prairie and shook his head.

"Dancer, you an' I will turn 'em. DuMonte, you and Abe help us get started, then ride to tell the others. Maybe we can hold 'em together as we retreat. Stampeding is better than burning. Let's get it done!" Cole's order was a battle cry.

Dancer went straight to Whistle and fired his pistol into the ground, inches from its head. The rangy lead steer with the V-shaped right horn didn't like the idea of going back; it shook its horns defiantly and kept plodding forward. Dancer fired again, this time so close the gunpowder sprayed the steer's nose. Like a ballet dancer, the animal spun around, and the closest cattle did as well. The point rider continued his prodding with gunfire and whooping, but Whistle had the idea and was already in an awkward lope southward, swirling the herd inside itself.

Cole Kerry, DuMonte, and Abe fanned out along the broad front of the herd, forcing them to retreat by firing guns, waving slickers, and yelling threats. As soon as the animals started back, DuMonte galloped down the left side, stopping beside each rider to give him the awful news. Most had seen the commotion at the front but not the flames. Abe took off to repeat the announcement down the right side. He slowed at the first position, looking for Oleen. The surly Swede was nowhere in sight, so Abe kicked his horse toward Jip Jersey.

Jip was at the flank position, watching the turbulence ahead of him without comprehending. Abe rode beside him and recited the story. Jip closed his eyes, stuttered through a short prayer, and drew his pistol. His movements were slow and measured, as if disbelief were grinding his mind to a half-pace. The herd was a mass of bobbing heads and horns in different directions; some of the beasts reversed themselves quickly, some slowly; some kept plodding forward. But, gradually, the herd was heading south.

Waving his coiled lariat to keep any steers near him from changing their minds, Cole watched the rippling turnabout of the herd with satisfaction. As far as he could see, Bar K riders were holding them into one thick line of thunder. Suddenly all that changed!

Behind them, soaring heat roared its authority and ripped into a row of cottonwoods, cutting off the sky with spiraling black smoke and whirling red blaze. Like a crazed war party, the charging wall of flames destroyed the solitary trees and screamed a desire for flesh. The closest steers bawled their fright as the smell of smoke reached them. Before Cole or Dancer could react, the fire lunged for the slowest animals. Fear snapped from steer to steer. Within minutes, the controlled retreat transformed into a wild explosion of unmanageable beasts.

Most of the cattle rushed forward along the trail the cowboys wanted, but others split east and west in their own terrified race for safety. Six spun around and ran mindlessly into the fire, as insects are drawn to camp lanterns, and disappeared. Riders worked to contain the flow, but hundreds more broke away. Steers stumbled and fell; few stood again as other fire-crazed beasts trampled them. Men, horses, and cattle thundered toward the morning bedground with clusters of wild-eyed beasts spinning away.

Their eyes smarting from the fire's advance, Cole and Dancer galloped with the back end of the herd. There was no need for shooting or whooping now; it was too late for anything but running and hoping a man's horse was surefooted. The intense bellowing of the herd, mixed with the loud pounding of thousands of hooves, took away any sense of reality. It was a crushing sensation; the fire bit at their heels, shoving heat and smoke against their minds and filling their lungs.

They were still barely twenty feet from the front edge of the fire, their horses terrified and racing without control. Both men's faces were black with soot, their backs singed with heat. In front of them, small blazes darted along the backs of cattle like evil fireflies. A bright flame jumped to Kiowa's tail. Cole saw the brightness out of the corner of his eye and swung his lariat to slap it away. The big sorrel reared, and Cole lost his balance. A stirrup flew from his boot.

He let go of the lariat and grabbed the pommel with his right hand and raised his left fist, holding the reins chest-high in a momentary war to stay mounted and alive. Only the return of a smooth gait gave him the opportunity to recover. Forgoing any attempt to retrieve the loose stirrup with his foot, he curled his legs tightly around the sorrel's belly and righted himself.

Dancer spun off toward the left to keep animals from running sideways. Cole went to the right for the same reason, finally shoving his boot back in the loose stirrup. He yelled, but his words were known to him alone. A burning ball of mesquite rushed past him and bounced into the herd. Flashes of red and yellow burst upward inside the brown sea.

Little more than a hundred yards beyond the newest flames was the chuck wagon! He was startled at its location. T. L. Hayden usually drove parallel to the herd, but the stampede had the wagon encircled and stopped. Cole was almost too scared to see if Ethan Kerry was safe. Then he saw the blind rancher seated stoically beside the cook. Was Ethan drunk? Didn't he know they were trapped?

Next to the wagon team was Jip Jersey, on a sweat-covered bay, trying to help Hayden turn the two agitated horses around to run with the herd until the wagon could swing wide to safety. A glistening white horn grazed one horse's belly as the stampede jammed past, and the horse reared in fright. Crazed further by the wound, it bolted, yanking the wagon sideways. Hayden flew into the air. Reins were soon dancing alongside the racing horses. Ethan grabbed at the seat in a wild attempt to stay in the wagon but bounced sideways and over the edge. Jip lost control of his dun and disappeared in the raging herd. The wagon teetered from side to side, a ship drowning in a stormy brown sea, dragged on by horses as frightened as the cattle.

Twenty steers collided with the wagon as it veered crazily to the left. The left rear wheel snapped loose, rolled steadily for ten yards as if on a mission, then lost its nerve and flopped to the ground. One steer's horn crashed into the water barrel, exploding it into wood shards and spitting water over the beast. The wagon shuttered as the tongue ripped completely from its moorings, letting the two harnessed horses drag it away in their terrified need to escape. Another wave of steers slammed into the wagon and it groaned and toppled over. The onrushing herd masked more destruction.

Cole saw Dancer come out of nowhere, weaving his way through the stampede. The lithe rider tried to get to the unconscious cook but couldn't penetrate the line of steers separating them before a white steer trampled over Hayden's body. A dozen more followed. Finally Dancer was forced to wheel his horse away and run for daylight to save himself from being overrun.

Cole panicked. Where was Ethan? He spurred Kiowa into a thin opening among the river of steers and weaved his way to where he last saw his brother. With its ears laid back, the big sorrel understood the destination and fiercely responded. Frantically, Cole looked for Ethan amid the entangled horns and flames. There! He glimpsed the blind man kneeling amid the onrushing steers. Cole was amazed at the man's apparent calmness: He looked like a rancher simply checking the grass for grazing.

Cole halted Kiowa near him and yelled out, "Ethan! Ethan! I'm here! I'm here!" His voice was raspy from the smoke, but it cut through the roar.

Ethan raised his head and waved his arm to send him away. "Go on, save yourself!"

Cole jumped down from the saddle, holding the reins tightly. Kiowa spun defensively in the direction of the passing steers, shaking its head with nostrils extended and snorting, wanting desperately to run. Rumbling past them was a blur of brown, chased by the prairie-eating inferno.

"Ethan, can you stand?" Cole asked, placing a hand on the blind man's shoulders.

"Oh, I'm not hurt. Just lost my wind. What the hell are you doing here? Didn't figure you'd care much—after the way I've acted."

"Get on my horse. If we don't get outta here, we're gonna fry—or get trampled. Come on!"

Ethan responded by putting his hand over Cole's, then patting it. His words were little more than a whisper. "Thanks, little brother."

"Here's my horse. We'll talk later. I'm going to need your help real bad after this—just like always."

Ethan raised his foot and Cole pushed the left stirrup under it. Ethan bounced slightly on his right leg and swung up, with Cole giving him support and continuing to hold the reins.

"Grab the horn! I'm coming!" Cole yelled as soon

as the rancher was settled and jumped behind the rancher. The skittish Kiowa took advantage of the reins lessening as Cole left the ground and bolted with him barely on its back. He grasped Ethan's arms with his hands; the rancher flinched and held his position so Cole wouldn't fall.

Ethan called over his shoulder, "I've got you, Cole. Hang on."

Laboring with the additional weight, Kiowa was soon running with its mouth open. Froth stung both men's faces. A half mile from the morning bedground, they rode down into a long arroyo and scrambled up its far bank. Years ago, water had proudly sang along the shallow channel's banks. Only a string of puddles remained to remind passersby of a more luxurious past. A quarter mile to the west, the arroyo broke proudly into a wide, shallow stream. Twenty steers were there drinking. A badly burned steer was lying in the closest puddle, nearly dead. Thirty more had discovered soft places in the bank of the creek and were rubbing their bodies in the waxy mud to remove the fire's sting. Another dozen curled their tails upward and jumped around the far knoll, like calves in spring.

Cole said, "That was the arroyo we crossed earlier, Ethan."

"Will it stop the fire?"

"I think so. As soon as we get to the old camp, I'll take a few men and see if we can't beat down any flames trying to jump it."

"Good thing camp is close. This horse is about done."

"This is Kiowa, Ethan."

"Son of a bitch! First it kills me, then it saves my life."

# Chapter Twenty-one

Both men were silent for several strides before Cole saw what had been the morning camp. Weary, smoke-covered riders were moving the portion of the herd that had returned into a circle and were gradually getting them resettled. Most of the steers within the widening loop were walking.

"Can you see if the boys are easing the herd into a circle? Or are the damn beeves running through?" Ethan asked.

"Circling. Looks like at least half the herd is here. More coming in, real steady-like."

"Good. They should be damn tired of running. Cattle aren't like horses—they'd rather eat than run. Do you see Luther?"

"No."

"I thought the remuda was in the rear."

"It was," Cole said, not wanting to say more or guess where his oldest brother might be.

"Look back. Can you see if the chuck wagon's burning? Cole, we're done if it's gone."

"I can't tell, Ethan, but it probably is."

Cole expected criticism from Ethan, but none came. He halted their horse next to a small, wind-bent tree, jumped down, and helped Ethan as he slid from the saddle. Kiowa shivered, shaking itself like a cowboy whipping a wet towel. Cole flipped the reins around a sturdy branch.

"Ethan, stay close to Kiowa. Haven't got time to unsaddle him. I'm goin' back to the arroyo!" Cole yelled, unloosening the thongs that held his rolled-up slicker on the saddle. He couldn't help noticing marks of the scorching fire on the animal's withers.

"I—Do you see Hayden anywhere?"

"No, not yet."

"You should've saved him—instead of me. He can cook. I can't do a damn thing. Except drink and make a fool of myself."

Cole put his hand on his brother's shoulder.

"Ethan, you're the one man who's going to lead us out of here, around this black hell. We're going to make it."

"Not if we lost the chuck wagon."

Without responding to his brother's dire statement, Cole pulled the slicker free from his saddle and ran to the nearest rider. Large-bellied Ferguson watched without expression or recognition as Cole come toward him. Ferguson's fat face was more black soot than the usual dirty sunburn; his hat was gone, leaving a bald head; his left shirtsleeve was a blackened strip that ended at his elbow. His uncovered forearm was spotted with blisters.

"Ferguson, help me up on your horse. We'll ride double, back to the arroyo. We've got to stop the fire there," Cole said, holding up his hand for Ferguson's help. The cowboy stared at the trail boss as if not comprehending.

"Ferguson, come on, man. We've got to back there. Fast! I haven't got time to find another horse."

Cole had seen vacant eyes like Ferguson's before; it was the same stare of shock some men got during battle. Instead of speaking, Ferguson pointed at a riderless dun, streaked with drying sweat, trotting alongside the herd.

"Thanks, Ferguson. It's gonna be all right."

Ferguson watched Cole grab the dangling reins of the passing dun and swing into the saddle. Cole looked around for riders to join him. There was no need, or time, to try again with Ferguson. DuMonte and Loop rode at the edge of the milling steers, and Cole waved to get their attention. They immediately loped toward him.

"DuMonte. Loop. Come with me. We've got to make sure the fire doesn't clear that arroyo."

A half hour later, the three riders returned to report that the prairie inferno had stopped for good. From the camp, an unending world of black death could be seen on the far side of the arroyo. Carcasses of downed steers were strewn throughout the smoking prairie, and a dozen tiny gatherings of flame hadn't yet realized their time of power was over.

Dark skeletons were all that remained of cottonwoods, except for one top cluster of branches that had managed to keep its leaves from falling prey to the fire. The remains of a buffalo was fifty yards north of the embankment. A lone deer walked gingerly along the north side of the arroyo, pausing to smell a dying turkey with its wing burned off. At the cut of the horizon was a downed horse.

Loop and DuMonte headed to the pond as soon as they entered camp. Loop offered to take Cole's dun, and he accepted. At the soggy edge of the water, the black man dismounted and pulled up his scorched pant leg. He grabbed a handful of mud and it rubbed on his burned leg. Loop had brought a scalded prairie dog with him from the arroyo, carrying the little creature in his hands. The prairie dog hadn't run or struggled when the young cowboy found it. Loop asked DuMonte what he should do, and the black man suggested mud like that he had placed on his leg. Loop immediately began applying small dabs to the little animal's belly and legs.

Exhausted drovers mechanically tended their mounts as if they were the last horses in the world. They might be for the Bar K, Cole thought. Where were Luther and the remuda? If the horses and chuck wagon were both gone, the drive was done. He guessed a thousand steers were missing. But without fresh mounts, rounding them up—or going on—was futile. Each man would soon be walking, much less not eating. His mind was as covered with soot as his body, and all he wanted was sweet sleep to forget this hell. But the men needed him to be strong. Now more than ever.

Old Ben Speakman wasn't in sight; Cole wondered if he might be with Luther and the horses. He hoped that was the case. Speakman's calf wagon had been abandoned not far from the morning bedground. A team of horses remained harnessed and the reins tied to the braking stick. Only one calf remained; the others had sought their mothers. Four cowboys watched the resettled herd, riding on spent horses. Some men were in the muddied pond, giving their mounts a deserved washing, or themselves a bath. Others were letting their horses graze without hobbles. Several drovers lay sleeping on the bare ground. One was Jip Jersey with his arm wrapped tightly against his chest.

Ferguson was one of the mounted drovers, but he sat on his horse unmoving, staring toward the black prairie. Feeling sorry for the soot-blackened cowboy, Cole walked over to him.

"Ferguson, how are you?" Cole asked, putting his hand on the horse's sweaty neck.

The fat man's eyes blinked, and he slowly looked down. He mouthed the word "why?"

"It's going to be all right," Cole said. "Go down to the pond. The water will feel good to you."

"Don't like water, Mr. Kerry. Makes me feel wet."

Cole couldn't think of any response. He shook his head, patted Ferguson's horse, and headed for the tree stump where a quiet Kiowa stood alongside two other tied horses. Someone had unsaddled the big sorrel and wiped down its back with grass. He guessed it was Abe who was wrapping Stovepipe's cracked ribs with torn strips from the cowboy's shirt. Ethan was beside them, helping hold the wrap in place as best he could.

Seeing the trail boss walking toward them, Stovepipe hollered, "Glad to see ya made it through Hades, boss!"

He winced and grabbed for his sore ribs. Cole silently thanked the cowboy for his grit, while Ethan told him to quit moving while they wrapped him. But the gap-toothed man wouldn't stop talking.

"How'd you like that dun, boss? He tossed my ass comin' across the hump. Not his fault, I reckon, though. A steer ran right smack dab in front o' him, it did."

"Stovepipe stay still. Damn. Son of bitch," Abe said.

Cole pushed back his hat and said, "Fine horse, Stovepipe. He's getting a washin' right now. Hope I didn't teach him any bad manners."

Stovepipe Henderson grinned lopsidedly.

"Where do you think that dad-gum Luther has hid them broncs o' his'n?" Stovepipe asked.

To worry—out loud—was too hard right now. Stovepipe's eyes belied the playfulness of his words. Cole nodded, and smiled thinly.

"I don't know. Haven't seen him," Cole answered, and pulled the brim of his hat back low on his forehead.

Abe said, "Damn, Cole Ker-rie. Big fire. Bad medicine."

Stovepipe tried to make it better. "Some o' them beeves'll drift in h'yar tonight, by their lonesome, boss. Seen it happen, I have."

From the ridges to the east, a silhouetted man leading a limping horse gradually become Jared Dancer and one of his buckskins. Watching him advance took the place of conversation. The small medicine pouch bounced on his chest as he walked. Dancer's hat was shoved back on his head, revealing a forehead layered with soot. Obviously spent, he walked slowly toward the group to report.

"Got to be three, maybe four, hundred head strung out along those ridges. I'd still be there, but my horse went lame. Sotar's out there. Oleen too."

Cole was the first to reply. "Thanks for walking him in, Dancer. Where's he hurt?

Taking the animal's left foreleg in his hand and rubbing it easily, Dancer answered, "Right here. Must've done it cuttin' in and out of that wild mess. Nothing broken, though. He'll need rest. Where's the remuda, and I'll get back at it."

For a moment Cole didn't answer, then he explained that they didn't know where the horses were. For the first time, Ethan spoke.

With his open palm, Ethan Kerry passed it along the tips of a cluster of buffalo grass beside him and said,

"Maybe we're licked, boys. You can tell me. I got blind, but I didn't get stupid . . . leastwise not more so. I've never . . . ah, been in a fire like this one."

Stovepipe acted like he wasn't listening as he examined Abe's wrapping on his chest. Dancer lifted the hoove of his horse's strained leg as if to check for a trapped stone. Abe looked toward the sky for a message from somewhere, then looked at Cole for the answer he hadn't received.

The trail boss's eyes sparkled with fresh resolve, and his response matched their intensity. "We're going to Kansas, Ethan. Nothing's changed."

The blind rancher shook his head and ran his hand under his nose. After inhaling and exhaling deeply, he said, "Cole, you don't have to—"

"So help me God, there's no way Winlow's going to stop us. Fire or no fire. That's the last I'll hear about quitting." Cole's eyes sought challenge anywhere among the gathered men.

Ethan was silent, rubbing his thumb against the end of his right forefinger as if it would release some special insight. Finally he spoke, and the uncertainty of moments before was gone. It was as if Cole's resolve had entered Ethan's body where his thumb was rubbed.

"Tomorrow, we can swing wide west, around that burn. Steers won't likely cross it. Horses won't, either," Ethan said.

"Any water that way?" Dancer asked.

"Should be. That stream—the one showing up in the west end of that arroyo—turns north along in there somewhere. Wasn't there water this morning, Cole?"

"You bet."

Dancer shifted his feet and said, "But . . . if the remuda's gone, we're done." He touched the medicine bag at his neck, bent over to pick up four pebbles, and rolled them in his fist, while Stovepipe watched curiously.

"What are you doing, Dancer?" Ethan asked.

All three men were surprised at the question.

"How did you know I . . . I was doin' anything?"

"Oh, I heard the rocks in your hand. They are rocks, aren't they?"

"Yeah, but . . ."

"I couldn't imagine Cole or Stovepipe—or even Abe—picking up something like that right now."

Dancer's face reddened. He grinned and glanced at Cole before responding. "Four stones. One for each wind. Thought I'd place 'em somewhere . . . for luck. Along with some tobacco."

Cole nodded agreement, and Dancer seemed content that someone understood.

Stovepipe challenged, "What if'n that goddamn fire dun chewed up all our supplies in the chuck? There ain't nuthin' around h'yar to git more."

Dancer stroked the neck of his horse absentmindedly and said, "What'll we do for clothes? All our war bags was in the chuck. An' most of the boys had their Winchesters in it, too."

Ethan sighed. It was the question he was wrestling with himself.

Cole realized that the three were waiting for him to speak. He wiped soot from the butt of his sidewinder-holstered gun. With no sign of frustration, Cole answered the concerns evenly.

"There'll be game bottled up in the lowlands, hiding from the fire. Abe, I'll be counting on you to find it. An' any wild greens worth eating."

The half-breed smiled. "Abe find. Damn. Cole Kerrie."

Cole continued, "We'll do fine. Nice change from

beans and salt pork. My Winchester's on my horse. So's yours, Dancer. How about you, Stovepipe? Yeah, I know it's there, I just rode your horse. Maybe others, too. Whoever has clothes that didn't burn can share them. We'll just have to make do. We can make it if we stay together. We can, I know it."

Ethan smiled thinly. "Might be more saved than we think in the wagon, boys. The way the missus packs things—and Hayden, they . . ."

The impact of the cook's likely death hit him, his words vanished, and his head lowered. He lifted it and said, "Boys, I don't like the idea of not knowing where Hayden is. Coyotes an'—"

Commotion at the far side of the camp stopped their discussion. The herd of horses streamed into the campground with Luther Kerry and Old Ben Speakman handling them.

"Luther!" Dancer exclaimed.

Stovepipe yipped with joy. "Yeah, it's the old rascal all right—and that old Rebel ghost hisse'f, Speakman."

"Where you think they've been?" Ethan asked.

Cole studied the oncoming horses before answering.

"I'd say they took 'em west down in the arroyo, where that whole stretch of water sits. Horses' legs are wet, an' it's not sweat."

"Savvy move," Ethan commented. "That's two to draw to."

"Well, boys, our first problem's been answered. Let's get saddled and bring in some cattle," Cole said enthusiastically. Dancer broke first for the herd, followed by the wounded Stovepipe.

After welcoming their brother and the one-armed Confederate officer, Ethan and Cole Kerry rode for the chuck wagon in the cleaned-out calf wagon. The two brothers would bring back what was salvageable in food, supplies, bedding, and clothes. The rest of the crew switched horses and resumed gathering stampeded livestock.

At Luther's suggestion, torn strips of an old saddle blanket had been wrapped tightly around each hoof of the calf wagon horses. The padding would provide insulation against the heated ground. Neither horse wanted to cross the scorched land, but with coaxing—and after careful pawing—they trotted gingerly onto the black surface.

Cole wasn't certain, but he felt something had changed with his blind brother. There was an unusual sense about Ethan, like when the wind quietly comes from the south instead of the north. When he glanced at Ethan, his brother's chin seemed to jut out a little farther; his back seemed a little straighter; his complexion, ruddy instead of wan. Or was it Cole's tired imagination?

When he thought about it, Ethan's mood had been different since their escape from the prairie fire. He wanted to look into his brother's unseeing eyes and determine if the old Ethan Kerry had returned. Could that be? Or was he seeing this change because he wanted it to happen? Was this just a momentary relief from Ethan's inner grief and he would lash out again just when Cole thought everything was fine? Cole rode like a man sitting next to a sleeping rattlesnake.

Ethan turned his head toward Cole and said, "Winlow's got to know by now that we weren't destroyed—and that we haven't quit. I think he'll forget being careful and come after us tonight—with everything he's got."

Cole was jolted by his brother's observation. He had been wrong to think his brother was weak or should be coddled because of his blindness. Ethan Kerry was every bit the leader he had always been. Only, his mind was more important now than his actions. Cole knew the idea of Winlow hitting them tonight made good sense—and that he wouldn't have thought about it. His mind was solely on preparing for the rest of the drive and steeling the men for sacrifice.

Finally, Cole spoke. "Well, boss, what you say makes a lot of sense. A worn-out crew would be easy pickin's—combined with a trail boss who was busy thinking about other things."

"Cole, if we can stop them now, it'll be the end of Winlow. If we don't, it'll be the end of us. I can't see, but I sure as hell can be of more help than sucking up the drive's whiskey. What do you think of . . ."

# *Chapter Twenty-two*

The rest of the day went fast and sunset found a subdued camp of weary men. They had regathered all but two hundred steers; Ethan and Cole were impressed and said so. Destruction of the wagon's contents had brought more real despair than the loss of the cook, although no one would admit it. DuMonte had insisted on burying Hayden and reading the Bible over his remains, even though his burned leg was hurting so much he couldn't walk and had to be lifted onto his horse.

Ethan's report of the surviving chuck wagon contents was thorough and from memory. He and Cole had brought everything worth saving back in the calf wagon. Most of the cooking gear was unharmed. Only two rifles survived: Jip Jersey's Henry and Speakman's old Springfield. Most importantly was the food. Half of the canned goods looked fine, except for singed corners and burned-off labels. One sack of flour and another of sugar were untouched; both were buried on the bottom. None of the salt pork looked edible. None of the hardtack was recognizable. They could find only a half sack of coffee that wasn't burned and a full one of beans. The small steel box containing trail papers and what money Ethan had was found unharmed as well. Ethan's diary was a stack of ashes within a curled leather cover.

When told of that sad discovery, Ethan strongly proclaimed, "Don't worry, Cole. I've got the trail in my head. Reckon I always have had it there."

"Hell, I know that, big brother. I was just wondering when you'd figure it out." They laughed, releasing the fierceness of the day.

Supper was Luther's infamous "son-of-a-bitch stew"—his version of Claire's home-cooked meal, and one he had been eager to prepare for some time. At Ethan's suggestion, a young steer had been killed. The whole thing simmered in one of the Dutch ovens for two hours. Wild onions, Abe had found, were added for good measure. Everyone said they liked it, and Luther shuffled around the camp puffed up like an old rooster, soaking up the compliments. No one noticed Loop digging a small grave by the pond.

After eating, the riders gathered around a small campfire, except for the two on night watch. *Funny*, Cole thought. *We ride like hell to get away from one fire and quickly seek the peacefulness of another*. He shared the irony with his blind brother as they walked toward the circle of cowboys.

"Men, Sam Winlow set this fire to stop us once and for all," Ethan said matter-of-factly. "By now, he knows that isn't the case—and come to finish the job he's been nibbling at since we left."

Tired faces searched quickly at the edges of the purple-slashed sky for verification of Ethan's stunning words. His voice was stronger than Cole could remember it being in a long time. Ethan had insisted on making this talk. The rancher stood as straight and stiff-backed as ever, and his younger brother stood beside him with his arms crossed. Jip Jersey whispered to Dancer that he thought Ethan could see again. The short point rider answered that it could be—the spirits had been trying to tell him something all day.

Squatted on a log, Oleen found his courage and said, "Yah, Mr. Kerry, an' maybe we should sell him this herd. This is more than—"

"We're not quiting, Oleen." Ethan's words were ice. "We're going to make them pay. For Hayden. For all they've done. Anyone not ready to fight can ride out now and consider the horse full payment."

No one moved.

Dancer said, "You know we'll fight for the brand, Mr. Kerry. We're damn tired of that Walking W bunch trying to stop us."

Jersey added a stuttered support, and Loop excitedly agreed. Sotar was quiet, as was Oleen. DuMonte surprised everyone at the campfire when he added, "It is time. An eye for an eye."

Assignments were quickly given. Sotar, Jip Jersey, Loop, and Cole would spread out into the darkness to the west and position themselves for the coming ambush. Ethan thought this would be the primary direction Winlow's men would come. Cole agreed. Dancer, Stovepipe, Oleen, and Ferguson would take the east. The rest of the Bar K drovers spread out along the northern perimeter. Luther and Speakman would guard the horses, making certain they were well under control. Ethan would go with them, even though he really wanted to be with Cole but knew he would be putting an unfair burden on his brother and didn't ask. Only a few had rifles left, and ammunition was limited to whatever each man carried on his belt.

Four horses were saddled and bridled so they would be immediately ready after the fight, in case there was a need to round up cattle or chase Winlow's men. Cole saddled Kiowa, even though he knew the horse was tired; the big sorrel would take him anywhere faster than any horse in the string, worn or not. Rolling what blankets and extra clothes were left into fake sleeping men, the Bar K drovers made the scene of a sleeping camp that the Winlow men would expect.

No one would ride nighthawk; the two assigned riders would be told to dismount and take a defensive position on the south side of the herd. If the steers bolted, so be it, Ethan declared. Otherwise, the night guards would be defenseless if the ambush came that way. Instead, two of the quietest horses were given fake riders; a thick branch was tied upright to each saddle and draped with a saddle blanket to look like a man riding.

The moon was a sliver of silver, with only three stars also deciding to appear, as Cole Kerry pushed back the sleep that kept creeping inside him. His elevated position gave him an excellent view of the rocky terrain ahead. Without moving, he could see a half mile of the arroyo, including where it curved northward, and even the thick grass west of it. Behind him on another, higher land shelf was a lone box-elder tree surrounded by a thicket of blackjack. He had decided it would make a good backup position if he needed to move during the anticipated fight.

For two hours, he had hidden behind three large, thick mulberry bushes fronting the access from the west end of the arroyo. Waiting. Thinking. Jip Jersey was the farthest to his left, about fifty feet away. His broken right arm was held in place with Luther's wrapping; his left hand held a pistol. Cole had suggested that Jip support Sotar by reloading his weapons instead of firing, but the stuttering cowboy insisted he could shoot with his left hand.

Between Jip and Cole was John Davis Sotar, twenty feet to his immediate left, kneeling on one leg behind a family of large rocks. If ever a man looked eager for a gunfight, Sotar did—and Cole knew men of the gun too well. He could see Sotar's right thumb and forefinger rubbing a constant circle in anticipation. Cole could even see a slight grin on the man's face as he scoured the countryside ahead for signs of movement.

Loop was fifteen feet to Cole's right, and Cole could sense the young man's nervousness. It seemed like years ago now that Luther had bragged about the cowboy "knowin' his airtights," meaning Loop had memorized the printing on can labels in the bunkhouse. The veteran point rider had said the young man could be a teacher, a high compliment from Luther. Of course, his standard was that the lad could count to a hundred. It was a long way from a schoolroom, Cole thought.

He remembered his own first battle, when he and his brothers waited for a possible flanking Union movement. The setting was much like this, only Luther was on his left, Ethan to his right. They were part of a patrol left behind to make certain Lee's Northern Virginia army wasn't flanked as they moved through the wilderness. He glanced over at Loop and wondered what was going through the boy's mind, recalling that his only concern back then was to not embarrass his brother, Captain Ethan Kerry.

It had always been that way: hoping to perform to his brother's expectations, Cole thought. Ethan's savvy leadership was always the anchor. Realization shuttered through Cole that he had never had anyone depend on him that way. Probably Loop was worried about embarrassing himself too, concerned about measuring up to Cole's expectations. Cole wanted to go over and reassure the young cowboy, like he remembered Luther always doing to him. But his mind caught movement.

Lying flat on the ground, Cole sensed the advancement of men before he actually saw them. They were coming on foot, along the lip of the arroyo. Their shadows gripped the ground and held it hostage as they silently crept forward. He guessed they had left their horses a half mile or so back down the shallow gorge. It looked like eight men in all, although the shadows could be lying to him. Probably another man, maybe two, with their horses. This is where Ethan thought the main force would come. And here they came. Just like old times, somehow.

Cole stared at Sotar and got his attention, but the Missouri gunfighter had seen them as well. Something in Sotar's eyes bothered him. What was it? Had he sold out to Winlow? Cole looked again, but Sotar was studying the darkness. If Sotar was with Winlow, he would certainly have a clear shot at him once the fight began. Cole looked again at the sullen drover. There was something about the man that was troubling, but he didn't think it was working for Winlow. Why did he think it was personal? He didn't know the cowboy from before—at least he didn't remember him. Cole turned his attention back to the faint shapes slipping closer from the lower ground.

This time they would pay, Cole thought. Inside, he was ice cold. Fear wasn't allowed to reside in this soul winter. He simply didn't believe he would be killed. A while back, Cole heard that the killer Wes Hardin had said the same thing to a friend: that he couldn't be

killed. Few men had this luck, this utter lack of concern, this uncanny sense of what to do in battle. Cole
did, and he knew it. As a younger man, it had made
him reckless. Now it served to make him a dangerous
man.

The closest shadow began to look familiar. Cole
could see his face as slices of moonlight cut into hard
features. The man's right eye carried a long scar. Yes,
it was the gunman called Cherokee from the saloon in
Uvalde. Cole eased his Winchester into firing position
but didn't lever it. The telltale click-click would sound
a loud warning in the stillness. Earlier, he had rubbed
dirt over the barrel of his guns to eliminate moonlight
from giving him away. He had advised the others to
do so as well.

Behind Cherokee, the others began to take shape as
men. He recognized Everett, the man who had beaten
Luther in that same saloon. His thick lower lip and
wiry muttonchop sideburns were unmistakable. Next
to Everett was a powerfully built man with his upper
body bare except for a vest. Even in the grayness, the
brawler's muscular arms and thick chest were intimi-
dating. Cole didn't recognize him but didn't intend to
let him get close. They were flowing over the arroyo,
with the intent of covering the entire camp before firing. Just like Ethan said they would do. Cole wondered
if this was the entire group. How many men did Winlow have in all? Twelve? Fifteen? Twenty? How many
would be left with the herd? Where was Sam Winlow?

He heard Cherokee whisper to the man closest to
him, "Where's that idiot Oleen? He's supposed to
standing next to their wagon. That's the signal everyone's asleep."

"Maybe something's wrong," came the response
from a gray shadow.

"Could be. You go on ahead and make sure," Cherokee replied, and motioned for the men behind him to halt.

The muscular cowboy quickly agreed. "Yeah, I ain't wantin' to face that kid brother of Kerry's. Heard about him. He's pure poison."

Another shadow spoke. "He ain't the only one. I rode with Sotar. He's in there. You won't like facin' him neither."

"Quiet," Cherokee ordered. "Go on, Everett. Take a look-see."

The blubbery-lipped cowboy hesitated, snarled his distaste for the task, but resumed walking.

Like lightning out of a clear blue sky, Jip Jersey stood up and screamed his anger. "Y-y-you sons of bitches-s-s! Y-y-you k-k-killed m-m-my friend!"

He fired awkwardly at the shadows thirty feet away. Moonlight shimmered on their moving gun barrels. In less than an exhale, Jip's challenge brought bright orange blossoms snapping death toward him.

*No, Jip!* Cole muttered, rose on one knee, and fired. Wham! Wham! Wham! His Winchester slammed bullets into the vanishing figures. The sounds connected to each other, like a loud train rushing through the night.

Staggering at the top of the arroyo, Cherokee groaned and toppled into the night. A second shadow next to him spun awkwardly and disappeared. From his angle, Sotar was firing into their exposed flank. A wild shot fluttered in Cole's direction, but he had already rolled to his left. Another shot ripped through the bushes where he had been. He shoved new loads into the Winchester and sought shapes that didn't match with the surroundings. Sotar was firing. The return gunfire was sporadic.

Cole waited patiently. A shadow head peeked out from the top of the arroyo. Cole fired, and the scream echoed down the crease. He couldn't see Sotar anymore, nor was he shooting at the moment. Cole expected that the Missouri gunfighter had also shifted his position and was waiting for targets. Cole expected as much from an experienced fighter. Where was young Loop? He didn't want to risk looking for him, even for an instant. He didn't think the young man had fired his rifle yet.

Somewhere on the east side of camp, sporadic gunfire clattered. Cole's mind asked if the herd was stampeding again and answered its own question that it wasn't. Didn't matter if they did, right now. Off to his far left was a faint rustling sound; Winlow's men were trying to outflank them! Where was Jip? Cole feared he was badly wounded. He hadn't heard any sound from his direction since the cowboy stood and yelled.

Gunfire appeared from the southern edge of the blackjack thicket higher than his position. Bullets hummed past him; one drilled his hat. In response, Cole slid farther down the slight incline where he crouched. He snapped a shot just to the right of the last gunburst. Acrid gunsmoke filled his nostrils. Nothing. Then he heard the distinctive crack of a pistol. Once, twice, three times. A shuddered cry cut through the night. He thought it was farther away than where he guessed Sotar was, but he couldn't be sure. Was he attacking—or being attacked?

A shadow loomed behind him, only ten feet from his boots. A glistening gun barrel sought Cole. It was Everett, but he wasn't certain where Cole was. His discovery came too late, as Cole rolled on his back and levered two quick shots into the cowboy's lean body. Everett shuddered with the impact of the trail boss's bullets. Everett's own gun exploded, and the slug drove into the dirt beside Cole. The Winlow rider sat down cross-legged like he was going to converse. He stared with glazed eyes at the crimson spot growing from his heart and spreading across his shirt. Everett's face questioned what was wrong when he tried to raise his own gun and his arm wouldn't cooperate. Cole kept his Winchester pointed at Everett's chest as the man's will separated from his body. Everett's head wobbled back and forth and came to rest on his chest.

Farther back, a second man fired wildly in Cole's direction and began to run down the low hillside. He must have passed Sotar, for his retreat was stopped by three quick shots. The fleeing man was thrown into the night like he had been yanked by an invisible giant hand. Cole emptied his Winchester at shadows returning to the safety of the arroyo. Galloping horses could be heard in the distance, so he scrambled to his feet and ran toward the gulch. He passed four prone bodies before reaching the arroyo's lip, shoving new bullets into the chamber of his Winchester as he weaved forward. One man was in the arroyo's floor, running and shooting back at him. Cole took careful aim and hit the man between the shoulders.

His chest pounded like a wildcat was inside him, fiercely ripping at his lungs. His eyes were bright with battle. Sweat peppered his face; his long hair was wet, strands stuck to his damp cheeks. The lower calf of his right leg was screaming in pain at being forced to run. Behind him came the sounds of struggle, and he swung to confront it. The bare-chested brawler had Loop in a crushing bear hug that would break his back.

Struggling like a crazed calf against superior strength, the young cowboy squirmed and kicked but was losing the battle. One unstopped compression of the man's powerful arms would snap Loop's spine like a stick to add to the campfire. Horrified, Cole ran a few steps, stopped, and brought his Winchester to his shoulder and fired. At that same moment, Loop's crazed gyrations were enough to free his right hand and grab the pistol in his holster. Wild-eyed, Loop fired into the brawler's stomach and then again into his heart from inches away—as Cole's rifle bullet drove through the brawler's head. A loud groan and the young cowboy's own maniacal yell were a single inhuman sound as Loop pushed himself away from the dead man.

"Loop, are you all right?"

"I—I—I k-k-killed a man. H-h-he's ah, r-r-right there. S-s-see? I—I—I killed him."

"We both killed him. If we hadn't, he would have killed you. You had no choice," Cole said, putting his hand on the young cowboy's shaking shoulders. Loop stared at the blood circles spreading in the dirt around the brawler's lifeless body, then at the splattered blood on his own face and shirt. He stepped away from Cole's hand and vomited. Sotar came running their way.

"Where's Jip?" Cole asked, looking at Sotar.

"Don't think he made it. I haven't seen him since this thing began. What happened here?" Sotar said. His smoking rifle was aimed briefly at Cole's stomach as he talked, then he dropped it to his side, holding the gun only with his right fist.

"Loop stopped that big hombre when he tried to break his back."

"Good job, Loop."

Standing a few feet away, Loop shook his head and vomited again.

"Are we going after the bastards?" Sotar asked.

His right hand searched the loops on his belt for remaining bullets. Eight, he counted to himself, withdrew one, and slid it into his Winchester's chamber.

Cole studied the long, dark arroyo before speaking. "Yeah. I'm going to get Kiowa—and go finish it."

"I'm going with you," Sotar snapped.

"Good. Let's go look for Jip," Cole said.

They found Jip Jersey, slumped against a large rock. He was dead. His body showed four bullet holes. Cole gently eased the limp body to the ground, straightening his legs and shutting his eyes. Loop was crying and not trying to hide it now.

"He was a good man, Jip Jersey was. Too good to die here," Cole whispered, and stood. "We'll come back and bury him."

Sotar muttered, "He doesn't care . . . anymore."

"No, I guess he doesn't. But we do."

"Come on, let's get to camp," Cole said.

Sotar grabbed his arm and said, "Cole, you and I have something to settle when this is over."

"I don't understand . . ."

"You killed my kin. That man in Abilene . . . Webster Stevenson, that was my cousin," Sotar answered, his face taut, his eyes narrowed. He made no attempt to move the Winchester at his side into play.

"I didn't want any trouble from him. The first time I even met him was when he came into the saloon with two friends and attacked me. I knocked him to the floor. He pulled a gun and tried to kill me. He and one of his friends shot first. That's why I got this damn limp."

"I don't doubt that was the way it was, Cole."

"Well, Sotar, you'll know where to find me. It's a shame, though. You've got a lot to live for."

# Cotton Smith

Sotar's face snapped and his eyes widened. He said, angrily, "You think you're that good, huh?"

"Yes, I am that good," Cole answered calmly. "Now I'm headed back to camp. This night is far from over."

# Chapter Twenty-three

"Boy, everybody's around the campfire! They must've had it a lot easier than we did!" exclaimed Loop as the three men cleared the soft ridge and saw the blaze ahead of them in the darkness. The bounce of youth was returning to his step. For the first time, he was aware of Cole limping.

"Yeah, come to think of it, I didn't hear much gun-fire—but I was pretty busy for a while," Sotar said, glancing at Cole for approval.

Thirty yards away, the campfire was roaring with fresh logs spurting golden light on the faces of Ethan, Luther and the rest of the Bar K drovers. Bright flames indicated that everyone was there, except Dancer. In midstep, Cole Kerry threw out both arms to stop Loop and Sotar walking on each side of him. Loop dropped his Winchester in reaction to the sudden motion.

Cole's realization came in a hoarse, terse alarm. "Something's wrong."

"What the hell?!" Sotar challenged as he stumbled and halted.

Loop's eyes were wagon wheels; the young cowboy dropped to his hands and knees, regrabbing his rifle and peering ahead for verification of Cole's declaration. He could see nothing suspicious. He looked up at the trail boss and asked nervously, "W-w-what's the m-m-matter?"

"Look at our boys around the fire. See anything wrong?"

"What the hell do you mean?!" Sotar barked. "They're just sitting there all easy-like and warm. Like we should be."

"Ethan . . . he's got his bandage off. Luther has a pipe in his mouth. Ever see him smoke a pipe? It must be Speakman's. Abe has on DuMonte's hat, I'd know it anywhere. DuMonte has a cigar in his mouth. Ever see the Preacher smoke?" Cole explained, studying the edges of the dark camp for answers. "Luther's holding something in his hands, sorta like a woman holds a flower. What is it? I can't . . ."

"That's Dancer's medicine pouch! Dancer'd never take that off unless something was fierce bad," came Loop's agitated observation.

Sotar frowned, shook his head in disbelief, and said, "Well, hell, man, maybe your brother can see again. The rest of it don't mean nothing. They're probably just funnin' with each other."

"No. It's a signal. All of it—to us. Ethan hasn't had that bandage off in front of anyone. Not once the whole drive. They're trying to tell us things aren't what they look like—without getting caught at it," Cole explained, paused, and finished, "Winlow's got the camp."

"You can't know that, just because of a sorry bandage or a cigar," Sotar snorted. "I don't see any Winlow men down there."

"I don't either. But I don't plan on walking in until we know for sure."

"Well, I'm going. Damn, man, I thought you were supposed to be so tough," Sotar snorted, remotivated about his personal obligation to avenge his relative's death and stung by Cole's earlier confident words.

"Wait. If you're going to go, put this in your boot. They'll take your guns, but they won't expect you to be carrying a hideaway," Cole said, and handed Sotar one of his silver-plated Colts.

"Damn, that is a fine-lookin' iron," Sotar purred. "Aren't you worried I'll kill you with it?"

"You can try."

Sotar hesitated, the words rattling in his mind. He shrugged his shoulders and concentrated on hiding the gun in his boot. As he did, Cole told him to tell the men that Jip and Loop were dead and that Cole himself was badly wounded and needed help. If he was right, that would bring Winlow out from hiding; if he was wrong, it would only cause a brief extra worry for the others.

"By God, you really think they're down there, don't you?"

"They're down there."

"Well, I think you're just plain jumpy after catching a little gunfire," Sotar spat. "Loop, you coming with me?"

"I—I—I'm staying with Mr. Kerry," Loop answered, remaining on his knees.

"All right. But don't expect me to keep everybody from laughing their asses off at you two for being like a couple of skittery women."

"Just tell the story. Tell it loud. They won't shoot. They'll need you to find me."

"Oh, I'll tell it, all right. Real loud. Then you can both look like the fools you are," Sotar said over his shoulder as he swaggered down the incline toward the half-circle of quiet Bar K men. Cole directed Loop to hide.

Luther stood as the Missouri drover neared, bringing a low reminder of "easy" from the darkness. Sotar heard the caution and knew instantly that Cole was right. Damn, he muttered, steeled himself for the worst, and kept walking. Luther leaned over and whispered to Ethan. Slowly, the blind rancher came to his feet. His face was drawn, his mouth a slit of worry; his sightless eyes blinked for clarity that wouldn't come.

As he neared the glowing campfire, Sotar announced loudly "Luther! Mr. Kerry! We turned 'em—but Jip's dead and so's Loop. And . . . Cole—he's hit real bad. Bleeding somethin' fierce. You gotta help real quick— or he'll die!"

Luther's head dropped against his heavy chest. Dancer's medicine pouch dropped from his hands. He yanked Speakman's pipe from his mouth, threw it on the ground, and spat into the fire, producing crackles of red. His rawbone shoulders rose and fell. Then he looked away into the darkness.

Ethan started to speak, but nothing would come out. The earlier resurgence of positive energy had evaporated. By the time he had realized Winlow's men were in control of the camp, it had been too late to do anything. Winlow's threat to kill all of his men—if Ethan, Luther, and Speakman didn't surrender immediately— had stopped him from flailing away wildly at his unseen enemy.

His one last hope was that Cole would survive, see

the clues he had engineered around the campfire, and escape. Now that was smashed into nothing more than a futile bit of make-believe. A prayer passed through his mind on the heels of the cold depression: "God, let me see just long enough to grab a gun and die with my brother, please, God. I won't ask for anything more. Let me die fighting beside him."

Sotar was proud of the impact his agitated pronouncement had produced. Out of the blackness came a confident command: "Hold it right there, cowboy. You can lead *us* to Cole Kerry."

It was Sam Winlow. His large frame became defined by the firelight as he stepped toward Sotar and the Bar K men. A flowing, white cattleman's coat and a high-crowned hat made him appear even larger than he was. The big man's bulging eyes, pointed nose, and ugly face were made more grotesque by the campfire's erratic touch.

Sotar's own face was torn between the anger at walking into the trap Cole had predicted and the need to act like he hadn't expected it. For an instant he wanted to attack, but the idea got no further than the tightening of his hands around the Winchester he carried.

"Take his guns, Oleen," Winlow barked.

"Yah, vill do." Oleen came quickly out of the shadows with a sheepish grin. He avoided eye contact with Sotar as he approached. The sour gunfighter was seething: How could he have been so stupid to walk into this trap after Cole Kerry warned him? Realizing Gus Oleen was a traitor made it worse. He braced for the Swede's attempt to take his weapons.

Sam Winlow's threat was stone. "I wouldn't try it, cowboy. We can find Cole Kerry with or without you."

Sotar's courage evaporated, taking most of his anger

with it. Oleen took his rifle and lifted the handgun from his holster. With both weapons in his control, the Swede looked at Sotar and chirped, "Yah, you vere the stupid one. I try to tell you this vould not be. But no, you vould not listen to Oleen, vould you? But they vill need you for the drive. I vill tell them you are good man. Oleen vill save your life, John Davis Sotar."

From the darkness, Winlow belted more orders. "Oleen, go with him. Bart, Wilson, both of you. I want that son of a bitch Cole Kerry dead. I want you to bring his dead body right back here so I can piss on it."

Sam Winlow laughed strangely, like a winter wind howling out of a hollow late at night. Sotar shivered and wished he had listened to Cole Kerry. Other laughter followed from the darkness, and Sotar could see a half-dozen men in the shadows. Six, he thought. Was that all? No, there were more. How many? Six . . . seven . . . nine. There were nine. Cole Kerry would want to know that. The thought of Cole Kerry waiting rekindled Sotar's confidence, and he took a step toward Luther.

"Give me a chew before I go, will ya, Luther?" he said.

Oleen reached out a hand to stop him, but Winlow gave his permission. "Let him go, Oleen. The cowboy's been through a lot, and I'm going to need him to move this herd to mine. Get it quick, cowboy. I'm not a patient man."

Puzzled, Luther took a tobacco plug from his pocket and handed it to the advancing taut-faced gunfighter. He hadn't known Sotar to chew. Taking the plug, Sotar said loudly, "I just need a chew, not the whole thing." He bit off a piece. As he handed it back, he winked and whispered, "Cole's idea. He's fine. So's Loop. Get ready."

Without turning around, Sotar asked, "Aren't you worried about scaring the herd with more gunshots?"

"Those beeves are so tired, you could ride through 'em shooting and nothing will happen. Besides, I've got three riders covering it now. Come on," Winlow answered. *Twelve,* Sotar thought.

With Oleen and the two Winlow men following, Sotar headed southward toward the battleground where Cole was supposed to be lying. As they cleared the ridge, Luther saw Sotar's shadow stumble and fall; he wondered if that was on purpose. He turned his face away from the fire, coughed, and muttered the news about his younger brother to Ethan. Lines in the blind rancher's face vanished and the hint of a smile appeared. He coughed too, to keep it from spreading further. Luther thought he heard the blind rancher say, "Thank you, Lord."

Behind Ethan and Luther, the barrel of a revolver glistened with red and gold reflections from the campfire as a bald-headed Winlow man approached. The fire's glow revealed a familiar plump face with a nervous twitch on the left side. He stopped a foot away from Ethan, his body shifted to a triumphant widespread stance.

"Remember me, Mr. Kerry? I'm the one you kicked off the drive," Ike Jenkins said with victory in his voice. "When the boss gits through pissin' on your brother's body, I'm gonna piss on yours."

Luther spat a stream of tobacco juice splattering onto Ike's boots. The angered cowboy swung his pistol at Luther's head, but the eldest Kerry ducked.

Ike Jenkins's threat was cut off by the strutting advance of Sam Winlow toward them. The ugly rancher took a long, black cigar from his vest, bit off the end, and lit the smoke with a stick from the fire. After several puffs, he took it from his mouth and examined it as if it represented a grand accomplishment. He stared at Ethan and Luther and chuckled.

A burst of gunfire rippled from the far side of the hill beyond the ridge around the camp, ending Winlow's pronouncement. Hints of light decorated the land and vanished. Another three shots sputtered in a separate volley. His evil smile gleamed with reflection from the campfire.

"Well, that's the end of Cole Kerry, the Kansas gunfighter," Winlow proclaimed, and his men responded with grunts of approval.

The big rancher took another puff and said, "You won't have to wait much longer, Ethan. When my boys finish dragging in what's left of Cole Kerry, then I'll shoot this stupid brother of yours. And then . . . well, maybe you will have to wait to die. Maybe. I'll just leave you here by yourself, blind as a goddamn rock. So the vultures and wolves can have you. Yeah, I like that idea. What do you think of it, Kerry?"

"Give me a gun, Winlow. I'll go against you man-to-man—right now."

"Now, that would be something, wouldn't it, boys? Me in a shoot-out with a fool of a blind man! You expect me to shut my eyes!" Winlow yelled at his men, who responded with hoots and ridicule.

Ethan spat in the direction of Winlow. The spittle blistered his boot top as the rancher jumped away. A chuckle from Stovepipe brought the swing of Winlow's boot in his direction. Winlow stepped closer to kick again when a Winlow man yelled.

"Hey, they're coming back, boss!"

Winlow stopped to observe Oleen and the two other men become visible against the top of the ridge. Oleen had a body draped over his shoulder, the limp legs tangled below his waist. Cole Kerry's distinctive gunbelt was evident even in the grayness. The other two men flanked him, one on each side. In their hands were smoking Winchesters.

"Lemme see, boys!" Winlow gloated as he watched the three men saunter closer. "I've been waiting a long time to see that bastard dead."

As they entered the yellow light at the edge of the camp, the man to Oleen's right tugged at his hat brim to lower it more across his darkened face. He muttered something to Oleen, whose expression was that of someone who had seen a ghost. Sweat trickled from the Swede's hat to his chin.

"Too bad you can't see this, Kerry," Winlow snorted. "Throw that garbage on the ground, Oleen."

"Hey, that's not Bart—that's Cole Kerry!" exclaimed a voice from the darkness.

On Oleen's left, John Davis Sotar—wearing Wilson's hat and vest—swung his Winchester toward the overconfident Winlow men and levered three quick shots. The man on the right spun toward the same targets and blasted away with his rifle. It was Cole Kerry wearing Bart's hat, vest, and gunbelt. At the "body's" demand, Oleen let Loop go and the young cowboy, wearing Cole's gunbelt, jumped to the ground, firing a pistol taken from his waistband.

Sam Winlow was dumbfounded; the cigar toppled from his mouth and bounced off his boot. He didn't notice Gus Oleen whimpering. Orange flames spat from three shadows; three others were down, and two hadn't moved. Luther slammed into the stunned rancher, knocking him down. He grabbed the revolver from the rancher's holster and joined in.

Ike Jenkins raised his gun to shoot at Luther. Sensing the movement, Ethan swung his extended arm backward and slapped the corner of the cowboy's face, forcing the gunshot to go wildly into the air. The blind rancher followed with his left fist, driving into what he thought was the man's stomach. His strike was accurate enough, and Jenkins's breath cried out, leaving him clawing to get it back. His gun clattered on the ground. Jenkins doubled over to ease the pain. Ethan felt for the man's exposed chin with his left hand, found it, and delivered a right uppercut that drove the cowboy off his feet and backward.

"Damn, I forgot how much that smarts," Ethan said, shaking his opened hands with satisfaction, but no one heard him.

As the Bar K riders scrambled for fallen guns, Stovepipe rushed to Cole's side. The trail boss handed him one of the Winlow pistols stuck in his belt. Levering and firing his Winchester with his right hand, Cole tossed a second extra revolver toward the advancing Abe. Even the religious DuMonte limped over to Sotar and took the offered pistol held out to him.

The blind rancher leaned down, searching frantically for Ike's fallen revolver. His hands brushed against the barrel and took the gun in his right hand. Grasping the handle hurt his bruised knuckles. With his other hand, he probed for Ike Jenkins. His fingers touched the cowboy's arm.

Cocking the hammer, he stood, aiming it at the downed Jenkins, and warned, "Ike, if I hear anything move, anything at all, the gun goes off. I can't see, but I hear real good. So you'd better hope no beetle comes to call. I might think it's you moving."

As he spoke, the fight was over. Four Winlow riders were dead; two were wounded; none of the rest wanted to stand against Cole Kerry and the angry Bar K drovers. Arms were raised in hasty surrender in response to

Cole's terse command: "Drop your guns or die. An' I'd just as soon you kept them."

From Cole's right, Luther suddenly charged into the vanquished Winlow attackers. The oldest Kerry's face was flushed, and veins knotted his forehead as he faced the closest man. Luther held up Dancer's small medicine pouch and screamed, "Are you the bastard that kilt my friend?"

Without waiting for an answer, he slammed his fist into the man's face. Before he could strike again, DuMonte grabbed his arm. Luther glared at him, and the black cowboy quietly told him to let the Winlow rider go. Luther hesitated, glanced at DuMonte again, and drove his fist so hard into the man's jaw that it snapped. Blood flew onto Luther's shirt and caught DuMonte's shirtsleeve as the Winlow rider crumpled.

"Sorry, thar, DuMonte. Reckon I jes' had to do it. Didn't mean to git no blood on your shirt, though," Luther said matter-of-factly, and looked around for another Winlow rider to hit. He grabbed a second man by his neck and repeated the process. DuMonte was stunned, watching Luther unleash a fury he had never suspected existed within the dull-minded wrangler. After the third slugging, DuMonte tried again to gentle the enraged Luther. This time the wrangler agreed.

With everyone preoccupied, Sam Winlow eased himself to his feet and took two steps to the edge of the campfire's ring of sitting logs, paused to determine if anyone was watching, and disappeared into the night. He wanted to laugh, to shout, as he ran toward the Bar K remuda. Three of his men remained uncaptured—watching the herd—but they wouldn't be of help. The Bar K riders would soon get them too. No, he must escape.

Back at the camp, Luther moved in front of the distraught Oleen and growled, "You slimy sonvabitch. I cain't believe ya dun solt out yur friends. How much did'cha git, Oleen? I cain't believe it."

"Yah, vell ah . . . L-L-Lut-ter, it vas mistake. Lut-ter, you know Gus Oleen—around money, I am foolish, please . . ."

"Ya kilt Dancer."

"No, no, Lut-ter. He—he vould not give up vhen they came. I—"

"You dun same as kilt 'im, Oleen. He dun reckoned ya was a-bringin' friends. I'm gonna put the rope 'round yur scrawny neck myse'f," Luther said, and shoved the Swede, forcing him to stumble backward.

# Chapter Twenty-four

Taking in the surrender with only his mind, Ethan Kerry stood next to the sitting logs and the unmoving Ike Jenkins. Gunfire had stopped. He heard his younger brother barking orders, the levering of Winchesters and the cocking of pistols, the scuffling and grunting of men and the whining of the Swedish drover who had betrayed them.

Behind him a hundred yards, he heard the bawling of nervous cattle. The herd was stirring some, he could tell. But that was to be expected. Thank God they hadn't stampeded again. Too damn tired, he thought. If Cole didn't send some riders back to watch them soon, he would remind them. He remembered there were three Winlow men assigned to watch the herd. They needed capturing too. He must tell Cole.

When he inhaled, the pungent order of smoke from the scorched prairie seeped into the night. He could hear his oldest brother cussing and spitting—and the distinctive speech of the half-breed Abe. Maybe he could get Luther's attention. This drive had been costly; three good men were dead: Jip Jersey, J. L. Hayden—and now Jared Dancer. It was difficult to believe.

Ethan wanted badly to be a part of this fight, to be what he once was, a man to step aside for. He was the only Bar K rider still captured—by his sightless eyes. His mind turned to Sam Winlow, the man who had caused him so much grief; it was almost like he could blame him for his blindness.

Where was Sam Winlow? His earlier listening had told him the big rancher had been a few strides away from the dying fire when Cole surprised him. Was Winlow still there? Ethan thought about walking toward where he thought the cruel rancher was standing and starting a fistfight. Maybe he was tough enough to withstand the blows that would come from not seeing.

His mind rejected the idea, but not the sense of desiring battle. Winlow should be his to deal with. Ethan listened hard. He squinted to push away other sounds and was certain Winlow wasn't there. Had he escaped during the commotion?! A defiant whinny at the corral told him the answer. Winlow was there! He had to be.

"Cole! Cole! Winlow's at our horses!" Ethan yelled, hating the fact that this was the limit of his contribution to the victory. In reaction to his frustration, he kicked at the prone Ike Jenkins. His spurs murmured like a coiled rattlesnake as the toe of his boot struck the cowboy's butt.

"Give me a reason to shoot, Jenkins. Move! Try something! Move!"

Ethan's pistol roared and the slug dug deep into the ground inches from his own foot.

"Come on, Jenkins, come at me. Come on, I'm blind as a bat. You can do it. Come on."

Ethan's pistol fired again, this time slamming into the dirt farther away. Ike Jenkins inhaled and held his breath in utter fear as his body froze in position. Ever so slowly, Jenkins let the breath escape, hoping the sound wouldn't reach Ethan's ears. Without turning his head, Jenkins stared at the wet spot at the crotch of his pants. His eyes frantically searched the dark for someone to come and assure the blind rancher that he wasn't trying to escape.

No one was around the horses when Sam Winlow arrived. Four were saddled, waiting for Bar K riders to return to nighthawking their herd. Across the black plains, the herd itself was stirring. Some animals were agitated by the recent gunfire but too tired to run without good reason. When the shots ended, so did the reason, and they returned to grazing. He could barely make out the silhouette of one of his riders. They would be soon captured or dead. He didn't have time to worry about them.

The closest mount was a fine one, he judged, taking pride in his judgment of horses. It should be able to outrun anything. The big sorrel trembled and blew its nose in reaction to the weight as he lifted himself into the saddle. Winlow growled for the horse to stand quiet, and it obeyed. His spurs jabbed the sorrel's sides, and the horse jumped into a fierce gallop to the south. Winlow smiled; he had chosen well. Into the night he ran.

Ethan's alarm cut into Cole's mind like a sharp knife. So close to victory, and the man responsible for their grief was escaping. Immediately, he knew his brother was right, and he raced for the rope corral. His eyes searched the night for any sign of the evil rancher.

Before he reached the retaining rope, he knew which saddled horse was gone. Kiowa. Sam Winlow had escaped on the big sorrel, the fastest and strongest horse in the remuda.

With one pop, Cole unleased the reins of a leggy bay mustang, one of DuMonte's string, bounced into the saddle, and kicked the horse into a hard gallop. With his Winchester across his saddle, Cole made no attempt to track Winlow closely in the dark. He knew well the distinctive mark of Kiowa's hoofprints and could see them attack the ground even at this speed, aided by the moon's cowardly glow. Winlow wasn't too far ahead, but his lead would surely grow with Kiowa's strength and Cole's need to measure his route. Cole's only hope was to get close enough to shoot Kiowa. He wasn't sure he could. Yet he had to.

He had kept Luther from killing the great red horse after blinding Ethan—and now he must kill it to keep Winlow from escaping. A shiver blasted through him at the thought. Kiowa had saved his life and had brought him safely to Kansas. The powerful sorrel symbolized this wild drive, even creating the reason for it being crazy in the first place.

His mind took him to the first time he saw Kiowa and the awful news about his brother's sight, then to the deep sand outside of Uvalde, to riding in front of the Bar K herd, to warning him about Oleen at the remuda corral, to charging into battle against the snipers, to carrying both he and Ethan from the terrible fire. How could he shoot such a horse? He would try for Winlow first, but at the distance he fired from, that was only a wish. A horse was the greater target. He blinked away his feelings for the big sorrel and tried to focus on Winlow only. It had to be. The rancher could not be allowed to escape. Such evil would continue to harm Ethan or try to.

Cole Kerry figured Winlow would not attempt to return to his own camp. There couldn't be more than three or four men guarding his herd, and they were most likely cowhands, not gunmen. No, Winlow would be seeking escape, not refuge. Kiowa's clipped hoofprints verified Cole's hunch: Sam Winlow was headed south. Cole cleared the first ridge, leaning low alongside his horse, half expecting a bullet. Instead, he saw a dark mound on the plains in front of him. His eyes soon confirmed that the mound was a body. It had to be Sam Winlow. Kiowa was nowhere in sight. Reining up twenty yards from the unmoving shape, Cole shoved his Winchester into the saddle boot and drew a Colt. He advanced slowly, trailing his horse behind him with the reins in his left hand.

"Winlow, get up," he challenged, and thumbed back the hammer. There was no response from the body. Cole stepped twice to his left, limping, before continuing to move closer.

"Get up, Winlow, and let me see your hands while you do it. Move fast and I'll kill you."

Still nothing. Cole studied more closely the odd position of the body. Winlow was dead. The severe angle of his head told the whole story. Enlarged eyes stared toward the fistful of pale stars challenging the moon but did not see them. Cole realized that the big sorrel had done it again. This time the rider had been killed. Kiowa had thrown Sam Winlow and he had broken his neck. Cole stood over the dead rancher for a long minute, releasing the tension of the extended battle.

"It's over," he whispered to himself, and pushed the Colt into his holster. It felt strange to have someone else's gunbelt around his waist. Suddenly he was so weary that he could barely pull himself up into the saddle. Halfway up, he trembled, grabbed for a handful of mane, and held himself in place until the weakness passed. Finally, he let the horse have its head, and soon they were loping toward camp.

At the ridge, the half-breed Abe met him at the ridge, riding a small brown horse, and greeted warmly, "*Tanyan yaun hwo,* Cole Ker-rie? Damn."

"Yes, Abe, I'm fine. *Pilamayan.*"

The half-breed smiled at the Lakotan "thank you" to his question about how he was. Close behind was Luther on one of Dancer's buckskins. Worry on his face became a solemn satisfaction after Cole explained what had happened to Winlow.

As they rode back together, Luther asked, "Well, boss, ya won't believe this, but none o' our beeves up-jumped an' left during all that shootin'. They's strange critturs, ain't they? Them Winlow hawks was real eager to he'p too, after we dun explained their choices." He spat a grand stream of tobacco juice straight down at his buckskin's hooves. "The rest o' them bastirds is all tied up, fancy as a Sunday-go-to-meetin'."

Cole realized he had completely forgotten about the herd.

"Don't mean to be pilin' on a worry ri't after we dun got rid o' a big'un, but what are we gonna do about the Walkin' W herd?" Luther asked.

"Good question. Seems to me we bring 'em both to Dodge, using whatever Winlow men are left to help," Cole answered. "We'll tell the buyers what the deal is. We'll take money for the gear of ours they burned— and some extra for our three boys they killed—and let it go at that. They can pay off his riders, too. We'll know who were drovers and who were selling their guns. Does Winlow have any family?"

"Bust my britches if'n I know'd," Luther growled.

"You figger I'm that ugly sonvabitch's nursemaid or sum'thin'?"

"No, I think you're the best man I know. You—and my brother. You know him? Tall fellow. Mean temper," Cole responded, a slight smile tracing across his face as the pale moonlight painted it like a Kiowa warrior's.

Luther grinned and spat again.

"Thar be one more Bar K feller that won't be a-ridin' in with us. We's gonna hang Oleen. You got a problem with that, Cole?"

"I'll kick his horse. But I don't want him buried anywhere near our friends," Cole answered, turned to Abe, and said, "Abe, I'd like you to . . . ah, to sing a song over Dancer's grave. A warrior's song. He'd like that."

"Abe like that, Cole Ker-rie. Damn. Give tobacco to Winds. *Lowan Wanagiya*. Song to go all way to Spiritland. Damn."

"Thanks."

Luther swallowed and added, "Yeah, he'd like that, I reckon. DuMonte kin say somethin' Bible-like over Jip's grave."

They rode farther without speaking. Ahead they could see a gray silhouette. Ethan Kerry stood near the horse corral.

Luther perked up at the sight and said, "Say, boss, I reckon we dun got ourselves a new chuck wagon. Them Walkin' W boys ain't got no need fer theirs no more."

"Yeah, I'll go ahead to make sure it stays in place while our herd is brought up," Cole responded, his weariness suddenly gone.

"Yeah, don't reckon thar'll be much hoorahing thar. They's only cow handlers left with Winlow's beef."

Reining up at the remuda, the three men dismounted and Cole retold the story of Winlow's demise to Ethan. Holding Dancer's medicine pouch in his reddened fist, Luther couldn't hold back the feeling anymore. He grabbed his youngest brother and hugged him. Cole returned the embrace and patted him on the shoulder.

"I'm plum sorry ol Kiowa's dun gone," Luther uttered, holding back tears as he stepped away from Cole.

"Yeah, me too."

"I reckon that red rascal'll meander back soon nuff," Luther said softly.

"Maybe. Maybe he'll just run forever," Cole said, and turned toward Ethan. "Reckon we're going to make it, big brother."

Ethan grinned and said, "What did you see first? Luther's pipe? DuMonte with a cigar?"

"I saw your bandage off."

"Well, get used to it. I'm not hiding behind it anymore."

"Yeah, we all saw your tricks. That's why we rigged up the little story Sotar told," Cole said, ignoring the Missouri gunfighter's disbelief at the time. "Sorry if it bit too hard."

"Finding out you were all right more than made up for it," Ethan replied, and asked, "Going to leave Winlow's body out there . . . tonight?"

"I'm a-goin' out thar ri't quick," Luther declared before Cole could answer.

"Oh, are you going to bury him?" Cole asked.

"No . . . something else." Luther's dark eyes sparkled mischievously. "All that coffee's bin a-hankerin' to git out."

Abe glanced from one Kerry to the other, then laughed when the words caught up with his understanding. Shaking his head, he led his horse toward the corral.

"I told the men we'd string up what's left of that bunch in the morning—when we ride on," Ethan said. "If that sounds right to the trail boss. They aren't cowmen, they're a bunch of gunslicks who ran into Cole Kerry."

"They ran into the Kerry brothers and the Bar K, Ethan. Say, coffee sounds good," Cole said. "Any left?"

Ethan responded, "If there isn't, I'll make some."

"Don't know if I can wait that long," Cole teased.

Ethan was the first to laugh, and he said, "Man, I had that coming. Say, while you're waiting for my coffee, I want you to give some thought to becoming my partner. You, Luther, and me. I got a big ranch. And I have a hunch the Walking W is going to be for sale besides!"

"Hellfire, thar's gonna be a bank up fer grabs too, I reckon," Luther blurted.

Cole grinned. He glanced at Luther, who was beaming.

"That's a mighty tempting offer, big brother. Are you sure . . ."

"Real sure. It makes all the sense in the world. It was Claire's idea."

"Claire's idea?"

"Yeah, before we left, she said that's what I ought to do. Just took me a long spell to get my head on straight. Of course, you'll have to put up with my trying to tell you how to do everything."

Luther laughed. "That thar lady's gotta a fine way of seein' things."

Cole smiled. "It sounds mighty good to me."

"It'll be good to have my brother with us again," Ethan said, and pulled a folded envelope from his back pocket and said sheepishly, "Cole, I've been carrying something that's yours—ever since the Red. Forgot it for a while, but I guess I just wanted to make you hurt—like I was. Feel like a fool hanging on to it." He handed the folded envelope to Cole. One corner was singed. Ethan rubbed his chin, stared strangely away with eyes that could not see, and continued. "Came in Claire's letter. Postal clerk brought it to the ranch after we left. I think it's from . . . what was her name?"

"Kathleen. Kathleen Shannon."

"Pretty name."

Cole stared at the envelope, and Luther exclaimed, "Well, damn, boy, open 'er up and let's have a look-see."

Without glancing his way, Cole slid his fingers under the sealed flap and separated it from the rest of the envelope. He pulled out two sheets of paper. It was from Kathleen. Moonlight was slid across the letter, pausing at identical brown hints in the middle of each page, reminders of how close the fire had gotten to Ethan. His hands shook in spite of his determination not to care what she had to say as he began to read to himself, hearing in his head the Irish song of her words.

*Me dearest Cole—*

*Two months have passed since you left and it seems like two years I do believe. I can only hope you get me letter. I be remembering your brother had a ranch near Uvalde in Texas and thought you might be going to this place. If not, maybe he can tell me where you are. It is me only precious hope and the one that keeps me heart going.*

*I am leaving Abilene forever tomorrow on the*

*stageline. Me mother knows but not me father. I
am coming to Uvalde, no matter how long it takes.
I must find you wherever you have gone. I am
trusting in the Lord above to help me.*

His brothers stood silent around him as he read.
Their faces showed concern, but only Luther dared to
ask, "What's she be a-sayin'?"

"That's private," Ethan cajoled.

"That's all right. She's on the way to your ranch,"
Cole said as he stopped reading and looked up. His
face glowed, and a wide smile followed. "She left Abilene on a stagecoach two months ago. Can you believe
that?"

"That's a mighty long stagecoach ride, Cole. She
sure must love you after all," Ethan said. His voice was
enthusiastic. "Maybe it's a good thing I didn't give you
that letter before. You would've headed back to the
ranch right then an' there!"

"Wal, shoot me in the foot, don' that jes' be like a
woman?" Luther exclaimed. "Hyar she plumb ran ya
off—an' now she's a-chasin' all o'r the country after
ya. Wonder what dun come o'ver the gal?"

Cole didn't answer. He was reading again.

*Father made me tell you about Webster Steven-
son. God bless his poor soul. Mister Stevenson
said he would foreclose on me Father's shop if I
did not marry his son. What an evil man he be.
Father borrowed money from hisself three years
this past March to start his wee store. Father actually cried when I told him that I would not do
this. I told me Father I could not live without you.*

*Father said that he and me mother would be los-
ing their home and everything if I did not do*

*this awful thing. I did what he asked of me but the minute I told you I knew it could not be so. When you left, I thought me heart was going to fall out of me body. I hope you can forgive me some day. I cannot live without you, me dearest. I dreamed every day that you would come back to Abilene and take meself with you. But I know that cannot be.*

*A week after the shooting, Judge Basin said your doing be self-defense, in spite of Mister Stevenson saying you were trying to kill his son. He made me Father to testify you were a cold killer and had threatened Webster and meself. I could not believe me Father would go so low. I asked to testify and told the judge what the truth of it be. Mister Stevenson tried to keep meself from it because I be a woman.*

*Jason Lincon, the other man you did shoot, be recovering well. Jason said he was paid to go with Webster. The other man I did not know. He left town before the trial. A farmer north of town, who be in the saloon when you did your fighting, testified Webster and his friends came after you. I did not know him but his name is Alex Wade. He be a good man, I think. So did two Texas men who saw the fighting and be saying how brave you be.*

*There can not be any gold worth giving up the honor of oneself like me Father. I moved out of the house that day and be staying at the boarding house of Missus Colter. She let me help with chores to pay me board. She be a fine lady and gave meself gold for the stage passage. I have promised to pay it back to herself when I can.*

*I keep me little red feather between me bosoms from the sweetest day of all time. It will stay there until the glorious day you find it. Do you carry*

*your feather in your hat or has it gone with the
memory of meself?*

Instinctively, Cole reached up his hat brim, knowing
the feather was gone as he did.

"What fur's the matter, Cole?" Luther asked.

"Nothing. Just a minute."

*I know you may not want to see meself but I
can not go on living this way. You can tell meself
to go away but you will have to tell this to me
face. Me every thought is being with you. I love
you, Kathleen.*

Cole put down the letter. His smile was entrenched.
"Well, I reckon there's two real good reasons for going
back to your ranch now."

"Whatcha mean, Cole? Tell us 'bout it!" Luther exclaimed, and Cole explained what had happened.

Ethan laughed deeply and said, "Well, Luther, looks
like our place is going to have a wedding when we get
back. I can see Claire just hustling around with ideas
already!"

Cole laughed, and Luther did too.

Then Ethan remembered Sotar's exchange with Cole
earlier. "Say, Cole, Sotar said he wanted to see you
when you got back. Said you had some old business
to tend to. What's that all about?"

Cole's shoulders rose and fell. He hesitated and said,
"The fella I shot in Abilene is his kin. He feels he has
to avenge him."

"Oh, hellfire," Luther exclaimed. "Lemme talk to
that thar Missouri boy. That thar's fool blood talk. We
sur nuff don't need no more dead men around h'yar.
He be no match for you, nohow."

"Don't low-rate him, Luther, Sotar is a bad man to have facing you."

Through the clearing came John David Sotar, walking slowly toward them. A silver-plated Colt was in his right hand. It was Cole's. Luther started to say something, but Sotar was already talking.

"Cole. Reckon you forgot about your gun."

Cole didn't move. Luther's hand slid toward the pistol stuck in his belt. Ethan stutter-stepped forward, attempting to get in front of Cole, but he stopped the protective move with a gentle arm to Ethan's shoulder. "It's all right, Ethan."

"Been thinking hard, an' it came to me that I was a lot closer to you than I ever was to my cousin. You're my friend. He was just a name. A fool, as I recall. You an' me rode together, we fought together, we near died together. I wanted to tell you that I'm mighty proud to be riding with you. I know you had to do what you did—an' there's no hard feelin's on my part."

"Thanks, John Davis. I'd have you at my back any time," Cole said, and reached to shake Sotar's hand.

From behind Sotar, hidden in the trees, stepped Old Ben Speakman. Only Cole realized that the big Walker Colt in his right hand at his side had been aimed at Sotar moments earlier. His eyes caught Cole's for an instant, but his wrinkled face gave no indication of his intent if Sotar hadn't done as he had.

Walking toward them, Speakman said, "Reminds me of the time—"

Ethan interrupted. "What about me? Anyone want this blind son of a bitch at his back? Might be the safest place to be!"

Everyone laughed.

Cole studied his older brother and said, "Ethan, you can see better than any man I've ever known."

# THE
# OUTLAWS
## WAYNE D.
## OVERHOLSER

Del Delaney has been riding for the same outfit for ten years. Everything seems fine...until the day he is inexplicably charged with rape by the deputy sheriff. Del knows he is innocent, but the deputy's father is the local judge, so he does a desperate thing—he escapes and leaves the state. He drifts until he runs out of money and meets up with two other wanted men in Colorado. Since he is wanted himself, he figures he can do worse than throw in with them. But these men are wanted for a reason and before he knows it, Del is getting in over his head—and helping to organize a bank robbery.

___4897-3 $3.99 US/$4.99 CAN

# *Broken Ranks*

# Hiram King

The Civil War just ended. For one group of black men, hope for a new life comes in the form of a piece of paper, a government handbill urging volunteers to join the new Negro Cavalry, which will soon become the famous Tenth Cavalry Regiment. But trouble begins for the recruits long before they can even reach their training camp. First they have to get from St. Louis to Fort Leavenworth, Kansas, a hard journey through hostile, ex-Confederate territory, surrounded by vengeful white men who don't like the idea of these recruits having guns. The army hires Ples Butler, a grim, black gunfighter, to get the recruits to Fort Leavenworth safely, and he will do his job . . . even if it means riding through Hell.

___4872-8                                    $5.99 US/$6.99 CAN

# BENEATH A WHISKEY SKY

# TRACY KNIGHT

Escaping the past is no easy feat. Just ask Sim McCracken. Sim is a jaded, weary gunslinger with a whole packsaddle worth of secrets and shame, who wants nothing more than to forge a new life. That's why he spared the life of the young pastor he was hired to kill. But that hasn't made the land baron who hired him for the job too happy. Before Sim has a chance to make a clean escape, another secret from his past catches up with him—a retarded brother named Charles, whom Sim hasn't seen since they were children. Sim has to travel across Missouri to escort Charles to a hospital, with his past breathing down his neck the whole way—and with murderous pursuers just one step behind him.

___4883-3                                     $4.50 US/$5.50 CAN

# MORGETTE IN THE YUKON
# G. G. BOYER

Dolf Morgette is determined to head west, as far west as a man can go—to the wilds of Alaska to join the great gold rush. He's charged with the responsibility of protecting Jack Quillen, the only man alive who can locate the vast goldfields of Lost Sky Pilot Fork. For Morgette, the assignment also holds the possibility of a new life for him and his pregnant wife, and perhaps a chance to settle a score with Rudy Dwan, a gunslinging fugitive working for the competition. But a new life doesn't come without risk. Morgette's journey has barely begun before he's ambushed. Soon he's beset at every turn by gunfighters, thieves and saboteurs. If he's not careful, Morgette may not have to worry about a new life— he may not survive his old one.

___4886-8                                  $3.99 US/$4.99 CAN

# DEATH RIDES THE DENVER STAGE
# LEWIS B. PATTEN

Clee Fahr has just arrived by stage in Denver City, Colorado. It is 1861 and the War Between the States has broken out back in the East. Torn apart by opposing military and political sympathies, the town is a tinderbox of treachery and suspicion. Eames Jeffords, an old enemy of Clee's from the South, is buying arms for the Confederate cause. Sam Massey, a mine owner, is raising a company of volunteers to march east and join the Union forces. Although he was born in the North, Clee has divided sympathies. But he's caught in the middle, and both sides see him as a threat—a threat that needs to be removed.

___ 4885-X                                    $3.99 US/$4.99 CAN

**Dorchester Publishing Co., Inc.**
**P.O. Box 6640**
**Wayne, PA 19087-8640**

Please add $2.50 for shipping and handling for the first book and $.75 for each book thereafter. NY, NYC, and PA residents, please add appropriate sales tax. No cash, stamps, or C.O.D.s. All orders shipped within 6 weeks via postal service book rate. Canadian orders require $2.50 extra postage and must be paid in U.S. dollars through a U.S. banking facility.

Name _____
Address _____
City _____ State _____ Zip _____
I have enclosed $ _____ in payment for the checked book(s).
Payment <u>must</u> accompany all orders. ❏ Please send a free catalog.
CHECK OUT OUR WEBSITE! www.dorchesterpub.com

# Man From Wolf River

## John D. Nesbitt

Owen Felver is just passing through. He is on his way from the Wolf River down to the Laramie Mountains for some summer wages. He makes his camp outside of Cameron, Wyoming, and rides in for a quick beer. But it isn't quick enough. While he is there he sees pretty, young Jenny—and the puffed-up gent trying to get rude with her. What else can he do but step in and defend her? Right after that some pretty tough thugs start to make it clear Felver isn't all too welcome around town. Trouble is, the more they tell him to move on—and the more he sees of Jenny—the more he wants to stay. He knows they have something to hide, but he has no idea just how awful it is—or how far they will go to keep it hidden.

___4871-X                                    $4.50 US/$5.50 CAN

# LAURAN PAINE

# THE KILLER GUN

It is no ordinary gun. It is specially designed to help its owner kill a man. George Mars has customized a Colt revolver so it will fire when it is on half cock, saving the time it takes to pull back the hammer before firing. But then the gun is stolen from Mars's shop. Mars has engraved his name on it but, as the weapon passes from hand to hand, owner to owner, killer to killer, his identity becomes as much of a mystery as why possession of the gun skews the odds in any duel. And the legend of the killer gun grows with each newly slain man.

___4875-2                                        $4.50 US/$5.50 CAN

**Dorchester Publishing Co., Inc.**
**P.O. Box 6640**
**Wayne, PA 19087-8640**

Please add $2.50 for shipping and handling for the first book and $.75 for each book thereafter. NY, NYC, and PA residents, please add appropriate sales tax. No cash, stamps, or C.O.D.s. All orders shipped within 6 weeks via postal service book rate. Canadian orders require $2.50 extra postage and must be paid in U.S. dollars through a U.S. banking facility.

Name_____

Address_____

City_____State_____Zip_____

I have enclosed $ _____ in payment for the checked book(s).

Payment <u>must</u> accompany all orders. ❑ Please send a free catalog.

CHECK OUT OUR WEBSITE! www.dorchesterpub.com